MANHOOD

MANHOOD

THE LONGEST MOAN

A novel by

L.M. ROSS

Q-Boro Books
WWW.QBOROBOOKS.COM
An Urban Entertainment Company

Published by Q-Boro Books

ISBN-10: 1-933967-03-X
ISBN-13: 978-1-933967-03-5
LCCN: 2006936046

First Printing April 2007
Printed in the United States of America

10 9 8 7 6 5 4 3 2 1

This is a work of fiction. It is not meant to depict, portray or represent any particular real persons. All the characters, incidents and dialogues are the products of the author's imagination and are not to be construed as real. Any references or similarities to actual events, entities, real people, living or dead, or to real locales are intended to give the novel a sense of reality. Any similarity in other names, characters, entities, places and incidents is entirely coincidental.

Cover Photo by Jose Guerra; Model J. Reed
Cover layout/design by Candace K. Cottrell

Q-BORO BOOKS
Jamaica, Queens NY 11434
WWW.QBOROBOOKS.COM

IN MEMORY OF ALL THE MIGHTY SOULS OF NEW YORK,

PAST, PRESENT AND FUTURE

LMR

Acknowledgments

This was and remains a work of love, of loyalty and of perseverance; a work of Jazz and dreams and poetry and the soft blue hue of a memory. If it makes you hot and angry, if it makes you yearn and smile, sometimes even sadly, then I've succeeded.

But as Billy Dee said to Diana in *Mahogany:* "Success means nothing, without someone you love to share it with."

To My Peeps, my Diehards and my True Friends, thank you for being. As I've embarked upon this journey, you've steadied my sometimes turbulent course, and I thank you for your unflagging love, your honesty, and support.

To my angels: Jodi "Wagamuffin," Lori, my "Wiz-Woman," Yasha "Pretti-Trini," Sweet Dani, and Lovely Linda "Kamai", thank you for the size and shape of your hearts, and for your fast fingers which helped to reassemble the bones and spine of this literary monsta.

To Kevin E. Taylor: "Kevinly," thank you for possessing the depth of *getting the Moan* on a much deeper level than the rest. I so appreciate your gift of Spirit and Light. To Candace: My Sista, thank you for Googling my name, finding my blog, contacting me, and for the efforts you made to resuscitate my first child.

Shout-out to every believer and nonbeliever in this finite talent o' mine. To the mental-feeders, soul-breeders, and long-time Spirit-teachers, I thank you. To the players, haters, singers, dancers, and martini-slingers, Saturday night heartbreakers, and you sweet-bitter long-blue-moan-makers, I'll holla.

And finally, for Jett, James, Cliff and Cunning: I do this in memory of y'all.

One Love,
Lin

PROLOGUE

NEW YORK CITY, OCTOBER 1976, 9:37 PM

The boy's brain screamed, *Fuck you*, *fuck him*, *fuck them*, *fuck all you motherfuckers!* as he bolted down the city block. Every part of him was hurting—hurting bad—and as long and hard and fast as he ran, he couldn't seem to make that pain stop. Fresh blood soaked through his pants, and yet still he ran. He ran and ran until he saw that decrepit old Lincoln parked at the next corner. The thoughts in his head ran louder and faster than an express locomotive. He followed the loudest of them all, and it told him to break into that car. And so breathlessly and hastily, he hotwired it, and soon he sped away into that cold and broken night. He drove with an uncontrollable madness, weaving in and out of traffic. It was for him, a needed act, and a mission to regain his sanity.

Maybe it was planned, or maybe it was providence he'd end up there, in that forgotten part of the South Bronx.

He left the car and stared at the carcass of the tenement that once housed his desolate childhood. Just then, a slice of icy wind blew in a gust so cold, it could wipe the *hope* clean from most anyone's eyes. As the wind wrapped its frigid arms around him, he knew he had to do *something* to keep that cold away.

Matches! He didn't have much, but at least he had those. Once, long ago, someone had told him that the blue of the flame was the hottest and most dangerous part. Maybe that *blue* could warm him now. He reached into his pocket and found a matchbook. Cupping his hand, he struck a stick. Suddenly, a blaze of red, yellow, and transparent *blue* loomed from that flickering spike. *Oh*, *yes* . . . he thought. How hypnotic it was, and *deadly* too!

As the menacing heat crept closer to his hand, he knew if he didn't toss it soon it would burn him. By then, though, he'd been burned so many times before his skin was now raw.

No more, *damn it! No more! Fuck you!*

But then, he saw it. It was just sitting there, as if it were waiting for him to claim it. He saw that can of paint thinner catching a most wicked light. He picked it up, and once again, he listened to his thoughts. His thoughts were his mind's gasoline that night. And the loudest, most profane thought of all whispered the word: *fire!* He quickly emptied the stringent elixir along those old wooden steps. He lit another match, and ooh, oh, hot-damn, he heard the *Who-o-osh!* And what a beautiful sound that *Who-o-osh* became inside his crying ears.

He watched the crimson rise and run to blaze and lick the stairs and beyond. The sensation of seeing what his anger had built transformed the mood in him. The fire raging inside of him had finally found its blazing twin. He watched it smoke and glow and burn and take on brand new flames. He saw the molded stairway fold and the collapse of wooden beams. He watched the scattered choreography of rats and heard the vermin scream. Something in the sleazy beauty of this began to strangely please him.

Jumping inside that stolen Lincoln, he quickly sped away. He looked back, just once, to see the flames of his past swoosh and crackle in the distance. Witnessing this fantastic monstrosity that his anger and a single match had made, the boy smiled back, brazenly.

CHAPTER ONE

Small and Bitter

MIDTOWN MANHATTAN, JULY 2002

The rhythm, the rhythm of the city's soundtrack swooshed and crackled just a little less loudly now. Strutting his urban atmospheric strut and fret, Browny glided his trick bones through another electronic night. It was a night like any other night of muscling crowds, siren sounds, and glimmering parallels of light. The Manhattan air grew thick with the musk of hot pretzels with mustard, and jasmine incense sold by Muslims and cats in silken robes. The traffic roller derbied down Broadway as mad people in mad machines streaked across the Time Square frenzy. It was almost postcard-picture pretty. But this was not *his* beautiful city anymore.

Little by little, Midtown was winning its war with sleaze, and shiny new erections molested the sky. Browny's mind flickered like a cheap neon sign.

Damn! Where can a brotha get a quick li'l hummer on a late summer night, yo? Can't a brotha even cop a bag, a vial, a hit of that herbal shit anymore? Why these bastards have to vacuum the streets and clean the dealers out of Bryant Park, yo?

All of his beloved haunts, the dens, and porn shops had been overrun by the Giuliani decency cops.

Man! Just look at this shit. Yo! Giuliani done blew up my spot!

It was true. The generals of Disney staged a coup on 40-deuce. It was a strategic maneuver; the working girls, the boys, the pimps, the tricks, the pervs, the dealers, and the junkies would never survive.

Browny had a mission, a purpose to that night. But he figured just maybe he'd kill some free time before his fated meeting downtown. He'd planned to bounce into Show World to rent a cheap view of stripper tits and coochie. But the glare from that most excellent hoochie plaza had vanished. It was like that classic Joni Mitchell line: "You don't know what you've got 'til it's gone."

Well someone had paved over *his* island paradise and put up a whole new neon world.

He could not get over it. Wasn't it just a year or three ago that this Great Gleaming City was flashing and spreading its legs wide open in fidgeting, glittering, clittoring eminence? He missed the night's red-lit arena, that throbbing crimson Times Square crotch, when whatever he wanted he could easily cop it there, and then be on his way. He missed his heyday so thick with urban sin and cinema, and suddenly this new place made him feel very old. The hot, greasy glamour had gone astray, and Faison Brown was duly pissed. So he went ahead and took the subway heading downtown.

Of course, it too was a different place now. A group of mad terrorists with screams on their lips had left a hole in its heart and gaping chasm where The Twin Towers had been. The skyline had changed, and the absence of those two shimmering signs, reach and commerce had become a most palpable thing.

But deep within its concrete skin, New York always had been and remained a den of diehards and do-or-die survivors.

He followed the lights. He ignored the faces. He'd long ago acquired the vague gaze and focused gait of a true Manhattan native.

Tiny taverns in the East Village glowed in soothing pink lights against skinny lines of varicose streets. The place he'd chosen and pre-arranged was as dark as a Poe short story. Behind the bar, bottles stood like brown and green soldiers poised on the frontline of a tidy little war.

It was indeed a "Browny" kind of place. It reeked of old dreams and nicotine, cheap booze, mean spirits . . . and even that stink of loneliness.

Stew, the bartender, was a larger-than-life presence, a compressed wall of a man with dead-end eyes and a sly, wry grin. Stew was part philosopher, part pugilist, who possessed the quasi-tenderness of a poet. Often he'd show his benevolence for stumbling bums—as he did this night with Browny as witness—by hailing a cab and paying the man's tab from his own pocket. When asked why, Stew said, "Hey, you never know the things that'll break a man."

A clouded barroom voice replied, "That damn bottle broke him."

But he knew the reason was far more complex, and so the cosmos inside of Stew replied, "His life was gentle, and the elements so mixed within him that nature might stand up and say to all the world, 'This was a man!'"

"Yo! I like that shit right there. That's Shakespeare, right?"

"Yeah. Old Willy Shakes. I only quote the greats."

It was then that *she* stepped inside the bar, in slow and careful samba, her famously long legs cloaked in black trousers. She was entirely clad in black, as if trying to be mysterious, or perhaps, still in her own quiet mourning. Her once famous eyes were obscured by wide Jackie-O shades, her hair wrapped in one of those *gelees* Tyrone had sent her from Africa.

No one recognized her.

She sat three seats away from Browny, who was one vodka shot away from drunk. He remembered her from back in the day. He remembered who she *was* and who she *used* to be. He turned in her direction, and he waited for her to notice him. It appeared she didn't. So finally, undaunted, he spoke.

"Yo, Bliss. It's me."

"Excuse me? Do we *know* each other?"

"Well, I sure as hell *know you*, Bliss Santana!"

Oh. It's him, that little, brown, hemorrhoid thing. What was his name?

"It's me, Browny. Faison Brown. You know, from the loft downtown? Yo, am I really all *that* damn forgettable? I never forgot *you*. Whenever I saw you, I'd think, yo, now Bliss, that's the real cream in Depina's instant coffee. So, wassup? How you doin' these days, Bliss? You doin' all right for yourself?"

"Was that *your* message on my machine? And how'd you get my number? It's always been private. You've been rummaging through his things?" Her voice wore the pissed-off strain of some utter invasion of her past life.

"Mami, please. No need to rummage. Yo! I had *your number* all along. Hell, I was in that inner circle. Yeah, Pass-cow and me, we go way back. In fact, I'm thinkin' 'bout writin' a book about me and the famous Mr. Pass-cow Depina."

"A book?" she asked, curling her lush upper lip dismissively. "Wouldn't that call for some *closeness* to the subject?"

"Closeness? Yo, I thought you knew. Once upon a time the two of us was down, like, like, Apartheid, so ya need to recognize."

"Pascal and *you* were down? *Friends?*" Bliss asked incredulously, lowering her glasses. "I seriously doubt that." She paused. "All right. I'm here. And I'm not even close to being *rich*, so any thought of blackmail would be crazy . . . and fruitless."

"*Fruitless?* Yo! Cool word. Kinda like how you musta felt when he left ya, huh?"

Bliss said nothing. She only rolled her ice-green eyes to the heavens, sighed, and let Browny continue as if she, or anyone could *stop* him.

"See, we all started out as *boys*. Nah. That's a lie. I mean to keep it real. Well, we *did* go to Performing Arts High together. Ya *know* I can sing, right? Oh hail yeah, yo. That shit's all legend. Like to hear me? Want a sample? Here it go . . .

"*On-hell-lee-toes . . . Angelitos? Negro—o-oes, lala la, skip-wahdeedeedah-da-dadday-ay-ay-eee-yoooo . . .*" He scatted to make sure there could be no doubt of his skills on the vocal tip. He didn't sound half-bad.

"So, after hearing *me* blow, yo, they *all* wanted me. Hell, to tell the truth, they was all a little *shady*. You know what they say about *show folk*." He let his wrist go limp for a moment to add effect. "But I blew with them for a minute, and the blend was tight, yo. That's when we started our little singin' group. We called ourselves 'Da Elixir,' right? But then, all hell broke loose, and—"

Bliss caught one hard glimpse at the small, rumpled, broken-down Browny and promptly choked on her gin and tonic. Though Pascal Depina had always downplayed his past, she knew he was once a part of a singing group, but she had somehow *forgotten* Browny's involvement. Now, suddenly, it *amused* her.

"Elixir?" she asked in a cough. Thoughts of him being *anyone's elixir* tickled her into a fresh gush of laughter. She couldn't help it.

"Yo! It was *Ty's* wise-ass idea. The rest of us hated it. But then Ty broke it down: 'See, the Elixir was a magic potion, like the Fountain of Youth, a feel-good balm, a healin' tonic.'"

She'd forgotten how good some clever drunks were at that game of emotional manipulation. *Ty*. She had and always would maintain a soft chamber in her heart for Tyrone.

"Go on," she said.

"Well Ty talked us into that name. So me, Pass-cow, Ty, and little David became 'Da Elixir.' Then Ty messed around and wrote us a fuckin' *hit*, and the rest is . . . well . . . that's music history, yo."

"Really?"

"Yes, Bliss. *Really*. And the more I think about it, just maybe Ty had that gift, that forward sight. You know, he was kinda . . . what's that word?"

"Prophetic?" Bliss contributed. *And this drunken idiot wants to write a damn book!*

"Yo! If that shit means he could see the future some, then yeah, *prophetic*! See, I think we spent most of our lives lookin' for that damn Elixir. Maybe everybody does, yo. I mean, check it: we both sittin' here sippin' on one right now. Whatever's gonna make us feel mo betta, yo—maybe *that's* the elixir."

The two of them sat marinating in the weight of that thought for a moment.

Then Browny added, "And you and me, we *both know* Pass-cow the Rascal had plenty of them elixirs. We used to have this li'l jokey-joke: Who say how many? Pass-cow gots a-plenny." Browny chuckled secretly. Bliss did not even crack a grin. "So, anyway, I figga ya might wanna throw in with me on this thing. Together, we could make this motherfuckin' story *sing*. What ya think?"

The notion of anyone *exploiting* Pascal enraged a deep and sleeping ire in Bliss Santana. She wanted to haul off and knock the shit out of Faison Brown. She wanted to forget the demeanor she'd long ago cultivated, and just simply wail all over him.

"Fuck you, you desperate little cold-blooded bastard! I

loved him. Do you hear me? Do you get that, *yo*? The answer is no. Hell no. And if you even think about slandering *my* name, I will see your little bone-picking ass in the highest court. You got that, *yo*?" she mocked.

"Yo! Bliss, so you name calling, now? Is that it? Is that your *new* elixir? You know what my boy Ty said about name calling? It's just a sad, desperate act of the guilty and insecure, baby."

"So now I suppose you were Tyrone's friend, too?"

"Ty and me? Oh, hail yeah! Ty? That's practically *family*. Yo, check it . . ." He leaned in nearer, his liquored-up lips uncomfortably close to her beauteous face. "I figga I'll start chapter one a little sump'm like dis: 'Yo! In high school some kids fit in, some stand out, and some just don't give a fuck.' What you think, Bliss? Is that the shit, or what?" He grinned, nodding his head, proud of himself.

"You know what I think?" Bliss said, leaning back.

"What?"

"I think it's adolescent. And I think you need a fuckin' breath mint."

"Oh! I get it. So, you Rosie Perez, now? Yo, everybody, Bliss got jokes! Well, I ain't laughin'."

Browny's face suddenly wore a dark and fearsome scowl she'd never seen before.

"One more crack, and I'll smack that pretty ass harder than Pass-cow ever did, yo. *Trust!*" And then, he was back to being Browny again. "So, yo! You wanna throw down on this with me, or what?"

"You could never write a book, Browny," Bliss Santana announced. "Seriously. You're not capable of it. Besides, all the pages would just flame from that Hell you've been living in. And now, I believe our little Algonquin roundtable meeting is through. And please, *lose* my number!"

She stood to leave, dropping some green on the bar counter. "Excuse me, bartender, his next one is on me. Just make it something stiff and bitter, and serve it in a dirty little glass." Then she clicked her hot tongue in Browny's direction and she exited the bar.

"Dumb witch!" he grumbled after her. "I guess you don't care that he used yo ass, too. Guess ya liked being a fuckin' *beard*, till he shaved you off with his disposable razor, and threw ya *both* away. Hey! That ain't half bad! Who needs her stank ass. I can do this shit all by my lonesome."

As he turned away from the door, Browny saw his reflection in the mirror. He noticed that annoying infestation of gray invading his once dark goatee.

Stew placed another vodka-shot before him. Browny drank it very quickly.

Despite his bullying bluster, Faison "Browny" Brown never did possess the knowledge, the skills, nor the self-discipline needed to write a *true* tell-all. Yet, even if he did, he was at best, a slighted and fairly minor character in a twenty-year saga.

But he was right about one thing: they all *had* met in a special place, a place that nourished the sons and daughters of applause.

NEW YORK CITY, HIGH SCHOOL OF PERFORMING ARTS, 1977-78

The auditorium smelled of turpentine and greasepaint. It was mixed with the tart funk of dancer feets' and the ripe sweat of youthful ambition. After third-period chorus, Tyrone Hunter remained behind to plink plink on the piano as he waited for Mr. Raines. A tall and lanky kid with warm toffee skin, Ty's brow furrowed into a studious brood as his long, tapered fingers stroked the keys. There was something playing in Tyrone's mind—a melody, a strangely haunting succession of notes that hadn't quite yet formed a tune.

Out in the hallway, a squat sparkplug of deep-chocolate bully who went by the name of "Browny" stalked the corridors most ominously. It was open season for Browny, who took his own antagonistic delight in chasing down "special punks." He'd just cornered another unsuspecting victim. Without provocation, as hard as he could, he punched the boy in the chest, then ran away, laughing.

As David Richmond glided by, he saw Faison Brown's heartless assault. Witnessing this scene pissed David off. His amber eyes blazed. *Enough with this shit!* he thought. *Oh . . . I got something for your ass, Black boy!*

Browny hadn't hit David—yet—but that didn't matter. David immediately stepped into action. He switched strides, contorted the usual freestyle grace in his gait and morphed into something more foreboding. He phased into his slow jock's swagger and just kept stepping as he approached the bully in question. Smiling most impishly, David balled up his fist, hauled off and punched him, far harder than Browny had punched his last victim. David did it for each and every "special punk" in that school who was too afraid to hit Browny back. This was no mere boyish punch. This was a quick left to the center of the chest, and Faison Brown fell to the floor, winded.

Meanwhile, Pascal "Face" Depina was poised inside his favorite place—the mirror of the boy's room. People had been telling him that he looked like a young Paul Newman—a young, bronzed, green-eyed Paul Newman. And Face was starting to believe the hype. He'd even taken to styling his fawn-colored hair to look like Newman's did in *The Hustler*. Sufficiently coiffed, he winked a green eye at his near-perfect reflection. When he exited the bathroom, it was just in time to witness the punch that landed Browny *hard* on his bullish ass. Depina saw David standing over Browny, and laughed his secretive crackle.

"You all right?" David asked, leaning over the stunned Browny. "Nah? You ain't? Damn boy. I guess you just got dropped by a "special punk."

Soon as he could, a dazed Browny rose from the floor with vengeance raging in his eyes.

"Oh, so it's like that, yo? Now, guess what? I'ma kick yo punk ass!"

With that, David ran. Only, it wasn't out of fear. He ran to show he could not only out-punch, but outrun a meaningless thug. He ran, leaving Browny to eat the gusts from his fairy dust. At the tail end of this run, David burst through the auditorium door, breathless, his every youthful muscle heaving.

Tyrone Hunter heard the abrupt commotion. He looked up, recognized David as that crazy-weird talented dancer cat with a knack for inventive fashion, and continued playing with the keys.

David stood in back, listening for a moment. It was a hummable tune with a kind of R&B edge. He didn't take long before he was nodding his head. Liking what he heard, he yelled.

"Hey! That sounds pretty damn good, man. So you're the dude with that stiff, bowlegged *Blaçula* walk from the ensemble chorus, right?"

It was some momentous introduction.

Ty didn't answer.

Mr. Thomas Raines, a round jovial nut-brown man in his mid-forties entered from stage right.

"Tyrone," Raines asked, "what's that you're playing?"

"Nothing really. Not yet anyway. I keep hearing this crazy tune in my head. I've been tryin to make sense of it . . . the notes, the melody. It's strange. But I do that sometimes—see things, hear stuff no one else hears and sees but me. Is there a name for that?"

"Yeah. It's called creativity. You should work on that tune, maybe give it a title, and the lyrics will come." Mr. Raines noticed David standing in the shadows.

"Oh, there you are. Care to join us, Mr. Richmond?"

With that invitation, David sauntered slowly down the aisle as if he were giving a grand performance. His maize-yellow sweat pants, tied high about his narrow waist, called attention to his noticeable V-shape. Though only five foot six, 130 pounds, he was extraordinarily muscular, and a skinny kid like Tyrone coveted David's well-formed biceps. Suddenly, David's long purple tank came off in a floating flourish, revealing an even tighter electric-blue one. As he walked, he hastily fashioned the bright purple top into a babushka around his head. On anyone else, it would have looked completely *ridic*, yet on David, somehow, it worked. By the time he made it to the stage, he was his own kind of performance art piece. At least Tyrone thought so.

Just then, through the door bopped a suave, well-dressed Pascal "Face" Depina, followed by a still winded and wounded Faison Brown. Browny was punching his fist and deviously eyeballing David. But David could not have cared less. His heart was too busy racing at the sight, the very presence of "Face" Depina.

Face and Browny seemed an odd combo to Tyrone, who was still fingering the keys. He wondered: *Why are they here?* But apparently they too had been summoned by Mr. Raines.

"OK, good . . . you're all present. Listen, fellas," Raines began. "This shouldn't come as surprising news, but each of you is dangerously close to flunking my class. Yes, Tyrone, David, and Pascal, I realize none of you are *music* majors, but you *don't* get to skate through my classes. Faison Brown, you *are* a music major, so, young man, you have no excuse."

"But, yo, Mr. Raines, you know, we all know, I'm the best singer in this whole—"

"Save it. Being the 'best' means nothing if you lack *discipline*," Raines admonished. "Now, Pascal, you being a senior, I'm quite sure you'd just love to see yourself swaggering, just-a diddy-bopping down the aisle in your cap and grown, right? You're on the acting track, correct?"

Thinking he'd yet another fan, Pascal grinned and nodded, vainly.

"Then leave the mirror at home, and try *acting* like an interested student here!"

Pascal's grin quickly left his handsome countenance.

"The semester ends soon, and if any of you want to pass, extra credit is due. You can come up with something individually, or work as a team. Either way, I want to see a superior effort from you all. It's sad enough we reject plenty of kids who would give their eyeteeth to be just where you are. No one gets a free lunch here. Remember that. You work hard for it, or you fail, and you'll soon realize you're not so *special* after all. So you'd better keep working at *being* special. Am I understood? Well? Am I?"

"*Yes, Mr. Raines,*" they all replied in a bored singsong unity.

Tyrone thought: *Well, it'll definitely be something individual. I'm not sure I even like these cats.*

Just then, David, seeing the horny benefit of working alongside the delicious and most coveted Face Depina, weighed in with an idea all his own.

"Hey, check it out. I know a way we could all get those credits and knock this thing clean out the box. All of us can carry a tune, right? Well, we could pool our talents, form a little singing group, and then do something really fly . . . like, flyer than The Temptations, even. Seriously, this guy right here, he could even write us a song," he said, gesturing at Tyrone.

Shut the hell up! Or are ya gay and crazy too? Ty wondered. Please, don't do this shit to me!

But Ty was too shy to speak those words. Face and Browny didn't say much of anything, and so their combined silence was seen as harmony.

"Great!" Mr. Raines announced with a loud clap of his hands. "Sometimes it's better when young people work together. Art is often a combined effort." He then placed one hand on Ty's thin and unsure shoulder. "So then, it's set."

No! Speak Ty! Open your mouth and say something, or forever hold your peace!

"But . . . but Mr. Raines. I don't write songs. I . . . I write plays. Besides, I don't want the pressure of having to create on a dime. Couldn't you just assign us a song from the radio?"

"Pressure? Please! If you're gonna be an *artist*, then ya best get used to it, baby," an eye-rolling David chipped in.

"Tyrone, are you serious? Any kid here can sing something from America's Top 40," Mr. Raines said. "Where's the challenge in that? Never be afraid of challenge, Ty! That goes for the rest of you guys as well. Challenge *yourselves*, daily, and get used to it, before the world outside these doors does the *real* challenging."

Ty stood silently, his creative light eclipsed by a floating orb of self-doubt. That school was forever challenging him, his abilities, his limitations and his own self-expression. He was at heart a loner who worked and thrived best when alone. Now he was expected to write a song for *them all* to sing? It was yet another task he didn't feel capable of performing. A shiver of anxiety raced with conflict and it coursed through the height of him.

"As young men of color, *challenge* will soon become your breakfast, lunch and dinner. Learn to be fearless. *Embrace it*, to eat it with gusto, and belch with the fume of success!"

It was corny teacher-speak, and yet in its own way, inspirational. Tyrone's doubts aside, the rest stood like young fruit on that stage, soaking in the sun of Mr. Raines's sermon.

David, the dancer, gazed longingly at Face Depina, and in that moment, David forged a little *challenge* of his own. In the time they were assigned to be together, he would do his level best to *make* Face fall *in love* with him.

"So, just to make it official, I hereby allocate the four of you to go forth, form a group, and be nothing less than *brilliant!* Synergy, gentleman, that's all I'm calling for here. I'll leave it up to you to choose a name, and design your own image. And yes, to perform a brand new song written by Tyrone. That's it. That's all. That's a wrap. Now, I think we're done here, gentleman. Have a good and productive day."

And thus, late that afternoon in the auditorium of the High School of Performing Arts, a shaky allegiance, and an alliance of sorts, was born between four boys—Tyrone and David, Face and Browny.

Still, once dismissed, Tyrone couldn't help but to think, *this is not the beginning of a beautiful friendship*.

THREE WEEKS LATER

"Yo! Hunter!" Browny kicked at the auditorium bleachers. "Why every time I see you, you and old man Raines got yawls heads together? Ya need to stop kissin'up, yo. People might start thinkin' y'all *funny* for each other. Always whisperin' together like a coupla bitches!"

Tyrone glared at him.

"Yeah, I said it. Whatchu gon' do, punk?" Browny challenged, fist clenched, upper body jerking in a pseudo-threatening move.

Tyrone had flinched the first few times Browny had done that, but he didn't flinch anymore.

"Keep talkin' that junk, man. Better yet, let *him* hear you. Then maybe he *won't* get his nephew, who just happens to be a producer at Sigma Sound Studios, to drop by the concert and take a look at us."

"What? Browny asked, eyes bugging out to twice their normal size. "Say what, yo?" His tempestuous tenor suddenly rose to new soprano heights.

"What's wrong? Is Depina singing too loudly in your ear again? Ya heard me," Ty said.

"But . . . fo real, yo?"

"For real."

"Shit, yo! I don't believe it. Yo, do Pass-cow and David know?"

"Nope. I just found out now myself."

"You know this could be big, right? I mean, Sigma Sound ain't no joke! Didn't Black Ivory record up in there?"

"Yup. And they were just about the same age as us."

"Yo! This could be crazy, fo real! I'm getting psyched and shit, yo!"

"Well, don't get too psyched. Just get it right, brother. Nothin's promised, and we still got a *lotta* work to do."

"Hell, the song is tight, the harmony's workin'out. Yo! It's smellin' like, like gold and hot shit in this place, man! Here . . . smell my finger, yo . . ."

Ty smacked his hand away.

Five seconds later, his finger un-smelled, Browny was zooming down the auditorium's center aisle. The troublesome cat had vanished, gone to that Happy Place that squat, talented, braided-domed black boys go when they dream of being stars!

He dashed into room 308 and yelled the news to David, who was deep into his ballet class. And David, in mid-arabesque, wondered: *Whaaaa?*

Browny then proceeded to zoom even further and he

hollered it in an echo to Pascal “Face” Depina who was staring in the third-floor bathroom mirror.

“Yo! A cat from Sigma Sound is comin’ to the Winter Extravaganza, and we gon’ be stars, yo!”

And so began the journey of four boys on fire, with very separate dreams.

CHAPTER TWO

Character is Everything

***Da Elixir* was the sum of four parts:**

Ty, Age Sixteen

Brilliant, Involved, Hopeful, Lucky?

Long before he'd ever heard of the playwright Bertolt Brecht, he'd written his own play that echoed that author's *Three Penny Opera*. It was Ty's entrée into the hallowed halls of P.A. He didn't *want* to be a cog in a machine of that entertainment factory whose prime produce was cranking out performers. But there he was, knee-deep in the hurried hubbub of wandering weirdos, eccentric adolescents, stage, screen, and television vets. Those halls buzzed with a combustible energy, a tangible excitement of the young, talented, and destined.

Strange, the things The Universe hands us.

Though he stood six-two and weighed a gangly 150, soaking wet, Tyrone had an almost coltish charm. His face was a thin presentation of toffee skin and curious features all trying at once to be handsome. To some, it was a cool face—a long, bony, hungry face. His crowning glory was a bank of pomade-assisted curls—a look some Latin chicos affected and Ty adapted, then resurrected from an old Sal Mineo movie. His almond-shaped eyes were a deep, dramatic shade of sable, and others were haunted by their directness. His most bewitching feature, though, was his lips—soft, puffy, heart-shaped lips. At times they seemed to be almost begging to be kissed.

A lexical cat at sixteen, Ty spoke with a crazy verbiage, as if his words were grits served with a dash of hipster syntax, mixed, peppered, *Tyronized*, and sitting on a china plate.

During his entrance audition into the school for performers, Ty riffed:

"Back in the day the Moms has all these fantasies of being a Blues Chanteuse. But truthfully, Moms was far more Piaf than Bessie, so the suits at Verve never called her back. By the time I shot out, Momma had a brand new bag: the camera. Man, she musta taken a million snaps of me, her half-cute papoose in a little blue homemade suit. She'd show them to everyone and anyone, though. I'm sure it was due to my cuteness, or her natural wizardry at fotog trickery. Ambition. This was her trip. Not mine.

"So one sunny afternoon in Harlem, she's standing outside the Kodak soul-freezing factory, perusing her latest batch, these new mugs of me, when some strolling lady asked for a peek. Lady turned out to be a casting agent. Freak thing, that. So, the Moms jet-speeds home, high on visions of better living room furniture, her eyes clouded by those spacey cataracts old dreams make, and she asked me, 'Ty, do Momma's baby wanna be on TV? Momma's baby boy wanna be a star, huh?'

"Now, I'm like, all of eighteen-months-old, but I must've goo-goo ga-ga'd something that sounded vaguely like 'Sure ma. Why the hell not?'

"Cut to page 133 in a Sears catalogue. That grinning brown tot is me. Ever seen that deep tan toddler in a wet diaper, making a mad telegenic sprint for a dry Pamper? That toddler was me. Hey, I didn't mind being exploited too much 'cause it helped with the bills, the ends, and such. But the expiration date in cute brown mutes ran out. And I was pretty much a has-been, rejected at age seven.

"So I'm here, writing plays about the haves and have-nots 'cause I've lived inside both those freaky skins, and I know the funky smell of them, intimately."

Ty had things to say. He was, by nature, creative. But he wore a mood the color of lonely.

David, Age Fifteen
Brilliant, Silly, Cute, Dancer

David knew from the time he could walk that one metro-golden day he would be a professional dancer. He'd spent his youth mesmerized by the flickering blue glow of early MGM musicals. Soon, he became addicted to all things light, spirited, and gay. He floated with an understated snare drum in his gait. Chest out, spine and shoulders straight, the aesthetic was never a problem for David. He was, in many ways, a kid chameleon. David Richmond could be very cool with his faggotry, unless he wanted to *play* the queen.

With the softest light-hazel overcast, David's eyes looked as if he'd just awakened from a dream. Often there appeared to be a private little comedy act going on behind his gaze.

Dance was his life, and he did it with élan. The kid was a

"firebird." Everyone who'd ever seen him said so. At his audition, David was asked to tell a little about himself.

"I tell people about myself through dance," he said. "I believe dance is freedom, plain and simple. Only, there's nothin' simple about freedom." And then he danced.

Tyrone just happened to see him audition, and one day he would write about it. What Tyrone witnessed was David Richmond, the Artist. David wore a raggedy leotard, and nothing else, and he was portraying the life he'd known—his whole damn life—in dance.

Tyrone wrote:

"I'd never seen anything like this strange and beautiful creature who would become my best friend. God! The muscles on him! Every finely-honed sinew of David's body became this instrument of poetic expression. See? When David danced, he told you exactly who he was. He moved from gleeful tap-dancing kid, to a ridiculed student, to an abused and battered teen, and he told you his story through dance. You could almost see the boxing ring and smell the sweat as he stomped and lumbered, sashayed and spun across the stage to the theme from *Rocky*.

I guess it was part modern—like lyrical—part ballet, and part something no one in that room could put a name to, but it made you believe him. It did even more to me. It made me want to laugh with him, cry for him, and pray for his beautiful spirit. I asked myself: *Who is this person, this freak, this strange and scary-talented cat? How does he do this, and that, and oh my God, that! And what is my limited ass even doing here?*

How do you compare a pin-light to a star? You don't."

Tyrone remembered that day, seeing David dance, even more vividly than David did. Ty felt that he was watching more than a dancer; he was witnessing an earthlike star. Soon, just to see him move and to watch him glow was enough to fall in love with him, a little. There was a light, a corona of brilliance that surrounded David Richmond. Tyrone Hunter would become not only a student, but a sponge to David's light.

Yes. David knew what he could do and how well he could do it, and he took pride in being a "wicked body-worker." That mad dancer's heart was full of hot rhythms as it sped, slowed, and sped again—when he opened the auditorium door, and there stood . . .

Pascal, Age Eighteen
Beautiful, Not Brilliant, Magnetic, Troubled

One fact was never disputed: physically, this boy was sumptuous. No matter your taste, your personal preference, no matter your sensibility or sense of aesthetic, when you stared at him, all you saw was pretty. Pascal Depina was a physically beautiful boy. There was a deep mystery, a racial ambiguity in that face. You couldn't tell his background. You knew Black was involved. But Black and . . . what? It confounded many. Was it African-American and Italian, or Spanish, or Irish, or something even more exotic like maybe Black and Tasmanian? Full of sharp angles and green-eyed mischief, he stood six foot five and weighed 180 pounds. Most entrancing was that chameleon-like skin in the sun, how the tones of tan turned to taupe and bronze. And everything just seemed to come alive when he smiled.

Folks said he looked like a junior Paul Newman, a strange Egyptian version, with eyes as green as Newman's were blue-green jewels and cool lime specks of light. When people noted his celebrity likeness—which they often did—he'd sometimes smile incandescently within, and he'd say,

"Well it's like this, I'm Mr. Newman's love child, 'kay? But we don't talk about it. Too painful."

Some people actually believed the lie, despite the fact that at six foot five, he was a full head and a cluster of curls taller than Newman.

Lie or not, in a place where talented kids would give their tender young tits to be even close-to-famous, Pascal Depina's line (along with those looks) brought him instant popularity. They noticed that face. That face launched a thousand crushes. That face got him props. That *face* became his name. He claimed he wanted to be an actor, but he already resembled a star.

His pulsar was evident.

Rumor had it that someone with clout had called in a favor to get him accepted within that special school. There may have been some truth to this notion.

For his audition—Depina read a scene from *A Raisin in The Sun*. And while no one present that day would forget the magic or luster of Mr. Sidney Poitier, Depina's strut and fret was deemed "passable." The reality: at most, it was a diligent application of a finite talent.

But Pascal "Face" Depina was a culturally miscellaneous phallic symbol: tall, erect, his presence recalling the athletic grace of ballplayers mixed with the insouciance of a minor prince. Ah! Yes, he of the beautifully cool and confident exterior.

Faison, Age Seventeen
Gifted, Unlucky, Obstinate, Unlucky.

Faison Brown acted like a street thug, a straight-up and decidedly unremarkable bully—albeit a short, squat, obnoxious, "damn he can sing his ass off" bully.

Upon hearing him, even David would relent to Ty:

"*Sheeee-it*! That boy *can sing*! Please, don't tell another soul this—'cause I'd have to kick your ass—but hell, I almost wanna *do* him when he sings!"

"Then I guess you're just a whore for a sweet voice. There

oughta be a name for sick people like you. Oh yeah . . . there already is. Groupie!" Ty chuckled.

"Umm . . . mm . . . a groupie . . . for Browny? Uh . . . not hardly. But *listen* to him. Really listen, Ty! It's like whatever is good and right inside Browny, it all comes pouring out when he sings."

"Well, he does have the makings of a true artiste."

"Meaning what, exactly?"

"Skill . . . like this crazy immense talent . . . and it's all dwelling inside a miserable human being. I gotta admit it, Davy, I thought he was all talk and full of shit, but then he opens his mouth, and he sings."

Things rarely came easy for short, dark, attitudinal boys who dream of being superstars. Yet Faison Brown had his hot, happy, happening future all mapped out. He was Faison Marcellus Brown, the Best Damn Singer in the whole school, and after one of those showcases, some top agent was going to hear him, feel him, love him, and sign him to a multi-album deal. In Faison's world, *cute* was wasted on the vapid cute-seekers, but real talent got you paid in full.

Browny, at his audition:

"When I was four, I started singin' in church cause I seen other bigheaded kids doin' it. I heard all that screeching high-pitched . . . shi . . . ummm . . . 'yah-yah-yaaah,' and I knew they couldn't really blow. But I could. By the time I was six, I was a soloist in all kinds of talent shows, and sang at people's parties, weddings, and funerals. Show business was my goal. See, I come from Harlem. We used go to the Apollo at least once a month, yo. Now that's show business. Everybody's played there. My pops used to date the Sandman's cousin's daughter, and once he took me backstage to meet Smoky freakin' Robinson. For *real*, yo.

"There he was—all suave, beige, and *smoky*-eyed. My Pops

told him I could sing. 'G'on sing for the man, Faison,' he said. But I was too busy messin' my pants to sing for a legend. Smoky understood, though.

"He told me: 'Keep at it, kid. I grew up in the projects, too.' That's what he said. Hard to believe with all the class and style Smoky got, he came from poor black folks like me.

"But I ain't no sweet-soundin' falsetto. Nah, I'm a mad natural tenor with a three-octave range. I don't just blow my notes, I ascend, yo. R&B ain't even ready for me. You know what inspires me, yo? Opera. Fo real. Black folks might not be too used to hearin' opera. But that's cool. I'ma change 'em. This is gonna surprise' ya'll but you know who inspires me now? Luciano Pavarotti. Luciano is like, the *man*! That's how I see myself: Faison Marcellus Brown, first tenor at the Met, performin' *Rigaletto*, yo, *Porgy and Bess*, all the greats. Just watch me, yo."

And he opened his mouth to sing, and this extraordinary sound floated out of him. It was high and pure and nearly angelic, and it soared across the room and into that place where excellence was nourished.

MANY FIGHTS, REHEARSALS, AND MORE FIGHTS LATER

Ty, David, Face, and Browny had become 'Da Elixir.' Personality-wise, they weren't a perfect fit, and conflict and acrimony was a constant. They argued over their name, their harmonies, and even what clothes to wear. David was often the peacemaker, and Ty, the strident defender of his song. Face Depina was bored by it all, and Browny, he just wanted to be heard, and *respected*, over and *above* the rest.

And just before the curtain rose, Browny was feeling *very* disrespected.

"Yo! Ty! You foul, man!"

"What now, Browny?"

"I just heard you and Raines. I hear you, yo."

"So. Try *hearing* when you're supposed to come in on the *lead*, OK?"

"Easy, bitch!" Browny hissed. "Yo, everybody! Dig this. Old boy Tyrone here is tryna ice the rest of us, yo. Oh yeah. Him and Raines was talkin' about how Ty *owns* the song and stuff. Like the rest of us ain't worked hard on this bullshit."

"It's called *intellectual property*, Browny. Look it up. It's not shady; it's the reality."

"Oh, so now I'm stupid, right?"

"Oh, you're some kind of *stew*, all right. And don't even think I'm *afraid* of you, and those loud-ass wolf tickets you be sellin'."

"Fight! Fight! Bitch fight!" Face chirped in.

"Say one more word, one more fuckin' word, and I'ma knock the piss outta you, boy. Ya hear me? I been itchin' to kick yo punk ass, Tyrone Hunter, 'cause you ain't shit, yo!"

"But you *are* The Shit? Right, Browny?'

"Girls! Girls! Please! A little decorum is needed here!" David interjected. "Must I break out the etiquette book? We're about to go on. So knock it off, ladies!"

"Go on? No, I'ma go *off* on Tyrone's bourgie ass."

"And I'm shakin' in my sharkskin. Show me what you got, Browny!"

"Oh damn! He's challengin' you, Browny. This shit should be *good*." Face chuckled.

And just before the fists flew, it was SHOWTIME!

As Mr. Raines had promised, his nephew, genius producer Tabby Freeman, was indeed present. Freeman sat attentively, digging the song, the moves, the staging, digging the whole act. These young cats had polish. David's studious choreography had whipped them in shape. Ty's sensitive yet soul-stirring song had legs. It was a smooth transition to see how four boys with vibrant personality, a killer song, and a light, sweet sophistication beyond their years might make it to the big time.

After the finale, Freeman approached Tyrone about making a demo of his song. A very hyped and excited Tyrone quickly agreed, but only if he secured the rights to his own publishing. His earlier show biz experience had given him a smart kid's knowledge of the business. Reluctantly, Tabby Freeman acquiesced.

But Ty had one more condition: "It's gotta be a package deal. We all worked hard on this thing. So, it's only fair that the other cats get to *sing* on wax," he said.

Again, Tabby Freeman agreed.

And together, Da Elixir made a very sweet noise. Their song was a rhythmic tale of teenage love, lust, and loss, sung with David crying falsetto, leading into Browny's soaring tenor, backed by Ty's solid baritone. And Depina . . . well, he gave *good face*.

When the song hit the airwaves, everyone was hyped. Suddenly, Da Elixir was Number 31 with a bullet. Premier East Coast DJ Eddie O'Jay caught the bug, then Paco, followed by Frankie Crocker. Then Radio Personality Vy Higgenson bit, and soon everybody was diggin' them, and digging it. Suddenly Da Elixir was like, The Shit!

By early April, they were the opening act at The Apollo. Local dance shows were biting for their delight, and even *Soul Train* was beckoning.

But by June, Da Elixir fizzled. Face Depina had just graduated, and aware of his matinee idol looks, he decided he was just too damn *pretty* for that group "bullshit." Besides, he'd already deemed that he "never needed any of them small-time motherfuckers anyway."

After Depina's departure, a disheartened David soon followed.

Ty thought it best to break the news to Browny, in public, on a crowded subway.

"Aw, na-a-ah! No! NO! Not like this, yo! Nah! We can't just punk out like this! No! Trust me. I am NOT gonna go out like this! Whose ass I gotta kick to stop this shit? David's?"

Ty wanted to say, *Ummm . . . but didn't David already flatten your ass once?*

But he chilled. Browny was miles past furious, and you didn't want to fuck with an ambitious *and* livid bully.

"We worked too hard, man. We on top, now! We 'bout to do *Soul Train*, yo! *SOUL TRAIN*, dammit!!! You gotta make these crazy motherfuckas come to they senses!" Browny was holding his head in both hands. He *had* to. He thought it might just explode if he didn't. "Ty, you could do it. Fuck Passcow! Never liked his pretty-boy ass anyway! You and David done got tight, yo. Make him stay! We got plenty of singers around us. We could just get another one. We could *still do this*, man!"

"Like I told you, Browny, it's a done deal. Now that he's graduated, Face wants to *act*. And David, he doesn't even wanna go on without Face. Remember what *happened* the night of the Extravaganza? Now David's all *strung out* over that cat. Besides, this summer he's got auditions and cattle calls on Broadway and beyond."

"Well, fuck 'em both. Yo, you and me. I know we had our *beefs*, but we cool. So we'll find us somebody else. Alright? *All right?* Ty? Don't you wanna be a star, yo?"

"Me? Nah. Da Elixir was just a freak thing. I'm a writer, man."

"Well, shit! What about *me*?" Browny asked, his voice trembling like lone brown leaf in the wind.

"Browny? You? You're the *real* singer, man. You've got chops for days. If you go to Juilliard and study hard, *I know* you could make it happen."

"Juilliard?" He threw up his disgusted hands. "Shit, man! People go there to *try* to be somebody. We *already* are somebody, damn it! Da Elixir's about to be big, yo!"

"Look, I'm sorry if this messes with your plans, but nobody else is really *into* it anymore." Ty placed a comforting hand on Browny's rumpled and hurt shoulder. Browny quickly knocked it away.

"Don't touch me! Faggot motherfucka!"

"Oh. So, that's the way it's gonna be now, Browny?"

Browny had no other words for him. He hated them. He hated them all now.

It made him sick to look at him. He wanted to hit Tyrone. He wanted to kick his ass all over the IRT.

CHAPTER THREE

Fire in the Pews

In the Latin Quarter the coolest kids danced *The Rock*, *The Patty Duke*, and *The Wop* as hip-hop came fully out the box. Spray paint cans in artistic hands tagged the South Bronx livelier than it had ever been. Urban kids spun on their heads as homelessness spun out of control. The boom of bass and the fume of freebase was spreading through New York City, and all over the place.

THE ROXY, NOVEMBER 1982

David was dancing on Broadway. Thanksgiving eve, though, he wanted to go roller-skating. So he called Tyrone, who, being in his sophomore year at Columbia, was full of new collegiate insights and metaphors.

"There was this *family* in the neighborhood," Tyrone told David. "A whole mess of them, called the Johnsons. The Johnsons was this gang of boys, all ambitious, all talented, and each in his own way, dynamic. They sang, danced, did impressions, mastered crazy instruments. They made a pretty black noise in a small segment of the world. Hell, they were like ghetto Jacksons. It was only later people discovered most of these Johnsons were never *really* family. They were adopted, trained, punished, rewarded, and conditioned to perform. Like lab rats. Then, little by little, those Johnson boys began to disappear, vanish, *poof*. People forgot all about 'em. But for a time, the Johnsons ruled the earth," Tyrone proclaimed, skating away from David.

"Tyrone?" David asked, catching up to him. "I know you're heavy into symbolism *this* week, but the point of that story would be . . . ?"

"*We* were the Johnsons, Davy. We *are* the fucking Johnsons!"

Two nights later, Davy devised an Elixir reunion where he, Ty, Face, and Browny would meet for a movie. The animosity was palpable, though initially misguided.

As the gang of four glided through the flashing Times Square scenery, it was plain to see that not everyone was strutting so lively in the city. A few tattered souls vividly knew the raw taste of hard times.

Browny yelled at a man sprawled on the pavement.

"Yo! Negro! Leave that pipe alone!"

"Easy, Browny! That's prolly somebody's old man," Face said.

"So what? Don't nobody give a shit about his wasted-drunk ass, or he wouldn't be lyin' out there like that!"

"There but for the grace of God, my brother," Ty reminded him. Just then Tyrone stopped his stride. He bent down and asked the man earnestly, "You all right, sir? You need a cup of coffee, a good meal, or something?"

The man stared up vaguely from his chaos, and promptly spat.

"Fuck you, punk!"

And the others looked back then broke out into laughter—loud, crazy, uproarious laughter.

"You wild, Tyrone! Yo! What was you gonna do, ask him to step to the movies with us?" Browny joked, laughing harder than the rest, holding his stomach and chortling into the night.

"Nice try, though, Ty. So what movie we gonna see?" David asked as the gang of four strutted along Broadway.

"Yo! I hear that new Chuck Norris flick's dope. It's 'posed to be def!" Browny suggested.

"No karate flicks! Blah!" David protested.

"I guess karate flicks are cool," Ty said. "But dang! When was the last time any of you cats saw a good *black* movie? Bet ya can't remember, can you?"

"I can't," David said. "Sometimes I just wanna holla, 'Yo Hollywood, ple-e-ease give us Negroes a chance!'"

"Ummm . . . it's 1982, Davy. Come correct! It's, 'Please give us *African Americans* a chance!'"

"No, Ty. I said it right the *first* time. I've been to *La-land*, remember? And trust me, we're still very much the *Negroes*, there. Hey, I know where we should go," David suggested. "Let's see the new movie, *Making Love*. I hear the two men actually, factually *kiss*," he whispered gleefully.

"Yo! Sports fans! Anybody see the *Knick*s game last night?" Browny asked, guiding the gab away from David and Ty's eternally queer talk.

Tyrone and David answered with a resounding, simultaneous, "Nah!"

Browny tried again.

"Yo, Facey, you used to run track. What you think of this new cat, Carl Lewis? That boy's bound to cop some crazy Olympic gold, huh?"

But Face was silent. Track? That shit was a lie he'd told

back in high school. Depina never ran track. But he'd also never copped to his athletic deception, and at that point, he couldn't see a reason why he should.

"Carl Lewis," David proclaimed. "There's something about that fast-ass black boy that I really *like*."

"I hear Diana's playing the Garden. Anybody wanna go? I'll buy the tickets," Tyrone said.

"Bet! Shit yeah, yo!" Browny quickly accepted.

"I can't, damn it! *Cats*, remember? I swear, all this steady work's puttin' a serious hurt on my social life," David complained. "Mondays are dark, though. I heard the new R & B king Luther's playin' the Beacon next month. And you *know* I loves me some Loofuh!"

"So, who the fuck *don't* you love, ya little queer?" Coming from Face Depina, those words brought a particular sting. David tried not to show it.

"Yo! Check it. This movie, the eats, the get high, hell this whole night's on you, right, Tyrone?" Browny made it sound like a given.

"Browny? Do I *look* like your Daddy?" Ty inquired, only half-jokingly.

"Yo! Come on, Tyrone! You's the one with all this new money, homey. You's the *only one* getting paid!"

"Browny, give it a rest," said David. "It ain't his fault he's brilliant."

"Fuck that shit! Tyrone? Yo, you payin' or what?" Browny hounded.

"I'll pay your way, Browny. All right? You *happy* yet?" Ty said. "But don't let this become a habit."

"Too late," said Face. "Already has."

"Yo! You mighta *wrote* the damn song, but ya didn't sing it all by ya damn self, did ya? We *all* shoulda been paid! Right, Pass-cow? Yo! Why ain't you sayin' shit? I *know* you feel the same way."

"And what *way* is that, Browny?" Ty's irritation was growing.

"Shit! Ya wrote the motherfuck, but the rest of us shouldn't be paid?"

"You know what, Browny? You're absolutely correct. I *wrote* the motherfuck. I *own* the publishing rights. Get over it. Or try to stop bitchin' long enough to sit down and *write yourself* a number one hit. Then *you* can spend the ducats anyway you want, ya hateful bastard!"

"Yo! I oughta bust you in your punk ass! Keep runnin' yo fuckin' mouth, Tyrone!"

Tyrone stopped in his tracks. "So you wanna *fight* me now, Browny?" he asked. "After *all* we've been through? Yo! *Yo!*" he mocked. "I'm talkin' to you, Faison! You wanna kick my ass? Huh? Then c'mon, let's do this, 'cause I'm sick with you and all your little petty shit!"

"Calm down, Ty. He's being Browny, like always," David said. "You know he's just jealous. Let's *try* havin' a good time for once."

But Browny refused to let it go.

"Depina! Yo, Face! Don't *you* want some of this?" Browny asked. "Ain't you got somethin' to say?"

"Oh? So now you *both* wanna kick my ass all up and down Broadway? Why you trippin' like this?" Tyrone asked, his face grimacing, then hardening in disgust.

"Well," Face said. "I ain't got no beef with you, Tyrone. It's *your* song, *your* money, man. But you know that shit was wrong."

Suddenly Tyrone was way north of pissed.

"See, David? Pay attention! What did I tell you about the Johnsons? Ain't no love, no brotherhood, no *nothin'* stronger than ignorant greed! The O'Jays had that shit correct. A small piece of paper carries a lotta dead weight. I said I'd take care of you all, and I *meant* it. Don't I break you off every chance I get? But it's never enough, is it? You'll always find something new to bitch about. You know what? Fuck a movie!" Ty said, then turned and walked in the opposite direction.

"Aw, Ty! C'mon! Don't be like that!" David called out.

"Yo! Fuck him!" Browny bellowed. "Don't nobody care about his bourgie ass! Walk away, bitch! Yo! David, *you* his favorite, why don't you wag your little ass behind him?"

"You know what, Browny?" David said. "That shit was small and fucked up, just like you! The *record label* screwed us, not Ty. When he breaks you off a grip, it's out of his *own* pocket. Tyrone is a fuckin' *prince*, but you can't see that!"

"Fuckin' *princess* is more like it!" said Face, nudging Browny into laughter.

"*Et tu*, Pascal?" Davy challenged.

"Fuck off, cocksucka," Face snapped. "Yeah, I said it. Now go home and cry about it like the little bitch you are!"

Turning their backs on David, Face and Browny headed for the nearest theatre.

Why you suddenly hate me so much, Facey? David thought. *God help me! Why am I so damn attracted to them pretty, damaged boys?*

Drawn to the dual plastic idols of good looks and cool swagger, David had a history of genuflecting before false gods.

There was a kind of magic about David Richmond, and it both fascinated and repelled, sometimes both at once. David was a character, a pure *original*. It mattered not if the boarding room in his head housed 127 personalities, each of whom "dressed for every occasion." Each of those people under his skin was a lithe, copper dancer, dancing, and sometimes tumbling toward grace.

Fey, silly, sexy, wise, whatever and whoever he was, he was always uniquely David. He'd breezed through tap and made a quick slide into jazz, then found an affinity for the rigors of ballet. When he was ten, he'd proudly been accepted into the prestigious Dance Theatre of Harlem's children's summer program. He'd worked hard, followed instruction, and by summer's end he was perfection in a Danskin. Back then, David believed that once he returned home he'd be a *firebird*—burning, flying, ready to soar.

Instead, his preacher father decided he was a tad too *merry* for comfort. So it became the Right Reverend Daddy Richmond's mission to make a "man" of his son. And he handed down an edict: "Boy, if you gonna float around here like some fancy sissy, then you gonna have to learn to fight!" The Right Reverend Daddy took David to a gym and *demanded* that he learn to box.

Daddy Richmond was determined to whip that little fairy clean out of Davy.

Boxing gave David a place to vent his anger over his father's implication that what he was, and all that he'd become, just wasn't good enough. Under those circumstances, the kid kicked much ass. He affected the swagger of a jock, and picked up the *shit talk*. It was a whole new role for David, an improvisation called survival.

The dancer-cum-athlete used his body as a brilliant artist would. With a cock of the head, a tilt of the neck, he *became* other people. He'd move from Pacino in *Scarface* to Vivian Leigh in *Ship of Fools*. People were there to be *fooled*, and fuck 'em if they couldn't take a joke.

But not everything was a joke. David took love, or the idea of it, very seriously. David truly, madly, deeply loved the idea of *falling in love*. Always had. Unfortunately, he had a knack for meeting the most unlovable people on the planet. Rico Rivera, for example.

A new and noticeably robust member of Daddy Richmond's congregation, Rico was a darkly handsome black Puerto Rican with a history of amateur boxing. Fifteen-year-old David couldn't seem to keep his eyes or mind off him.

APRIL 1985

David was a queer individual in many ways. Among his curiosities, he actually *liked* attending funerals. For him, they were these social events. And didn't David always look *fly* in black? He'd slip on his one modest suit, step into a parlor, sign the register, and should he be asked, he'd say, "Such a kind man, wasn't he? I used to stop by after work, and we'd talk." This apparently was more socially acceptable than the truth.

But this day was different. More than anything, he longed to say, "When I was fifteen, I used to collect his sweaty jockstraps from the locker room floor. I sniffed them and masturbated myself to sleep. And *you* would be . . . ?"

For this funeral, David meant serious grieving business. But like those times when he was fifteen, other thoughts intruded. As David listened to the mourners' solemn sentiments, he began to remember Rico Rivera in his prime. Ah, Rico—a five foot ten, russet-skinned, thick-printed *wonderman* . . .

David had already learned to box some, but that quite wasn't enough. The Reverend had a notion that Rico just might be the right influence to *set David straight*.

"Take my boy to the gym," he told Rico. "Turn the little sissy into a fighter!"

Rico, a middleweight with quick hands and a hot and deadly glare, once had a shot at the pros. This, in Reverend Richmond's eyes, made Rico a worthy role model. It mattered not that Rico had recently been paroled from prison, where he'd been sent for breaking and entering. He'd paid his debt to society, and "let those without sin," and so on. The Reverend trusted Rico to get the job done.

David's interest in boxing suddenly grew.

After a rigorous workout, Rico would head for the showers, leaving a trail of ripe clothing in his wake. Behind him, David would gather those damp sweaty articles, adoring them, sniffing their musk. Rico's jock, and the heady stink of it, became the source of endless fascination. Once inside the shower, David would watch Rico as he stood under a jetting nozzle. His eye perused the exquisitely rounded globes, a rich caramel color, the hot carved legs splayed apart as the water ran down his body in jeweled rivulets. David stood there, out of sight, envying the slow movement of that water.

And when Rico turned to face him, David found himself staring at a portrait of True Masculine Beauty. In David romanticized eye, what Rico possessed was more of a *prize* than a penis. It was sierra-skinned jackfruit. Oblong, soft-pulped, its magnificence called out, almost beckoning him from beneath tufts of wild black grass. Perfect in its mold, yet peculiar, full, and David noticed how its fullness seemed to be enlarging. Yes, Rico's piece was changing before David's very eyes. The dense bronze Spanish bar was elongating in its skin, growing hard, then harder, until hard as wrought iron.

Was it begging, was it saying, or was it hissing, "*Suck me?*"

Just then David let his presence be known. Against the rapid sound of the pounding in his chest, he'd asked so timidly, "Ummm . . . are you OK? Do-do-do you *need* anything, Rico?"

Rico didn't answer right away. Seduction was a quiet dance around the ring of David's libido.

"No. Get outta here, kid!" Rico finally said.

And the world ended.

But then the world began again one fated day after a workout when Rico said, "C'mon, Davy. Let's me and you take a long ride."

David's impatient heart became a drummer of new and exciting rhythms.

Rico drove fast that dark night, and his silence and the speed began to scare David. There had always been a tension between them. For David it was part mortal fear and part undying admiration. For Rico it was something else entirely.

Once safely at Rico's apartment, the boxer said, "I think we've done enough foreplay, don't you?" *Foreplay?* David wasn't sure of what he'd meant exactly. Then Rico led him into a small gym-like room, complete with a punching bag, mats, the stink of sweat, and the stained memoirs of old conquests. He tossed a pair of gloves at David, and demanded, "Put 'em on, kid!"

At that point, the *last* thing David wanted to do was to box. But he did as he was instructed to do. Immediately, Rico slugged him on the chin, hard, hard enough to make it sting, hard enough to make him cry. Rico then began tagging him forcefully with body blows. It seemed as though he wanted to beat, to hurt him with those repeated blows, and David tried like hell to shake them off with his shoulders. But then Rico cold-cocked him dead in the nose . . . and David fell hard to the mats.

"We've sparred long enough. Now drop those fuckin' sweats!" Rico commanded.

"No! Fuck you!" David spat, lying on the mats, his feelings, his body, everything in him hurting. Everything, except for his jackfruit, and Rico could plainly *see* that.

Unaccustomed to hearing "no," Rico crouched down low, and he quickly ripped Davy's sweats in two. It left him exposed and bulging in his jock. "Look at ya . . . all hard-up for me!" Rico grinned and quickly commenced running his tongue eagerly along the warming cloth. This felt strange and new to David. Strange and new, but he clearly didn't hate it. But then, all at once, Rico yanked down the jock's combustible panel and he gobbled up its hot and salty contents.

Suddenly, David's trembling member swam in the impulsive current of a man's mouth. This was what he'd wanted, and what he'd dreamed. Only he could not have dreamed the *feeling* of it. A warm sweeping motion consumed him, as a thousand sensations melded into one sighing moan. All he could do was *moan.* To be steeped in that crush of tongue and saliva was the most *authentic* thing he'd ever known.

It was realer than religion, realer than sin!

But this new, warm, wet sensation was getting the better of him. David suddenly, very quickly, a little *too* quickly, shivered, shuddered, and spurted all over.

This was more than just a climax. David had climaxed many times before. But this, *this* was *a Nut For the Ages*!

Afterward, ever the sweet talker, Rico warned, "I'll kick yo fuckin' ass if you ever tell, or if you *do* this shit with somebody else! Hear me? I swear, I'll fuck you up!"

And those hot words were like *romantic* music to David's burning ears.

One week later, Rico would redefine the meaning of "Breaking and Entering." But David would be the first to admit his little sugar plum was ripe to be plucked. What David remembered were plaid Bermuda shorts and Rico's legs—strong and dark, they shone with mad-sexy muscle. And those deep sable eyes with their endless lashes were all over him.

They parked in the woods on the edge of a lake. Rico's large hand crept up David's trim thigh and it burned there like a brand.

"You hot, ain't you, Davy? I can tell," Rico said as his hand delved inside David's Fruit of the Looms. David wanted to say, yes. Yes. YES! But he didn't have to say it. Rico took his thumb and held David's chin, and he kissed him, for just a second, on the lips. David felt as if he'd levitated.

They left the car and walked into the woods. They stopped in the dense part. There, they stood and removed their shorts. There, they stroked, they massaged and prowled each other's bodies. There, they rubbed their inflamed sticks together, hard, harder, until they seared and made sexual fire.

Next, there was kissing . . . long, slow, liquid kissing. This day Rico gave David a whole new appreciation of hands. Hands were as paramount to lovemaking as they were to the art of dance or of boxing. Each finger became an individual lover, entering him, probing so slowly, then deeper, so deeply that David soon begged for the genuine article.

"It'll sting a little at first," Rico warned. "It's supposed to. But don't worry, you'll get *used* to it."

Was he speaking about fucking, or was he speaking of *love?*

Rico mounted him with quick and eager purpose. David thought he was ready, but a part of him was not. Suddenly, a large brown blade of lightning sliced through David's core. "A-a-aw!" Pain inclined the dancer's spine into leaning. Pain came hard and pointed. David tightened, physically protesting pain's every thick and brutalizing inch. "Relax! Dammit, relax!" Rico demanded as he brusquely kicked David's legs apart. Soon his limbs spread and stretched like those branches hovering just above him. The rough husk and scratch of grass pricked and pounded, piercing, crushing him. Bark and limb and cherry were broken in that grass, and a burning boy yielded into moaning.

"That's it. Now you got it! Mmm. Just stay still, Davy, and let me make love to it."

David heard Rico clearly. He'd said *make love!* Make love, as opposed to fuck, which was what he was actually doing. Somehow, David's agony was lessened by the fact that he was *pleasing* Rico. More than this, Rico loved it, so in David's mind, Rico must've loved *him!*

From the moment of that erect and zealous shudder deep within him, Rico Rivera became a minor god, the beau ideal, and the shining bronze prototype for David's future choices.

Perhaps we all want some form of the thing which first wanted us. Or maybe we just long for the one thing we *never* truly *possessed*.

That summer, David learned the rhythm of bliss, and the elation in what his father called "sin." He'd learned how to please, and to find some painful contentment inside that act of pleasing.

Life was wonderful, and so was love, even when it was a secret love.

And then Rico, very shortly after, unexpectedly married the church's second organist. David's father, the Right Reverend Richmond, presided over the ceremony as David watched, quietly shattered, from the pews.

And now, a man with Rico's older, sadder face lay soundly, most profoundly dead. David Richmond wanted to scream: "*Liars!* Rico didn't die of any damn cancer! You sit here grieving a lie . . . and half of you probably know it . . . especially the young boys in here. And what are you crying for . . . *who* are you *really* crying for?"

But David had been taught good Christian etiquette, so painfully he swallowed his ire, and he chilled.

And then, before this *ceremony of lies* was completely over, David rose from his seat. He excused himself and quickly exited that stained glass grievatorium. After all, it was Wednesday, and thus, Wet Jock Night at Limelight.

CHAPTER FOUR

The Condition of One's Loafers

BROOKLYN, JULY 1977

As they often did, the New York contingent of the Hunter clan gathered at Tyrone's Aunt Viv's place for Sunday dinner. That particular day, all things seemed familiarly tribal as they commenced digging into the mutilated bird. But then, another kind of foul entered the festivities: Uncle Jerome. A small, reed-thin, pop-eyed man in an omnipresent porkpie had stumbled in to perform his long-running one man show entitled "Let's Piss on the Family Dinner."

"Aw-w-w! Y'all done started without me again," he said scratching his backside while Aunt Hattie clicked her tongue in disgust.

"Don't worry, I ain't got no fleas, Hattie," he countered. "I's scratchin' my ass 'cause it itch, damn it. Don't you fat, black church people's asses ever itch? Or do prayer *cure* that shit?"

No one said a word. Tyrone could feel his cheeks puffing like blowfishes. He wanted to laugh, but he knew enough to chill.

"Well, where my chair at, huh? Ain't I 'posed to have a chair in this here courtroom?"

The eating continued.

Jerome ambled, arms stretched out as if he were walking a tightrope to the china cabinet, and fetched himself a plate. He chose one of Viv's finest dishes. Then, staring at them all, Jerome purposely let it fall to the floor. Every person present jumped.

"Yeah, I drinks!" he proclaimed. "Damn it, I'm a drunk!" He gazed around the table at the faces of his family, faces that refused to acknowledge him. "Guess I be the only sinner in this room, huh? Well, ya ain't gotta feed me and ya ain't gotta love me if ya don't want. Guess what? I don't need ya. I'ma find me someone and we g'on live our *own* long, blue moan."

Ty wondered what a "blue moan" was, and what-in-the-inebriated hell Jerome was talking about.

"Ain't nobody said you ain't got feelings, Jerome. Now let me fix you a plate," Viv said.

No one else spoke. To Ty, it seemed to be a contest. Which Hunter family member could best ignore Jerome's drunken ass? Aunt Viv fixed him a plate. And after cussin' them out for "turnin' they backs on they own," Jerome left. And everything resumed as if his anger weren't still lurking in every corner of the room.

Once the sweet potato pie was finished and the young'ns, including Ty, were dismissed, the women started in on the Jerome conversation.

Ty followed his cousins sluggishly and heard his Aunt Hattie say, "Shit! You need to put his puny ass out!"

"What am I g'on do? Better he stay here than in the gutter!" Aunt Viv responded. "Girl, where else he gonna go? Don't nobody want him . . . 'cause he fucks with men."

The phrase was blunt, concise, and shocking as "The Truth, Black Folks Style" often is. No pussy-footing, no vague allusions to Jerome liking show tunes, or to the condition of his loafers. No creative euphemisms to pretty-up his vulgar reality. And Ty knew by the sound, the *inflection* in Viv's voice, that it *was* vulgar.

Suddenly, he understood why his Uncle Jerome was the eternal family outcast. Why Jerome drank the way he did. Why Jerome was barely tolerated. Yes, now he knew. And he wanted to weep for his uncle, and for himself. The lesson lay in four short words: He fucks with men.

Go ahead! Be a faggot, and alienate everyone you love! Once outside the walls of family gossip and rejection, a tentative Tyrone approached his mysterious uncle. He knew to tread lightly. He didn't want that violent fool living inside of Jerome going off on him. So, he made his presence known by clearing his throat, and it stirred Jerome from his momentarily reverie.

"So Unk. Let me ask you somethin'. What's a 'long blue moan?'"

Jerome cocked his head, and clicked his tongue in mock annoyance. In some sober part of him, he was secretly glad that Ty had found the gonads to ask.

"Bwoi, ain't you ever heard *real* jazz befo'? I don't mean just Billie, or dat new stuff they be teachin' you in dat school. I mean 'Trane, and Bird, Clifford Brown, Little Jimmy Scott, Art Tatum and dem cats? Dem's some special jazz angels right there. Sometimes, when just when you need it, they make music . . . and the sound floats so deep inside ya, you can *feel* it, deep in ya weary bones . . . and it gets re-e-e-e-eal personal. It becomes your sound, alone. It UNDERSTANDS your blues, your sadness, your joy, and everything you feel. It knows all about you, everything you are, or wanna be, and'll never be. When that happens, all you can do is *moan*. Moan, 'cause, finally, something or somebody in this crazy world understands you, and feels like you do. And that feelin' is good, bwoi." He closed his eyes as if reliving a Good Moment, a serene and profoundly pristine moment, wrapped in a blue neon glare of his past life, and then he sighed. "Don't nothin' beat a Long Blue Moan, bwoi. Ain't nothin' else like it. Now, some people, I mean *real special* people, they can do that too. They can give you that moan. They can wrap it up and just give it to ya, like a gift, 'cause they understands you."

They walked outside, and Jerome gazed at the setting sun. His eyes squinted at that bright orange orb hanging so low in the Brooklyn sky. Raising his bag, he toasted that sun and his own sad and plastic freedom. He toasted it with the bottle in his brown paper bag. "You think I'm dumb, but I ain't. I see you, *clear* as this day. And lemme tell you this bwoi," he said in a whisper. "Don't let *no man take* your manhood."

Ty wondered if his Uncle Jerome was crazy-drunk. He didn't sound like it. But like those times when he was truly crazy stupid-drunk, Ty didn't quite understand what he meant.

Yet Jerome had the look of a fool in his eye, and Ty thought it best to go back inside.

Later that evening, Jerome cornered Ty, having recognized traces of himself in his teenage nephew. Tyrone expected the usual mindless drunken gibberish.

Instead, Jerome grabbed him by the collar and said, "Can't nobody live yo life, but you, boy. So don't you let nobody steal yo motherfuckin' joy! Ya hear me?" He took a long anguished swig from the brown paper bag he carried through life. "See, they don't like me," he declared, his brown eyes more sad than red. "They don't like me. Never did. My own brother, and sisters, Ty. You think I did somethin' to 'em? I ain't did shit but tried to live *my* life. That's all."

Tyrone wanted to say something comical or comforting to blow it off. But he knew it was true. He felt an incredible sadness, as if he were looking in the mirror of his own future.

Jerome. What a lonely existence he must've been for him. This was not what Jerome wanted. This was not who he wanted to become. Ty understood that now, and in a secret part of his heart, he wanted to embrace the lonely drunk wobbling in front of him.

"Bwoi, *look* at me! You g'on live your life. You go'n meet some men, and dem men go'n feel just like *you* feel inside. And some of dem men will *like* you, for a minute. And that minute is tricky. Don't you go believin'in no minutes, bwoi! Even when dem minute men make you feel like you ain't alone. *Respect* yourself! Don't you go takin' all kinds of *minute men* inside you, bwoi! Find you somebody that understands you if you g'on go through dis pain out here. Find you somebody, and hold on to dat. Don't make you no mo or less a man. It don't make you a punk if you pitch or catch. You understand what I'm sayin'? Just don't you *never* let no kinda bum inside you who ain't *worth* it. And make sure nobody go inside you without no rubber. Ya understand me, bwoi?"

Ty nodded, embarrassed as all hell. But now he understood. He understood that his crazy, drunk, *bent* Uncle loved him . . . whatever the condition of *his* loafers.

Jerome wandered off down the block, nodding as he passed Omar Peterson.

Ty, his cousins, and Omar—nineteen, well built, and deeply hip—often sat on the same stoop watching life, kids, men, women, and fools go by. Beyond noticing him, Ty was *feeling* Omar. He dug his tough boy Brooklynese swagger, and how his deep-mahogany skin caught a shimmering light. Omar had a moist little habit of grabbing himself through his Levi's when he thought Ty was looking. Yeah, Omar was kind of hot in that "I don't have to try to be, I just got it like that" way. At least Ty thought so. Sometimes, he'd shoot Ty *The Ray*, that special gaze some gay boys gave each other, and it made Tyrone wonder just *how hip* Omar was.

After Jerome passed, Omar strolled over toward Ty, handed him a note on the sly, then walked away. That night, as Ty lay in bed, he opened Omar's surreptitious note.

Do you want to be a 'faget?' I could show you. Nothing wrong with being a 'faget' long as you keep it secret. I can show you the 69 Saturday. Come to the Brooklyn Library, and we could hook up. Just don't tell. If you don't want to, it's OK. But just DON'T TELL anybody. Peace. 'O'. P.S. Throw away this note. I'm serious! Saturday morning after 10 o' clock, call me. Let my phone ring once then hang-up if you coming. Tyrone? Throw away this note. I'm serious!

For one belly-aching moment, he imagined it was a cruel hoax. Or worse, a setup! Maybe Omar and his big, bad Brooklyn boys would show up and wail on his "faget" ass, punch him in the throat and kick him in the dick.

Then his mind took a *negativity pause*. Maybe Omar *was* gay. Ty considered the secrecy, the constant grabbing of the dick, and how, when Omar said something funny, he'd look at Ty as if measuring Ty's glee factor, *Ty's delight*.

Everything made a vague kind of sense. *Yeah! Omar could be that way!* The prospect excited Ty because from the first day Ty saw him, he dug him some Omar with his hard-boy, dark-chocolate, crotch grabbing, cool-ass self.

Tyrone read and reread that note, pushing, pulling and rubbing his stiffness into those words, pulling and tugging until the ink began to smudge, blur, and flood the page.

Saturday came. Ty dialed the digits, let it ring once, and abruptly hung up. Butterflies aside, he told the appropriate lies and hopped a subway to the Brooklyn Library. But if Omar fucked around and wore the wrong outfit, didn't comb his hair, brush his teeth, or any other equally unappealing shit . . .

Hello. Omar appeared, and he did not disappoint. In his black Levi's and white T—one sleeve rolled up, two Kools in the crease—Omar was Brooklyn heat personified.

"Hey," he said. "So you wanna do this?" His voice was full of confidence.

"Bet. Let's go." A warm thrill rose in Ty's belly, a slightly high, slightly ill feeling of nerves, anticipation, and curiosity. They walked side by side, but not too close, and neither had much to say.

No one was home at Omar's crib. But he didn't know exactly when one of his brothers, his sister, or heaven forbid, *his moms* might return.

"Wanna beer?" he asked, playing the host.

"No, thanks," Ty replied. He never much liked beer, and besides, he already felt on the verge of retching. So he sat on the couch, pretending to be enthralled by the longhaired Asian chick shaking her tail down the *Soul Train* line. Omar stood near the telly, slowly, blatantly rubbing that notorious thing he rubbed.

Ty looked, saw that growing soul train line in Omar's Levi's, and said, "So, whachu wanna do, man?"

Omar glared at him as if to say, *Damn boy! I know you a virgin, and this shit is new for you. But are ya stupid, too? We ain't about to do the nasty in the middle of my mama's livin' room, fool!* But what he said was, "Follow me."

So, Ty followed him down that long, thin hallway indigenous to Brooklyn apartments. Omar stopped where the deed would be done, at the end of the corridor, in an empty space near the closet by the room Omar shared with his brother. A slant of July sunlight streamed inside and hovered in that space, giving them just enough light to see, admire, trace the contours of each other.

Omar removed his shirt. The brother's chest was a terrific traffic jam of dark, hard, muscular lines, one swerving into the hard, dark next. Already there were black ringlets splayed across it, and rich chocolate nipples sat erect and stony as two hardened Brooklyn projects. Suddenly there were crazy beats inside Ty's chest. Omar's skin in that limited light was close to indigo, and like smoke, it swirled in Tyrone's eyes. Omar held him inside a stare; cogent of his physical appeal, yet only partially aware of this spell he was casting upon Tyrone's very soul.

Did he know what a prize he was? Did he know how his full lips were like soft, puffy rafts Ty wanted to board and, if he could, sail away on from every secret he'd ever kept?

More than anything, Ty wanted to kiss those ripened lips. But he didn't know the rules yet. Still, it seemed Omar was willing him to kiss his neck, to lick his pulsing jugular. Looking at the radiance which seemed to emanate from him, Ty recalled those summers of pickup B-ball games, the funky Converse All-Stars, and the shooting gush of hydrant waters washing him clean, washing *them* clean.

But they were boys then. And as far as he could see, Omar was now *a man*.

And the man unfastened his pants. And the man wore blazing red nylon briefs. And those briefs were swollen and stretching and taut. And red nylon never hugged a man's dick tighter. And that dick was large. Unexpectedly, breathlessly large!

Omar pulled at Ty's T, grinding his largeness into Ty's thigh. Backing away, Ty removed his shirt. Omar placed Ty's hand upon the girth of his growing projection. A rush of adrenaline zoomed up Ty's spine. Ty rubbed and Omar's piece grew and spiked through the skinny shroud of nylon.

"Stand back," Omar warned, as if this giant phallus he possessed needed more room for its big debut. Ty stepped back.

And Omar rolled those red nylon briefs slowly down his hips, his thighs, his calves . . .

And there he stood. Beyond large. Beyond hard. Beyond words. The deepest, darkest, mahogany rod bobbed long though exquisitely flawed. The dim light illuminated its bulbous head just so. Omar was *much* more man than Ty had ever bargained for.

"Now, let's see *you*," Omar said.

Ty was, by then, hard as hard could possibly be. Seven-and-a-half inches of taut, teenage buoyancy. He unzipped, reached in, and produced his erect and leaking fruit.

Omar slapped his custard apple against Tyrone's, flushing him with heat. They stood, foreheads touching, breathing hard and stroking, rubbing. Breathing hard and slowly grinding, their swollen lips wanting kisses, wanting everything. But afraid, withholding. They stood *closeasthis*, breathing, sweating, breathing, waiting, erect with lust and expectancy.

Omar moved first. A dip, a bend. A pinch. A raw and hungry gnaw of nipple, he made the slow descent down chest and belly and bush. And with one breath through the kiss of Omar's lips, Ty's dick disappeared inside a hot shock of moisture. Slippery. Hot. Gliding. Hot. Heading for the throat hot! Ah-h-h! First time blow job. Everything inside Ty quickened, suddenly alive, dynamic, active, and supreme. Brand-new bliss slid, surfed, and sloshed along him. His amorous hand slid across the spiraling waves of Omar's spinning skull. Thoughts of something like *Love* began whirling in his belly.

Then, looking up, his eyes fixed inside that *need*, Omar smiled and said, "Now, you try me."

He pulled Ty down, and they lay upon that cool wooden floor, contorting like dark and salty pretzel boys. The taste of Omar's sweat kissed the thirst of Tyrone's lips, and then, with one deep, memorable breath, he made that glide down pounding chest, heaving belly, down scratching path of pubic naps to that tremulous tip.

Oh! So *this* was what was meant by *69!* Breaths quickened into labored panting, into strident bucks, into pitching hips and lips sighing, "Ah! Shit!" Omar's strong hand shoved Ty's head further, then further down his long and slippery wedge. It felt so warm, so wet and so strangely heavy to his tongue. The act became a challenge for Ty; a test to see if he could possibly possess Omar, in all of his totality. He soon learned that he could not manage it. Yet, through a river of sweat with a current of veins and the wildest pulsations, he tried.

Ty was inside of Omar's lips, and he could feel that grip grow stronger as its suction became tighter. Omar commenced sucking like street-tough roughnecks never dared to suck. Soon, he was fighting the pitch of Ty's dick-happy thrusts, and he was winning.

Tyrone devoured what he could, his lips and tongue running, his head and neck pumping against the heat of skin and drum of veins. This was, its own way, miraculous. That this brother he knew as Omar, would want Tyrone with the same passion that Ty found himself wanting him. "Ah-h-h! Ahh!" Ty shuddered as his eyes closed and the softest chrome blue light came inside of his lashes.

It was then that Omar shifted from homeboy into a smoothly erotic angel. This metamorphosis felt very real and yet somehow magical in Tyrone's soul. In that moment, Omar became a *long blue moan* caught in the pit Tyrone's throat, and Ty didn't want that sweet choking to end. Omar plunged deeper, and in unison they caught the same fever, the same rhythm, the same fire. And they moved together, tough and tender, angry and sweet, hurting and yet, cured.

Omar pulled away, and Ty followed. Their excited hands commenced to beating proud wet stalks. The verge of eruption seemed but a stroke, a breath away. Ty volcanoed first, bursting, filling his fist in hot spiking rivers of white. Omar followed, shaking, shooting and pitching his gift. And Ty watched him, shuddering, as he sprayed the seed of need, turned satisfaction, like a black Uzi to the floor.

Ty lay there with a man, a full, bucking, squirting man. He fell into a silent study of Omar's face. Beads of sweat aside, it was a dark and beauteous face, and Ty found himself landing on the softest reaches of its tough owner's soul. The *thud* was so precise, it was unmistakable: Ty was falling *in love* with Omar, and five minutes before he hadn't known that feeling could ever exist for him. But his mind sighed, *Oh, Ty. You love him. You do. You love Omar. Yes! But . . . uh-oh! You love him, and he's a roughneck.*

But posturing roughneck not withstanding, Tyrone had become Officially Queer. That day he felt he was at last, sexually baptized as a new and radiant "*faget.*" A happy to be nappy, albeit closeted, citizen of the other side.

"What time is it? Quick, man! You gotta get dressed! My sister'll be back from doin' laundry any minute," Omar said briskly, killing the mood, but never the memory. The two of them quickly dressed, and it didn't matter much to Ty if the brother had no post-fellatio etiquette. Tyrone felt sure they were destined.

Three weeks later, after much suggestion, coaxing and slow neck kissing, Ty *gave it up*. He would experience the agony of the anus with a man inside it, because, for Omar, it was mandatory. The idea frightened Ty, as he remembered his Uncle Jerome's warning. It didn't stop him. But he insisted rubbers be involved.

Giving it up to Omar was the biggest, most painful, most necessary lesson of Ty's sexual schooling: Men are dicks. If you prefer them, dicks are cool. But let one inside you, and it hurts, physically. Yet sometimes the deeper, most unforgettable pain comes from the depth of the emotional bang.

After its stretching and after the pleading, after the insertion, after the voices and after its agonizing culmination, after all this, for Omar the challenge was gone. Thus, their queer relationship abruptly ended.

Omar had fucked himself another virgin. Mission complete. Omar checked Ty off the list, like his mama's dry cleaning.

This incident caused a shattering of sorts. At first it confused him. When Omar wouldn't take his calls, when Omar made excuses, or simply ignored him, when Omar took to squiring homegirls around from the block, when Omar locked his arm around their shoulders in Tyrone's presence, it hurt him deeply. After a few weeks of this treatment, it pissed-off, sickened, crushed, and then, ultimately toughened Tyrone.

"Omar might've been a roughneck, but he was a *bigger punk* than me," Ty would later say metaphorically. "He took me to the dark end of the fair. I was scared as shit, but I dug him. I was willing to walk beside him into that haunted house of voices. But he refused to go in with me. Fool! He turned out to be nothing more than this cowardly clown. I could've shown him how to step outside the center ring. But he fucked around, got scared, and missed the whole damn carnival."

CHAPTER FIVE

"Face" the Facts

As it turns out, Mr. Paul Newman didn't go slumming through the South Bronx and leave his seed to nest inside some sweet café au lait creature resulting in a pretty-ass Face Depina. However, Face still did possess a color-rich pedigree. His mother, Matilda "Mattie" Dupree, was part Creole and part Caribbean. She bore a striking resemblance to Lena Horne. His father, Alphonze "Fonzy" Depina, was Portuguese and a quarter German. A real good-looking cat, Fonzy played a mean jazz sax and was a preeminent studio musician back in the day. A chronic drugger, boozer, and womanizer supreme, he put aside his pills, potions, and pandemic penis as soon as he'd first laid eyes on Matilda. At least, he did, for a time.

"Dupree, huh?" he'd asked. "So, just exactly how French are you?"

Ah! Mattie of the flowing black hair and flashing hazel eyes. Their love was real, dizzying; it was lyrical, sublime and so very jazzy. But their lover's concerto caused nothing but clashes of disharmony, as neither of their families would condone their coupling. Mattie, though fair, was deemed too dark for the boldly beige Portuguese Depina clan. And Alphonze was so high-yella, he was damn near white. Besides, the man was a musician—by definition, *a fancy-ass vagabond.* Yet nothing could stop two crazy kids in love.

And, ah! The things that bloom from the flowers we love.

Face: "Family? What the fuck is that? Movin' from one broke-down project to the next? One more set of people that didn't know who I was, or *what* I was. Just 'cause what I was didn't *look* like them. And it was all right to call me 'half-and-half,' 'octoroon *maricoon*,' '*mixed spick*,' '*butter pecan nigga*.' I heard all that shit and worse. And *this* was *family*. Every last one of 'em was stone-broke and hopeless as they fuckin' jokes! Treated me like shit. I used to run away just so I could get lost somewhere, anywhere. Never got all the way lost, though, 'cause don't people try to find you when you lost? I don't remember nobody ever tryin' to find my poor yellow ass."

Pascal Depina was punted back and forth between relatives like a worn-out soccer ball. He heard it all, from "You take him. I got six kids, and I never did like his daddy anyway" to "Foster parent? Well, how much do it pay?"

Finally, he landed in the streets of East Harlem, keeping company with stripper chicks, dealers, pickpockets, and cons. He lived by his wits, stole what he could, panhandled when he had no choice. More than once, he slept in a dumpster. Other times, he relied on the kindness of carnal-minded strangers.

Then, one day *she* saw him.

FEBRUARY 1974

"Boy? Whatchu doin' out here on these streets? Ain't you got someplace to be? Somebody home waitin' for you, son?

You hungry? You ain't on nothin', is you? Fess up! Don't even try to run no game on me!"

Lavinia "Precious" Stone was a streetwalker who saw a lost, green-eyed boy trying his best to be brave. And that green-eyed boy awakened a memory in her. She imagined Pascal as the *What if?* on the other side of her first abortion. She saw something in him, and to her, that something felt *personal*. She offered him room, board, and a taste of her terminal freedom. And because he was looking to love someone, Pascal loved her.

She had the softest hazelnut skin, too soft and pretty for the dirty work she did.

"They rent my body," she told him. "That's it. Not one of these played-out three-minute sons of bitches evuh gets *my* heart!"

Then she smiled a smile reserved only for him, and he snuggled in her bed to sleep with her. He was fourteen; she was thirty-three. She was everything: mother, father, teacher, protector, provider, and finally his lover. Some nights she'd let him suckle her, and she'd pacify him to sleep.

But that kind of intimacy began to feel wrong to Pascal.

"People *always* put they damn hands on me," he told her. "Women was playin' with my peter when I didn't want nobody playin' with it."

The men were no better. Nor were the crazy aunts and cousins, and uncles, and the kids down the street. He was a pretty, yellow, green-eyed novelty, and *that* was all anybody ever wanted to know about him.

"I remember my only birthday party. I was six. Aunt Claire made a chocolate cream cake. Don't remember how it tasted. All I remember is crazy Aunt Vera yellin' 'Happy Birthday Pascal' and jammin' her fuckin' tongue down my throat. They made me run around naked, and they pointed and laughed at me. 'Let's see if little Pascalito's pee-pee's grown!' That shit was wrong! They was supposed to look *out* for me."

Lavinia listened, the shielded pieces of her heart unraveling to him.

"I'm sorry, honey. I thought you *wanted* to be close to me. I . . . I didn't know," she said, lightly kissing his shoulder. "I swear on everything left to believe in, Pascal, I won't never touch you wrong again."

She kept her word. And she died of cervical cancer the following spring.

So Pascal Depina was fifteen and back on the streets when he wandered into a midtown parish. It was said to be a *safe house* under the care of good Christian men, with care-giving eyes and arms spread wide open to welcome children of the ski-marked night. But despite their robes and talk of God, they were no different than the rest who saw beauty and abused its golden, boyish body.

Pascal met Angel at that safe house. Angel, a vet at ten, had the safe house thing tricked out by thirteen. He was a street-scarred sixteen when he got into a fistfight with Pascal. They battled to a draw, and slowly Angel's iciness thawed a bit.

Some might say Angel was not only a graduate, but the valedictorian from the school of "*Do Ya Wanna Get Fucked Up and Do Fucked Up Shit?*"

It was the winter of a growth spurt. Pascal went from five foot ten to six foot three, and Angel dug how the new height, the deeper voice, and premature mannish beauty got them inside liquor stores, movie doors, and the cool restricted clubs. Yet, it didn't take long before Angel grew to resent that shit, too.

When you're walking down 42nd Street and the whores tease *your* boy, oohing and ahing at his prettiness and offering to fuck *him* for free, it can piss you off. Everything seemed to come effortlessly for Pascal. Angel would gawk at that dreamy puss, looking so damn smug and so fucking pretty, and he'd almost want to fuck him himself. He wanted to kick his ass, then fuck him. But Angel couldn't, because Angel was straight. So Angel kicked his ass and left him in the gutter.

MAY 1975

Erik Von Ness was Viking blond, ice-blue-eyed, and brick-headed. He was New York's other extreme, Fifth Avenue-bred, a former pilot, mountain climber, full of daring-do. Von Ness was born with a fortune, and added to it by investing well. He met Pascal outside of the Port Authority, where Pascal was running his latest hustle: picking pockets under the guise of helping travelers with their bags. The tip was usually fifty cents, a dollar, a five-spot tops. But Von Ness *looked like money*. Pascal swooped up Erik's Ralph Lauren bags and placed them into a waiting cab, deciding to leave his wallet alone. Von Ness, liking Depina's moxy, intrigued by the mad, young cobra lounging in those shrink-to-fit, purposefully tight 501s, handed him a fifty-spot.

"Keep it. It's yours."

"For real? Thanks! Thanks a lot, man."

Then Von Ness wagged his finger. Pascal knew the move. He viewed men who wagged their fingers at him in a *c'mere* gesture as men with sex on their mind. To him, they were, in fact, wagging their dicks, *the dick of their fingers*, when they asked, "Would you like to take a ride?"

Opportunity smelled of subtle sweat and high-priced cologne.

Pascal told Van Ness his story, emphasizing the parts rich, white, liberal, horny people would want to rectify.

"So . . . what about school?" Erik asked. He was clearly fascinated by the kid's tale of urban survival.

"School? Man, it wasn't my scene. When I went, they called me 'ghetto trash' 'cause I didn't *look* like them or wear the *right* clothes. Hell, I don't *got no* decent clothes."

"I don't *have any* decent clothes," Von Ness corrected.

Pascal told him he was going to be somebody "large." Maybe even an actor.

"In junior high, they put on that play *Guys and Dolls.* I was Nathan Detroit. Folks say I was good. Man! I sure *felt* good on that stage, with that applause, and all that good shit! I wasn't ghetto trash no more. They got schools for kids with talent. I know this kid who goes to one. So maybe if I can save enough cash, I'll find a place, cop some fly rags, and look into something like that."

"Well, you certainly have *presence*," Erik said. He stared at Pascal and saw a grit that wasn't yet grimy. Inside that contemplative eye-fuck, Von Ness was trying to decide if he could trust Pascal. But who didn't want to trust a face so damn pretty? "Listen. I travel quite a bit, and my houseboy recently went back to Singapore. Would you like to housesit for me? Just for the summer. I'd pay you, and you'd have full use of the pool, the tennis court, the entire house. What do you think?"

"What? No shit? You serious?"

"Yes, I'm serious."

"That's fuckin' WOW! What do I think? I think, yes, man! Hell, yes!"

Erik laughed, and Pascal laughed. They sealed the deal with a handshake and a rigorous ass-fuck. The whole time, Pascal closed his eyes and imagined himself lord of that magnificent manor. He could see himself living and ruling over such a place, and the vision of it all was almost erotic.

Soon, Erik was grunting, groaning, and gushing excitedly against his belly, and Pascal, in turn, detonated over the whole vision-of-richness trip. The two of them lay heaving, staring at the high marble ceiling, as Erik issued one warning.

"By the way, kid, this is crucial: my business must always remain *my* business. So, no company. No sleepovers or hanging with your friends. No one-night stands here—ever. Should I find you've deceived me in any way . . . well, for your sake, I hope you never do. Understand?" Von Ness gazed at the set of ancient *machetes* adorning his wall just above the fireplace.

Pascal did understand. So he never talked about the orgies with Fortune 500 guys, or the day a man he watched raise a family on TV showed up at the door, ready to get his not-for-prime-time freak on.

And so began Pascal's summer of living less dangerously. A summer of cleaning pools, dusting masterpieces, and waxing fine wood floors. He answered the door, took Erik's calls, and a poor boy got to live a part-time life of Riley. He was a *good* lad *most* of that summer. It paid to be. Erik, bless his horny, liberal soul, managed to get him into that school of performing arts, and purchased him a fly new Italian designer wardrobe to boot. For Pascal "Face" Depina, youthful ambition proved to be a very *fruitful* thing, indeed.

CHAPTER SIX

Singin' for The Panties

When you're not the boy all the girls adore, what do you do? Do you shrug your shoulders, and just say "fuck em?"

Fuck 'em was all Browny wanted to do. He'd been wanting to since he was 12, when his older brother "Trick" would bang the girls quickly in the small Harlem room they'd share. There, just a few feet away in the twin bed opposite his, Browny would listen to the sounds of lust. To his ears there was no music in it—rhythm, yes—but no music in the grunts and groans, the sighs, the moans, in the shrieks that begged "STOP! Yes!! NO! MORE!"

Who were those schizophrenic Lolita's anyway? And why couldn't they ever make up their damn minds?

But so what if it didn't play like music! The sound of sex aroused him, made him feel curious and all jumpy inside. He wondered what it would be like, and when he'd get his chance on that schizophrenic female carnival ride. He had no rap, no game, no plan, and no discernable play. He didn't have the dazzling looks or the height or superior ball-court skills. And though willful, in many ways, Faison Brown felt inferior to all the other boys on the block. But he *did* possess the one thing those other cool boys did not: Faison could croon, and with his voice, he could sing for his pussy.

His brother Trick Brown first took him aside and schooled him on this phenomenon.

"You see Eddie Kendricks, the pretty one in The Temptations. Women love that cat. I'm sure pretty as he is, he *always* got the draws, and it didn't matter that the boy could sing, too. But not everybody's Eddie Kendricks, yo. You think you *look* like Eddie Kendricks? Hell nah! But you can sing, even *better* than his ass, and that's for sure. Women throw they drawers at Eddie. But what they throwin your way, brotha? Well, besides the middle finger, yo? Ya needs to *work* for them panties. Ya needs to make 'em melt down they wet thighs, hell, ya needs to make dem shits fuckin' vaporize! And you can do that shit, too. You can melt the panties with that voice of yours. Now, I don't mean none of that opera bullshit! Besides, where a BLACK man gonna get a fuckin' job singin opera, yo? All you gotta do is sing real sweet to 'em, nice and low and quiet-like. I'm tellin' you, bro, if you finesse that shit, you could be like the new pimp of Harlem."

Trick was seldom wrong about anything, especially when it came to getting what he wanted. No. Browny wasn't Eddie Kendricks, nor was he Eddie Munster. But he thought *maybe* he could be the *Black Eddie Fisher*, because Browny's mother once *loved* her some Eddie Fisher, and though he was no pretty boy, he'd once sang and snagged the beauteous ass of a young Elizabeth Taylor.

Singin for the panties . . . it sounded like a plan.

Faison Brown took to singing everywhere he went. He sang to himself while walking down the street. He sang quietly on the bus and on the subway. He sang and people began to take notice, the women especially.

At 15, he'd landed his first job in a local record store in midtown. He was hired to replenish the stock and sweep the floors after school. Browny was not a big fan of cleaning up after people, but one of the perks to the gig was that he could listen to all the newest music, for free. Browny not only listened, he sang along.

He liked the reaction he saw in people's eyes when the music stopped and this glorious sound continued, wafting from *his* lips. He simply loved the attention. He felt as if he was finally winning the favor of people, in particular that of young women.

One such woman was Verna Stevens. Verna was a bright-skinned girl with pretty hazel eyes, 'that good *Indian* hair' and yes, a slight overbite. And Verna, at nineteen, was four years older and another lifetime more experienced in all things carnal.

Jon Lucien's captivating "Song For My Lady" poured from store's speakers, and Browny, a talented mimic, sang along, copying that enchanting island patois, and all:

"Mornin' sun, oh tell me what you've brought my way today . . .
Is it perfumed blossoms for my lady's hair?
Wasn't she smilin' when ya looked upon her face today?
Was she singin' praise of Mother Nature's way?"

Verna heard that voice, and the slow vaporization of the panties began. She didn't think Faison Brown was beautiful, but God, he was beyond sexy when he blew those notes!

"Baby? You could tame the fuckin' birds from the trees with that voice! So what yo number is?" she giggled.

Browny could not remember a single time when he'd ever made a girl *giggle* with delight, so perhaps this was the first.

It was almost closing time, and Verna, mesmerized by the kid with the velvet in his throat, waited outside the store. She wasn't in love, and she wasn't a whore. She just wanted to connect with the person, with the owner of that voice, to hear it rub against her ear, whisper sexy refrains between her legs, and to take her slowly to another world. That was it. That was all.

"You really should be arrested for molesting women with that voice," she joked as Browny stepped outside. Browny smiled. It was a Good Moment. "So, where you off to?

"Home. Why?"

"You still live with yo mama, don't you?" she asked.

"Ummm . . . yeah." Of course he did. He was still a kid.

"So, you in a hurry to get back there?" she asked suggestively, chipping in a wink.

Rookie or not, Browny felt very sure he could have him some of this curious bright-skinned chick with the pretty eyes, good hair and that slight overbite.

"I'm Verna," she said.

"I'm Faison," he said.

And that was all that either of them said.

Back at Verna's apartment, she put on an Isley Brothers record. Ronald Isley was not just her go-to voice when she was feeling frisky; Ron Isley was her God. And little did she know that Browny could mimic him, too.

"Oh Lawd, boy!"

He didn't remember her clothes coming off. It was like he sang, and they just disappeared. He didn't recall who kissed who first, but suddenly his singing tongue was lodged down her throat. He was pushed against the living room wall, and her hands were all over him. "Keep singin!" she said. And he did, between kisses. And he did, between nibbles to her ear. And he did, between sucks to her tits. And he did, and soon, he was fucking her. Fucking her. Fucking this stranger named

Verna, who felt soft and wet in those places where he hadn't even touched her.

This was like discovering a new planet. This was mature pussy, engulfing his penis. This was like being launched into a whole other orbit. She sighed, and he felt like crying. "Keep singin!" she said, as if his singing were the only magic she'd ever know. "Keep singin!" And he did, between each restless, breathless stroke.

He kept singing, but he didn't sing long.

Faison Brown finished singing before Ron Isley did.

He arrived on her belly with a grunt and great massive shiver, the size of which he'd never known.

"Damn, boy! Just damn! You sure *sing* better than you can fuck!"

Browny didn't care. Well, not really. He'd just discovered a new dimension to his gift. Ahh . . . the Power of the Panty-melting Voice!

The rest would be sexual history.

CHAPTER SEVEN

The Book of Ty

FALL 1979

Trick Brown was hip, down, street-smart, industrious, and seemingly more sophisticated than his brother. More than this, Trick was the one Brown Tyrone actually liked. Trick had that mean, independent gene, and was way too enterprisingly cool for anybody's "lame-ass school," so he quit in the tenth grade and hit the pavement making a way, and his own brand of street hustling pay.

Trick was five foot ten, two hundred pounds of mocha imperfection glazed in cinnamon, and Ty dug his flavor from the start. Maybe it was those sleep-sexy eyes, or those big ol' puffy lips, or maybe it was that wide, well-muscled body full of mojo. He looked like a fullback—all arms, chest, thighs, and butt. Homey had bluster for days, and one glance at him rolling down the sidewalk sporting his Trick grimace and cool-ass simian bop was enough to fluster most into crossing the street. Maybe it was that mean, I might just beat yo ass and take your shit toughness. Maybe it was that the brother was straight rebellious.

But there was more to Trick Brown than met the naked eye. Trick had a habit of calling Ty "Junior." Ty had been called worse, but he hated that name, that word coming from Trick. "Junior" inferred that he hadn't attained enough hip points to hang with a brother.

But suddenly Ty was seventeen, with a pencil-thin moustache, a fluent vocab, a minuscule bit of celebrity, and a head full of pomade. Tyrone magically achieved his *cool-enough* credentials from Trick. They became not only boys, but boys who slap-boxed down Lennox Avenue, who flowed with an easy homeboy cadence, and who liked to dance.

Trick couldn't read so well. He was, in fact, illiterate. And once Tyrone discovered this secret shame, it became his mission to teach a brother. In that teaching, Tyrone managed to reach a brother, and a brother reached back. They'd meet twice a week in secret, at the Shomberg Center in Harlem. Their lessons began slowly, as Trick's pride and frustration were obstacles. But Tyrone never judged him, and once Trick could trust him, baby-steps became larger steps, and larger steps became bounding leaps. Pretty soon, Trick was reading *Native Son*. He was asking questions, venturing opinions. And Ty found himself having a secret romance with Trick's impassioned mind.

"Trick, you never were stupid, man. Truth is, you're one of the smartest cats I know."

"Yeah, right. Don't bullshit me. I'm just gettin' by. But you get props on that," Trick acknowledged. It was his way of saying, "Thanks, Ty. You made a diff in my fuckin' illiterate life."

"Someone just failed to teach your ass basic phonics. Once you got that shit down, you were off and jettin' like Bob Beamon, man!"

Often, Trick would look at Ty, when Ty was unaware of being watched, and he'd think, *What's up with him? All this good shit is because of him, and the cat's humble. He's gotta be that way. Gotta be, or I wouldn't be diggin' his vibe. Look at him. Man! I can feel all the good shit this cat brings.*

Away from reading, they would get wasted on talk and chiba, and it seemed talk, weed, and each other were all two homeys needed to be content. Soon they became true aces, smiling covert smiles, keeping what the rest would never understand close to the vest. Besides, it was nobody's business if they were secretly queer for each other. Whenever they found time or someplace to be together, it became their oasis, even if that oasis was the back seat of Trick's metallic green Deuce and a Quarter.

SEPTEMBER 1979

Trick's ride was parked on 169th Street.

"You afraid of it?" Trick asked, with a touch of the braggart-with-a-big-ol'-massive-bozack in his voice.

"Afraid? Nah," Ty said. "I've done this before." But his mind was howling: *Don't you know the truth, man? It's got nothing to do with the size of your joint. Which is huge by the way. The truth is, I'm in love with you, fool. And I gotta tell you, lovin', really-lovin' another man scares the absolute shit out of me. Where will all this secret love and lust take us? It feels super-scary, stupid-dangerous to me. But, there you sit, bruh. There you sit.*

Yes. And there sat Trick's pickax, protruding high from his lap in the backseat of that dubiously owned Deuce and a Quarter. Eyes met, then lips and tongue were drawn to its crest. He tasted like stewed plums, like sex and honey and chili, like secrets and sweat, and a little like the pulse of love. Ty never took sex or sexing lightly. Emotions, senses were all involved in the mix. He wanted to remember every fold, curve, and twisting vein of Trick. And of it.

That always lush romantic ditty "Get Down Tonight" played loudly from Trick's cassette: K.C. and his Sunshine Band urging Ty to get down, get down on Trick's freaky fat freakishness.

But, oh! The hot things two horny brothers can do in the back of a '76 deuce. That deuce with its lime-green metallic sheen rocked, sighed, and drove Tyrone full-speed into a whole other kind of liberation.

Each sneak-end they would live out their hippest dreams on the dance floors of the city. The two of them became larger when they danced. They transformed, shifting into something bold, bronze, and handsome. With a fly glide to their stride they would slide inside the drive, and you knew them by their walk, that sheen in their game. They meant serious disco business.

It was an unusually chilly October afternoon. A breeze was kicking in from the north and Tyrone acknowledged that shiver on his skin as he left Empire Barber Shop, having had his fade tightened. Fine vines and sharp hair were all that really mattered in 1979. Ty was taking notes from that notorious spiral bound slang book being passed around school. When he finally got a glance, it read like a rumor of who was cool, and who was phine, and who could vine, and who wasn't phine, and who couldn't vine, and what they thought, and what music they listened to, and who threw the best gigs, and who knew how to dance, and shit like that. And the coolest kid, the hippest dude in the whole damn school, already at the height of his legendary drool factor, wrote, "Appearance ain't everything. It's The Only Thing." That attitude fit Tyrone for a cool autumnal season.

That particular night, he dressed to finesse—his skinny pimp frame in a suit of shiny blue rayon. Even Niagara Slim, the elegant Neighborhood Bum, tipped his bag in Ty's natty, ghetto-dapper direction, saying, "Boy, ya lookin' like a hundred-dolla bill!" and Ty beamed all the way to West 117th Street.

With a quick lively bop into Trick's building, Ty rang the buzzer to the sound of "Whoisit?"

"It's me, Trick-diesel. Let me up!" The buzzer buzzed. Ty entered and climbed the tedious project steps leading to the third floor. Tapping on 3-H, he hollered, "Hope you're ready. I ain't payin' no full admission tonight. Let's roll!"

Trick Brown opened the door, looking like a squat, powerfully built white tornado—totally out of season.

Though the impression put a rise in his rayons, Ty lectured, "Trick. You're the Black Travolta, all right? But, it's fuckin' October, man! And it's hawkin out there tonight!"

"But don't a brother look fly in this?" Trick asked, fishing for props.

"You look like a fuckin' star," Ty said and he meant it. But those gushy words sounded too sweet.

Trick didn't like it when he sounded too sweet.

"A fuckin' star?" he asked dubiously.

"Yeah. A thick-ass co-star on top of a thick-ass ghetto wedding cake. Where's the wedding, huh?" Ty turned his sweetness around.

"But, yo, Poetry Man, check the twill of this polyester. Damn. I look good in this here motherfucka! Good enough to be buried in this here bad boy!" He grinned his gap-toothed Trick grin, checking his cool quotient in the mirror.

Ty stood beside him, gazing at their dual cool images as he said, "Whatever, man. I'm tellin' ya, it's after Labor Day, it's cold out there, and you'll look played-out. But don't let that stop you."

"All right. I'll sport the money-green jammy. Still say I

should be buried in this here white one." Dropping his pants, he gave Ty the so-you-want-some-of-this-before-we-go gander. Ty declined with his eyes. The night was so young it was infantile. There was juice in the Deuce and plenty of time to rub dicks in the crazy dark.

"Let's do that club in the eighties. Remember? That joint, Pegasus?" Trick suggested.

Fifteen minutes later they were on the block, floating by cool jerk juveniles juiced on bravo and possibility. People dug their style, decked out like ghetto kings. Kangols tipped acey-deucey, with Trick in his lime-green marshmallow shoes.

It was a typical Friday night's hang in a straight disco, where enthusiastic white girls became urbanized sirens, and the men resembled blasé gigolos. It wasn't supposed to be their scene, yet the two hot-danced themselves electric on an evening full of speed and the promise of ecstasy. Trick stood, full of elements, taking a rest before grabbing the tallest chick he could find and dancing his thick ass off. On the night's hungry dance floor, he and Ty reigned like kings, players, Somebodies. The floor was full of sex and its strobe-lit possibilities, party freaks, and cliques of hedonistic hands reaching out to touch them. So, Trick and Ty, they'd look at each other, chip in a few Latin hustle steps, and no one dared try to best them. Along the mirrored walls and under red specks and flashing blue balls of light, they caught glimpses and dug themselves in all their profitless beauty. When you're seventeen and nineteen, with moves like fuel-injected pop lockers, you tend to believe in your own providence.

Girls, chicks, the few sisters present awaited their turns to burn inside Trick and Tyrone's radioactivity. Trick and Ty would grab them two at a time, spin them wild and fast like 78s . . . until they'd be all dizzy, man. Dizzier than *Gillespies*.

And for a while, those chicks would be crazy dizzy in love with Trick and Ty. Ty and Trick. They owned those clubs and joints they inhabited. Both boys were bad and fast becoming legends.

If "appearance was the only thing," Trick Brown didn't appear freaked or stressed that Friday night, though he'd vaguely mentioned "a debt."

"Man, I hope big-headed Razor Morrisey don't bring his crazy ass 'round here, riffin' 'bout that damn debt. Spotted me a little loan. Nothin' heavy. But, sheeit. He can't get what I ain't got, right?" he yelled between beats.

He said it with that quick nervous energy he had, like that of a speed addict having just popped a fistful. Trick laughed it off, so Ty laughed with him. Laughing was the second best thing they did. They laughed hard in the bricked-up face of their circumstances. Mostly they laughed at themselves, because they were young, strong, horny, and testing the limits. High, stupid, and completely ridiculous, they laughed and danced as the music played its loud and thumping bass for the swaying, rhythmic populace. Ty was in that wild place he'd go when he was dancing and feeling alive!

Ty was still in that wild place, dancing, spinning, and drawing a charismatic sweat when Razor Morrisey bopped in with his big head lidded under the cruel shade of a beaver-fur fedora. Razor's rep, like the rats in the city, infected the community at large. Razor was a local hot-boy with juice. He had his hot hands in a little of everything: drugs, extortion, numbers, prostitution, chop-shops, loan sharking—anything as long as there was profit in it.

Ty never saw Trick and Razor's animated conversation, or how Trick's graceful hands began to fly like frightened birds, trying to explain themselves. That absurd night's fractured pantomime went unnoticed. And Ty was too busy dancing to see that long slow drag out past the doors of Pegasus. He never witnessed that quick flicker of panic darkening Trick's gap-toothed smile. Never saw Razor break mean with a switchblade.

Ty was knee-deep inside the screams and whistles of a frantic dancing room where he and Trick reigned. He didn't feel Trick's absence, sense his terror, or know something was horribly wrong until someone tapped his dancing shoulder and said, "Trick's hurt, man. Razor and his boys, they stuck him. Real bad."

Ty ran like a brand-new madman. He ran with a wild heart beating in his ears. Outside, there was a fresh smear of blood on the pavement. It must've been six feet long. Strange. Ty felt a twinge of relief, thinking: That can't be Trick's blood. Nah. Trick ain't that tall!

But further down the street, he saw something. A small ball, bloodied and still. They'd beaten him badly. They'd slashed his throat. Blood was all over his face. If it wasn't for the bloodstained money-green suit, Ty would've never recognized him as the same Trick he'd laughed with, danced with only minutes before.

"Trick? Trick. Get up, Trick! Trick? No-o-o!"

The human voice was never meant for that kind of frenzy. Ty held his hand, and there was nothing but cold. He held it until he couldn't hold it anymore.

A large thing was welling up in him, a tightness in his chest. Tyrone couldn't breathe for the rage in his broken heart. He thought he was going crazy. Maybe he was. He wanted to hit and spit and whale on everyone, every thing and every person on the street. He walked around, pacing in his raging skin. There was no sane place left in him.

Ty: "I still have dreams of the blood. A million times in my dreams, he's stabbed in the slowest motion. His arms, they flail in a kind of flourish, a sad and fractured ballet. And everyone just dances around him, or stands there, watching his life drain away. They just stood there, letting the blood run. Did any one of those motherfuckers out there know who he was, or what he was going to be? He was somebody's son, somebody's brother, somebody's friend, and I could trust him, and we could dance. Didn't they care that he'd never fuckin' dance again?"

Theodore "Trick" Brown was buried in that fly white suit he'd so admired himself in. Tyrone and Faison served as pallbearers. Ty eulogized: "He was a smooth, chocolate heartthrob with crazy legs. He was tough and tender too. But when he put on a suit, there was a new glide in his walk. He never stuttered when he talked and the poverty in his pockets didn't show . . . much."

SUMMER 1985

Many times Tyrone tried to write it all down. He'd tried, but the words stared back from his word processor until even he didn't recognize them. That's when he'd sense Trick. His presence, or pieces of him, began to hover inside that writing room, seeping into Tyrone's consciousness. Trick Brown was haunting him, slowly.

"Why don't you just write the fuckin' truth, man? You taught me how to read. But I could always read you, Ty. What were we? Best friends? Just two cool dancin' fools? I don't think so. I did you, you did me, and didn't we both like it? Damn it, Poetry Man. Start again: 'Once upon a time, there was this dark-skinned, Harlem-bred, thick-muscled, big-dicked brother named Trick, who rocked my fuckin' world.'"

Omar was the first, but Trick was The Memorable One, the long, blue moan that caught in Tyrone's throat.

CENTRAL PARK, AUGUST 1984

Ty said to David, "Even though it was only my second voyage onto those warm, slippery shores of The River Fellatio, I was convinced it would be OK, because he *liked* me. I had a bad case of love's wicked itch, and no one could scratch that shit like Trick. He showed me I could dig a man deeply as a friend and still want to be kissed, touched, sucked, and fucked. I could talk and laugh, be silly or intense, and just be. And given time, I know he would've realized and admitted he loved me, too."

"Baby, that's so queer I could gag on the beauty of it," David joked. "You were such a mental boy, even back then. I remember you tellin' me once that you could never love a vacant pretty boy. And I thought, how tragic. Sex and beauty are the key components of our culture, baby boy! And here's my little rebel, breakin' the laws of our God-given superficial nature.

"Why? Because he wants someone to talk to who can talk back. Dionne Warwick and me is both gonna say a little prayer for your sad-ass." Tyrone laughed.

"I'm not blind, baby. I recognize fine when I see it, ya beauty-whore! I just choose not to chase after it with my mouth wide open, 'cause it's only fast food. It can't sustain us. Beauty's just a cock or a pussy staring back at us from the crotch of time. It's gonna rot and shrivel and dry up sooner or later. And when beauty hits the wall, Duchess, it can be plug ugly. Substance lasts. Believe me. The quick, meaningless fuck is highly overrated. 'Kay? Self-identity is sexy to me. I knew more than the biggest part of him. I knew the best part of him. Sometimes he'd look at me, and this pure and brilliant love poured from his eyes. It was spiritual. Besides, the pretty ones are never very interesting or dynamic."

"Or dangerous," David added. He knew Ty's choices even better than Ty himself. "Trick wasn't everybody's pretty boy, but he was pretty dangerous. Hell, he personified that shit. He was black, hard, and tough, and yes, that can be beautiful. But, he didn't look or sound or act in any way gay, baby. You liked that, too. Ya still do!"

"Nah. Trick looked, acted, and sounded like himself. And I dug that. Dealing with my first Real Man was some serious shit. I wasn't just lookin for a quick hummer in the backseat of a deuce. For me, the brother had to be down—"

"*Down*-so-low-nobody-but-a-seasoned-queen-could-even-tell-he-liked-dick, you mean. I know men just like Trick. Even if he'd lived to be one hundred-years-old, he would've never stepped out of his cool cock-clutchin' closet. Don't kid yourself, baby boy. Cool-pose was his god. And if you think you could've changed that, you's a fool. Please don't take this wrong. But the day I met you, I knew you were that stiff, 'God please don't let me mince or switch or let my wrist fall limp' type. Sometimes I think you're just another uptight straight boy trapped in a queer man's body.

Tyrone looked at David, with his mouth opened wide, and was clearly appalled.

"It's OK. That ain't a judgment. This is your best friend talking. I see all, feel all. You never *wanted* to be gay. That was one of those hilarious jokes the Creator played on yo ass. If you had your way, you'd be straighter than John fuckin' Wayne. But you can't be, so you settle for being quietly queer. You got a bit of that Johnny Mathis/Rock Hudson complex in you, boy."

"That's bullshit! For you, anyone who doesn't come into a

room leaping and screaming like a freaking siren is a closet case."

"No. But the siren of my buck-wild blatancy must scare you."

"What?" Ty chuckled. "Nothing about you *scares* me, David."

"Oh really? So . . . why do you think we've never bumped nasties? I *know* you love me. Hell, who *wouldn't*? And without gettin' all Hallmark about it, I loves you too, Porgy. But I'm so far from being your type that I might as well be from Uranus!"

"That's the first thing you've gotten right all afternoon," Ty fumed.

"Problem was, and still is, ya want too damn much. Ya want dick. Oops, excuse me. Penis. But not just any penis will do. Will all the big, black intellects in the house please whip out your long, thick, ten-inch IQs? If you're queer, but not too queer, Ty would like you cleaned, stripped, and sent to his tent."

"So I'm asking for the impossible?"

"No. Not if you happen to have Barbara Eden's bottle on hand. Listen, you want love. Believe me, I do understand. But trust me, not prayers, not a genie, not even the best, most upstanding queer cat on the planet can deliver all the stuff you want."

"I'm about ten seconds from kickin' your soft ass all up and down this fuckin' park! What the hell does that shit mean?"

"Simple. Do ya want a roughneck, or a rough wit? Trick was a budding roughneck. But in your mind you've painted him with all kinds of intelligence, sensitivity, romance, and Technicolor movie shit. Because that's what you *want*. But you ain't bein real, baby. *Hello!* Trick was a hustler, a get-in-where-you-fit-in type of Brother. He'd do what he had to do to survive, look good, drive a fly ride, and stay high. Obviously that was the real bait, the boyfriend juice back then. But you can't accept that, can you? You're afraid that truth would cheapen what you felt for him. You're afraid if you write that shit, he would only come off as a colored cliché."

"I hate this conversation. I hate you. You know me too fuckin' well, ya li'l spooky bastard!"

"Hey. We're all products of pain. But the question is, what you g'on do with yours? Damn it! Tell the truth, and shame the devil!"

CHAPTER EIGHT

Suddenly, That Duplicitous Summer

JULY 1985

Inside the walls of Don't Tell Mama's, under dim lights and hipster chatter, this one cat spoke the staccato of the fatally cool. Sitting at Ty and Browny's table, he kept running his fool mouth, riffin' and vampin' 'bout his music. His voice itself was a kind of scat as he prattled on about Diz and Prez, Bird and Billie, the whole ethnomusicology of jazz.

Although Ty didn't know him from a can of paint, he seemed a little too everything: too pretentious, too slick, too fake, too much like a player. In dark shades and a carefully cocked beret, he was way too precious for the room. But, Ty's Uncle Jerome had taught him to live by the c'mon get happy phrase, "No fools, no fun," so he left himself the freedom to be amused. But the dude began stroking Ty's thigh under the table, and though he was smoothly shady with it, he sent Ty a vibe that said: *Yeah. I see ya diggin' me. Bet you wonderin' how you can be down with all this?*

Ty pushed his hand away, gave him the Mixed-Negro-Please! look.

"Yo! What's your prob, boss?" the stranger rasped. "What up with the stank attitude?"

"Don't ask questions if you'd rather not know the answer," Ty cracked.

"Well, fuck it, I'm askin'," Mr. Too-Suave-For-The-Café insisted.

"'Kay. The low-budget Miles Davis lounge lizard trip. It ain't real, ain't authentic. No disrespect. I think ya fakin' the funk, bruh."

"You don't know jack! Authentic? Miles is my daddy!" he said in a hurt voice, getting up and walking away in a slow bop.

Ty turned to Browny, who'd brought him along to sample a new play.

"You know that cat, right? So what up, Browny? Was he legit or what?"

"Hell no! Sucka! He *clowned* you good! You don't know who that is? That's *Pass-cow*! He's in the play. See? Fuckin' mouth got ya spittin' out Tang before you know the flavor!"

"Pass-cow? *Pascal?* That asshole was Face?"

"Yeah. Some people call him that." Faison still held a secret grudge. After all, his name was Faison. Why didn't people call him Face? So what if he wasn't gorgeous? He had talent. Why were people too damn lazy to shorten his fucking name? "Call me Face," he'd tell them. But it never stuck.

But that hidden resentment went unnoticed by Ty, because for him the night had just become electric. All at once, his head was flooded with memories of that fine-ass Depina boy. When he first met Face, Ty was leery of him. He'd thought Face was all mutton and no chops or potatoes, and not nearly as talented as he pretended to be. And those tales of his background were shaky to Ty's discerning ear. Face had the best haircuts, the most expensive clothes, but why did he always have to turn his well-formed nose in the air? Still, he made a beautiful entrance, and he had the uncanny gift of being whatever you projected him to be. Blink your eyes and he became a duke, a thug, a crush, a get-high partner, a potential lover, a friend, maybe even a savior. When he tilted his fine head and smiled, no one except Browny was immune to his charm. He was the bomb-diggity.

Most handsome.

Best dressed.

Mr. Popularity.

Ty felt that odd excitement reminiscent of an earlier time, a time of promise. In that romantic state, he'd almost forgotten the ugliness of Da Elixir's demise. Then he realized.

Oh damn! I just embarrassed myself, right here in Don't Tell Mama's! Face Depina, of all people, just clowned me!

Suddenly, he'd lapsed into that hopelessly uncool high school chump. But now, as a highly evolved, socially adroit college grad, Ty had to do something. Improvise. Say something quick. Recover from the stigma of being punked.

"Face, huh?" he acknowledged, in a decidedly beige tone. "That low-budget Mario Van Peebles wanna be! Homey needs to go back to Acting 101. I didn't buy his rap, his spiel, his thing."

It was Browny's turn now to shoot *Ty* the quick gas face.

Then Depina took to that small, blackened stage, and something unexpected happened. He was absolutely riveting. He'd dug deep, applied himself, studied, hung out with musicians and junkies, and junkie musicians, and, as a result, all you could see was a sad brilliance. He was strong, authentic, and so radiantly real that Ty believed every word he rasped in his portrayal of a doomed jazz musician. Ty was tripping on that experimental theater stuff, but no one told him there'd be a nude scene! Hello! Pascal "Face" Depina stood naked, as if it was the most natural thing in the world to be naked, and blowing his sad horn as the other clothed players ignored him.

But Tyrone did not ignore his ass. He couldn't.

Naked as new birth, Depina gave new meaning to the phrase Les Jazz Hot, and *long* too! His sleek body had a Palomino-like quality—all shiny, defined, and gleaming. Ty's eyes clung to the skin of his dangle, lingered on the tense, light-skinned mold of an ass strong enough to crack walnuts. *Ah! To be, or not to be, a fucking walnut!* Tyrone thought.

When Depina's character died from an overdose, nude, alone, even his gonads became collapsing actors. Oh, yes, Face did his thing. He'd worked his performance into Tyrone Hunter's most sensitive of review areas. When the show was over, Ty was the very first to stand up and cheer.

"Bravo! Bravo, my brother! Encore! Encore!"

"Tyrone! Calm your monkey ass down! Shit! He wasn't all that good!" Browny said.

But Tyrone felt he'd just watched the dawning of a star, because whatever star quality was, Face Depina was lousy with that shit. Against the roar of usually jaded New Yorkers, Ty wanted to bolt upright, charge like a mad new fan to that stage, and just take him. But he chilled.

"He's good, huh?" a stranger sitting at the next table asked.

"Good? He's fantastic!" Ty yelled back.

Shortly thereafter, at Ty's insistence, he and Browny tipped backstage to sing Depina's praises. As they approached the door, Ty wondered, *What will Face say? How will he act?*

Face opened the door, saw them, and immediately flashed his newly improved, well-capped actor's grin. "Tyrone Hunter." His arms flung open and the two embraced, hard and full, like old friends, or lovers even. The warm reception seemed odd to Ty. Before that night, before Face sat at their table and affected his rasping strange jazz cat act, the last time he and Ty had seen each other they'd argued over mon about the money. And like Browny, Depina had of it. But apparently Face had let go of his gru was another story.) At least that was how it seem night of unexpected reunions. Ty hadn't decided some little mind game, or maybe another act. He knew wasn't the brightest of cats in the alley of his old acq tances. Yet Face Depina was a kid of the streets, and not ab his own fits of duplicity. He wondered this, because Face *ap peared* genuinely happy to see Tyrone again.

"Tyrone Fucking Hunter." Face was still holding him.

Fuckin' homos, the hater in Browny hissed.

But then, in a shock of all shocks, Face pulled back, leaned forward, and kissed Tyrone full on the lips.

So he was one of them bold fuckin' homos now? Browny thought.

Ty was stunned.

Browny couldn't believe it. Face . . . and those fuckin' kisses! Browny remembered back when they were Da Elixir—singing, dancing, spraying their post adolescent sexitude for the terminally teenage masses.

But even then, it was all about "Pass-cow." At some point David had decided to test the power of his boyfriend juice.

"I think I'll have me a piece of Depina," David had told Ty and Browny on the subway. David assessed his own appeal. "I can bag him. I'm cute, verging on adorable. Plus, I'm a dancer. Check the gams. And my ass? Please. "See this?" he pointed. Rico once told me I could open a jar of *caviar* with this thing."

Yes, dancing had indeed given David a superior ass. But would all that ass be enough to *bag* the coveted Face Depina? David thought so. Ty and Browny didn't.

Then, the night of the big show, for some queer reason, Face decided, in the middle of the applause, to do the unthinkable, something most popular-cool teenage boys would never dare to do. He turned to the only openly gay member of the group, little dancer who'd patiently taught him the moves, and, to eryone's amazement, he picked David up and kissed him rd on the lips.

The crowd went wild. The secretly queer kids went ballis-tic. And David went on a jag of love from which he never fully recovered. Tyrone was most amazed by that spectacle. It didn't mean Face was gay, necessarily, only that he wasn't afraid to be gay-friendly. On that count alone, Depina scored fifty extra cool points, and Ty lost a bet. He had wagered fifty bucks against the possibility of David ever cozying up to the smooth cool of a dude like Face Depina. But upon seeing their supposed closeness and hearing the wild crowd frantically chanting, "Face! Face! Face!" Ty thought, *Wow! I bow down to the queen. Look at that. Little Duchess and big fine Face. Damn!*

Browny stared, too . . . but for entirely different reasons. He saw it as one of Depina's putrid displays. It was all a pose. Everything in him dictated that this was a blatant move by Face to be the showstopper, the one people remembered and the one they talked about. Browny was never a fan, nor groupie and hardly a Depina devotee. He had tolerated much, just singing and dealing with the other three, but in that moment, he *hated* him some Face Depina. *High-Yellow Bastard!* As Depina brought David back down to Earth, Browny thought, *Maaaaan. I should just hit one good long note, and then these motherfuckers'll know who the real star is, yo*!

But he didn't, and so they didn't know.

Now, watching Face plant a long wet one on Tyrone, he wanted to say, "Yo! Ty! Don't kiss him back! You don't know where them lips been, fool!"

But like that time on stage, he just watched and he chilled. Besides, now it was too late. There was something almost vampiric about Face Depina, at least to Browny. He'd seen the effect Face had on others after simply kissing them. He'd seen supposedly normal people become slaves who craved that abusive attention. Now it was Tyrone's turn. Hell, Ty had just been kissed, and thus, he too would soon be indoctrinated into the Face Depina cult.

"You was the half-black *Oliver* up in this motherfuck tonight," was Browny's forced critique. Browny was keen enough to *know* the difference between Sir Larry and the fictional street urchin. He clearly *meant* the latter. "Didn't even know you had it in you. So, you got an agent now, or what?" *And yo, how long did you have to blow the motherfucker to get this fuckin' role?* is what he really wanted to ask.

Depina ignored his question. He was too busy staring at that skinny kid from school, the one with more *luck* than talent. He was busy falling into the new idea of Tyrone Hunter. Damn! He grew up good, didn't he? Recovering from that Vampire's Kiss, Ty offered his breathless assessment.

"Man! I got no adjectives for you tonight. You did the old school proud, bruh. Sure had me fooled. Sorry for being such an asshole earlier, but—"

"Don't stress it, man. Fuckin' with people's heads, seein' how they react, gives me new material" Tyrone thought that admission alone was very telling.

Face Depina looked different than that piece of jazzed-out strange from earlier in the evening. He had a mad mane of curly springs all over his head, as if his hair couldn't decide whether to be an Afro or dreads that week. His chest was flawless and dusted with just a hint of sweat. And his arrangement of riches looked damn good in those tight black jeans. As he began stuffing belongings into his *Actor's Trick Bag*, he grabbed his script and to *most* everyone's surprise, a copy of a popular stroke magazine fell to the floor.

"Uh-huh! I knew it. Fuckin' *closet* case!" Browny hissed, just loud enough for Ty to hear. But the sight of the magazine was a happy vision to Ty.

"Uh, that's not mine," Face lied. "I know somebody in there, though."

"Small world, ain't it, sister? Ty the Tyke is still writin'. Ain't you, Ty? Only now it ain't about music, yo. It's about the smut thing. You scribble a little sump'n in them queer magazines, right?" Browny teased.

Both Ty and Browny witnessed a small sensation as they watched Depina's face brighten into an intriguing Cheshire cat smile. He was beautiful—very, very beautiful—when he smiled. "Damn! You mean our uptight, Ty? First you write a hit song and now you pennin jerk-juice words, too?? Damn, boy. You must got a wild imagination!"

"Don't be fooled by that boy, Pass-cow! Under that game face, he's a true freak, just like you." The bitch in Faison was trying to annoy them both.

"It's Face, man. Nobody's called me Pascal in years," Depina said with slight irritation in his tone. "So, you're a freak now, Tyrone? I mean, you seemed pretty lame back in the day. You were always runnin' around with that li'l effeminate thing . . . what's-her-face?"

"David!" Browny said. "Come on, Pass-cow, you remember that shit, yo!"

If I have to tell this half drunk Negro-bitch my fuckin' name one more time, I'ma have to jump on that black ass and kick the shit outta him! Face thought.

"Yeah. Ain't seen him in so long, guess I forgot. David. Yes, David. The Dancer. Wild little pussycat, that one. Whatever happened to him, anyway?"

"Oh, he's tapped in, man," Ty bragged. "He's always working or touring in a revival, or doing something showy. Right now he's in L.A. shooting a video."

"Cool. Cool," was all Face ordered at the news of David's progress.

Later that evening, the three shared a cab uptown. Ty wisely sat in the middle. The ride was quiet, considering all the things and places and people they had in common. Browny whipped out his flask of vodka, which he finished by himself, never offering the others a swig.

Ever since the group's break-up, Browny had been working on a whole new act. That act was known as: the eternal victim, drinker, attitudinal brother with a perennial bruised look. He had his reasons, though some called them excuses. He'd been trying to break into the music business, without success. He was still dreaming, still trying, and still getting his drunken heart smashed to smithereens. Everything bad that ever happened to him was someone else's fault: crooked agent, lazy, crooked manager, lousy crooked songwriters, the advent of crooked videos, fear of the Straight Black Dick. Everyone, in some way, had conspired against him. Plus, he was dark and small. For that he blamed God.

"Where the hell a brother gonna sing opera? How'm I gonna flex my fuckin' chops in the fuckin' chorus of the New York Philharmonic, yo?"

Watching him, Tyrone suddenly remembered, and missed, the singer with the crystal tear in his voice, the three-octave tenor who reached operatic heights. He missed that other side of Browny, the one who soared over the hater he'd become.

Browny got out first, on 28th Street, stinking of liquor and a foul attitude.

"Yo, Pass-cow! I would give you my number, but you'd just lose it again. Tyrone, I'll buzz you later, bro. Peace out, Pass-cow," he taunted, and with that he slammed the door.

"Diz-zamn! What vile bug crawled up his ass tonight?" Ty asked.

"Hell if I know," Face said. "Browny will never change. See, we cribbed together for a minute. Ya know, two strugglin' artists tryna make it. Then he fucked around, got in some deep shit with Razor Morrisey, and I had to bail his little drunk ass out. Motherfucka never even thanked me."

"Razor Morrisey?" That name still sent a little tremor through Ty. "But . . . he's.. he's the one . . . who stuck, who killed—"

"Yeah, Trick. I know. That's right. You used to hang with Trick, too, didn't you?" Face paused. There was something secretly sexual brewing inside this pause. He was remembering a rumor he'd heard on the street . . . a story about Ty and Trick. And it intrigued him, a little . . . this thought of Tyrone fucking with someone so dangerous.

"Yeah . . . too bad about Trick. But, I guess Browny's love of dope musta been stronger than his love for his dead brother. No disrespect. So, anyway, *I got Razor off* Browny's ass. Took a whole month's rent and *then some*, but I did it. After that, Browny's ass had to go. Too much heat around him. You know yourself how it is when you do a solid for somebody and they end up resentin' you. That's why I'm cool now with you and the song-money thing. I can't resent you for winnin the song lottery. You wrote it, and it hit big. But Browny, that cat will hate seein you and anybody else succeed until his dyin' day, yo. That's just who he is. So, anyway, enough about him! What's goin' on with you? Were you diggin' me up there? Did you really like my performance?"

But there was a *lot* coming at Ty, and none of it sounded *legit*. Why would Browny want to deal with Razor Morrisey on any level . . . other than mortal combat? Face had played the role of *Saint Depina* and helped Browny's ass out of a jam? Ty felt as if much of what Face said was an attempt to jerk the truth around and make himself out to be a hero. These events, as Depina narrated them, could only occur in an alternate universe.

"Well?" Face asked. "What did you think? Do I got the stuff, or what?"

Ty remembered now. It was *all* about Face. He had almost forgotten that it always was, first and foremost, about Face Depina. In that space between answers, he thought of David, his "*li'l effeminate friend.*" Why did Face have to say it *that* way? David wasn't so effeminate. Didn't Face *get it*? That was just David being playful, and in love.

David, at the age of fifteen, had lived, breathed, and dreamed of only Face Depina:

"I mean, da-a-a-a-mn, Ty! Why, oh why does Face have to be *so* damn fine? Face is, like, from the planet *Super-fine-taurius*! Tell me this: did you ever jerk the gherkin thinkin' of Facey? 'Cause I do. Regularly. So, you think Facey likes boys, cause something about him just makes me feel all wet and giggly inside. Who is Facey fuckin', anyway? You think Facey fucks as good as he looks?"

"He probably fucks as good as he dances," Ty had replied. "Which ain't bad for a white girl, from Long Island, but . . ."

Ty's slightly bitchy, if truthful critique would only fall on deaf ears. David couldn't and wouldn't hear, nor compute anything vaguely negative about his "Facey" . . . not even from his best friend Ty.

Yet, years later, there was Face, disrespecting David, calling him Ty's "*li'l effeminate friend.*"

In the taxi, Face's question remained: what did Ty think of Face's acting skills? Ty hadn't yet answered. Face wanted, almost needed to know, and the question, left unanswered, still hovered like a gadfly. Face sat closer, one strong knee pressed achingly against Tyrone's.

"Your skills? Your skills are tight, man. You were really on point tonight," Ty finally said, and he meant it.

But what Ty didn't say was, *Yeah. You're tight, all right. Tight and toasty. Ever have any man-honey on that toast?*

"So, you think I got what it takes?" Face pressed.

"Sure. Why not? It's all a crap shoot. When I wrote that song I never expected it to be a hit. Besides, I—"

"I mean, because I go the whole nine, you know? That play is *hoard* on me, so many lines, emotions and shit." *Hoard* was Facey-speak for something extra hard, arduously hard, *super-crazy*-hard. "Now, I just need to kick it," he sighed. "So, you got any ideas . . ." Face's voice trailed off strangely. He was trying to be sexy, Ty could tell.

In that silence, some slow and unspoken fire was crackling between the two of them. Tyrone had sensed it, but he had no clue of what to do with the heat of it. Then, it came, out of nowhere. Without warning, Face's hand crawled up Ty's inner thigh in a smooth and confident glide. There was an undeniable humidity in that hand. Face Depina knew deep in his balls that he could have Tyrone Hunter, right there, or most any other man or woman he desired. His shiny green eyes stabbed through the dark, focusing on the intended target.

Damn, Face. That's your hand on my thigh, dude. Whatchu tryna do?

Next, that slow and meandering hand settled on Ty's lap. That hand slowly commenced rubbing, caressing the strap of Ty's thang. Face smiled. Tyrone glanced forward to find the taxi driver ignoring them. Just then, the exhibitionist in Face had made him bold enough to unzip Ty right there in the backseat.

The first touch vacuumed Ty clean away from the reality of

a New York cab ride. His head spun. His thoughts collided. *Face Depina is touching my dick!* There was always a certain strain of wildness, a fearlessness in Face, and maybe Ty had forgotten that too. *Yo! Mr. Tax-driver! Do you see this? He's stroking me off, man!* Heat was baking every atom in Tyrone's body. *Oh, my damn!*

It was a mighty bumpy, bouncy ride through the downtown streets of Gotham. Tyrone wanted to grab a shock of Depina's hair and drive his beautiful lips there, to that percolating place. *Does he give head, too?* He could only imagine the wet slick warmth of Face's mouth and lips going down on him. But this, this was cool too because Depina's manipulations were making him drool. Ooh! He had skills in those hands! Ty was moaning low and he hoped the cabby couldn't hear him.

When the monumental moment came, Ty pushed Face away swiftly, and suddenly, forcefully, he sprayed in a thrust to the floor and the seat and his jeans. His breaths came coarse. He was breathing harder, and faster than a long distance runner. And the deed was done, he thought: *Whoa! Just whoa! Look at me! I'm a fuckin' mess, but I don't care!*

If anyone had told him what he had in store that night, or with whom, Tyrone Hunter would have thought them crazy. *Whoa! Did that really just happen? I can't even believe this shit!*

"That's act one, baby. Tonight's your lucky night. Let's swing by Mirage," Face whispered. Tyrone and his shocked penis consented.

A few minutes later, they'd checked their clothes down to their jocks and hiking boots. Ty was in deep lust with Face's physique. His eyes perused the lean, almond-hued sweep of him. Face's outstretched supporter loomed abundant with unseen buttered-pecan treat. The club songs began to pump, and they hit the crowded floor. It seemed like every hot, horny cat in Manhattan was out cattin' that night.

Face was slowly, boldly wooing Ty, and together they moved and grooved their hips as if the two screwing. The music, its beat became more primal. They progressed to writhing in their jocks. This was a kind of mating dance, a dance of two beasts, in heat, in sweat, on fire with a rhythm most intimate. And through all the smoke and the steam Ty couldn't help thinking: *Damn! Even this cat's dancing has improved!*

It was too loud to truly communicate, to talk, to reflect upon anything other than sex. And so their grinding did the speaking *for* them, and with their eyes they *signed* in lust's most suggestive sentences.

And then, inside that mid-nasty-groove, Depina grabbed the back of Tyrone's neck. He did it in a fit of blatant aggression, pulling Ty's face into his. They stared and they breathed, and then they kissed. That kiss was long and hot and daring and wet.

Ty's heartbeat became fast with impatience, its beat as lewd as music's bass line. Face clutched Ty's behind and pushed his winding body forth. All Ty could feel was that long bank of meat, mounting, stirring beneath Depina's damp jock.

Lost in the thrill, in the chemistry of him, Ty became a sweaty victim to this strange new passion ignited between them. Following the charge of his own libido, Ty planted sucking kisses all over him.

He let his tongue run wild across the taut, savory, tantalizing sweep of Pascal "Face" Depina. Ty lacquered the elongated neck and glided the spanning sweat-wet shoulders. He licked the dense dark wires of Face's pits. He feasted and nibbled on those delectable tits.

Face, for his part was digging it; yes, digging it, far more than he'd expected.

"So . . . ummm. . . ya wanna fuck around some?" Face

Depina howled, so bold, so straight-out with his shit . . . and Tyrone Hunter and his anxious dick howled back and answered,

"Hell, yeah!"

Depina's green eyes slyly darted the crowd, and noticed a few eyes on him. This was his element. He then locked his thumbs at the waist of his jock, and he slowly flipped down the front . . . and motherfuck! It was a tan, very long and still erecting tower. It took Ty's breath, and ran away with it.

"Diz-zamn dude!" was all he could say. From his view in the audience, Tyrone assumed Face was blessed. He'd just never expected an Urban-Legend pitched between Depina's thighs. But there stood close to ten-inches of lean, ghetto-bred, uncut manhood. It reached out for Tyrone, willing him, daring him to do something hot, something inspired, and something risky with it.

Just then, Depina tucked his prize away. With the both of them sufficiently excited, they exited the dance floor on a mission, in a quest for just a little more privacy. Their pricks stabbed a path through the dancing, prancing, romancing mayhem, en route to the back room.

But that back room was jammed. The high reek of sex was everywhere. Kissing, groaning, moaning men caressed and coupled in a reckless synergy. Some boys stood panting against the walls, as other boys worshipped them, falling on their knees. Still others engaged in fits of coitus within a masculine merger of musk and energies.

There stood Ty and Face Depina in the mix of it . . . two tall, erect ethnics who wouldn't fit comfortably inside this serpentine mass. Even if they were to engage in that makeshift orgy of men, total strangers would be all over them, like bacon on greens, like hot on salsa.

"Hey. I used to DJ here," Face said. "There's this old booth upstairs. Real private," Depina gestured in that direction of those stairs.

Ty nodded, and Face led the way.

Inside the darkened glass booth, he switched on a red lamp. Face looked even hotter bathed in red light. There was an old turntable, a leather chair, and a gang of vintage disco albums. A small army of spent condoms littered the floor like defeated latex soldiers. Face dropped his jock. His piece pitched upward—tall, tan, and lovely as its owner. He sat in the chair and led Ty's head down, down . . .

"Suck me off, if you can," challenged Face Fine-ass Depina. Ty was hypnotized. Yes, naked was Depina's color. Still, there was that shadiness about him. Ty didn't know where the hell he and his elegant pecan prick had been. So, he reached for his wallet, pulled out a Trojan.

"What the hell is that for?"

"Safety. I'm not down with the DNA slurpee. Don't you read the papers? All kinds of diseases out there, man. You gotta suit up if you wanna play with me. Besides, you don't know where I been either."

"No glove, no love, huh?"

Face smirked. *Fuckin' punk! What's wrong with him? I'm clean and he's lucky I'm payin' attention to his fortunate ass!* Depina thought. But he didn't say anything as Tyrone rolled the rubber down his lengthy span. Then, in a New York minute, Depina grabbed Ty's chin and fed him warm raging knob and extended shaft, then more shaft. Damn, how much shaft did he have! And with more shaft came more vibration. Rising from the chair, Depina and his pinga bucked and struck the back of Ty's throat. Ty choked it back, then lapped to the sound and beat of the bass at his feet. As the flaunt and strut of sexy, sweaty men freaked below, Ty ingested the tip and shaft of a dream. Was it real? Was he really gagging on a spit and red-lit dream?

"I knew you dug me back in school. I could tell," Face said with hubris as he stood pushing Ty against the desk. Then, all at once, his moist lips locked on Ty's naked schlong.

"Wait! Wait! Don't you want me to put a rubber on?"

But Depina didn't care. Like some reckless predator, he was all over Ty, smacking his ass, twisting his tits, throttling that mounting piece with lips, mouth, tongue, and throat. Ty never imagined one man could be so sexual. Face was a rattler—licking and hissing through Ty's prickly bush. He was rough, full of slobber and rushing breaths, but a suck-sore Ty was surprised at just how much he liked it.

Then, he switched turntables, mixed it up, scratched it, and surprised Ty with a brand new beat.

"You know," he began. "I *done* a couple a men before. They just love to sit on this long hot motherfucka and r-i-i-i-ide." His voice wore a tough guy catch to it, when he said that. He smacked *his lovely* to Tyrone's thigh. "And I just love to hear 'em squealin' like first time faggots!"

Is this your seduction rap, Face? Cause as good as you look, that shit could use some work.

"I got that fuckin' part down cold," Face said. "Now I need to know the rest."

"Ummm . . . the rest?" Ty, asked, not quite feeling his lead, his flow, nor his intentions.

"Yeah. The *rest.*" His hands sailed down Tyrone's belly. He grabbed Ty's limb and jerked it into a long, strong, wicked hardness. "Get up. I want you to fuck me."

It had been a night thick with surprises. But Tyrone couldn't quite fathom this one. Face, with his long straight bone so pleasingly erect, lay, face-up, his back on the table.

So he wanted to be Ty's bottom. As fantastic as it seemed, this was something that Tyrone could, and most willingly do. But, looking directly into the erotic beauty of Face Depina, head-on, would've made Ty arrive too quickly, so he ordered, "Turn around."

Face did, and Ty slowly massaged the red-lighted slopes of a perfectly glazed rump. He could smell the excitement on the air. Depina tensed and taunted and began teasing the hell out of a previously-sedate Tyrone, who, was now quaking at the sight of him. Ty looked down at his own piece, slightly amazed at the juicing hardness Face Depina had made of him. Tyrone, who never left home without his rubbers, slid a shield quickly along his anxiously pulsating maleness.

It was show time for Tyrone and Face Depina. And Ty was primed and ready for his close-up.

Crouching low, he divided Depina's cheeks. Then slowly, very slowly he descended, allowing his crest, and then his shaft to submerge inside that knotted Cheerio of flesh. The clasp, oh, the maddening clasp of it was beyond all he knew about the concept of intensity.

"Aw! Oh, Shit man!" Depina groaned that groan of anguished pleasure. Ty began his ride then, easing in and sliding out, giving Face more and then more of his measure.

"Aw! Shit!" Depina shouted.

Ty pierced him with abandon then, sending his piece deeper inside of him with one long impatient thrust. Face grunted hard against the slice and slide as a warm and engulfing tightness fully enclosed Tyrone. Like some deep and magnetic furnace, it seemed to will Ty, to pull him deeper into its heat. Being inside Depina was like plunging one's dick into the eye of a crushing, twisting cyclone. It was exciting and it was havoc. It was freeing and it was dangerous.

Not one to freely allow himself be totally dominated, Face turned himself around. Then, with a sense of sexual sorcery, Depina glared defiantly at Ty.

"Come on! Punk! Hit it! Damn it! Fuck! Fuck me! Harder! Harder, damn it!" he demanded.

So Tyrone hit him rougher, lunged in him deeper, and fucked him harder. Applying more muscle, more force, more bravado, Tyrone began to tear inside this grotto of lust and surprising need. His hips thrust harder, his body plunged deeper as sweat popped across his every lunging sinew.

"Come on! Fuck! Is that all you got? Fuck me, dammit!"

Ty set an even meaner rhythm then, grabbing those shoulders, pushing Face down, and sending his every inch forcefully through him.

Depina rose up, devilishly winked, and gnashed his teeth against Ty's nipple.

"Aw! Face, man! That shit hurts!" he complained as Depina rolled the other nipple between his strong, menacing fingers. This caused an old and forgotten excitement to charge inside of Tyrone's mind. This wild activity only coupled with his long tarnished history of curiosity about Face. It all merged with the intensity of actually *being inside him*, and this sent Tyrone to that racey spacey edge. He could *feel* his whole body flooding with ecstatic wonder. He could feel each pulsation against the physical rub. He could feel this groove deep inside of Face Depina. Ty could feel his own arrival coursing through his body; feel its alternating rushes of smoothness and friction.

He had maybe three strokes left within him, and that was it. He lunged and instantly, he felt his shudder. He could feel himself slipping into that strange shiver-place. And with that sensation, he grabbed Depina's long hard dick and he pistoned it quick, quickly, then quicker still. A willfully strong and vibrant charge rumbled through Depina's erection, and its seismic quivering was about to set Ty off!

Depina heaved and erupted like wild, the skeet of his bounty blasted, flying, filing into the air, courtesy of Tyrone's presence, and Tyrone's fist.

For one hot, sticky moment of transference, Ty felt as if, with that power in his fist, he controlled the heart, the mind and the body of Pascal Face Depina. And with that power in his grasp, Ty pulled back, then slammed, and shook, with the whole of his entirety he shook, satisfied.

I can't believe it! I can't believe it! I just did Face fucking Depina!

"Man," Face sighed. "That was wild, baby. Real wild. I guess I brought out that wild boy in you. That's pretty hip." He laughed, and then his aspect turned and it shifted from the humorous.

"But, don't go fallin' in love with me or anything, 'cause you know I ain't like you, right? I mean. I ain't gay. So you *need* to keep this shit between us. All right?" he said, his green eyes staring back at Ty in complete and utter seriousness. "This was just one of them experiments. You know, like, this is just an *actin'* exercise."

Something very strange had just happened. It was a kind of murder . . . a murder of a good moment. Tyrone heard him. He watched those pretty lying eyes trying to convey some truth that he knew was the height of mendaciousness. But it was all sort of dreamlike, or more like *waking up* from a dream, where everything sits in its own quiet haze and nothing is quite yet real.

"I mean, it felt all right. Don't be hurt. Can't say I was really all *into* it. But—"

"What? Come on now, Face! This is me, Ty. You don't need to bullshit *me* with this whole I'm-that-tough-hard-*straight*-street-cat trip of yours anymore. That shit won't play in Peoria, and damn sure won't play with me. You give head, man. And you take it up the ass, man. Last time I checked, that's you a pretty damn *gay* man!" Tyrone fumed.

"See, the old Face would be kickin' yo punk ass right about now. But I'll just call that shit a compliment. You're all hung-up on labels. Ain't you heard Tina Turner's new cut: "What's Love Got to Do With It?" Well, what's *gay* gotta do with it, huh? I ain't like you, Ty. Hey, you ain't gotta believe me. You can ask any one of my *many* chicks. See, I'm up for this role as a gay athlete, and I'm supposed to *know* what the hell I'm doin', right? Besides, shit, man, I went to P.A. I was *surrounded* by all you fuckin' guys. And down here, steady dealin' with the artsy farts, I'm always bein' hit on. I've been around the block, man. People do what they do, and that's their biz. I've seen it all. So, not much turns me off anymore. Anyway. See, this part, it ain't no buck-wild dick-swingin' porn. But I'm supposed to be a young, queer cat. I have to *get* what being a queer is about. I mean, what's it like to kiss? Did that. You close your eyes, and it's like kissin' your damn arm. But I had to go *deeper* than that. I needed to *know* what it feels like to be with another man. Now I know. See. I'm in this for real. I'm tryna be an artist, not some fly-by-night. I'm dead serious about my craft."

Tyrone stared back at this *actor*, this supposed thespian, and for the first time since he'd know him, Face didn't seem so damn pretty anymore. *Who was he, really?*

Maybe Ty should've felt clowned again. But the laugh, this time, was on Depina. Tyrone wanted Face to know *he knew* for sure now that Pascal Ornate "Face" Depina was *not* legit.

"*Acting?*" Ty said. "Nah. Pascal, trust me on this: you were never *that* good. Yeah, sure, maybe sucking dick, once, might be an experiment. But sucking it twice, and then taking it to the rim and demanding *more* just makes you another deluded faggot! You think you played me? No, bruh. Ya played yourself!"

Ty began his shrivel process. That eight-inch thing which let him know how it felt to be black, gay, and alive was descending into a little brown sliver of pissed off twine.

"Come on, Ty! I picked you outta all the guys I coulda picked, 'cause I knew you'd keep it quiet. So don't feel used. You enjoyed it. I know you did!" Face blustered as Ty walked away. "Yo! Just keep it between us, and don't be all mad at me, brotha! Hey! Ain't you never heard of *The Method*?"

"Whatever's clever, *sista!* You played yourself, but whatever's clever," Tyrone said, heading back to the room filled with men who knew, acknowledged, and who embraced what they truly were.

CHAPTER NINE

Claims and Proclamations

FALL 1981

Tyrone was studying journalism at Columbia, which was cool and all, but journalism, at best, was literature in a hurry, and Ty was in a hurry to make literature. In his nineteen years, he had been through so much he *knew* there had to be a novel (or two) in him. He had just spent a long, hot, industrious summer *feeling* and writing. So now he stood, in the offices of a publishing house, holding his own little piece of earth, believing it to be the whole fucking world.

For his date with destiny, Ty had worn his hunter-green corduroy jacket and carried his serious-business briefcase.

He hadn't expected the editor to be so young, so darkly handsome. But Constantine Feld was.

As Feld leafed through Tyrone Hunter's Great American Novel, all ninety-three pages of it, Ty began to *feel* the buzz. He imagined it was greatness swooping down from the air to kiss his angst-ridden ass, embrace his teenage tragedies. He could smell the fresh ink on the pages of his contract, hear the champagne uncork. Constantine Feld was going to rise from his desk, call in the big boys of literati, alert the media, and, damn it, phone Liz Smith! Yes, Ty could feel it. All that good shit and glory was just a page-turn away.

But then Feld, his eyes never leaving the page, delivered not glory but a hard smack of condescension.

"You want to write, kid? Learn *how* to write. Finish school. Get a life! Pay attention to things around you. Question everything. Lose your hang-ups. You're young. Be promiscuous! Then try celibacy. Don't speak for a year, maybe two years, and then *shout* everything. Write. Rewrite. That's the best advice I can give you, kid. Now, good luck, and good evening."

Ty couldn't believe it. He'd put blood, sweat, and a summer of hot tears into that manuscript, and here was this man disrespecting him and it. *Typical. Fuckin' fat-cat elitist! And that page of advice from the Bohemian's Handbook? This is the '80s, in New York City, and he wants me to go out . . . and be promiscuous?*

Every man has his own Petri dish. And while Ty was born to experiment, none of his experiments were of the *très* kinky variety. Instead, he took turns embracing the various "isms." He had this mad itch to learn more shit than anyone needed to know about mysticism, vegetarianism, Buddhism, Jungism, plus a whole lot of other "isms" most people couldn't even pretend to understand. That past summer, after reading *Das Kapital*, Ty had been down with the proletariat. David was in East Oshkosh at the time, dancing for the money as hard as he could. When they touched base long-distance, all Ty talked about was embracing socialism, while all Davy talked about was embracing the long, brown, thick dicks of chorus boys. Some ideologies, like some cocks, fit for a season.

Inside that fancy Forty-second Street office, Ty imploded. And for one, self-doubting, introspective moment, he thought, *Maybe I don't have what it takes*. But his Uncle Jerome's voice piped into his consciousness: *"Bwoi! Don't you let them motherfuckas steal your joy!"*

So Ty, who'd *thought* he was a genius since he wrote that freak hit song, said to this high-and-mighty editor hunk: "Excuse me, sir. I've worked very hard on this. You read one page of one chapter, and you say I can't write? Maybe I can't. Or maybe you don't read so well, which is pretty sad, for an editor." And with that, he snatched back his prized, if unappreciated, manuscript in an indignant blur.

Ty returned to school, taking a deeper, more soul-investigation interest in people, everyday people as well as the city's *perceived* freaks of all types, classes, kinds. He sat in the parks and observed the way people behaved when unaware of being watched, listened to. He spent time on the streets and slept in a shelter. He volunteered in a soup kitchen, hung out with skid poets, underground artists. He submitted his short stories to major magazines, and was never more alive than when sitting on fire, exchanging ideas with writers in workshops. Ty was determined to sharpen his literary chops. Whenever he could, he spent time around young kids, desperate to never lose touch with the rejected seven-year-old child within. He was accepted at four writer's colonies, and he never stopped working. Homeboy wrote and scribed his aspiring ass off.

Tyrone became a kind of urban chameleon. Every day brought a different suit. He'd try it on to see if it fit, sometimes reaching beyond the drag and assuming the identity.

Like Langston Hughes, forever the dreamer, seeker, the searcher, Tyrone Hunter searched for rhythms, and life, and the rhythm of life in nitty-gritty ghettos and cold dark grottoes, in synthetic goddesses, in plastic heroes, in uptown bars, in dim Jazz clubs, in the larynx of Billie Holiday, in the crying sax of Charlie "Yardbird" Parker, in the sensitive phrasing of obscure artist Jimmy Scott, in the regal posture of Nina Simone, and in the ethereal intelligence of Coltrane's horn.

Along the way, he met Jamaal. No last name. Just *Jamaal*—a struggling poet-radical visionary artist-thinker-primal screamer who shouted Allah and Nationalism to the casually beige clique downtown.

Jamaal said it *loud*, shrouded his body in kente cloth, wore his political hair in knotty, unkempt, and I-don't-care locks. He was a dark, towering performance art piece with a deeper voice than God's or James Earl Jones'. His trip was to anoint avenue blocks with his Big Black Sound.

"Why? My Black people— my beautiful Black people, why are we beaten . . . and gunned down in these streets? Why? Black people, my beautiful Black people, why the HELL I can't *hear* your screams? I ask WHY? Whhhhhhhy? Black people, my beautiful Black people, why are we running? Why are we *running* for our lives?"

Yes, Jamaal was an angry Black cat, and he had his righteous reasons. Black people were becoming daily statistics, victims of crime, malice, and wickedness. It was, in some segments of the city, open season for the abuse and slaughter of Black people.

Few could call his outrage unwarranted. When Jamal spoke, screamed, and hollered, it wasn't just a radical's hyperbolic gusts. Black people *were* indeed running for their lives.

In time, Black Michael Griffith would be pursued by a ruthless pack of white men, chased into the merciless traffic of the Belt Parkway, then hit and explode into carnage and injustice. Black people *were* running for their lives. Doors were being broken down by cops, as the Black grandmothers behind them, like Miss Eleanor Bumpers, were brutally shot to death. Black people were running for the lives. Young graffiti artists, like Michael Stewart, were beaten into comas from which they'd never awaken. Black people were running for their lives. Prejudice and ignorance combined with kicks, fists, and baseball bats to take the last breath from sixteen-year-old Yusuf Hawkins. Yusuf Hawkins was just a Black boy, who made the fatal mistake of shopping for a used car, on the *wrong* side of a Brooklyn street. Black people *were* running for their lives.

Jamaal spoke out against those and other racial atrocities. He was a freedom seeker, seeking like-minded thinkers and new Afros in a terminally Jheri curl city. He'd talk *Revolution!* to most anyone who'd listen to his cry, and Ty, oh Tyrone was down with the sound.

Ty was a young Black man with eyes, ears, a heart and a mind. Jamaal recognized those signs, and he tried with righteous conviction to awaken the sleeping radical in him. Theirs was an educational hang. Ty was a knowledge groupie, and Jamaal was big on dropping the science.

Being five years older, Jamaal took a liking to Ty's anxious mind. Jamaal was a known criticizer of most everything and anyone who did not play a part in Uplifting the Race, yet he was torn between the *Koran* and the *Kama Sutra*, between hostility and lust.

There was something beyond the rhetoric that stewed in a soup, a callaloo of possibilty between then. Hands grasped a little longer than was customary between two brothas. At times, both sets of eyes fluttered inside the momentary silence of: What If.

But whether straight or bi-curious, Jamaal was far too much the warrior to let the white stain of male-on-male surrender soil his favorite dashiki. And Ty Hunter, for his part was *not* seeking the position as Royal Cocksucker to the new African King of Radicals.

In an East Village bar, he struck up a conversation with a longhair, who had once ran with The Beats. But something the man told him sounded a warning in Tyrone. The history he recited was about love. It seemed that Allen Ginsberg's love and admiration for Jack Kerouac was so deep, Allen would fellate Jack under the Brooklyn Bridge.

Upon hearing this, Ty wondered: Did brilliance shoot out? Could Ginsberg swallow it and from the bitterness be somehow better?

According to longhair legend, whenever those acts were performed, it was Allen going down on brilliance. Jack never gave brilliance back.

"Oh . . . Hell, no! I'm not gonna fall for Jamaal or any other on-the-fence angry straight man, no matter how brilliant his ass might be. Nah! See, I do not crave cock in that blind, love-me-short-time way. Hell, I've got one too. No reciprocation is the first sign of lack of sexual respect. What's the fuckin' profit in that shit?"

The subject was moot, as far as Jamaal was concerned as well. While walking with Ty through the village, they happened upon two young Black men holding hands. In Tyrone's eyes, it was a beautiful vision. But the sight of this only sickened Jamaal. For him, there was nothing vaguely cute or advantageous in being Black and *openly* gay. And so he said, loudly, as the couple strolled by them:

"Ain't no evolutions nor revolutions to be gained by taking it up the ass!"

"Why did you just do that, man? They weren't bothering anybody," an embarrassed Ty countered.

"The hell they weren't! They were bothering me!"

"Why, Jamaal?"

"Cause Black men should *be* Black men! Not runnin here around here, fuckin' each other. There's too damn much work to do, if we ever gonna see The Revolution!"

"But *Revolution* is change," Ty said strongly. "Change redefines things by the nature of word. Your version is the old version, and it's gonna have to *change*, man. Love is so much wider than your narrow definition my, soldja!"

"Oh yeah?" Jamaal smirked indignantly.

"Yeah. And I'm sick of people tryin' to tear love apart, like so much meat. It *is* what it is. Love is *love*, brother. Man lovin' woman, woman lovin' woman, and no matter what face you put on it, men lovin' men is *love*."

"It's deviant. . . . And just wrong, and I ain't with it."

"Man, all this time, I thought . . ."

"You thought *what*, Ty . . . that I was . . . *queer for you?*" Jamaal stopped walking and dared Ty to *say* it.

"No. I thought you were this righteous *forward* thinker, but your shit is just as archaic and judgmental as the rest. You don't *get* it, do you? You try, just *try* to maintain any kind of a *lasting* revolution without *love*, my homophobic brotha, and you'll see it's gonna fail!"

"That's just some fuckin' psuedo-intellectual sissy-talk."

"Nah, man . . . that's just the truth," Ty said.

As the two glared at each other, Ty witnessed a misdirected hatred in his new friend's eyes, and with it, came the end of his *revolutionary* crush. Ty had much too much pride to pursue someone who hated, to the bone, a part who he was, and who he *suspected* Jamaal was as well.

Tyrone boarded his next train . . . *alone*.

CHAPTER TEN

The Season of Bliss

JANUARY 1986

Once upon a time there was a sweet-faced *chica-sista* who went by the name of Bliss Santana. Bliss was a very sassy, sexy girl. As Face would so indelicately put it:

"All I know is she's hot, yo. When my Akita, Sasha, saw her . . . even *he* popped a boner! Before that, I thought Sasha was a fuckin' *queer* hound!"

Maybe it was all that long, cascading gypsy hair, blacker than a raven's wings, or maybe those liquid eyes, as stunning and hypnotically green as Face Depina's. Whatever it was, the moment Face laid his mean greens on hers, he heard the noise of a galloping heart. In Bliss, he saw his feminine equal. Naturally, he was attracted. On the surface, she was refined . . . tall, lithe, and her breasts were real strident girls. She had a scratch of a voice that made him think of a cool *dame* belting back bourbons with the boys in a smoky pool hall, a cue in one hand, a Camel in the other. And when Bliss Santana laughed, it caused little earthquakes under the skin of men. This was even true for Face Depina.

He liked her from the beginning, when she turned, did a double-take, and asked, "So, what your bag?"

Acting was hers. She excelled at that gig, but often she portrayed *real* so much better. Bliss Santana was a fighter, *cusser*, shit-talker, and a take-no-prisoners brawler, if you pissed her off. That wild streak gave her a hipper edge than the rest. On the exterior, she was another pretty actress with chops. But when the lights went down, she turned the player off. Then she became that Jersey girl, burning with the spirit of ambition, who'd worked on herself, cleaned up her act, and went from tough chick with pool stick to daytime TV's leading young Blacktress.

She began that trek at Arthur Murray's, teaching samba and other Latin dances, but decided after one more misplaced brogan landed on her baby toe, *Fuck this scene! Hell! If I can fake-teach these rhymically-retarded bastards how to dance, and all the while smi-i-i-i-ile like I'm fuckin' Rita Chita Rivera Moreno then maybe I can be a freaking actress!*

So she paid her dues as a waitress, barmaid and hat model while she studied the craft and read *Backstage* and all the trades religiously. She found parts in plays, a few showcases, copped an agent and prayed for that big break.

She *never* fucked her way to the middle.

Face had never met a more confident woman. He called her a "complex carbohydrate." Later, he'd compare her—as he did all women, screwed and unscrewed—to a car. Bliss was a Jaguar: expensive, fast, lovely, and yes, *trouble*.

They met when he auditioned for the boyfriend role on her soap. Face was nervous, and this condition showed in his aspect. He had that frightened gaze of a half-assed player who'd forgotten what the hell he was doing onstage.

He's damn cute, though, Bliss thought. *Hmmm . . . maybe a little too damn cute for comfort.*

"So, what's your bag?" she'd asked, followed by, "Calm down, honey boy! It's just a read-through. Tell you what: Imagine everyone here except you is buck naked. Look at these bastards. They look pretty damn ridiculous, don't they? Now breathe. Breathe . . . There. That's better."

That was how it all went down. But Face Depina would change the story in later years to protect his facade.

Face didn't get the part.

"He's a bronzed Ken doll, only stiffer and less talented," said the casting director.

Maybe Face didn't snatch the role, but did get to roll in the snatch.

"Wanna know why you didn't get cast? I saw the test. You were prettier than *all* the rest. Hell, you were prettier than *me!* And ya *know* we can't have that shit!" Bliss teased.

"Bullshit! No one's prettier than you. I sucked!"

"Well . . . yeah. You *did* suck. But you're just starting out. I'm telling you, you're just too damn pretty. People will think you're a pretty *gay* boy or something. Are you? Gay, I mean?"

"NO! Hell no! Want me to prove it?" Face quickly snapped.

"Puh-leeeease! All actors can *act* fuckin' interested. It's okay, hon. Really. I've lots of gay friends. Well, a couple style-conscious bastards and ballerinas whom I love, dearly. Come on. You can let me buy you a drink . . . and tell me your story," she said, swinging a big bag over her shoulder.

She pulled Face's arm and he followed her willingly down the hall, into the elevator, and out the door. It was winter, and darkness had fallen on the West Side like a cool translucent shade. Despite her low-key beret and dark specs, Bliss was instantly recognized. Her fans waiting by the studio door, called out:

"Zina! Zina! Don't let that new bitch get the best of you!

"Zina, when are you gonna find out you were switched at birth?" "Zina . . . excuse me, Ms. Santana, may I please have your autograph?"

Face watched this scene unravel with an envious fascination.

"How that shit feel, Bliss? They love you! Damn. Must be a fly life, so many people *lovin'* your ass . . ."

"It's all very sweet and gratifying. But *love me?* Please! They love Zina, the eternal doormat with the nice wardrobe and the good heart. They got no idea what makes me . . . or my heart tick . . ."

"Well, *I'd* like to know," a suave Face countered.

He took his finger and dabbed lightly to her soft cheek, smoothing away a fallen lash.

"Hey . . . let's make a wish," he said.

"You can't be serious."

"Why not? Shit! Life's a crap-shoot . . . sometimes we could use all the luck we can get," Face attested.

"Well, you go ahead. Make a wish, pretty one."

And so Face did. He gazed at the tip of his long index finger, closed his eyes and blew.

There's something strange about him, she thought as she watched him. *Something distinct and disturbing. Something as bright and beautiful and as harsh as sunlight.*

And she said, "Careful what you wish for, pretty one, because you just might get it."

Together they walked the neon and navy street, and it occurred to her that she didn't even know his name.

"So, what's your fuckin' tag again?"

"Face. Face Depina."

Upon hearing that, Bliss Santana began a long and wicked journey into laughter. She couldn't help it. A loud burst of it just rolled up out of her, and she guffawed down West 57th Street. Face watched her lovely green eyes tearing. He saw the cords tighten in her long delicate neck, and he felt cheapened by that sound. He was used to laughing *at* other people. It had been a long while since anyone had laughed *at him*. He'd forgotten what it felt like: that creepy sensation of Stupidity, standing still.

Is she high or what? Fuckin' crazy-ass actress! She better stop that shit! What's so fuckin' funny, anyway?

And still she laughed, stopping only to catch her breath . . . and then resume into another chorus of it. The subway rumbled under their feet, and he could feel the train, that fucking train, speeding like a dangerous thought. For one equally dangerous moment, he wanted to haul her cackling ass into the nearest storefront, and to rip that noise from her laughing throat.

Finally, she saw the wounded look that had claimed his handsomely confused mug, and thought it best to cease. "I'm . . . I'm sorry, baby. But that name, it's . . . it's too fuckin' precious! *Face Depina?* That can't even be your real name. No one could do that shit to their kid; sounds like you wanna be a fuckin' porn star."

"Well, my real name is Pascal," he said. "But everybody calls me—"

"Pascal. Pascal?" she asked, repeating it in her mind like a schoolgirl nursing a mad little crush. *Bliss and Pascal . . . Pascal and Bliss . . .* "I like that. I guess I'll be calling you Pascal," she determined in the moment.

Face Depina had always hated that name. But hearing it purr from those full, lush lips of Bliss Santana's, suddenly, he didn't seem to mind it so much.

As they continued to walk, a fashionably dressed male couple glanced at them. Bliss felt sure that she'd been recognized, yet again. *Oh well, get out the pen.* But their eyes settled on the studly Face in a slow and deliberate glide. Feeling strangely protective, Bliss immediately grabbed his arm.

What is it about your sway? I see Adonis. But who or what do THEY see, Pascal?

"So, you never told me. What's your bag? What do you do when you're not busy being so damn cute?

Face couldn't tell her he installed carpets, DJ'd and "modeled" some. His sexuality was already in question, and modeling would give fire to the kindling of her suspicions.

And so he lied. In that huge inky universe of Big Black Lies, it was a small high-yellow one.

He said, "I'm in advertising."

All at once, it no longer mattered what he did. Bliss quickly shuffled him through the doors of Bloomingdale's and headed straight to the lingerie department.

"What's your favorite color?" she asked.

"Green," he said. "Money-green. Mint-green. Just green, baby."

He studied her innately exotic skin, her tight-boned erotic beauty as she meticulously browsed the racks for just the right article: a mint-green teddy. She held one up. Face nodded in approval. Bit instead of whipping out her slew of credit cards, she turned to him and said, "Come here and kiss me." Face eagerly obliged, and as their tongues searched the newness of each other's mouths, she stuffed the teddy inside her big leather bag.

Oh shit! She's wile. This chick is wi-i-ile! Maybe she's even a little craz-e-e! I dig her. I can see myself fuckin' the hell outta this chick. So you think I'm queer, huh? Well, you bet your sweet ass you won't when this night is over.

Hmmm, he's a pretty good kisser. Nice soft slow tongue. Not too wet. I wonder what else he's good at.

The couple then returned to her lair on the West Side, a trendy little symphony in avocado green. She was still in her 20s, yet she had acquired *things*. There were several citations honoring her work, photos with New York swells and power brokers. And, most notably, there was that larger-than-life-size portrait of Bliss, in the nude, which seemed to ask: Are *you* man enough for all of this?

Observing the quietly elegant way she lived, Depina was made all the more envious and hungry for something better.

Bliss fixed them a pitcher of stiff martinis. She sipped hers slow and purposefully.

They kissed some more, this time for accuracy, for Bliss to see if she really *liked* him. It wasn't long before she decided she did. However, she saw no physical signs of his arousal, so she boldly said, "Why don't you remove your clothes, Pascal . . . I think I'd liked to see all of you."

He looked at her then, as if waiting for her to say "please."

Instead, she took the request up a notch, and demanded, "Strip, damn it! Let's see if you're *pretty* where it counts."

Face stared back at her then, licking his lips, lowering his eyelids, doing all the shit he *thought* made him sexy. He ran his hand through his newly shorn hair, which was now shorter and curlier and framed his chiseled countenance most flatteringly. He played with his left nipple and blatantly winked at her. It all might've worked if he hadn't tried so hard.

What the hell is he doing? Oh, no! He's posing for me. Oh Gawd! He's definitely gay . . . or bisexual at least. But damn if he isn't a very, very cute one. What the hell . . . it's a slow night in Bliss-ville. I'll do him as long as he's wearing a freakin condom.

Then Face very slowly removed his shirt.

Oh! Yes. Now this is interesting. I like this. Pascal works out. Hell, the boy could be a model!

Face intentionally saved his best for last. Even if he wasn't *hard* as a steel beam, just yet, he knew he had the inches. He slowly rubbed his swelling crotch, watching her, watching him, anticipating that stunned look of awe on her face when he finally whipped it out and she could see what he'd brought to the party.

He unzipped, reached down deep, and then he thrust forth . . . the Depina Jewel.

"Oh! My damn, Pascal! Look at you. You certainly are a growing boy, aren't you?"

"That's what they say," he grinned.

I don't doubt it. But who *says it?*

Ambition, adrenaline, and martinis mixed in a very heady cocktail. Face sipped it all, looking at Bliss as the Depina Jewel slowly lifted, propelled and gradually projected, and finally it rose most prominently to the occasion.

They kissed with their eyes, and their lips and their hands until they kissed their clothes away.

Face saw this as a command performance, the deed, the work of a Method Actor. He very gradually guided his piece slowly, yet deeply inside of her. A quick and breathless catch just once then moved with an easy intimacy along the length of him, and it. What began tentatively as making love, soon accelerated into quick and rhymic fucking . . . and the fuck and the fucker fucking her was just fucking fine for Bliss.

But Depina had yet to really discover the full map of a woman, or how to be freaky-free with a female. That was OK. He was young, hung and willing to please. Bliss Santana just knew, with his clay in her hands, she could mold this hunk called Face Depina into a more pleasing and pleasuring shape.

When she disappeared into another room, she'd left Face laying on her living room floor, spent and musing on the event.

It had been a while since he'd laid a chick. And so what if she didn't blow him as good and juicy-gooey-slick as the men he'd known who loved his dick. She was soft and fluid, and giving . . . and yes, the sly filly in Bliss seemed satisfied by his stallion acrobatics.

Yeah. Guess I proved myself tonight. Depina wanted to jump up, click his heels, open the 17th floor window of that luxury building and shout out to all The City:

"I'M FACE MUHFUCKIN DEPINA, DAMN IT! AND I JUST FUCKED THE HELL OUTTA BLISS SANTANA!"

But he realized that would've been *très* unsuave, uncool, and uncivilized. So, although the urge was vivid, he chilled.

When Bliss returned, wearing her pilfered mint-green teddy, he noticed the Black and Latin cultures fought for possession of her nose and lips and the tones of her skin. She looked, in her stilettos, like a fine and sultry gazelle. And she had a little something extra to enhance that carnal spell.

Bliss wasn't the first to introduce Face to the jolts and joys of fine cocaine, but this time he indulged in ways he never could have before. Bliss's stash was choice, Columbian and copious. They sniffed and snorted, sniffed and giggled, sniffed and cooed. When it came time for round two in their sexual Olympics, things began to turn for the better.

Face made *Love* to Bliss, and the effect was like losing time. He sat on her couch, and she mounted his impressively long thighs. She liked being on top, in control, her back and shoulders arched across her expensive coffee table. She liked her clit stroked by a warm and knowing hand . . . and placed Face's hand to her pleasure spot. She stared boldly into the green of his eyes, and the thrust and slide of him made something ecstatic, something come alive inside her. It claimed her pussy, claimed her belly, her face, her breasts, it claimed her skin, and began to claim a soft and wet corner of her soul.

"Oh . . . oohhhh . . . Pascal! Yes, papi! Yes!" she sighed.

Face sunk slowly, deeper inside her, tunneling her tight wet grip of her woman's clutch. He liked it . . . and he felt most assured that it liked him, too. Staring into her eyes, he wanted to laugh, as a good feeling began rising in his head. It was safe, and wet, like crawling around in warm womb water. And for as long as the effect that fine white powder lasted, the thrust, the pitch, the sex improved. His lost groove was found, and like a boomerang, she threw it back to him. The cock of his walking manhood was regained between wet skins as her thighs wrapped his back like a coffee-colored boa constrictor. "Ah! Yes! Oh! That's it! *Pascal*! Yes!"

But Bliss wanted more. She wanted shooting stars, comets, and solar showers. She wanted all that shit. And penetration alone would not take her to that silky Milky Way. Face had to go that extra distance, *downtown*, and *not* the Lower East not West Side.

Into a tree-lined village he stared, without a map, knowing his performance would be the telling act. The telling act that determined, that separated the men form the boys—-especially the boys who like men's dicks. But a dash of coke on the tip of his tongue numbed him enough to ignore his basic distaste for what he was about to do. Besides, this shit pleased Bliss, and she and her body and her guile and her mind and her wild treasure trove of substances had done her part in pleasing him.

So he did it. He went to that downtown place. With her steady hand sliding him, guiding him, he went flicking, fluttering and *freaking* all the way.

Face Depina wasn't seen again for nearly three weeks.

When he resurfaced, he was well on his way to full-fledged coke addict status, with a classy new wardrobe and fresh traces of expensive pussy on his breath.

Bliss, being a successful working actress, provided an entrée into the Higher Life. A life filled with New York intellectuals, budding directors, fashion fixtures, style icons, about-to-happen playwrights and a whole crew of chilly new friends willing to pull a few strings, and do most anything for a friend of Bliss.

One such individual was Claudio Conte, a long-maned,

red-hot model-of-the-moment. Claudio was supposedly from southern Italy, only by way of the Bronx. But to his credit, he was cool, hip, and just *Italian-enough* to talk the talk. Face did not like him at first. Claudio Conte stepped hard on the long frail toes of Depina's ego.

The insecurities arrived once introduced, as both men stepped back to slyly appraise the other. It was like two good-looking alley cats might, eyeing, sniffling each other out, trying to decide whether to fight or form a fraternity of two.

There was too much sausage in the room.

Face and Claudio were both just too damn fly to share the same space. It would only invite confusion and then, much comparison. At whom would people gaze at first and for how long? Who would they want to befriend, mother, take home, play with, think sexy things about? Which one would they really want to fuck?

But on the sly, Face was checking Conte, because for a supposedly European cat, he had a lot going on, or at least appeared to . . . and Face knew certain things about people. Life on the streets gave him the education.

Claudio. Who was he, really? With that Michelangelo-carved jaw-line and a freaking granite chin that seemed to stretch and enter a room before the rest of him, he looked like a man who was capable with his fists. His shoulder-length hair was Conte's trademark, and that night, it was meticulously slicked back, making him look like a big arrogant hawk about to strike. He was almost as tall as and taut as Face—thus, another reason to hate him. But Face didn't hate him. Face was suspicious of his ass, though, especially when Bliss grabbed Claudio's hand and the two retired to another room.

His first instinct: *Follow them.* He needed to know what their story was, and if Claudio Conte was fucking Bliss. It was possible. After all, he and Bliss weren't exactly exclusive, then. He also wondered if Claudio was really, truly, all-the-way-straight. But some playwright was busy babbling about his new play, and Face needed to at least appear interested. The man's conversation lasted all of three minutes and thirty-one seconds. Face was checking the clock over the man's balding dome, computing how long it would take that tall hot Italian male model to fuck Bliss.

When the door opened, he reasoned there hadn't been enough time for anything sexual to have occurred, except . . . maybe a little . . . head.

Is that it? Was she in there, givin' that slick muhfucker head? Is she stank like that?

Strange, it didn't make him mad or angry or insecure, the thought of Bliss giving Claudio Conte head. Maybe when he kissed her, he'd know for sure.

What he needed, really needed was a tried-and-true gay detector, like li'l David. David could always spot a fag . . . no matter his bag, his drag, or the hag with him. David would simply *know.* He could walk into a crowded room, blindfolded, and scope out all the queers just by sniffing the cologne on the air. It was a gift, and David possessed it. But David wasn't there. And as Face Depina watched Bliss and smooth cat Claudio approach him, he silently begged the *gods of gaydar* to grant him a little *momentary* Davy power.

But the gods didn't come.

And so, once the two were upon him, Face thought it best to try the gentle insult. Staring at the dense, bone-straight line on Conte's brow, he asked. "So, it's Fabio, right?"

"No. It's *Claaahhhdio* But I get-a-that all-a-the time-mah."

"*Well Claaahhhdio* . . . you plunk those eyebrows yourself, or does somebody do that shit for you?"

Bliss appeared slightly mortified.

Unfazed, in a heartbeat, Conte chimed, "I have-a them waxed-a, twice a month, I'll give-a you her name-a. She can-a take-a care of that pesky *unibrow*-a thing for you, no?"

Face wanted to hit him. *Hoard.* Bliss laughed a short polite laugh, as she sipped her third martini. Then stepping-nose-to-nose with Face, she kissed his offending caterpillar brow.

"That's all right. I love my baby's . . . ummm . . . *growth.*"

It was just close enough that Face could NOT smell any trace of MAN on her breath.

"So what do you think, Claude? I mean, really? Is he not The *New* Gorgeous? Don't you think Eileen's people should take a look?"

"He might-a get-a some work," Claudio shrugged, his lips curling as if he too were sniffing Depina, his cool quotient, his temperament, his eyes, his lips, his sexual preference. "But he might do-a better with a more-a . . . ethnic agency, no?"

They way he'd said it, it made face want to hit him, *hoard. Twice.*

"Please!" Bliss said. "Eileen could use some café au lait with all that buttermilk she's serving up. Step into the '80s! Pascal would be perfect. This, *is* The *New* Gorgeous!"

"What are you two talkin 'bout? And who's this Eileen chick?"

"Eileen Ford. You know, she's the legend behind Ford Models. It's Claudio's agency . . . and personally, I think *you're* Ford material."

"What?"

Face still hadn't revealed that he had, in fact, sort of modeled, though not very professionally. But Ford was the apex of the industry's prettiest posers. You were *somebody* if Ford represented you. Maybe the acting thing could wait. After all, no one was beating down his door to see him, read him, ink him to a three-pic deal. And even he knew there were far greater talents out there screaming to be noticed. Modeling just might be a feasible solution. Yes. He could make some very decent scratch . . . and maybe travel, and roll around the city, with style.

But as thoughts of cover-boy glory popped like blinding flashbulbs in his glittering skull, something began to darken the Depina facade.

Back when he was seventeen, still a student, he would go into Manhattan to make the rounds. There he'd be trying out the actor's life of casting calls, interviews, go-sees, and such. He had nerve. Young Pascal Depina was incandescing with the hot flame of an "I'm gonna be *somebody*" fire. He thought little of lying about his age, his past, his sexuality, and his credits. But his inexperience showed. And he remembered his last modeling gig. The photographer was dark, gay, and notorious for depicting naked men of color in twisted pornographic shapes. The money was decent for a kid. But Face didn't much like the end result: his young cool queer ambiguity, spread naked, as another man was about to mount him. That man was a big thick chocolate brother, with a large camera-friendly penis.

He sometimes thought about that day . . . and those pictures . . . and wondered if they would ever come back, like ghosts often do, to slowly haunt him.

"What's wrong, Pascal? Aren't you interested in modeling, baby?" Bliss asked through coke-clouded eyes.

"Well . . ." Face hedged, and then shook off that troublesome thought. "Me? Be a model? Wow. Who the hell wouldn't?"

The rest would become pretty boy history.

As it turned out, Ford didn't want him. But Boss Models did.

The agency marketed him as an ethnic Paul Newman. His curly hair was dyed a lighter chestnut shade, which served to accent his retro cool, and the pools of those seething hypnotically money-green eyes. He provided quite the fantasy object, and his moist lips were like soft cocoa pillows a man or woman might lay their lustiest wishes upon.

It didn't take long. By June, Depina's likeness was everywhere. It was suddenly *The Face*. You couldn't escape it. Not those smoldering eyes, perpetually wet lips, sumptuous pecs, stony belly, and certainly not that large cum-hither crotch appeal.

His fineness was all over MTV, VH-1, and the billboards across Harlem, Times Square and Chelsea. He became the moody mysterious look of sex in the East and West Village. You couldn't escape it. Everywhere one looked, they could see, the face. The Face! The camera loved him, and he'd learned to *fuck* it back with that ceaseless intensity of his eyes. He whetted the appetites of all who gazed, glared, stared or fantasized. With the power of his fierce 50-foot façade, he ignited the dreams of those who let their curious eyes slide to his designer codpiece.

It was an achievement for pretty, not-quite-Black-or-Latin men everywhere. He'd ascended ("quested" he called it) into a whole other stratosphere of existence.

And there could be no doubt about it, Face Depina was all of a sudden, like, *The Shit*.

He'd walk into a place, carrying his new arrogance like a long bronze dick, whipping it out, and waving it around the joint. Not literally (in most cases), but figuratively, he was this new shiny erection, one with which to be reckoned. And along with it, came the best tables, the best seats; the best champagne and finest cocaine. The hottest chicks, the biggest dicks . . . this semi-fame was the ultimate trip.

But Face never owned his grace. The industry queens could haul him in, dress him, primp him, powder him, light him, and suddenly he was a million bucks worth of sex and sophistication, class or trash. His personal style became one of full-length minks over top-of-the-line Nikes or Armani trenches topped by Kangols. One would've thought he had stock in Kangol. He owned every style of hat, skimmer, cap, beret and tam Kangol ever made. Ironically, *beavers* were his favorite. He took to wearing showy trinkets, wrist-glistening bracelets, and wouldn't be caught dead without his five-carat diamond and platinum crucifix. He was bold enough to wear big hoop diamond-studded earrings in each lobe. No one dressed the way he did back then. He predicted those with money soon would. He was often photographed with this double-gauge nipple rings showing.

From day-to-day, week-to-week, you never knew what flavor he'd like, what color his hair would be, whether he'd be clean-shaven or scruffily goateed. Every day brought yet another mood, another friend, a new acquaintance, a biker, a banker, an Asian babe, a B-boy, a B-girl, or some brown boy who halba'd no ingles. When he'd run into someone he'd fucked or fucked over, left emotionally stymied, he'd hit them with:

"Oh yeah. Of course I remember. We had a wild time, didn't we? I like to fun. You like to fun, and so it was cool that we funned together. I'm tryna do fun right now. So call me later. I mean it. We'll fun again. Peace. By the way; you been hittin' the gym?"

Or with women, he'd end the identical riff with: "And you look fuckin' great in that color."

Once Face and Claudio Conte had gotten to know each other, Conte dropped the faux foreign pose. Game recognized game, and Face found his first real adult hang. Claudio was five years older and already a jaded member of the nouveaux riche. Modeling was just a hip, trippy day job where he got to cheese and pose, and party and pose, hobnob and pose, and snuff expensive sniff up his arrogant nose.

For Claudio, distribution was far more lucrative than shooting attitude and modeling.

Hanging with Claudio, Face never had to purchase coke. It

was here, there, everywhere he looked—in the car on the way to a shoot, in the dressing room before and after the shoots, in the back rooms and the bars, the dive, and hot spots, not to mention spread out on the coffee tables and end tables of Conte's apartment.

To the ghetto-born Face, Claudio was the coolest white dude in the whole damn city, with his affected continental air, fake European flair, and that stony chiseled face of model-man confidence. No matter his mood, emotion and whatever his demons, his fixed expression never deviated from the snide self-satisfied Conte, in effect.

Face wanted to *be* Claudio Conte. And Claudio was the ideal counterpoint to have along when dressed to the nine, stepping lively inside the China Club. Claudio was the one to call when the night needed a good talking to, a rush, or a toot to make things just a little bit better, stronger, realer.

Face had never been a people person, a natural friend-maker, or keeper, so he mostly let his fame and hunkdom handle the intros. He'd pay attention to the way others handled themselves, what talents they exhibited, and find a way to exploit them as a part of his growing entourage. He tried enlisting Tyrone into this menagerie of men, because Ty was a writer and who better to handle his press?

Ty, however, declined. He'd lost all taste for Face Depina.

Yet David had no such misgivings. David was ready to jump on the bandwagon, and become the President of the Face Depina fan club, if any such organization existed. If not, David would have gladly started one.

He was looking for something to do with his pent up creative energies. His show had closed, unemployment reigned, and money was too tight to mention.

Ever the innovator, David had formed a troupe of avant-garde dancer and artists. They performed for free, passing the hat in Washington Square Park, on 34th Street, in Columbus

Circle, wherever, for whatever, until the cops came. But it didn't amount to much, and living hand-to-mouth was a particular brand of New York bitch. David would go on audition after audition, but when he'd finally land a job, he'd find out the gig didn't pay. Finally, there came that moment of a deeply talented queen's greatest indignity: *begging* for a waiter's gig in a midtown steak house.

For that reason, and others, David could not have been happier than the night he'd gone clubbing, and glided into Face Depina outside The Tunnel. In David's eyes, it was kismet.

"Facey? Facey Depina? *Damn, baby*, is that *you*, looking good enough to eat? Raw! Like sushi! And *ya know* I'm not a fan of the fish."

Face was high, and actually kind of glad to see that cute copper mug from his past again.

"Hey, David! How the hell are you? And what you doin these days, kid?"

Waiting tables, and for your tall fine-as-wine-ass to jump off that sexual fence you've been sitting on, baby? So . . . when you gonna leave them snow-queens alone and finally confess your fierce undying love for me, ya pretty bastard?

But what David said was, "Well, I finished my run in *Europa*, but I'm still out there, auditioning. And you know how grueling that is. But I've been doing some extra stuff, too. Like, I'm working with this new dance troupe . . . , PBS, Performing Black Sissies, and . . ."

"Yeah, yeah, great . . . listen, it must be fate, runnin into you—"

"You know, I was just thinking the same damn thing."

"You still do make-up, don't you? Because, cousin, I could use you."

"Yes. Yes. Use me, Facey! Beat me, whip me, make me write bad checks!"

"David! Seriously. Stop *playin, man!* Every artist needs an artist around 'em, and hell, they don't get no more artistic than you. Here's my card. You need to get at me about this. Seriously, son. This could be very . . ."

His mind stranded by it limitations searched for just the right word. "Very . . . beneficial yeah."

David took the card, and yet it felt as if he were holding a winning lottery ticket. Seeing Face again, and receiving that invitation from him, David hoped he wasn't dreaming the entire episode.

"Take care of yourself, Davy," he said, kissing David's cheek.

Then Face Depina disappeared inside the crowd. And David, he just stood there, with a stunned smile, being jostled inside that mini New York club riot.

Who knew David's winding journey would include riding shotgun inside Face Depina's Cool Carnal Corvette? David did! Now he had Face's *digits*, and a job offer too. All he'd had to do was, be *himself*, and stand there, looking *fabu*.

And so, David was officially indoctrinated into Pascal Face Depina near-cultish menagerie. His roles: makeup man, personal stylist, and undying loyalist. Sure, maybe it wasn't Broadway, or even off-off-Broadway. But for David Richmond, this was a gig he would've done free.

CHAPTER ELEVEN

Confessions: When the Aria Arrives Too Late

This scene was a new and disturbing one for Ty. This was Riker's Island Prison, and there was nothing vaguely cool or comical, poetic or musical behind those gray enclosing walls. Tyrone tried to conjure some better vision, to romanticize it, to add color to the spectrum of his preconceived idea of prison. But once behind those walls, he could find no poetry there. When he sniffed the foul air, he could only detect the smell of hardened men, and wasted dreams, and that sad odor of souls rotting.

He was there to see Browny. Browny, who could never seem to jumpstart his own damn dreams! Browny, who, to most, had become an afterthought. "Poor crazy Browny," people would say, knowing that curtain had closed on his fantasy career of being a singer, an operatic tenor. Browny could never seem to grab that fabled brass ring for the lure of his siren, his bitch and his mistress: crack cocaine.

Another arrest for *possession* had landed him there.

When he entered the room and appeared behind that glass partition, Tyrone thought Faison Brown had never looked smaller, and more defeated. His right eye was swollen shut, via his latest in a string of brawls to protect what was his stalling manhood. Even his lame attempt at a simian bop and to play the prison tough had failed to win over his audience of one.

"Hey Tyyyyyyyyyyyy, up in here, yo. Checkin' out how we gangstas live, huh? Better not be puttin' me or this scene in no book, yo?" he joked.

"You? You . . . inside any book of mine, bruh? Not hardly. How you doin, Browny? I mean, really, man?" Ty asked, his words wearing that genuine cologne of concern again.

"Hey. I'm cool. You know how I do . . . make the best of every situation, yo."

"Well . . . I guess that's what a man's gotta do."

"So what's goin on? I want some news from home, yo. Tell me all about you, and li'l David."

"Me? I'm OK. Working on a new play."

"Yeah, that's you, all right. Always creatin' and makin' that crazy money, yo."

Ty thought he'd discerned a certain and most historic resentment in Browny's tone.

"And David, he's doing his thing on the road. But that's David's bliss . . . always traveling and entertaining the masses," Ty said.

"Yeah. Seems like you cats is doin exactly want you wanted to do, yo. More power to you. And . . . ummm . . . what about the other one, that bastard, Pass-cow Depina? What his slick ass been up to?"

"Face?" Ty shrugged. "We don't travel in the same circles. Apparently he's some kinda male model, on his way to superstar status, or some such concept. I see his face on mags and billboards all over the city."

"Yeah. That lucky fuckin' bastard! Always knew he'd cash in on his looks, yo. Some cats make me wonder, though. Pass-cow, especially. Don't know why *his* ass is so blessed, with all the foul shit he's done."

Tyrone sighed, and pondered how some things and some people never seemed to change. For as long as he'd known him, Browny always held some strange and often bitter feelings for Face Depina. No. Face wasn't one of Tyrone's Top Ten or Top Forty people either, but Ty didn't hate him or wish him any ill-will. Yet, to Tyrone's mind, Browny did in fact, hate Face, and for what, Ty wasn't completely sure.

"Seems like motherfuckas do people dirt, and instead of gettin' punished, the motherfuckas get rewarded, yo. You ever notice that shit?"

"Notice what, exactly, Browny? You got something to say, just spit it, man!"

Browny always did have a way of telegraphing certain things, in a not-so-subtle way. He was deliberately gliding the conversation in the Depina direction. Ty could see it now. Yes, Browny was *working* on something. There was, indeed, some *devious* angle to his dangle.

But Faison Brown had picked up a few things about this concept called timing. He'd learned long ago that some info was better divulged in drips and drabs. Yes. He had *something on* Face. It had long been a part of Browny's M.O. to try and amass enough information on most everyone in his circle . . . and then, to use it to his own device when *the right time* came along.

There sat Tyrone, totally ignorant to this secret only Browny and Face Depina held. Tyrone, the "bourgie one" who thought he was *so damn hip* . . . and yet he didn't have a clue.

"What you want me to spit?" Browny asked with a most surreptitious smirk.

"You got some business with Face, maybe you should take it up *with* Face. Don't be calling me here to *this place*, to gossip about that cat. I've got better things to do with my time, man."

"See, that's the thing with you, yo. Always so damn busy! Sometimes you too busy to notice when people do you dirt," Browny hinted.

"Man, please. Look, if Face Depina said something foul about me, fuck him! I couldn't care less. This ain't high school. This is the real world. And I know you have a lotta time to reminisce in this place. I get that. I do. But you really need to stop concentrating so much on the *past* and focus on your future, Browny. Seriously."

Browny chuckled. Ty didn't get it. "The past informs the future, yo. And that's my point. Sometimes you *need* to look back to the past, and see how some stuff people *did* effects the future."

Growing more impatient with the tediousness of Browny, Tyrone sighed, looked at his watch, and pondered why this visit was even necessary. He *did* have *better* things to do than to sit there and reminisce with a bitter Browny, who was clearly living in a bitter place, behind a bitter plate of Plexiglas.

And Browny could sense that uneasiness in his quasi-friend. He didn't want to make a new enemy of Tyrone Hunter. What he wanted most was *a comrade* in his growing hatred of Face Depina. And so, he'd chosen now as the time to reveal an ugly truth from the past.

"Yo, Ty . . . remember back in high school, when we formed the group, and we became Da Elixir?"

"Of course I do."

"Well, you remember that night when we cut our demo? Remember how hyped and happy we all was, after it, yo? We was all hangin out and drinkin' and smokin'. We was havin' a good-ass time, and nobody wanted the night to be over. Then you said your people was away at a funeral or sum'm. So you told us that we could party at your house. Remember that, yo?"

Ty nodded an exasperated nod.

"Well we was all over there, getting looped, drinkin your daddy's cognac, and smokin Depina's weed. We was all hyped and havin a pretty cool time, too. And we didn't have that many *good* times together, yo."

"Yeah. I remember."

"Yup. Thought you would. But, later on, maybe we was tired and too blasted to stay up, 'cause I remember feelin all groggy . . . and when I looked over at you, you was knocked the fuck out, yo."

"Okay. I don't remember it that way . . . but . . . go on."

"Well I guess David fell out after you and me. But Depina, you *know* he was still up, and up to doing some *devilish* shit, yo."

"Really? Like what?"

All right, Faison. This is it. Bre-e-athe. Brace yourself, Ty! Cause I'ma about hit ya with a bullet, yo. Hope you ready for it.

"Well, Ty, lemme axe you this: "You ever remember anything *missin'* from your crib, after that night?"

Tyrone Hunter began to rack his mind about that time long ago. Until then, with Browny's curious inquiry, he'd never once had the tools to put it all together. The puzzle pieces never quite fit. And then, suddenly, a very *sick* and twisted feeling invaded his belly. He didn't want to think it. He didn't and hadn't even imagined it . . . but here was Browny, providing the key, and the missing puzzle piece to that mystery.

"See . . . cause the next day, when Pass-cow and me was on the train headin' home, he was wearin' this stupid-ass, sneaky grin, yo. Like he had a secret or some shit. I got tired of seein' that damn grin, so I asked him what was up." Browny paused for dramatic effect.

"And he looked around to see if anybody was lookin, and he reached inside his Members Only pocket . . . and he pulled out this . . . piece . . . this fancy piece of jewelry, yo."

That sick feeling crawling in Tyrone's gut had crept so deeply into his marrow, he felt as if he'd vomit, right there. He had to *know* for sure . . . and so he had to ask.

"What did it look like, Browny?"

"Man, I don't know. It was a while back, yo. But it was this . . . fancy thing . . ."

"Was it a pin, an antique broach? Did it have small . . ."

"Small emeralds and pearls in a circle . . ." Browny finished Ty's thought. "And hell, I don't know much about that antique shit. But it looked like *money*, yo."

That was it. There was a fire in Tyrone's being . . . and it blazed and it raged and found a place in the lasers of his eyes.

Browny kept talking. There was something else . . . Ty saw his lips moving, and he heard the words coming out . . . but by then Tyrone had *murder* on his mind.

"And I said: Yo, where you cop that shit, yo? And he laughed and said he snatched it from yo mama's jewelry box. And I said, yo, that shit ain't right. And it was prolly real special to Ty's moms. And I asked *why* he did it. And check this, man: he just shrugged his thievin' shoulder, and he said: '*fuck* Tyrone *and* his whole bourgie-ass family!' And then he laughed, all high and crazy-like. It was like he *showed* me who he *really* was that day. And when I looked at him, yo, I could *see* it, man. It was like he really *didn't give a fuck*. And that shit struck me, yo. Then he had the nerve to ask me if I wanted to go with him to the pawn shop . . . and maybe use some of the money from yo mama's pin to cop some good blow. And I said, 'nah, man. That's dirty money, yo . . .' and I told him that he was foul and fucked up. And I got off at my stop, yo . . . and left his grinnin' ass on the train."

Having finally confessed this, Faison Brown felt every bit the ghetto superhero. Only, the cape was dingy with Browny's own excrement.

"And *you* knew this, and you *never* said a fuckin' word about it?"

"Well that's what I'm doin' right now, ain't it, yo?"

"Browny . . . all this fuckin' time, *you knew* he'd stolen from my family, and you ain't said shit, right? Damn you! You, you fuckin' . . . coward! You never rise. You never step the fuck up! Do you? Never!"

"Yo! Tyrone! You need to watch your lip. I ain't *about* to be too many more *cowards* up in this muhfucka. I'm tellin' you *now* . . . so don't kill the messenger, yo."

"But that broach *meant* something to my mother. And she was so sick about it. And it broke her heart . . . because *she thought* my father *gambled* it away. And even though my father *swore* on *her Bible* that he didn't . . . she blamed *him* for it . . . even to this day. And you! You sit there tellin me you fuckin' *knew* Face took it? And you didn't say shit to me about it? I mean . . . what the fuck! How could you . . . just? Why, Browny?"

"I ain't no snitch, yo. You know I ain't got no kinda love for Pass-cow. But I'm from the street, yo, and I don't snitch like some weak punk-bitch."

"But ya *snitchin' now*, bitch!" Ty fumed. He could no longer even *see* Browny. All he could see was *red*.

"I'm tellin you *now*, cause I had some time to *think* in this place. And right is right, yo. So, I just thought you should know."

Tyrone knew enough about that little man behind the glass. He knew Faison Brown was loyal to no one, but himself. He played people, and loved nothing better than to see them go off, as long as the direction of the explosion was within viewing distance, but not directly *at him*. Ty knew to know that confession was meant to serve no one, but Browny.

"Besides, Pass-cow is grown, and makin' all that big model money. He don't need *me* to keep his dirty li'l secrets, yo" Browny added.

"So, you thought the time was right to *strike*, huh?"

"What?"

"You know, to rise up, to say something; to right the wrong."

"Yeah. That's me, yo. Just tryna right the wrong."

"Yeah, yeah. That's you, right? Fuckin' coward!" Tyrone hissed. "Got all that damn *mouth*, and ya never know when the fuck to use it!"

"Yo! You know what? Fuck you, Tyrone!" Browny blared.

"No fuck *you*! You *coulda* stepped up. You coulda *did* something. *You* coulda been a fuckin' *man!* This is so fuckin' *historic*, it's almost laughable. It's just like *that night* at the showcase, when *Face* was grabbing all the glory . . . and you couldn't handle it, could you? So, you thought, maybe if you could hit that one high note, and let people know who you were, you coulda grabbed the spotlight. All *you* had to do was *open* ya damn mouth and *sing*. But ya froze up, like a lil *bitch*, didn't you? And you didn't sing it, and you didn't do shit! And that's your claim to fame, ain't it? How you coulda, woulda, shoulda hit that note . . . but ya didn't do shit! Cause maybe you *ain't* shit, but a *fuckin' coward*! And maybe *that's* the story of your fuckin' life."

"Yo! You just better be glad this fuckin' glass is separatin' us . . . cause I'd be all over yo punk ass! Trust!"

"Fuck you, ya li'l weak bitch! I'd never let a coward kick my ass!"

Browny's plan of forming an *allegiance* with Ty in his hatred of Face Depina was failing. Miserably. He'd *thought* he was doing Ty a favor. Instead, Tyrone had turned all shades of *ugly* on *him*. Browny expected Ty to be pissed, but not this . . . not so damned *livid*.

Tyrone rose from his chair with a mixture of fire and tears in his eyes. Even the dark, puny sight of Browny sickened Tyrone now. With an anger that he'd rarely known, he stared at Faison Brown, and promptly, boldly and with much force, *punched* the glass between them. Browny jumped.

Tyrone wanted to spit on that glass. He wanted to kick Browny's cowardly, terminally criminal ass. More than that, he wanted to *murder* Face Depina.

He left the visiting room and the walls and smells of that prison, vowing to never return.

Browny was right about one thing: the past *did* dwell; the past did have a way of determining the future.

The events of that night, the night Face Depina had stolen from Ty's mother suddenly replayed in Tyrone's aggravated head. The night, and his own ignorance of the events had caused a permanent rift, a tear in the fabric of the Hunter family, and it had changed it forever.

When Mrs. Hunter discovered that prized broach was gone, that heirloom which had been in her family for several generations, dating back to slavery, she was beside herself. She had searched everywhere, and when she couldn't find it, her mind went into another realm of suspicion: Mr. Hunter. Surely it must have been him . . . him, on one of his mad gambling binges. He must have taken it, lost it to some flunkie, and refused to admit his guilt.

There were confrontations and denials. There was church and prayer and more church and more prayers. There was a deep and profound loss of trust. Finally, after one loud and pivotal scene at the family's dinner table, when she told her husband she'd forgive him, if he'd only *admit* his culpability . . . things hit the fan.

Tyrone had watched it all unfold, and he, believing his father HAD taken the broach, sided with his mother.

And in the end, Mr. Hunter felt betrayed by both of them. He was an *innocent* man, condemned by his nearest and dearest loved ones. How does any man recover from that accusation?

Mrs. Hunter demanded that he take his "lying gambling cheating ass" out of their home, and angrily, Mr. Hunter left. That separation only caused a deeper bitterness in them both. The trust was gone . . . and soon, there was nothing left to the foundation of their marriage. They would divorce two years later.

And why? Well, thanks to the years-late confession of one Faison "Browny" Brown, it was *Face Depina*, who had, with one stupid malicious teenaged act, single-handedly destroyed the core of Tyrone's family.

And though the fire in Tyrone's mind dictated Depina would have to pay for this, *murder* was too damn messy and undignified for Ty's revenge. But something . . . something *had* to be done.

Tyrone prayed on it. Confronting him seemed a useless enterprise. For one, Face was rarely in the country. He was always off being fabulous in some exotic locale. Grabbing Face by one expensively ear-ringed lobe, dragging his ass to Ty's mother, and confessing what he'd done, that too would prove too little, too late.

Ty thought perhaps karma would handle the mean and ugly things that manifested from Face Depina. Maybe he'd go down in a fabulous jet. Maybe he'd meet a fiery end. Maybe the elements would conspire to take away the one thing Face treasured most: his own *physical perfection*.

Some *thing* close to a curse was playing on Tyrone's mind. He never housed such dark, unspoken thoughts before. But short of murder, what else could Tyrone do? Face Depina had to pay, one way or another, for the ugliness he'd done.

As pretty as he was physically, ugliness was something Face Depina applied so often in his relationships, one would've thought he had a Master's Degree in Ugly, and sick and twisted ways of it.

CHAPTER TWELVE

Love & Fists

In the summer of '87, amidst a city's outrage over police shootings and racial violence, some people managed to fall violently in love. But Ty's inner soundtrack blared, "I Still Haven't Found What I'm Looking For."

By the fall, people were hurting out loud and right in front of him. They were hurting in shrouds and Salvation Army overcoats, hurting under newspapers, on the concrete, and before ghostly trash fires. Tyrone would open the door and find people were hurting all over the place. But the few souls huddled that cold night outside the Blue Note were probably hurting *most.*

But inside that renowned jazz emporium the music was *live!* Some bluesy cat on a slide trombone played a snazzy riff. Heads bopped, fingers snapped, people was diggin' it, man.

Then, the mood changed as a thick cinnamon-skinned man stood center stage with a sax. He took a breath and blew its horny horn in a long and *hurting*, yet so clear, melodious, pristine, and perfect note that it reminded Tyrone of a trembling tear. Maybe this sustained resonance was that fabled "*long blue moan*" his Uncle Jerome had spoken of; the penetrating sound of sex and sadness, sin and surrender. Ty listened, and it seemed that angry, lonely people cried out of that horn.

After his solitary date with a mood at the Blue Note, Ty headed home. On his way to the train, a Great Hulking Giant of a Man bumped into him so hard it nearly knocked him to the ground. But the Giant just kept stepping.

Damn, dude! I believe the phrase is, excuse me! Ty thought. But he didn't dare say it. Only a suicidal *fool* would have said it. That offender of his space seemed too big, too mean, and far too dangerous. This man looked as wide and dangerous as the street itself. And so, Ty chilled.

He didn't know it then, but the Giant had a name, and it was Chaz. Chaz Williams.

Upon returning home, Tyrone remembered why he'd left. The place was a mess. His desk was a wasteland of stillborn chapters of a wasted book about a wasted generation that Tyrone was far too emotionally wasted to complete. But the act of *writing* had become, for him, the only confirmation that he was still alive, and so that act consumed the crippled hours of his wasted days.

He checked his messages. David deeply wanted to trip the erotic light nostalgic. Ty listened repeatedly to David's voice. How hopeful, animated, and *silly* it sounded, as if nothing in the world mattered but dancing to his *own* promiscuous groove.

"Ty, you there? Pick up, ya cave-dwellin' bastard! Listen, this hot, hot, *hot* new club just opened on West 12th. So take your hand off your penis, 'cause it's time for some hot new dick. What are you savin' it for, baby boy?"

Ty detected a sadness in David's voice, as if he pitied his friend's isolation.

"Ty, if you're *still my boy*, when you get this, you better holler back. I repeat, hot new dick, West 12th. Be there, or be queer, and alone. Again!"

Hot new dick? Doesn't he even give a fuck that we're in the middle of a goddamn crisis? Tyrone commiserated inside his room with the ghost of Trick Brown.

"I just don't know about him, Trick. There's nothing out there but crowds and cliques of loneliness. I see it on every corner, on every street, in every section of every borough, and it sits on every fuckin' fire escape. Sometimes I leave home, and it tricks me, man. I almost begin to feel cocky that it's gone. But it plops right beside my ass on the subway, and rents space inside every spectacular square and rectangle in this diseased city. Hell, Trick, I've got fifty different versions of lonely scrawled in fifty different matchbooks—and those are just the ones I've kept. But you wanna know something? If I wasn't so afraid for David, I'd almost envy his little wild ass. But my friends are dead or dying. And I'm celibate, and alone, and I guess that's a kind of death too."

Meanwhile, in the meatpacking district, Chaz, the giant who'd nearly flattened Tyrone, walked his formidable gait beyond the doors of another blackened building. It was a den where the players played in leather. He walked, and the place rumbled. For years, he'd known the smell of pitch-black rooms where lust bent his limbs into falling before some long, hard, thick anonymity. Shiny metal studs oiled with sweat, chained and nippled-ringed men flexed for him. But he was sulking, stalking the night for the right size, the right skin, the right illusion. What he needed was a precise partner endowed with a hard, heavy hand, with just the right strike and burn to it.

As a Corrections Officer, Chaz Williams had to *take a man down* that day. It was rough work, breaking a man's spirit, breaking his legs, his will to flee. The blood was never pretty.

But hell was never *supposed* to be pretty. Now it was time for body and soul to even the score.

Inside that darkened labyrinth, men noticed the fierce six-foot-nine, 325-pound frame, and some feared him, not knowing what to make of this dark and grizzled mesomorph, crowded by slabs of hard muddy muscle.

Yet, inside a darker room, where candles flamed and burned down the wick of night, he yielded his might to a world of submission. He was seeking redemption, and it came warm, hard, and thick across his lips, its weight, its girth, its taste taunting him. There in that room of men and masks and plaintive howls, against the growls and grunts and sinsuous contortions, Chaz Williams surrendered his will to the succulence of anonymity. And the seam of a leathered crotch began its swelling. And two men were *driving* him, wrecking him with digits, plugs and latex phalluses. A sudden burst of amphetamine crackled within him, and against that sweet pain of yearning, he wanted, needed to know. Who were they? One man wore a hood, the other dressed in cop gear. They were taunting, teasing, tormenting his flesh with hot hands, hot tongues, hot candle wax. And that large knot grew and mounted more robust beneath leather.

Soon all three stood erect as sightless cobras, each rearing in the air.

"Suck him off! Suck it good, boy!" the cop demanded of Chaz.

"Don't call me boy!" Chaz spat.

Still, Chaz did as he was demanded to do, and he did it the vigor, spittle, and breathless abandon.

A sling awaited him. Blindfolded, hands and feet fastened by ropes to the chains of the sling, he heard the charged crack of the cop's whip, and waited for the burn. He needed to burn. To feel the burn would be . . . *paradise.*

Paradise arrived, crisp and sharp as the bullwhip blazed across his buttocks.

"Aw-w-w! More. Yes. More! Harder! Shit! Make it burn!"

Every whip, each snap made him hump and snarl, compelled him to tremble, to cry out loud, "More! More!"

Lashing ceased. Williams unleashed a gut-deep groan. Sweat and electricity boiled on his skin. A warm coating touched down slowly—slimy, slick and filling. Chaz was probed, pried and opened by fingers, by thumbs, and then, by fire. A rotund bolt of heat and lightning came sharp, so sharp and singeing. It was surpassing his limits—surging beyond pain's threshold, lashing through sweat-cloaked sinews, as he twitched, trembled, *begged* for more.

"Yeah. Take it. Take it!" grunted the cop.

"Surrender to it, bitch," the executioner said. Waves of naked flames delivered a lovesick strain of pain, baking his center, slamming his being. The gloved intruder shoved deeper then, bringing shocked pleasure and a full-bodied frenzy.

Excruciatingly keen, a twisting pain pushed through curves, through grooves, through gullets, rudely reconfiguring this giant of a man.

In a state of climactic trance, everything in him lurched. A sound beyond a scream echoed in his brain, and without knowing he would, he erupted. Quick and hard, the clotted cream careened out of him in a physical burst that felt like freedom.

Chaz was then untied, his blindfold removed.

It was then that the lean Executioner promptly took aim on a night when lust became an animal entity, a sharp and reckless thing, too hot, too strong for precautions, for warnings . . . or even for rubbers.

Long steel prong pierced bluntly. Long steel prong thrust severely. There were more thrusts and each thrust came bar-

baric and swift, and it sent the sling's chains rattling, as Chaz bellowed, "More!" In savage discord, other slave voices screamed inside that howling cacophony.

He wanted it dark, kinky, forced, and this was the sex of his mind's design. He grunted and he groaned to the synergy of these men, piling him, driving him, ramming him, slamming him, each so exquisite in their abuse. Each lunge began thrilling his senses, shifting them from pleasure to pain, from pain to pleasure. A rain of sweat and stinging tears filled his eyes in that room of masks and howls and erect and nameless men.

It was then, inside that carnal madness that Chaz knew, Nirvana was just a few thrusts away. The Executioner drumming him quickly grabbed Chaz's ears. Everything else, stilled. The hooded man jammed his willful tongue through the mask's slash and he gnashed his teeth to Chaz's tongue. The shock of him was palpable. Sucking bleeding tongue, the hooded one pummeled and slammed, pummeled and slammed and a bleeding Chaz wanted them to bleed and come *together*. He said it with his eyes wide open. The man inside him glared back, *understanding*, and then possessed by a feral whim, Chaz shot wildly, and the man shot wildly inside him. That raw hot wound in Chaz Williams felt balmed and appeased as he slowly convulsed. The man collapsed on top of him, jism connecting them inside the throbbing candlelit gossamer.

And then, the man who'd shot inside him removed his mask. Chaz Williams' eyes shot open with a hotly strange recognition. He felt as if he'd *seen* the face of that man before.

It was Face Depina. And his cop partner was Claudio Conte.

"Yeah. It's me. Face Motherfuckin' Depina. And I just made you my bitch!" he sneered, wagging his sperm-polished knob at Chaz. Then, bunching up phlegm, he hauled off and spat on Chaz's writhing belly.

It was the most *romantic fit of poetry* Face could have ever recited to Chaz's masochistic ear.

Chaz Williams wanted to burn his life away. Face Depina carried a blowtorch.

From that night on, Chaz was yin to Face's complicated yang.

CHAPTER THIRTEEN

Fire In Young Men's Eyes

CASA DE LA DEPINA, WEST VILLAGE, MORNING, DECEMBER 6, 1987

That magnificent kid between the sheets *said* his name was Ishmael. Maybe it was. Maybe it wasn't. In dawn's first trick of peculiar firelight, he looked twenty or twenty-one. Was he? Face wanted him to be. This "Ishmael" had been good at granting wishes. Hot, brown muscle boys were becoming proficient at fulfilling Face's sadomasochistic stateside wishes.

Chaz was away at another funeral. But Depina never liked funerals in his head, nor in his bed. Facey was bored. This new and glamorous existence often left him feeling jaded and longing for the next thing, the new excitement. Even when he was high and wasted, he longed for something different, something worth *remembering*.

He'd seen too much, done too much, fucked too much, and all, too quickly. When he'd get bored, he needed to play with *life*. That morning, after the groggy night, Face wanted something else. If men were going to be with men, then they should *fuck* like men, hurt like men hurt. Save that soft shit for chicks. To his mind: the bigger the danger, the bigger the thrill. Whenever Face found a partner willing to up the *thrill*, willing to take that dive into a *deeper darkness*, he was a very, very hyped boy.

"I'm bored." Face announced, exhaling his first Newport of the day. "No one should be this fuckin' bored. You don't seem like such a boring cat . . . at least, you wasn't so borin' last night. But this mornin' . . . I don't know, yo." He yawned and stretched his arms. "Maybe I need to be fucked outta my boredom," Face said, glancing under the sheets, witnessing two healthy morning erections. "Maybe *you* should tie *me* up and give me a good, hard fuck. Yeah. That's it," Face decided, his voice never losing its forcefulness. "Think you can handle that?"

Ishmael smiled and nodded, as if this too was what he'd secretly wanted.

Depina was shackled by handcuffs and ankle restraints. He motioned for the red ball which he usually saved for his sessions with Chaz. It seemed the perfect accessory, all the better to gag him with, to silence his howls. And so Ishmael applied it.

Upon entry, Face smiled and received him like a hot and stinging dagger. Yet, as inch after long, hard, angry inch penetrated him, it made Face want to cry out loud. The urge to protest was replaced by one of sexual bravado: "Harder, deeper, damn it!" But the gag prevented it, and so he *demanded* it with the green of his eyes. But something inside those seething eyes turned inward on Ishmael. Something in the act itself triggered an explosive reaction. Depina was just one more john, exacting something from him, *telling me what the fuck to do!*

Ishmael was *not* going to take it anymore. All too quickly, his attitude hardened, and the thunder of his thrusts increased.

In Depina's eyes, Ishmael was suddenly that enigma in hot leather. Strange, how he reminded Face of his long ago homey, Angel. That glazed look inside the hustler's eyes began to frighten and excite Depina. But that look was soon accompanied by a violent anger. That anger began to claim Ishmael's limbs, his hips, and his dick. In the middle of a thrust, his anger became an implement of war. Everything transformed. He was fucking something else in that moment: *prejudice*, *ignorance*, *disrespect*. That hot piece of tan ass writhing below him was real, raw and tangible. He could hit it, and it wouldn't hit back. There could not have been a tighter or more *right there* place to use as an anger receptacle. Depina's anus represented the world, and Ishmael commenced fucking it hard and rapidly with body, cock, belly, gut, knees. He banged his fists into Depina's chest. He picked a cockfight with his own conflicted emotions, calling Face "punk" and "*faggot*."

"You like it, faggot? Huh? You feelin' me yet, faggot? Huh?"

Face always hated that word, when it was directed *at him*. This was not what he'd paid for, nor what he'd requested. Depina wanted to hit him, hit him *hoard!* Draw back and knock the shit out of this crazy motherfucker. But his hands were locked. Yet, somewhere between the force, pain, and degradation, everything changed. They not only changed, but crystallized. Face Depina realized nothing was ever perfect. Nothing, except anger. The anger he'd known as a teen, the anger boys like Ishmael know, live with, live through, and somehow survive. Now, Ishmael was Anger incarnate, ten inches of vigorous, vicious rage, engaged in perfect fury.

Yes, Face had raged himself, many, many times before. And so, in some deep and visceral place—just beyond his near-ruptured sphincter—Face Depina understood.

The hustler exploded in a flurry of white-hot sparks. He shot and shot as if his cock itself were spitting! The pellets riddled Face's body like collateral damage after a hellish war.

As Face lay bound, gagged, unable to please himself, Ishmael grabbed his long, hard, tempestuous member. Gripping it tight, he silently, violently jacked it. Face spewed wild white chunks. Then cruelty slowly left the hustler's face, and he realized what had transpired.

Ishmael quickly removed the gag.

"Shit man! I'm . . . I'm sorry, man . . . I . . . I just needed to throw myself into something." His apology tumbled from his mouth like blood.

"Don't sweat it, kid. And don't *ever* apologize! Understand me? Don't' say nothin'," Face huffed, his body wrecked by the urban hurricane, his skin a six-foot-five skid mark, his cock leaking pain.

He found himself staring at the floor, which he did sometimes when the gods of language kidnapped his voice. He stared as if whatever he was supposed to say was written there like cue cards for a brain-damaged actor. He gazed at the leather jacket on that floor, its scarred, distressed leather like the kind Fighter Pilots wear. For a moment, he saw his equal.

Before Depina was ready to let him go, Ishmael left, taking the three hundred bones he'd earned with him. Sadly, Face watched him exit, knowing both had new poses to affect, new tricks to leave sore and wanting more. Were they separated at birth—two lost twins, no longer looking for love? *Love?* Whatever that shit meant. Ishmael was a hustler, and thus not interested. Face understood that.

Being with a young cat like Ishmael conjured up memories of an earlier life; that other life, when "Face" was Pascal. He remembered how he'd worked his own hustle then: swinging on a few unfortunate white boys, snatching purses, committing little acts of miscellaneous mayhem. It wasn't about copping new *Jordans* then—just a way to make ends.

SOUTH BRONX, OCTOBER 27, 1976

Even then a boy could see that Jimmy Carter and those other politicians were lying. Revitalizing the South Bronx was *not* a top priority. The place was still an urbanized Hiroshima. Sirens raked the streets, sending wild cries through an indifferent borough. Yet even fear and dread had a rhythm, and danger had an excitement all its own. The Son of Sam was wreaking havoc. The fire escapes had eyes. Good people walked beside the corrupt, drums pounding in their chests. It was not a pretty place, but Pascal called it home.

Sometimes, the sounds of Tito Puente's timbales would salsa Pascal coolly down East 183rd Street, and he felt high. That night, in fact, he *was* high, spinning off cheap wine, good reefer, and sounds. He was feeling no pain and almost breathing the syntax of singing. That was when the streets, the people, and all of it became sort of *beautiful*, and poverty put on a better suit of clothes. Tito's energy and the lively sound of timbales could do that for him. Then there were those times he passed by a "Black people's church," a storefront where the music, the shouting, and the hope never stopped. It, too, in its own goose-bumping way, was beautiful.

Pascal had smoked most of his dime bag, but he planned to save a joint to blow with Angel. When he was high, his mind became this free-from-musical review. But suddenly the music stopped as he approached a shadow, too obvious in its femininity. It was Rosalita. All summer she'd been shooting risqué offers to take the kid home and "make a man" of him. To her eyes, he *looked* fucky enough. But, always he smiled, and said as usual, "No thanks, Rosie."

Homeboys huddled on the next corner—their eyes vigilant, attentive as coyotes, ready to jump and strike at anything that moved.

Pascal bathed inside the bright yellow fluorescence as he stepped into the nearest bodega; his mission to cop more rolling papers. But he saw a familiar face from his earlier childhood. He wanted the graying man behind the counter to remember him, to recall some thing, some gesture, long ago kindness. He gazed at the man as he rang up the register. He waited for that glint to come into his eyes, that squint, that instant of recognition. But it appeared this man didn't remember him.

It saddened Pascal just a little, and a part of him wanted to say: *Hey. Mr. Rodrigo. It's me. "Pascalito." Remember that snotty nosed, dirt-poor kid you used to throw a pack of Lifesavers, for free? Well, he's sixteen today, so how about a free beer, for old times' sake? It wasn't* that he'd really expected that. Yet, it would've been so nice to be remembered, to have been told that he'd grown up well.

Still, it was *his* day, his return to his native, and *someone* should give a shit. But it appeared to be just another day in the slaughterhood. The tediously humming boulevard of his forgotten life throbbed on dispassionately. Except someone *had* remembered, and that was his reason for being there, to grab a piece of chocolate cake, kiss his Auntie Claire's aging cheek, and try to ignore the reek of mothballs in her apartment.

"Look at this handsome boy in my do'," said the small, café-au-lait colored woman with large, hazel eyes and a touch of poverty in her time-worn smile. "Well, he ain't a boy no mo. You's a handsome young *man.* That's what you is. Son, I ain't had time to make you no cake. But there's a pack of Hostess cupcakes in the breadbox. Hid 'em in there, just for you." She winked.

How fuckin' special. A whole pack, just for my ass? Damn. Could you afford 'em?

Then, as if to smash the cupcake of his dismal day, that fuckin' *father* suddenly emerged. A stooped and ticking shadow of decayed glamour, it seemed he'd come only to renew the fuckin' hatred. Though the man was about as welcome as a cockroach crawling over the Thanksgiving turkey, Pascal had just received the wonderful news of his acceptance into a *special school* for performers. It was a dual cause for celebration, and Pascal thought, *hoped* maybe his father would lose *that look*, that cruel, accusatory grimace he always wore. Maybe just once, he might embrace the boy, tell him how *proud* he was. But the senior Depina didn't care about any birthday. He'd only just come to hit his sis up for a loan. Cocaine was getting to be an expensive habit.

When his father made eye contact with him, for a moment Pascal felt warm.

Shadowed by wasted years of loss and misunderstanding, a father drew closer and whispered in his son's ear, "Ya think that school's gonna make ya something *special?* You can *perform* all ya fuckin' want. It won't change shit. You'll still be a little murderer."

He'd said it as if Pascal had *asked* to be born, as if he, as a innocent infant had the power to kill, or murder anyone, much less his own mother. That accusation was as historical as it was *hysterical*, and it made sense to no one at all, except, Alfonze Depina.

And yet, in that one whisper, Pascal knew *nothing* was forgiven, or forgotten—except what day it was.

His father left, and Pascal looked in the mirror expecting to see the same wickedness his father saw in him. But he didn't see it. All he saw was his face beginning to crack with tears. *No! Don't you fuckin' cry like some punk bitch! One day they'll be the ones cryin'.*

He lifted his chin, and in defiance of tears, something close to flames appeared in his eyes. Suddenly he was sixteen and livid, hell-bent on hitting, spitting, shitting on something. Maybe tonight he'd throw himself off a rooftop and see how well he could fly. Would his body crash and burn, or glide like an angel? But teenage suicide fantasies could wait. Different day, same shit. It didn't matter, though, because Pascal's boy Angel was fresh out of juvenile hall and full of ideas on how to get the party started correctly. So, the plan was to get fucked up, and then do some fucked-up shit.

"This is how it's gonna go down, *mijo*. He knows me. So you be cool, and let me do the tawkin'. Once we get him all hard and bothered, the pants is comin' off. This dude's always packin' *big* bills. We might fuck around and get a couple of Gs off him tonight. He likes you light-skinned boys, so you'll be over like Grover. All ya gotta do is act interested. Believe me, he ain't gonna run too far with no fuckin' pants on. I'm tellin' ya, this mutt-fucker is an easy mark."

But the mark was Pascal.

Someone had obviously ignored the "PLEASE DON'T PEE IN OUR HALL" sign. Nevertheless, Pascal followed Angel through the stench of piss, up four flights to a door at the far end of the hall. Amidst the drone of '60s Motown and the smell of bourbon, a dark face appeared at the door. Strong, blue-black, hypnotic, with a menacing sheen, its lips looked permanently down-turned. Its slow eyes trailed Pascal's face, then his crotch, like an overgrown boy eyeing a shiny new toy.

"Hey, dude. Wanna double your pleasure tonight?" Angel asked.

The stranger glowered at Pascal and thought, *Yes! Good work. Good fuckin' work!*

The door opened. He was in his forties, and about the biggest brute of a man Pascal had ever seen in person. Pascal himself was tall, but this guy, *he* seemed more like a Giant. He must've been something like six foot ten and three hundred pounds of muscle and threat. Earlier, Angel had said he was in law enforcement. Suddenly, Pascal wondered if that was true. There wasn't much furniture in the little room—only a bed, a night table, and a dresser with a TV on top. Pascal gazed at the man skeptically, and then he saw it. *Damn! What's goin' on in them jeans motherfucker? You got a big, black fist in there?*

Angel loomed in the background, like an extra in a Technicolor porn movie starring Pascal "The Punk" Depina.

"Here, drink," the Giant offered.

"What's this?" Pascal asked as he sniffed the dirty glass.

"Bourbon. A *man's* drink." Even his voice seemed tall.

Pascal passed it to Angel. Angel downed it quickly, not a grimace in sight. The man poured another, passed it to Pascal. Trusting Angel, he drank that one.

"Angel tell you what I like?" the giant asked.

"Yeah, I told him," Angel said, locking the door.

"Good. 'Cause I know you fuckin' want some of *this*!" the man taunted, holding the biggest, hardest part of himself.

"Nah. No way, man. I ain't like that! I stand still, and you do me."

"Fuck that shit!" the stranger spat. 'Tonight, you my faggot-bitch!"

Why did he have to call him *that?* He wasn't some faggot-bitch. He wanted to hit him, and show him, prove he was no one's faggot. But to hit him would have been crazy. Beyond crazy. To hit a man of that size would have been a retarded thing to do. And he didn't like the way this man was looking at him. Sensing danger, Pascal shot Angel a look that said, *Come on, man! Let's do what we came to do, and book.*

But Angel just stood, idling.

All at once, the man gripped the back of Pascal's neck and applied a fierce pressure to it, forcing Pascal to his knees.

"Yeah. Give it to her, Rock!" Angel suddenly shouted, a strange, new bluster claiming his voice.

This stranger must've had over eleven fearsome inches.

Pursing his lips, Pascal clinched him away. That's when he felt that cold metal poke under his chin. *What the fuck?*

"Angel! Angel, get this motherfucker off me, man! He's . . . he's got a gun!" Pascal cried. "Angel? Angel? Let's go, man! I . . . I ain't down with this!"

"Shut the fuck up!" Angel shouted, folding his arms and looking on.

The man placed the cocked gun into Pascal's mouth, choking him into terrified submission.

Oh my God! He's gonna kill me. It's my birthday, and this motherfucka's gonna kill me.

But he didn't kill Pascal. The man had another kind of death in mind for him. What transpired in that room was never supposed to be about sex, but some wilder, meaner, *other act* entirely. The Giant eased the gun away as Pascal slowly rose.

"Let's go, Angel," he whimpered.

Angel grinned, then struck him so hard, so unexpectedly, he hit the floor, stunned temporarily unconscious.

In seconds, Pascal's jeans were around his ankles, and an ache like no other ache in the whole long, wide, thick fucking world was building, flaming, breaking inside him. He wanted to *scream*, but only a grunt of anguish came to the surface. He felt rug burns on his chest as he was lunged repeatedly into the carpet. The Giant lifted his sweater, and laid his sweating skull on Pascal's back. The moisture ran down, smelling of bourbon and sweat and victory, as the Giant pushed and slammed and thrust.

A dread—a fear for his life—gripped the soul of Pascal Depina. All he could feel was pain. All he could hear was the sound of a pounding body and the eerie noise of Angel's laughter.

A piece of Pascal Depina *died* that night—swallowed up by the pain, the distress, by the cold sweat and tears. Betrayal carved a hole in him. That betrayal felt so large, it was unforgivable. And he grew angry and *hard* beneath the grunting, smashing weight of this Giant fucking him. He was hard and hurting and the whole room was spinning. *The bourbon*, he wondered. *Was it laced?* Everything hurt too much to think about, and everything hurt for hours.

"All right. That's enough! Let the bitch go!" Angel ordered. Angel, of all people, was *giving* the command. Lunging at a more punishing pace, the Giant exploded, and then, unexpectedly, so did young Pascal, branded somehow by the violence of it. He rolled over, buried his confused head in his arms, and wept like a violent child.

"All right. I'm through with her. Did you like it?" the Giant asked. "Musta. You a fuckin' mess. Tonight you got broke-in by Rock, kid. Now run tell your *daddy* about that!" Then he spat on him.

"Yeah," Angel chimed. "That's right, punk-ass. Welcome to the world. And, oh, yeah, happy birthday, motherfucka!"

When he was let out of the room of blood and laughter, the dazed and bleeding boy ran. He ran in pain, his hurting brain screaming, *Fuck 'em all!*

But fuck *Angel* most.

Soon a stolen Lincoln sped away inside a crucified night. He drove with a madness as his only passenger, as he wondered *why* his boy, his partner, his *ace* had turned on him. Was it that wiseass comment he'd made earlier about homeboy getting "done" in the joint?

"Did you like it? Bet ya did," he'd cracked. It wasn't an accusation. He was only ball-busting. But hadn't he *noticed* how something shifted and darkened in homeboy's mug when he'd said it?

"Fuck you, man!" His boy had snapped. That was all he'd said, but his head had been full of its own private madness.

Still Pascal drove, and before he knew it, an old tenement

stuck up like an unmarked, unremarkable gravestone above the corpse of his earlier life. As he stood before that vacant building, that place where he'd first met Angel. He kept glaring *fuck you* at it, as memories of a hopeless childhood burned within him. That night, just once, he thought he could make that flaming incandescence *stop!*

Maybe the only real *angels* were the careless workmen, the alley people, or the bums who'd left behind that *can of paint thinner.* An icy wind wrapped his skin and every cold event of that night embraced him. *Fire* was needed.

Fuck Angel! Fuck 'em all! he thought.

With one strike of a match, *Who-o-osh!* This became such a beautiful sound, a beautiful vision of crimson rising, running, licking, engulfing those stairs and beyond. He saw it smoke and glow, burn, take on a new flame, and it made him shudder all over. He watched for a moment the scattered choreography of rats fleeing in all their sleazy beauty.

And then he drove away in that stolen Lincoln, driving harder and faster than ever. In the rearview mirror he could see the blinding red monstrosity he and a *stick of anger* had made. And Pascal Depina smiled a little.

CASA DE LA DEPINA, WEST VILLAGE, LATE NIGHT, DECEMBER 6, 1987

"The College Girl" had been a new breed for Face. He remembered she was cute, if a little too quiet. He couldn't recall her name, but he liked the way she giggled when she said, "You look a little like Paul Newman."

"She had a very pretty *boceta.*"

"Bo-what?" Claudio asked.

"*Boceta.* It's Portuguese for pussy. There *are* some pretty ones, ya know."

"Hell, I appreciate a good twat, but *pretty?* Most of 'em look like Audrey, that man-eating plant in *Little Shop of Horrors.*"

"Well, *hers* was pretty. Fine hairs, all fresh and dewy. Dewy enough to know she *wanted* it. But somewhere in the middle of wantin' it, she changed her damn mind. You don't do that shit! You don't stop my passion, my thrust, my best shit with some scared bullshit! Little tease! She was only a fuckin' freshman, though. Maybe I was her first real man. At least I didn't go at it full force. Gentle was all right for a minute. I think she musta wanted a *boyfriend*, but I knew I was never gonna see her again. Shit! It's the '80s. Nobody's supposed to give a fuck."

"Right. Right. So why are you still thinking about it?" Claudio asked in that chronically bored voice of his which telegraphed, not only weariness but a disdain for sentiment.

"Because she seemed so . . . so *pure.*"

"Don't kid yourself, man. It's an impure world."

"But there was somethin' *brand new* about her. I was high and doin' my thing. But she was cryin' near the end, and it made me feel weird."

"And . . . so what! You gave it to her good. That's all."

"Nah. This felt like something else. Almost like I was *forcin'* her."

"Bullshit! Look at us, man. You need a mirror? There's not a chick out there either one of us ever needs to force himself on. And all this talk is bringin' me down, man. When did you get a fuckin' conscience?"

"I don't know. I think about stuff sometimes. Like when you're sittin' around, or you're in the shower, washin' your dick, and rememberin' all the places it's been . . ."

"Oh, yeah. Sure. I've done that. Takes half the damn day."

"You too? Well, it got me thinkin', that's all. I get into some pretty kinky shit sometimes. You *know* that. But no matter how hard and fast I *do wild*, it's always been . . . what? Help me, buddy. What's that word?"

"Consensual?"

"Yeah. Consensual. I never wanna think I forced somethin' foul on somebody. Maybe I'm just depressed or somethin'. Give me a 'lude."

Claudio complied.

"Thanks. You know, the world can be one big bowel movement. Sometimes life is one smooth shit and everything's goin' good—ker-plop. But me? I can't be happy with kerplop. I'm always lookin' for the belly-achin' diarrhea."

"You know what, man? You're nasty! Try not to use that ghetto toilet talk around the chicks, OK? Unless they're skanks, they hate that shit." Claudio dipped his silver straw into a long, white line and sniffed. *Ahhhhhhhhhhhhh* . . .

CHAPTER FOURTEEN

How Do You Say "Faith" in Your Language?

CAFÉ WHA, GREENWICH VILLAGE, JANUARY 1988

Adapting to the skin of the melancholy soul he'd become, or perhaps always was, Tyrone often made a lousy first date. You couldn't shut him up to save his miserable life.

"These days, I'm alone . . . but I'm so lonely. People, who know me, call me a *romantic*. But that's not entirely true. Hey man, like most everyone, there are times when all I really *want* or *need* is some head. You know? You meet someone. You dig each other. It's purely animal. You're not even checking each other's credentials. Somehow you just click, and before you know it, you're rubbing genitals inside the risky hole of night. The sex, it's so hot, it almost has *meaning*.

"And then, you shiver. It's over. He looks at you. You look at him. And all you've really shared is sweat and cum and this pregnant pause that never gives birth to anything real.

"Just once, I wanna *feel something real*. I want to shudder in the cool, blue hue of the moment. I wanna just breathe and rest in it, and not worry or wonder or stress my impending mortality.

"See, the truth is: I do not *identify* with 'The Life' out there. Would you mind getting to *know me* before you suck my dick? Wanna know what kinda freak I am? I'm the kind of freak who actually wants to *talk* to people, see them in broad daylight. I wanna see every beautiful flaw. I wanna know who they are, and who they wanna be. Why? Because truthfully, knowing who someone is, and what they dream, that's the *real* intimacy. Maybe that sounds like bullshit, but I'm serious. That's the kinda freak I be. People want sex as if it's ultimate. Meanwhile, we're all just fuckin' each other into an early grave. Hey, is it not considered *fabulous* to wanna be kissed, just kissed, by somebody who knows how, and who *means* it?

"But nothing is that deep or spiritual anymore. Maybe it never was. These days, you front and pose and maybe you'll get blown, or you'll fuck and pray 'Oh God! Please don't let this condom break in the middle of all this meaningless shit!'"

"You want my history? Bet. Here it is: In 1980, I was still shell-shocked. My best friend had just been stolen from me. But before I knew it, it was time for college, when I wasn't even ready for the fuckin' world. I was eighteen, man, and a fuckin' closet widow. Wasn't I supposed to be young and full of dreams, semen, and good cock-strong intentions?

"In late '81, every now and then, I'd hear these whispers of a 'gay cancer.' Queer little oxymoron, don't you think?

"In '82, while at school, I had everyone using that motto: 'No fools, no fun.' I was young, fairly cool, somewhat hung. But I didn't suffer fools, and never gave myself permission to have big fun.

"The first season of young white men in the Village who wore the latest in purple sores was 1983. They were sweating, losing weight, and falling by the wayside of this fuckin' urban wasteland. Remember? By then they'd given the cancer a proper name.

"By 1984, I was walking petrified. People I knew, people with whom I'd been really, really intimate with had died from an intimacy disease. At first I freaked. And then I grieved, and I've never stopped grieving. And suddenly into the cage of my skull came that shrill and urgent voice. That one I couldn't seem to turn off. That voice told me: *Get thee ass to a clinic!*

"So I tested. For two weeks, I did nothing but sweat. I prayed, made promises to God, on my knees pleading, crying—for myself, for all the unlucky rest. And thanks to the grace of God and providence, I tested negative.

"By 1987, I spent most of my time reflecting upon this choir of my new and tragic friends. In my dreams some screamed and some roared, and others moaned that the songs they had to sing were left unsung, unfinished. Each of them vocalizes somewhere now, in purgatory . . . Maybe it isn't a dream.

"These days I'm too afraid to fuck without meaning or rubbers or prayers. It's 1988 now, and I'm celibate. There's no shame in surviving, is there? My friends are missing my life. Hell! *I'm missing my life.* I *need* to know the reason why I'm still here and they're not. I have to believe they were just unlucky. I do know this: They never got the chance to be *realized.* Now, they're gone.

"But some things you hold on to . . . like *him*. I wear his tattoo where no one can see it. And the one you *can* see, I reserve for an intimate few. See this? See this blue stain inside my bottom lip? It's really a tattoo of a name. The asshole tat artist fucked it up and etched the word 'Tick.' It's *supposed* to read 'Trick,' damn it! But sometimes I wonder if it *really* was a mistake, because maybe it signifies *tick*, *tock*, *tick*, *tock*.

"God! Am I crying? Do you have a fear of gay, African-American men with chests full of rage, and eyes full of tears?

Shit! Hey, playa, better tell me now if you do. You. You sit there with your cool, strong face, like no one and nothing can break you. Just wait. It *will* happen. If it doesn't—or worse—if you don't let it, then wherever you are, I'll feel sorry for you. The last thing you want to be is one of those solitary old queens alone by a fence on the playground, alone in the park, or alone in the streets, just always, always alone, with your old overcoat of dreams hanging 'round your shoulders like a death shroud.

"See, it just doesn't pay to affect the role of the cool desperado. You have to love and *let* someone, some fool, somewhere LOVE you. That's it. That's all, man. See, just when I thought two people, two *men* together was some kind of a miracle, I *found* him. My big, black, thick-skinned, crotch-grabbing *miracle!*

"Well, he's gone now. And maybe I've already had my quota of miracles. But you have to go on, right? I mean, don't you? That's what I'm doing here tonight . . . *trying* to go on!

"I just wanted you to know, besides these tight jeans, my eight-inch erection, and the cock-ring that glows in the dark, I am *more* than this, man. I am more than this.

"So what are you?"

"What am I, you ask? I'm a designated war correspondent. This is a war, you know? I guess it took death to get me off my pacifistic ass. But I'm finally fighting because I have to, even with a pen full of bullets.

"So if you think I'm cute, or that I'm an easy fuck, please, don't get it confused or twisted. I'm just isolated as shit from fighting this war. That's all."

And Ty's first date of the New Year asked, "Yo, man. It's gettin' late. So, you still wanna fuck, or what?"

TYRONE'S CONVERSATION WITH A GHOST

"Well. It's me again. The Duchess says all the time, 'Ty, just try puttin' your dreams and desires out there. Tell The Universe.' Shit. When was the last time the fuckin' Universe listened? Trick? Are you listening? I don't need the eyes of a saint with a godlike body, or a wet dream with a Watusi's dick. I'd like to meet the man who can help me be the *best* me I can be. Someone who makes me smile with just a glance, just one crazy-ass look. I'd like to meet the man who *gets* that I'm not perfect and never will be, but who'll love me and my imperfect ass anyway.

"I'd like to know that man who owns his mistakes and who knows by doing so, it only makes him stronger . . . who's lived life, loved life and is willing and ready to do it all again, with me by his side. And if he even exists, let that man call me my naked name, and make me feel like I'm laid out on the hottest, most quixotic get-away inside my skin. See? I had that once. I'd like that again. Where can I find someone who can catch a knife in his throat . . . without *spitting up blood*?"

TY'S KITCHEN

The following morning, David regurgitated the tale of his latest conquest.

"'I hate to be indelicate,' I said, 'but how much dick you slingin'?' And he just chuckled at my ass. *Love it* when they laugh right off like that, cuz I know they like me a little already. Then it's 'Hey, check me out, baby. I bring *all this* to the table, *and* I can dance.'"

"Oh, yeah, Duchess. You can dance. I've seen you shakin' that ass. Ever think maybe you shakin' it a little too fast?"

"No. I shake-dance, just fine. Thank you. You just can't get with my rhythm. People are tryna find something certain out there, something to celebrate, baby bubba. Laughin' releases endorphins and shit. I swear Ty, *you* really need to try it—along with *several* tequilas."

"Nah. We're diff, bruh. I can't be you. I'd never jet-propel myself toward anyone who clearly showed signs of disinterest in my thrust."

"True. We *are* diff. Verrrrry diff. See me? I *get laid* on the regular. Wanna know why *you* don't? Sure, I bet you thought it was that long-ass, sad looking horse-face of yours. But, nah. It ain't even that. Your problem is you talk too damn much! And, most of what you say comes off as high and mighty."

"Get outta town, David!

"No. I like it here!"

"So, what are you saying . . . that I'm judgmental? Because, if you are, you're a liar."

"No. Not exactly, judgmental, but maybe its close second-cousin. Hey, I love ya. But face it, baby. You're one of those particular, uptight queers that less uptight queers don't particularly like."

"Oh? Guess I can live with that reality."

"And I see you do. Is it workin' for you, Ty? Is it gettin' you laid?"

"Hey, I get my share, probably more than you think. I'm just not so wide-open, like . . . ummm . . . *some* people."

"Hmmm . . . Say what you will, but my ass is getting waxed, and I am just lovin the buffed afterglow of it."

"No kiddin? You tell me and everyone who'll listen about your adventures in . . . ummm . . . getting buffed. But being discreet and being *easy* are two completely different species of whore. Never took you for an easy sissy."

"Oh stop it! You just don't get it. What you call, easy, I call *free*!"

"Yeah, right," Ty scoffed. "Next time I want my *free* ass kicked, I know the secret password: 'I hate to be indelicate, but how much penis you slingin'?'"

"Dick! The word is dick, damn it!" An infuriated David threw up his hands.

"Easy! Calm down! Bre-e-athe! What are you, fresh from lockdown in some woman's prison?"

"Me? Me, Ty? I'm *not* the one in prison. Shit! That's why ya gets no play. First, learn to say *dick*! Learn to look at that ridiculous thing between your legs and love it, and share it, and laugh at it, and maybe someone else will do the same. Laugh, Ty! Remember how? See me? I love the sound of my laughter. I plan to keep on laughin' till the day I die."

"I *have* a sense of humor. I never gave up that habit," Ty protested, and then he lapsed into melancholy. "But that habit abandons a brother a little more every day."

"Well, get out the fuckin' house! Step into the metro! Hit a bar, spot a tall, dark, intelligent mother's son, and make that eye-fuck count! Mosey up and say something smart-ass caz-z-zuel, like, 'Do you wear Jockeys? I love the sight of expandin' Jockeys in the mornin', don't you?' You'd be surprised, he might smile, start a convo. Hell, you might even get some."

"You know, Duchess, not everyone has your sense of buffoonery. Not everyone has your need to shock, or that straight-out raw fag dawg mentality."

"Well, they should!"

Everywhere Tyrone went, be it a train, a club, a jazz bar, even the street, he heard that same blue moaning note. Maybe it was only in *his* ear. If so, what was he supposed to do with that sound? Was it an emotional tear only he could detect? Should he compose a new song? Trip into lust, just go crazy and fuck a stranger? Should he manufacture new tears? Who were all those solitary men on the street, blaring their horns in sad and haunting dirges? Ty imagined those dirges were postmortems for the boys who were lost, getting lost, or would soon be lost in the fray of the times.

FEBRUARY 1988

Ty often took the number 1 train. The ride was longer than the number, and it gave him time to read or think or people-watch on the sly. That's when it occurred to him: There are all kinds of brothers out there—brothers who aren't screaming retribution before revolution, or holding their bozacks on street corners. Brothers who aren't living lives of denial, coping with lies and failure through drink or clever chemistry. They aren't out there jackin' people's shit, or suckin' the devil's dick, and they don't care or give a damn what Alexis Carrington-Colby is wearing. Ty had almost forgotten there were others left, worlds away from his orbit, with little interest in doing the *très* artistic thing. Yes. There were others, with middle class leanings, a growing fraternity of them: elevated, educated, well-bred brothers becoming buppies.

He immediately caught Tyrone's eye on the subway platform—his big, thick, nut-brown body swathed in gray flannel. On the train, Ty noted how comfortable he seemed in his skin. He didn't swish, lisp, or emit an ambiguous impression. Quite simply, he was the ideal specimen for a long-repressed GBM with hopes of love's second coming.

Then came a question: "You finish that yet?" It seemed to float above the static rumble of the car.

Tyrone looked up into full questioning lips and liquid eyes. It was that ol' lovely near-chocolatized brother, and he carried sex on his face, his lips, and his legs like a stallion that never slept.

"Grisham. He's a good writer. Don't you think?"

"Uh, actually, I haven't read it yet," Tyrone replied. The

brother peered around the indifferent straphangers for a seat. Then his eyes settled on a narrow space next to Tyrone.

Does he want to sit with me? Ty wondered as the train stopped at Fourteenth and the car emptied considerably. He could've sat *anywhere* then, but he chose to sit right next to Tyrone.

"I was in law for a while. He writes the way a lawyer thinks," the man said.

His history was exotic: "I was raised in Germany until the age of six, Italy through thirteen, then all over the U.S." A chic, well-spoken cat, he bragged of sharing classes and "notes once" with John Kennedy, Jr., and he'd even been to Africa.

"Really? I'm *dying* to go," Ty said.

"I'd highly recommend it, as long as you're not afraid of needles. You'll be in for a battery of them."

This man never stopped talking about himself and how he figured into the world of high finance, mergers, and cutthroats. Before he knew it, the next stop was his.

"I get off here," he said, standing and beginning to rise in his jeans.

"Hey. Here's my card. If you ever think about dabbling in the market, I'm your man."

"Thanks. Maybe I will."

They shook hands, and as he left the train Ty glanced at the card. It read: ZAIRE T. MONK, ESQ.

Sometimes, The Crude and Basic Law of Manhood is simply this: the penis wants what it wants. No talk. No prelims. Just do it! But Ty was not overtly looking to bag himself a buppie. Finally, he decided, Just *maybe I'll tip home, bust a nut, and be over it.*

There was an old Sam Cooke song his mother used to play when Tyrone was just a tyke: "Another Saturday night, and I ain't got nobody . . ." Well, it *was* another Saturday night and it seemed like *years* since he'd had anybody.

What he *had* was a hard-on. There he lay in bed, alone, inside that stillness, that post-midnight hum, minus probing lips, nor a lover's tender lingering kiss, without benefit of imagery or mindless flicks of coitus, and he'd somehow manufactured, an erection.

This strange *phenomenon* came on—uninvited—whispering lust, fully, by its hot and naked name. It came, unexpectedly . . . . like a sigh, or a whine, like a shout or a SCREAM! It came like a wild awareness of his own impatience to be touched, to be kissed, to be loved by someone who meant it.

That yearning played like a hot and edgy song throughout his body. It played in a whisper, its lyrics composed of fantasy and wonder, longing and a thousand different images of things, of people, and of ghosts he could see and feel, but he could no longer touch.

Tyrone was more than just horny. His loneliness was a song of hot and raging beats, dictating its lone and silent scream of: "Play Me!"

It was times like these that his body became fire . . . and he'd catch hold of its heat in his hand, and he, being alone, he would try to extinguish it, manually.

And so, he played with his fire, as if it were his my oldest friend. His midnight friend with perfect posture, his midnight friend, turned hostile king, turned punk, turned bully, prone to spitting.

And like a bully's aggression, the physical posturing, the internal insurrection, erections often derive from deep and lonely places. And like a bully, the penis will ultimately rise up, puff up and fight for attention.

Some nights, he tried to resist, and then thought: *No!*

Few men, not even Ty could ignore their king, their punk, their bully who's prone to spitting!

Any Loneliness unaddressed can manifest in aggression, or worse, a Hard-on; a Terrible Erection of The Soul.

And so, it was left to him, to all of us, to massage our gods, to rub them slowly. Though we sometimes quickly brush them away, like an embarrassment . . . or a fear . . . or more like the tactile trace of a tear.

Sometimes Ty found himself daydreaming about that cat on the train. His thoughts would drift away from him, like a kid's helium balloon in the wilds of Central Park, and they'd linger in the rarefied air.

He'd often wonder about the man who wore a suit as if it were tailored and pressed in a Designer's Heaven, a brother who bore the strange name of Zaire Monk, ESQ.

The fated thing about the city is that sometimes people you haven't seen in ages suddenly show up shortly after the thought of them has stroked your mind.

Months had passed, yet the recognition factor was instant. Ty nodded and Monk included a smile in his nod.

"Yo, bruh. How you doing? Listen, I've got a great inside tip for you."

Ty was so happy to see him that Monk's words didn't quite register . . . at first.

Monk was beyond warm for Ty's long lean form. Sometimes a lonely, needy, carnally interested brother has to stand with his horny dick in hand and just say, *fuck it!* Besides, Monk's "great inside tip" was steadily rising inside those Brooks Brothers.

"Why don't we shoot by my place, and I'll tell you all about it?"

Inside Monk's apartment, the hard glide-'n'-slide of Monk's thickness sputtered against Ty's thigh. He grabbed Monk's bountiful ass and slammed into him with a desperate violence. He just about *lost it* to that sweet slide of heat and need and want.

But they hadn't really talked. They hadn't explored what made the other tick. This had always been paramount to Ty's conquests. He had to decide if they fit. He needed to know who people were, and he wanted them to know him. He told himself this made him less a whore or predator. Less a flighty person who lived from one meaningless fuck to the next. This, in Ty's mind, made him *Less a David*. He loved David madly, but he never wanted to *become a David*.

But here he was, grinding, sliding, his libido unleashed, as the freaky sensation of Monk's wide tip swerved against the fine hairs of his breach. Was *he makin' that move? Of course, he was! But did Ty really want him to?* Monk's ripe mouth gently brushed the swell of Ty's upper lip. Monk's skin was smooth, his bozack so hard and so damn tempting . . .

"We don't have to fuck, Ty. We can do whatever you want, man. We could just jerk-off together, and that could be hot too," Monk said as he skimmed his moist lips along the slender nape of Ty's long-unkissed neck.

Wow! I knew I liked you!

And so, though both men were eager to do the deed of men in heat, they'd somehow refrained from attending to their baser needs.

Ty left Zaire Monk with a warm kiss and a promise to continue their journey into whatever was fated to happen to them. They exchanged numbers, and Ty couldn't wait to call him, that very night.

Tyrone usually considered first *real* conversations, as first dates. There was that whole *audition* process, where people tended to send in our personal ambassadors to do the grunt work. It was hard to be authentic . . . which made it a bit uncomfortable for him. He was someone who made a living *in* communications. For Tyrone Hunter, words could be his lure and his most shining of features when he'd finesse his verbiage, to a degree. But sometimes in spite of himself, he talked too much, or said exactly what was on his mind; and being so candid didn't make him very popular with other gay men, itching to get physical.

Yet as soon as Ty heard Zaire's voice, a wave of calmness came over him.

"I wanna thank you for putting on the brakes, man. Seriously. I don't know what got into me."

"Well, I know what *didn't* get into you or *me*," Zaire chuckled. It was a hearty, manly chuckle. No signs of a secretly girlish giggle stashed away.

Initially, the two of them engaged in short icebreaking tête-à-tête. But it didn't take long before the really began to talk about things that mattered, and they dialogued well into the early morning hours. They began to vibe without barriers, and between them, the conversation between began to fly. Ty told him about the things that made him happiest, and the things that made him cry. Ty told him about Trick. Zaire empathized. They talked about the risks, and of losing people they cared for, and Ty spoke about his fear of never finding True Love again.

Zaire's family was from Haiti, and he told Ty of his island roots, about the times of poverty and indigent strife. He spoke of coming to America, at age nine, and of his hunger to succeed. He spoke of feeding on new knowledge, of excelling in every class, of being accepted into the Harvard Business School, and the college sweetheart who became his wife. Zaire had lived a different life than Tyrone: one of world travel, of marital bliss, and producing a male progeny. Once the marriage turned bad, he questioned his core sexuality, and just where it would lead him.

Most of all:

"I have a very serious work ethic. Friends kid me, tell me I'm too buttoned-up and need to have more fun. But most of them are caught in this vicious cycle of looking for the next lay, the next party, and always living hand-to-mouth, Me? I'm doing well. I intend to own my own townhouse before I'm thirty."

"Mad ambitious cat. So what drives you?"

"My family. They mean the *world* to me. We come from nothing, and we've made it. Their support has crucial. I want to set them up, in style. They weren't too pleased when I *came out* to them. But, they've adjusted, little by little. I'm really not *in* The Life. But, I'm not in the closet either. I mean, the people who *need* to know, know. I'm just not into this whole one-night-only bullshit. Yanno?"

"Oh. Trust, I know. But I've slipped and been guilty of it once or twice. And *only* once or twice," Ty admitted.

"You're human. And a beautiful one at that."

"C'mon. We don't have to go there, Zaire. I've known enough beautiful people to *know* I'm not beautiful."

"Excuse me? You are beautiful, Ty. But I wasn't strictly referring to your exterior. You have something about you, man. I read it as compassion. People like you are damn rare in this city. And when I run into them, I want to attach myself to them, in a real way. Damn! I hope that doesn't scare you!"

"Nah. I'm not scared. I've spent too much time, doing that, being scared."

"Being scared is no place to live."

"But lately, when meeting new people, I become so damn Tyrone-conscious, and I begin this whole internal dialogue thing."

"Well, shut it off! I want you to trust me enough to tell me what your internal voice is saying, right this minute," Zaire challenged.

"Really?"

"Really. Give it a try. I can handle it if you can."

"Well, right now, it's saying: I make a lousy first date. I live in my damn HEAD too much."

Laughing out loud, Zaire said, "You need to come out more often."

"People keep telling me that lately. Hell, not just lately. Maybe I should take heed."

"Hmmm . . . Maybe you should. Go on. What else does your internal say, about me, in particular?"

Tyrone pondered before answering.

"I wonder if this cat, this Zaire cat is one of those *wonderful* people offering wonderful things, my best friend David keeps telling me exists out there."

"Well this David sounds like a wise cat. Ty, writer or not, you can't always live inside your head, man. You've gotta believe in people, and most of all in possibilities."

Well into the third week of their courtship, Zy and Ty's conversations were lovely in their essence, and Tyrone recognized their loveliness right away. He cherished that period of a new relationship when everything was fresh and so precious, before time or other distractions somehow tainted them . . . or made them common and tragically pedestrian.

"Of course you *know* you're seducing me, right?"

"All I know is my *spirit* erects whenever I speak to you."

"Wow! Tell me this: If I were there, present in your presence, right this moment, what would you do?" Ty asked.

"I'd hold you very tightly. I'd cry with you. I'd kiss you. I'd tell you to *believe* in possibilities. I'd try to imagine why I would ever let go of holding onto you."

"I'd let you do all of the above."

"I'd love to do all of the above."

"Zy . . . You say these things, and they stroke my heart, man. Things, I'd secretly imagine myself hearing from someone... sometimes even before I imagined them."

"Souls have no comprehension of space and time . . . they

just meet when the time is right . . . and when the two vessels housing them are receptive to it, then gravitation takes control."

"There's a depth in that, man. Reminds me of one of my fave songs, that line: "*Pulling closer . . . sweet as the gravity . . .*" from *The Closer I Get To You...* by Roberta and Donny."

"OH. MY. GOD! Yeah, we're gettin' married!!! I can't believe you pulled that song out of thin air, Tyrone!"

"Perhaps our souls danced to it, in separate places before."

"You don't understand. That song is one of my FAVORITE songs of all time!"

"Same here, baby. It's a classic fave."

"Well maybe, just perhaps . . . it's time our souls danced to it, together."

"Oh, you fuckin' poet! I'm rubbing my inner thigh... as I lie here, imagining it's your beautiful hand," Tyrone heard himself say.

"It's a matter of time before we can rub each others legs, hands . . . hearts . . ."

"Lovely thought, my Lovely Man."

"God! It's 1:37AM! It's 1:37 on Tuesday night/morning! How does this happen to us?"

"We're both a little insane. But you're right. It's late. We're being crazy. It's time for us to *be* sane again!"

"So, my favorite crazy brotha, are we finally gonna get together this weekend?"

"Sounds like destiny's plan for us."

"Good. Cool. Cause all this romantic rambling we do is leaving me very *hard* and frustrated."

"So, go to bed."

"I *am* in bed!"

"Well, go to sleep!"

"OK. I'm off to sleep. I can't tell you how much I wish you were here right beside me."

"Sleep tight. And goodnight, my *husband*-to-be."

"I hope that was the *sane* part of you saying that!"

"It's late. I'm never sane at this hour."

"It's all a matter of time. I promise to play that song at our first candlelit dinner, Ty."

"Yeah-yeah. Whatever! Now go to sleep, you crazy-sexy-romantic-poet-man!"

"Well, are you gonna kiss me goodnight, or what?"

"Zy! Zy, we're not in junior high. I don't do kisses over the phone," Ty laughed, yet he was strangely enchanted by the idea of it.

"I could fall asleep kissing those lips of yours, every single night."

"Damn! Damn you for making me smile . . . and making me hard . . . and making me dream."

"Well, I might have to take things in hand between now and our next conversation. But just so you know: I'll be thinking of only you, baby."

"Such flattery *might* just get you the draws. Goodnight, my sweet sexy-poet."

Zaire was full of sweet sexy poetic things, and he was never shy of reciting them to Ty. And after a while, it didn't feel as if he were just running a line on you. He was actually being romantic. Zaire Monk needed that outlet, and the object to express it, just as much as Tyrone needed to experience it.

Is there anyone, woman or man on the planet who didn't want to feel completely, utterly, unabashedly *desired*?

Their first *real* date was a trip to The Blue Note. The artist of note: Premier sax-man Grover Washington. Ty was agog and Zaire was beyond impressed. The brother played, he swayed, and he made a charismatic thrill of his signature song, "Mr. Magic." He held the room spellbound with one willfully long,

long exceedingly long *superhuman* note. Ty closed his eyes and floated away on that note. It was sexy, sensual, seductive and sad.

They'd planned to stay behind for the second show. But jazz and passion together made for mad-hot bedfellows.

And together, they would make their own sexy composition: rhythmic, funky, hot, and sweaty. They moved like two experimental jazzmen, their improvisational hands stroking the other's pulsing keys. The attraction between them was so strong they could've stood grooving, moving, lunging, lusting, and come like that.

But Zaire's slow hand descended Ty's belly, clutching what stood waiting hard and hovering. Zaire's fingers played down Ty's spine and the music rose. With a quickness, he dipped and blew Tyrone's lonely horn, hard and loud, pausing only to lick the engorged reed with a slick *uncorporate*-like madness.

"Oh yes. Suck me!" Already, Ty was edging—a deep crescendo rattled his balls. Running his hands along infinitely dark shoulders, he eased Zaire away.

Theirs was no staid meeting of the Mutual Penile Admiration Society. Ty knew it was time to get wild—wilder than the tangible urge to scream: *No!*

They took it to a primal place—the floor. There, face to face, legs akimbo as they straddled each other, Ty entered him. "Aw! Ark, Ah!" Zaire's mighty arms lowered and rose as he undulated downward, controlling Ty's impact. And soon their hips worked in pumping, slapping, thumping unison. Ty thrust, Zaire humped, Ty hammered, Zaire surged and his eyes never left his partner's. Soon their music reached its thrashing crescendo. Zaire rocked and rolled, smiling as Ty plunged and pummeled.

"Aw! Ah! A*w-w-w!*" Tyrone groaned. Zaire brought his feet to Ty's chest, grimacing as Tyrone lit into him. "Aw-w-w! Come on, baby. Work it! Throw it on me!"

Their legs entwined, breaths echoed breaths, heartbeats

collided, and tongues drummed the skin of lips, prying, dashing toward warm rattling wetness.

And after climaxing, Zaire Monk, Esq. said, "You just don't know, man. I've been celibate for almost two years, and that, that right there was ah-h-h, my brother!"

Ty couldn't help but smile.

Yes. They were a rhythmic *song* for a while. Zaire and Tyrone. Ty and Zy. But not everyone was diggin' it or trying to hear their music. Zaire's parents, for instance, just straight up didn't *like* Tyrone. Oh. They knew *who* he was and *what* he was, and what he and Zaire were *doing together*. That was never the issue.

NO, Ty was simply deemed not quite up to snuff. He didn't play the right sports, or belong to a fraternity, let alone the *right* fraternity. He did not vacation in the right spots, or own the right suits. Hell, Ty half expected the old brown paper bag test to see if his skin was light enough.

The Monks decided, after one chilly dinner of Cornish game hens, that Ty's golden-brown luster lacked sufficient polish. And after three months, apparently Zaire—a grown-ass man with a grown-ass career (and a grown-ass penis)—complied.

"Damn! Damn you, Zaire Monk! Damn you for making me smile . . . and making me hard . . . and making me dream."

And so, with the crashing of another dream, masturbation became his most faithful of midnight friends.

Months passed. David would tease, taunt and berate him into once again stepping out into the "risky hole of night." Finally, after much insistence, the two agreed to meet up at a new bar in Chelsea. Only David became quickly enamored by a certain proud papi he'd met on the train. David Richmond's libido had its own time clock. He never showed, and had forgotten all about calling Tyrone to inform him.

It was just as well, because that night, Destiny intervened.

The bar's soft, blue, neon light, *his* face shone like a hot, dark carving full of ancient mystique. And Ty thought, *if I were a sculptor and molded that face, I'd call it Africanus Man*. There in a room full of eyes, attitude, and spiked crotches, Tyrone saw the closest thing to *home* as he checked their reflections in the mirror. They were different shades of the same color. He was six foot two, Tyrone's height, and his naked head caught an arresting light. A white Lycra shirt clung to his body like a possessive lover. His posture was so erect, so regally dignified, so sexy that his presence evoked the image of a majestic piece of mahogany sculpture. He gazed back at Ty with unfathomable lush-shiny eyes, and Ty couldn't imagine why the others weren't all over him, fighting to embrace his magnificent succulence.

It occurred to him how still this man stood in a night full of pretense and games and movement. Was that regal stance only a pose? If so, he seemed to be posing for Ty alone. A faint suggestion of a smile crossed the man's face, and Ty played it off by looking in another direction. When his gaze returned to the mirror, the man was gone. *Shit!* he thought. *Fuck me! I'll never get it right!*

But as he turned away in disappointment, the mahogany sculpture had come to life. It walked up right behind Ty, and with a slight accent, said in Ty's ear, "I'm Imani. Let's dance." He extended a large, firmly carved hand, and Ty took it.

They danced slow and hot, skulls touching, hands striking the unfamiliar maps of each other's bodies. Ty sighted what he hoped was an intangible moan. The man hardened, a slip of precum coating sweet, warm promise on his secret skin. Then, this man called Imani stepped back, and his full-frontal *lovely* was *massive*! Pulling Ty close, he ground that excitation into him. Fires rose, set, and caught flame against their flesh. His eyes were heat-seekers darting over Tyrone. The shrouded vision coursed a seductive trail further down his thigh, asking the one essential question of the night.

Hungry as the evening was, courageous as desperation sometimes makes men, Ty wanted nothing more on this deep brown earth than to touch *it.*

Sometimes, by nature, or by a silent shout of the eyes, by God or by fluke, people *do* manage to find each other. They are not always at their best, but they are men, full of urgent limbs, flaming minds, and bone-erect complexities inside their jeans. They smile, and solitude takes a sabbatical.

"I'm Tyrone."

Ty wondered: *Do you think I do this shit all the time? I don't. Do you know how long it's been since a man, any man, has entered the wet, warm asylum of my mouth? Do you know that the taste of your neck is like solitude's serum? What did you say your name was? Oh, yes. Imani!*

They hadn't spoken another word. Yet Ty had a feeling that both he and Imani were well-versed in the Blues. Did Imani feel it too—that sensation of falling? Ty stood outside himself, watching himself recede into some dark, hard calamity of need. But he *needed* to fall into something or someone who could support his scared-shitless descent into carnality.

"I do not live very far away," Imani said. "Come home with me tonight. Let's be sexual men together," he offered, his long lashes sweeping over nearly Asian eyes. Ty was charmed by the way Imani said things.

Inside an uptown apartment building, on the seventh floor, there came a pronounced BANG against the wall, and with it, Imani cooed, "Take it easy!"

But I am gagging on you, you beautiful African fool! Ty *was* gagging, gagging on his story, his truth, his vibe, and those slow-traveling brown eyes sang down on him with such lewd tunes. Strange . . . how he and this man vibed with these seemingly new rhythms.

Were they really new? It felt as if they'd *rhythmed* before.

As Ty's eyes drank him in, he wished more than anything that he were an artist of fine sculpture then. He wanted his hands all over him, shaping, molding, adoring him. He let his mouth go wild. His tongue spun art upon the new flesh; this dark god who called himself Imani. Yes, Imani, who could have inspired fire in the loins, the heart, and even in the mind of Michelangelo.

"Yes. Yes. No! Not so hard," Imani begged between sighs. "Please. My deek! Take it easy!"

But it had been a long time since *easy* was Tyrone's for the taking. A plunge of his hips told Imani just how deep, how sooty, and how boundless *longing* could be.

Tyrone closed his eyes and let nothing exist but that *deek*, that Island of Imani on his tongue. Imani threw his hops in slow, rotating dances, and oh! Ty danced along. He imagined tangy plantains, sassafras root, savory mangos swaying in a swift breeze. He imagined Imani's sweat trickling, and then running like the Nile down the brawny continent of his flesh.

You're close. You're so close . . . I can feel you!

Imani pulled away and his bounty vaulted high, filling the room with the voice and vision of his coming. He managed to still the air pumping in and out of his lungs just long enough to say, "Oh! You don't know how much I needed that!"

"I think I know." Ty said. "I think I know."

Ty's hungry eyes glimpsed his naked body, taking in all that dead-gorgeous African manhood standing before him. His nipples hard as rock candies, his panting chest washed in luminous sweat, his sweeping shoulders pitching with the very caps of them jumping from that explosion. Imani's face was a thunderclap of dark, haunting masculinity. His was a terrible beauty, so sharp it hurt the untrained, unappreciative eye. Ty was suddenly his art groupie.

"In my country, we've got no places such as the place we

met this evening. I like this country for its freedoms and its opportunities, but I miss my home," Imani said sadly.

He'd come to America from Liberia to study medicine. He had one semester left, and then it was on to his internship.

"I want to go back. I must go back to treat the villagers. Though some parts of Liberia are quite rich, my village is small and very poor. I am needed there, and so I must go." Imani peered back at Ty, his gaze a silent howl.

And then, both of them stared at the dick that Tyrone's emotional fist had pumped into iron. In one rash move, Imani gobbled Ty down as if he were the raw esoteric food of a god.

"Ah-h-h! Mmm, yes!" That coiled tongue seemed to have been created for pulling deep pleasure from another man. Ty could feel his *life* inside Imani's mouth. The room spun and took on color and light, then heat. *Yes! Keep spinning! Keep swirling! Keep sucking me outta this world!* Ty's skin sizzled. Whirling his hips, gradually, sensuously, he felt Imani humming a most hot and savage hum.

"Oh! I . . . easy! E-e-easy, baby! I'm . . . I'm, I'm gonna come—I don't want to come yet!" Ty said.

"Then I must stop. Together we are far too good to end so quickly," Imani said, looking at Ty and smiling.

I love your accent, your smile. Imani, you are a Long Blue Moan maker, that's for sure: shy, intelligent, cool, hot, happy, and sad at the same damn time.

Imani's vine rose mightily once again, and Ty decided it was best to say what had to be said before the two of them went any further: "I don't get fucked," he said plainly and just a little too forced.

Imani looked a little stricken by such dick-deflating candor.

"Understand, it's not a faggot issue. Really, it's not."

"Are you afraid of catching something from me? You need not worry. I am nearly a medical doctor and I am, how do they say it here? I am clean."

"No. It's not that, really. It's just never been my . . . erotic orientation," Ty managed.

"Are you afraid? That the plague is never far away?" Imani's eyes searched for an answer.

"No. But I think a man should know what he likes, and, well, I don't like ass sex very much. For me it's a gift a man gives to a man he loves, and even then it's a gift that hurts, and looking at you, Imani, I figure I'd hurt for a decade or two." Ty laughed nervously, trying to take the shade off the mood.

"Sometimes a man needs to hurt," Imani stated.

Oh damn . . . Is he gonna try and rationalize or finesse me into this shit? Nice try. Won't work, though, my erect African King!

Imani didn't know Ty's history. He'd no clue of Tyrone's trust issues. Omar.

Omar had hurt *a lot*. And did Omar *dig* him? Not.

Now Ty stood before this man called Imani, and it seemed Imani was waiting for him to say something. But Ty couldn't tell if his no-fucking-in-the-ass policy had pissed Imani off, or if Imani was the type who was *going to* that night, with or without permission or policies or prophylactics. Was the man merely being philosophical when he said, "Sometimes a man needs to hurt"?

"Well, have you . . . been tested?" Imani asked, slowly, as if wanting to know, yet dreading the answer.

"Yes. Many times. I'm negative," Tyrone said. "And you?"

"I am negative also. So you see . . . things aren't so bad. Do you have any condoms?"

In the dreamy afterglow, where cream pooled on bellies and ran down mocha thighs, they kissed, hot tongues igniting like venerable flames.

They became fast, furious friends. Imani seemed to be the answer for Ty, the elixir for what lay dark and alone inside.

Strange how a good, cleansing, bone-shuddering climax can sometimes kill the scream of lonely chaos.

Many times, Ty collapsed contentedly into Imani's firm stretch of sun-roasted skin, thinking, *Damn! He's so fuckin' strong! Where does all that strength come from? Is it something they teach young boys in Liberia? Maybe I can learn something* better *from his naked example.*

"Imani. That's a beautiful name, man. It's Arabic, right? What does it mean?"

"Faith," he'd said. "Faith."

JUNE 1988

The doctor did indeed go back to his country to tend the villagers. He and Ty wrote long, sad, beautiful letters, swearing they'd be together again—one day.

But "one day" was thousands of miles away.

CHAPTER FIFTEEN

The Discontented Season

DECEMBER 23, 1988

Blood never looked more murderous than on that snowy concrete in back of the Windsor projects. But to hear Faison Brown tell it, the stunned and bleeding motherfucker had it coming.

"You know that cat, Ty? Huh? Well, that motherfucka is boys with the cutthroat motherfucka that ripped holes in my brother's chest."

Suddenly a part of Ty, a part Browny couldn't see or understand, was also stunned and bleeding.

"And he's gonna *step to me*, smilin' and cheesin', talking 'bout 'Your brother shouldnuh went ta Dairy Queen if his po ass was lactose-intolerant!' Yo! What kinda shit is that? Like it's all some fuckin' joke to him? Fuck it. Let him press charges, I don't give a shit! Ain't no fuckin' punk gonna throw shade on *my* brother's memory and grin in *my* motherfuckin' face, yo!"

Ty understood. But, damn it, here it was Browny's first day back in the world, and already he was throwin' up his fists.

He'd called Ty and asked him to pick him up, and, of course, even after all the ugliness, Ty acquiesced.

Despite their miniscule bout with high school recording fame, and Ty's getting *paid*, and Browny resenting that shit; despite the prison confession, and Ty washing his hands of Faison Brown, Browny decided in his hour of need that Tyrone was the only person he could depend upon in a clutch.

The only *real* connective thread between Tyrone and Faison was Trick. But now Trick had little to add to the relationship, except his absence, which was *a felt thing* whenever Ty spent time around Faison. Yes. Trick and Faison looked alike. That same angry dark child grimace claimed their foreheads whenever something upset them. And they had a similar hyperkinetic energy. But the similarities ended there.

I knew Trick. You'll never be him. He never went looking for a fight. Hell, Trick was the coolest nig I knew.

But the times were rapidly changing.

Earlier, the sky was a vast and limitless blue page. All at once the intrusion of slate colored the day as the sun grew red and low in the horizon. And there Faison Brown was in a T-shirt on a cold winter's night. Tyrone saw a sad kind of irony in the nickname "Browny." *A brother out of season.* He dropped him off on 110th Street in Harlem. As Browny was about to leave, Ty shook his hand, slipping a new one-hundred-dollar bill in Faison's palm.

"Merry Christmas, Browny."

"Thanks, man. You too, yo . . ."

For Faison, everything seemed just a little sweeter, if more barren, than when he'd left. It was Christmas time, yet the city stood uneasily still, like a shark at leisure, wearing a garland. Where was everyone?

While he was still in prison, his mother had died, and on that day, he'd promised himself to live a more *righteous* life. But it was going to be a tough promise to maintain. The only people hiring were Mickey D's and Burger King. Less talented brothers were bringing in five tax-free Gs a week, slinging vials and baggies on the street. His people were genuflecting to a different king now. *The Pipe* was lord and master. No one was paying much attention to the signs or the Keith Haring billboard over 125th Street advertising: CRACK IS WHACK. Sheeit! Half of *Bush's America* was strapped, high, dying, or dying to get high.

During his incarceration, Browny had grown addicted to smuggled porn, and thus, he'd become a ruthless masturbator. *Titties, titties, titties!* He was obsessed by thoughts of sucking on *somebody's* titties. He remembered one chick with big ol' chocolate beginning-to-sag-some titties. She didn't have too many flies on her yet. And from what he recalled, she wasn't too particular either.

Juanita Lewis was a woman, a sista, and a single mother who *owned* her sexuality. Because of this remarkably feminine trait, she wasn't averse to taking in the occasional brawler, baller, less-than-gentlemanly caller. Though some mistakenly considered her loose, she was never a member of anyone's cliché Ho Club. She'd also long ago transcended the stigma that her four kids were by four different men.

"What I got to be ashamed of? Shit! All I'm guilty of is four bad choices. I love my kids to death!" Juanita would say.

She was an urban Assegai woman, a makeshift warrior fashioning spears against corruption, and making an example of herself. No one, much less a man, ever raised a hand to her, and she'd never once rode the welfare merry-go-round. A woman of purpose, she organized rent strikes, spearheaded a neighborhood watch, and once clocked a man dead in the jaw who'd dared to spit on her freshly swept sidewalk. She was an attentive mother *and* father, too, simply because she had to be. Most of all, she was a woman who held on to the same elusive dream even overweight sisters with four screaming kids and big-beginning-to-sag-some titties dream. Many nights alone in her bed, she'd sometimes cry those "I Just Can't Find Me No Good Man" blues.

"Hey, Faison," she said, almost inadvertently. "Heard you was back."

"Feels good to *be* back, yo," he said, thinking it a positive sign that her apartment door was done-up in green aluminum wrapping paper and a big red velvet bow. When he entered, it *felt* like Christmas. "Nice tree," he said.

She could smell jail all over him. It was unmistakable: a musk of desperation, coupled with a dash of bravado to disguise the stink of fear. But Juanita wasn't scared. She liked it. Brothers fresh from lockdown usually gave a good fuck—for as long as the fuck lasted. Unfortunately, most of them blasted quick loads and pimp-walked out her door, not calling again until a hungry night implored and begged for more. But Juanita had grown used to it.

"Ya hungry?" she asked.

He nodded.

She wore her hair in a short natural. Her eyes were large, black saucers, but they weren't cold, arbitrary eyes. She could cook too—cooked like nobody's mama's business, and she knew about nineteen positions to a one-night stand. All but six she might perform if she *liked* you. She had a warm smile, too. It was that lovely kind of smile that didn't make a man like Browny want to do polluted things to her mouth; well, at least not right away.

When dinner was served she brought him a li'l something to nosh on in the form of a heaping helping of smothered pork chops, collard greens with ham hocks, potato salad, macaroni and cheese, hot cornbread, red beans and rice, a slab of peach cobbler, *and* a Diet Coke.

Yes, the food was smokin'. But Browny had been so long tucked away on an extended Hell's Holiday, and there sat those breasts; those luscious Juanita Lewis *chesticles*. Strange how they kept staring back at him, like two bomb shells encased and stretching out a pink sparkled spandex turtleneck ensemble.

Look at dem shits. I need dem shits.

Juanita's kids were at her sister's, and she was thinking she *might* just give him a piece.

Faison looked different to her. She liked his newly hard prison bod, and that he had *enough class* to bring her a six-pack (and not a single one had been opened). She didn't even mind that little nervous Browny habit of tapping on things—the table, his stomach, his thighs. She liked how he wasn't so concerned with time, or checking his watch like those other fast cocks before him.

She turned on the radio. DJ Frankie Crocker, the Chief Rocker, was smoothing it out on the R&B tip, and radio station WBLS was settling into "The Quiet Storm." Faison decided it was time for his old standby. Yes, he chose to bless Juanita with a song, because history had told him when he used his voice the sexual magic would happen. He knew his vocals were his aphrodisiac, and so that night, *it was on.* The song of seduction was "Never Too Much," and Browny was never too shy to sing it:

"Oh My Love . . . a thousand kisses from you
Is never too much . . .
And I just don't wanna stop . . .
Oh my lovvvvv-uh-ooh-ooove . . ."

Oh my da-a-amn, bruh! Make a sista feel all gushy and wet and serenaded and shit.

She felt special, felt like . . . *Negro! Why don't you just . . . just go on and take me?*

Soon he attempted to bust that move. He fell, as if freefalling into *all* of her, into every crease, every pleat, and every comforting ripple. He was falling into this sweet voluptuous dream of a long awaited pussy paradise. But all of a sudden, that dream of gliding inside a soft moist poontang heaven abruptly . . . stalled. When he pushed inside her, he went all limp.

Memories of prison, prison memories, damn them! *Oh, Nah! Oh, damn!* Browny rolled over, embarrassed and devastated; he pressed his frustrations into a pillow.

Juanita, understanding somehow, slowly fingered his back, as if trying to stroke his phantoms away.

"Faison Brown, listen . . . you ain't got to prove nothin' to me," she said tenderly.

He wanted to scream, *It ain't you, stupid bitch! I need to prove this shit to me!*

A soft sweep of her gargantuan breasts swayed across his restless shoulders. How huge, damp, and comforting they seemed. This was it. This was *attention*, at last! This was what he'd dreamed of, yearned and prayed for as he lay in that cell, night after cold and lonely night. This was what he'd craved and needed for so damn long. And there it was, touching him, stroking him, calling out to his sleeping manhood. Swiftly, he rolled over and he began to kiss her, hard. His tongue sailed down and darted each earth-brown mountainous tit. He was probing, lingering on that luscious chocolate areola. Yes, even more than his love of chocolate, he needed *dem shits*, he needed dem shits! And dem shits were making everything come back to *life*, *rising*, *quickening*.

He mounted her then, much like a rusted bike in the rain, remembering the wetness of the ride. Inside her sopping-wetness, inside her spicy folds, he lost all sight of those random prison visions and every brutal memory. Hard time slid like random precum from the dick of his mind, and he almost wanted to cry against the awe-inspiring float of those breasts. *Ah, yes Juanita*! *Throw it on me, sista!* And throw it on him was exactly what she did. As she juggled and jiggled about him, he pushed and he grunted and finally, he shuddered his way slowly back into the world.

She was *A Find* when the rest of his clique was doing time inside a prolonged nightmare of living crack whores. *Show her some attention, some simple, genuine respect, and Juanita and her cooking, and her kids, and her pride—and her titties—could be yours.*

All women were strange fish to Browny. This one drove him delirious, turned him into an elastic, spastic, sputtering madman between those grateful sheets.

Only afterward, he wondered, *Is she for real? Do she got the gift to see my gift?* Could she look beyond the rust and swagger, see into the faint signs of his luster and recognize he had a shinier future in mind? Or did she possess the power to turn on him? Would she try to stick a brotha for his papers? *Papers?* All he had was enough for cab fare, admission to a titty bar, and maybe a lap dance. His only prospect was a homemade demo tape of his unhappy ass singing. *Papers?* Soon he imagined he'd be making crazy-mad papers singing his bruised heart out. Where would those chicks be then? Biting for his *rich*, dark delight? *Women.* He didn't trust them very much. Yet, now and then, one would fuck around and genuinely *surprise* him.

"You can stay here if you want. Sleep right here on my couch. At least till you get back on your feet," she softly volunteered. Brown was far too needy to refuse. She let the truth be known as she prepared the sofa with blankets and a pillow. "But you got to get a *job*, Faison. I ain't yo mama. And I don't plan on takin' care of you."

"You all right, Juanita," he said, looking at her, and for the first time seeing *more* than just titties, titties, titties.

"I *ain't* your ho, and I ain't no Saint Juanita either." She turned off the light, leaving him warm, satisfied, and thinking—thinking about a *future*.

What he did not know, and what Juanita in her generosity

was afraid to tell him, was of her connection to a man who once broke mean with a switchblade.

The journey of Faison Brown was paved with dreams and demons along every street corner. Browny was not a lucky man, nor was he a gracious one. But his history with ambition had the impetus in a little colored boy's most noble intentions.

It came as an epiphany of sorts. One Sunday night, Faison Brown was sitting in his small Harlem living room with his mother, watching Ed Sullivan. Earlier that evening, The Temptations had crooned their hip new tune "Cloud Nine" and a young Faison was digging it. But later on, during the same show, some man he'd never heard of was singing a different tune, a different set of notes, and something in the sound of him made Browny notice. It made him sit upright and pay attention.

It was a man named Robert Merrill commanding the stage, and what he sang was an aria from *Othello*. The sound was so compelling that it enchanted young Faison Brown. But much more than that, once the song was done, he turned to his mother and saw tears in her eyes. *Tears?*

"What's wrong, mama?" the young boy asked.

Sniffing slightly, she replied, "Ain't nothin, son. Just, happy tears is all. Strangest thing, though. It's just somethin in the sound that man made, it touched some place deep in me."

It must have been a *very deep* place, indeed . . . because Faison thought, what a *powerful thing* that man possessed to have had that effect on his mother, a woman, he'd never once seen cry.

The Temptations were going just fine on "Cloud Nine."

They'd succeeded in making Black and White folks worldwide tap their feet and dance with a coolest fury to the beat. But The Temptations hadn't made Faison's mother cry. *Opera* had.

"Well, I wanna touch people, too, mama."

"Awww . . . I'm sure you will, son, one day."

"No. I mean for real, mama. I'm gon make people cry happy tears."

Upon hearing that, his mother laughed, and perhaps she shouldn't have. But her thought was: *Lawd please! What would a young Black boy in Harlem know about any damn opera?* Yes, she was aware that her son could sing. Everyone whoever saw him and heard him, said it, proclaimed it in the pews and the aisles of her Baptist church.

"Sistuh Brown, that boy of yours is sho nuff blessed."

"Girl, that child can sang!"

But better that he learned a skill, and continue to sing on Sunday mornings. That would be fine . . . even better than fine, because that feat alone would have made her proud.

Oh Lawd . . . did ya hear him? Ain't he a mess? Why you give me a crazy child?

She didn't say those words, yet there was something just a little beyond *ridiculous* in Faison's promise of one day singing opera, and so, she laughed.

But the harshness of that laughter hurt Faison to his core. It felt as if she was, in some way, circumcising him, slicing into the skin of his dream.

As he sat on the couch next to her, he made a silent vow to himself. The vow was: to someday *erase* that dismissive laughter from his mother's belly.

People had always dismissed him in some form or fashion. They'd dismissed and made light of him because of his height, and the dark tone of his skin. They'd dismissed his wanting to sing in the church teen choir, when he was only ten. Yet he'd proven that he could not only sing with them, but exceed and soar beyond the best of them. One day people would have to stop being so damned *dismissive* of him.

Now, there sat his own mother, laughing at his most earnest ambition. He resigned right then, that he would *show his mother*, and show them all. He would *become* an opera singer; a young *Black* opera singer, from Harlem.

If you tell yourself something enough times, you can almost *will* it into reality. Faison Brown had long ago convinced himself that one day, he'd *be* a star. Yet, within the cosmos of his existence, were always those naysayers and the nuisances, the distractions . . . and the demons.

JANUARY 1989

Strange how it seemed that no one wanted to forgive him for his weakness, much less extend any offers of a singing gig to an ex-con.

Browny had to humble himself. He was living with Juanita, and thus, his finding work was *a must*. He had little choice. He took a janitor's job at his old high school. He hated returning to the loudness of that place, to the ghosts of ambition singing a cappella in those hallways. He hated not wearing a custom tuxedo, not giving a grand concert in the old auditorium, and not talking to the students of his ascent into legend status. That was how he'd always imagined his return to be . . . and it was a lovely reverie, indeed. But this custodial situation, was not, repeat NOT his beautiful dream!

He tried to make his own glamour by singing arias from Puccini while buffing floors.

Meanwhile, he'd still audition, and still those bigger doors continued to close with loud-ass *slams* in his hopeful, black face.

Rejection could depress even the best of brothers, let alone The Maestro of Low Self-Esteem.

And then, as hard luck would have it, one day while walking home in his stained janitor's uniform, he ran into a man, recently in the green. It was a man, with a familiar face and an even larger arrogance than even he'd remembered.

"Pass-cow Depina! Yo! Is that *you*? Ah, shit! Look at you," he appraised, his envy evident. "Hey! Digs the ride, man. Hot to death! This is slick!"

"Hey, Browny. Steal any Jettas lately, or you an entertainer now?" Face asked, laughing to himself.

"Yeah. Well, all that's about to go down real soon, man. You know me, I'm still doin' my thing. Got prospects out the ying-yang. So, uh, what you doin' 'round here? Somebody told me you's the next big thing! About to be large!"

"I am large. It's the petty li'l motherfuckers I used to run with that got smaller," Face jabbed. But suddenly the David-styled hairs on the nape of his beauteous neck stood on end.

Browny noticed Face looking around nervously, and he detected those green eyes shifting, looking up and down the street.

"Yo, man, now's not a good time," Face warned.

"But yo. This must be fate 'cause I got this tape and you sho gonna wanna hear it."

Face panicked. "Yo! Shit! Get in. Just get in, now!"

Seconds later they were hauled back out of the car and Browny's hands were forced behind his back. He despised being touched, especially by cops, and what the *fuck* were they trying to *shackle* him for? He was nobody's choirboy anymore, but for once in his life, he was living clean.

Yet there he was, Faison Brown, fighting off a cop, being "one of those aggressive negroes." Cops always hated that shit. So they yoked him, and then pushed him face-first to the pavement.

He was Mirandized and shoved right next to the man who'd never *really* been his friend nor his *boy*.

A vivid terror spooked inside those green Depina eyes, as all Face saw were vile visions of a life behind bars. That vision was not, and never was a part of the Grand Depina Plan.

Then something in the craziness of the moment made Face remember an old debt, a long ago debt that Browny had yet to pay back.

"Pssst. Motherfucka, you *owe* me. Just tell 'em the duffel is yours. Cop to this and I swear, you'll never want for nothin' again. I can hook you up," Face whispered to a stunned, confused Browny.

"What, yo? Whatchu talkin' bout?"

"Razor Morrisey. Had ya cryin' like a drunk bitch, beggin' for your life. Broke as I was, I bailed you out. Remember?"

Browny's mind quickly shifted back in time.

He and Face were living together, right after P.A., trying to be artists, co-existing. But Browny had fucked up, got hooked on coke, and his foolish ass ended up owing *Razor Morrisey*'s boys—Razor, of all fucking people. Now there was no rent money, no cash for food, no nothing. Face was deep into survival mode, looking to pay rent, looking to not be homeless again. Browny was in survival mode too, but even more literally. He *needed* that money.

Where can that little fool get that kinda money? Pascal wondered. *And what the fuck I'm gonna do 'bout the rent, my acting lessons, and food, and some fuckin' get high?*

Of course, there *was* someone who could help. It was someone with money who probably wouldn't even sweat him about paying it back. Someone who'd liked him back when he was still "Pascal." But what would he want in return? Maybe just a little suck-'n'-fuck for old times sake? Hell, Face could do that shit with a quickness and be on his way . . .

LONG ISLAND

Erik Von Ness lay in a chaise lounge on his deck, his jeans undone, his Hamptons-tanned feet propped up. Once more, Face Depina had provided him with a more than decent suck-'n'-fuck session. But after the gush, Von Ness wasn't gushing over the possibilities he once saw in Face anymore. "The Kid" had provided a service, and that was all Von Ness wanted from him now.

"Erik, listen . . . I hate to ask, but I really need to borrow some cash. See, I'm tryna be an actor, and it's *hoard* out there. Rent's due, and there's food and . . ."

"Save it, kid. I'm not your daddy. I'm not even your *friend*. Was once, a few summers back, until you got what you wanted from me, and disappeared. Maybe you don't *do* friends very well, kid. Hell, I almost *admire* you for having the nerve to come here and ask me for another favor. And for that, I *will* give you something. What's the going rate these days for common boy-whores with uncommonly pretty green eyes?" He reached in his pocket and threw a fifty at Face. "Goodbye Pascal," he said, turning his back and walking into his stately home.

Face stood there, feeling cheap, insulted, feeling reduced, fucked, and fucked-over. *Oh yeah? Ya stuck-up fancy faggot son-of-a-rich-bitch! Nobody disrespects me like that no more!*

Besides, Browny *needed* that money. Browny would be as sure-as-dead without it! And Face needed some cheddar too. So he was *going* to make that visit pay, even if it was in a fancy piece of crystal, like that Lalique vase, or maybe some artsy-fartsy knickknack. Or something, for damn sure! Face was determined he was gonna *get* paid—and a helluva lot more than a fucking fifty.

So Face followed Von Ness inside. And once inside, things

went faster and crazier than either he or his suitor had ever bargained.

Why did Von Ness have to get physical? Face wasn't trying to fight him. He just wanted to *use* him, again. Why did he pull that *machete* on Face? And when Face moved towards him, *why* did he have to slice into the boy's arm? Blood pooled through the sleeve of Face's shirt. *Oh shit! Oh shit!* By instinct, by mania, by the sight of his arm, Face *had* to hit him then. He hit the man so *hoard* it knocked him down and the machete flew out of his grasp. Face was in pain and still so mad, he struck him again, that time in the belly and Von Ness flew across the living room. His head hit very hard on that hardwood floor, and it knocked him unconscious. Face took a Cartier watch, some diamond cufflinks, a gold slave bracelet, and some other shit he knew Von Ness had probably insured.

Von Ness was still out when Face left, never looking back.

In his pain, in his anger, and in his haste to take what he could and get the hell out of there, Face hadn't noticed that, in his fall, Von Ness had knocked a burning candle to the floor.

The burning candle! The flames! The curtains! The flames! The floors! The hardwood floors! The flames! The flames!

Face saw it all on TV that night. As the reporter mentioned the man's name, something in him recoiled in horror.

I didn't do that. That wasn't me . . . was it? I know . . . *I didn't do that.*

"Oh, Erik. Oh, fuck! Fuckin' Erik!"

But for Depina's tragically dirty work, Browny was saved from that deadly slice of Razor's blade. And for yet another month, Face's rent got paid, on time.

* * *

“I paid him off, and I never called you on it, did I? Well, I’m puttin’ in my fuckin’ marker now, brother.”

I didn’t think you hadda fuckin’ heart, Browny thought, *till you took it out yo crusty pocket and showed it to me.*

And in one mad, greedy, ambitious, desperate moment, Browny shook his head. Before he knew what shackled him, he was back behind bars. But this time, he had a promise, a guarantee from Pass-cow Depina.

CHAPTER SIXTEEN

Heard It Through The Grapevine

JANUARY 1989

The people Tyrone once knew were slowly disappearing. It was almost becoming a deadly new trend. Browny was back in the pen. Face was off in Europe being vain and fabulous again. David was often busy traipsing after him, and it sometimes caused Ty to wonder what happened to David's *own* driving ambition.

People were indeed disappearing and with their absence, Tyrone began to feel a very real strain of isolation.

Back in the early '80s, when Ty had arrived at Columbia, though undiagnosed, he was clinically depressed. It wasn't easy living the special loneliness of being an eighteen-year-old secret widower, grieving in a place most people couldn't see, let alone begin to understand.

Somehow, by sheer will, he'd made it through—one step, one class, one day, one semester at a time. By Ty's junior year, he had a new roommate, and slowly that presence changed the complexion on the skin of days. This roomie was an almost constant source of comic relief, and his name was Jasper "Jazz" Thomas. Jazz swept into Columbia like a fresh breath of real illy Philly air. A sanity saver, Jazz was a buff, handsome, ebony brother with a smooth rap, a mischievous grin, and a fast-ass zipper, which impressed many campus women. Jazz was also a bit of a freak, and experiment junkie.

Yeah, Jazz. He was probably the best *straight* friend Tyrone had never known.

Now, for old times' sake, Tyrone placed a call to touch base with Jazz. He'd missed those days of laughter and light, and the folly of two Black boys being totally ridiculous. The more he thought about it, the more he needed to speak to Jazz, and so he'd thought he send a shout from NYC to his boogie boy from the wilds of Philly.

"Hello . . . Ms. Thomas? Ms. Nina Thomas? Hi. I hope you remember me. This is Tyrone . . . Yes, that's right. Ty Hunter. Jazz and I were roommates. I'm so glad you remember me. Oh, that's very sweet, Ms. T. 'Charming?' Really? I'll have to tell my *own* mother you said that. So, how are you? Well, I haven't spoken to Jasper in almost two years, and I just wanted to find out how my big head boy's doing . . . and what he's been up to . . . which is no good, I suspect." Ty laughed.

But there was no laughter on the other end.

"Yes. Yes, Ms. Thomas, I'm sitting."

And her voice was heavy with a mother's pain. And every word she spoke wore a faint trace of something wrong, something not right, something insane, something *unbelievable*. And as she spoke, her pain became Tyrone's own new pain . . .

Oh, no! No, Ms. Thomas . . . not Jazz!

Ty's mind drifted back to one day, one particular day at Columbia . . .

APRIL 3, 1984

Ty was just coming back from giving a poetry reading in the village. It hadn't gone well, and he felt as if the words he'd written weren't being truly *felt by those who'd heard them*. He hoped once arriving back on campus, he'd see Jazz, and Jazz would say something comforting, or stupid, and just make it all go away.

But instead Jazz was fresh from a shower, a cleansing in an effort to make the most horrible news of the day just wash away.

"Ty? Did you hear?" he asked. His face was that of dark and sad and tired ghost. He didn't look like Jazz in that moment.

"Jazz, man, you're not gonna believe that bullshit reading, man. I shouldn't've even went to the damn thing. And people were like . . ."

Suddenly it occurred to Ty that something bigger, *far larger* than a poetry reading stood between them inside that room.

"I'm sorry, Jazz. Did I hear what?"

"Did you hear about Marvin? Marvin Gaye?" Jazz asked.

"Oh yeah. *That!* I was just passing by the student lounge, and some chick swept past crying that she'd heard it on the news. But that's crazy. But it's just some crazy rumor, right? It can't be true."

"It's true, man. It's true."

"Say what?" Ty asked, astonished before his mouth went completely ajar. "Jazz, that's not even funny, bruh. Please tell me this is one of your lame-ass jokes!"

That's when Ty noticed the radio station was playing "What's Going On?"

"They say his father shot him. Shot him dead. They say the old man's under arrest. They say a lotta shit, but none of it makes any sense."

"*What?* That's, that's just *insane*. Marvin . . . is like . . . family. He, he can't be gone."

"But it's true, Ty . . . and his father shot him. I mean, damn! What could make a man do that shit to his son? I've been sitting here, raw . . . and listenin' to this music. I keep rememberin' all the good times I had as a kid, a tyke, and a man with Marvin in the background. I can't believe he's gone, man. It just don't make sense."

Jazz had called several of the girls, the chicks, the "sorority freaks" he'd fucked but had never once *felt.* They either off-campus, or they wanted to be left alone. He thought he'd wanted, needed to fuck something or someone. But what he wanted was a friend. Tyrone was his best friend there. Often he'd look at Ty, at how normal and real and down he was, and the fact that Ty was gay no longer mattered. He loved Tyrone. He needed Tyrone. And finally, there was Tyrone.

Jazz was still wrapped in his white terry cloth towel from his shower. He stood, staring at Tyrone in silence. One spot, one single spot of a clear elixir slid down his naked thigh . . . like a transient tear.

Tyrone saw that single tear and he wanted to touch it, to touch Jazz, to wipe it clean away. He wanted to pretend that it was all a lie, a mistake, and Marvin didn't die. A part of him was crying then, crying like that perfect and clear single tear sliding down Jazz's thigh.

Jazz stared at Ty, as if the weight inside his friend's eyes was somehow holding him up.

What were best friends for, if not to provide some sense of lucidity against the madness?

Jazz stared and looked to Ty for confirmation that the world would one day make sense again. It was then that he hugged Ty, tightly. As Jazz's large dark hands drifted across Ty's back, it felt so good, so right, and so necessary to be holding each other.

There were times when Ty's mind drifted to the dream he'd had before he really began to know Jazz. Jazz, provided an intriguing fantasy; the rich dark skin, the easy smile, the graceful physicality of him. In Ty's dream, Jazz was upset over some girl; some dizzy chick had mysteriously broken his heart. There were tears in his eyes as he'd stumbled in from boozy night of heartbreak. Drunkenly, Jazz had gotten into Ty's bed, and after realizing his mistake, Jazz didn't care. There were tears falling from his eyes, down his chest; tears and a moisture, like sweat, poured all over his crying fresh.

And in that dream, Ty awakened, and silently wiped those tears away. Jazz grinned and the light from that smile glowed in the dark. He took Ty's hand and placed upon his broad indulgent thigh. His skin felt iron wrapped in the smoothest silk. He gently placed his hand in the back of Ty's neck, and Ty so slowly descended. And in that dream, Ty blew Jazz, like a saxophone, sadly.

Now, Jazz was drowning in the wave of tears and emotion and Tyrone that could not save him, or anyone.

In reality, in an act of confusion, and bewilderment, of need, and music remembered, all they'd shared was a tight embrace of souls. And after that needed embrace, after their shared grief at Marvin Gaye's passing, the two broke away.

On the radio, the song "Sexual Healing" played, and it was all either of them could hear.

"Hey, what is this . . . a fuckin' homo moment?" Jazz asked with a sad smile.

"You wish," Ty said. "You wish."

How many times had Ty wished to be lost inside a moment, a mood, a swoon, a reckless decision that ended with them huffing, puffing and lock inside of each others arms?

But if something were to happen, a fluke, a freak moment, a mistaken move, each of them knew it would only be an act of healing some loneliness one or the other sought so desperately to remove. It would be some unwritten rule between two cool best friends, to never acknowledge that it happened; to trust in other that it would never be *spoken* of again.

Years later, hanging up the phone, after listening to a mother read her son's obituary in his ear, Tyrone cried in such wild and wasted tears.

He reflected upon the hurtful irony that sex was not healing a damn thing anymore. Sex was killing people. Sex, or drugs, or both had killed Jazz a year-and-a-half ago. And Ty hadn't even known.

Just ten short days after hearing and trying to process the death of Jazz, at twenty-four, there came the glib call from Ty's estranged and gambling father. The message was simple:

Uncle Jerome was dead.

Oh, no! Not Jerome.

Tyrone had been feeling optimistic about him. After Omar, visits to Brooklyn had become less frequent over time. But the last time he'd pushed through, he'd noticed that something was beginning to melt the frozen claw that had a hold on Jerome's life. A casual observer wouldn't have perceived the change, but Tyrone did. It gave him a strange sense of hope for his Unk, because inside those ancient gin and juice ruins, Jerome had found love. Or love had found him. Suddenly his uncle's heart was full of vaguely remembered palpitations.

Love was decked out in long and happy bones, taped glasses, and brand new teeth. Love was found in a tall, skinny dude named Clifford. He was a friendlier man than Jerome. Cliff was an ex-drunk, with one lazy eye, and a positive influence. But he was crazy, too . . . crazy with spring. He was like a live cock squawking and chasing after a new feathered friend.

Seeing them, Ty was struck by how oddly precious they were together, whether arguing over what to have for dinner, or debating over the blues and old jazz greats. Jerome's posture had improved, too. And he had a brand new porkpie to match the new stride in his step. With Clifford, Jerome didn't seem so hell-bent on killing himself with and self-pity. It was really *something* to see. It confirmed in Ty, a slender thread-thin belief that strange and wonderful shit could actually happen; furthermore, it could actually happen to anyone, even gay, *Black*, drunken men.

Two men together could work, beyond fucking or sucking games. So many people were marching through quick, ineffectual lives, snug in their collective blindness and racing with a chaos that passed for heartbeats, but Jerome had found *love*. Or love had found him. Finally *love*, on that loveless Brooklyn street, at last.

Ty imagined they would *bond* and form a life, Jerome and Clifford, two black men *together*. Yes. It was crazy and sweet. It was possibly calamitous, and yet so deep.

And he never believed in it, until *they* gave him that possibility.

Now the possibilities were falling down all around him, like mortal dominoes with well-loved faces.

After the tragic news of Jazz and Jerome, Ty retreated into his own self, his darker, most introspective self.

He got himself tested and retested, and he continued to read negative. It didn't matter. Fear was the mother of all paranoia. Maybe those tests were all *false-negatives*, because something felt very wrong inside him.

Did he have *it*? Did that cute boy with the trusting brown eyes, who'd slyly bit Ty's nipples a little too severely, did he *have* it? That uncertainty lived in Ty's every pore, because real or imagined, every siren represented another death. Every siren became another broken heart, another kind of pain, another unfinished work of art, another unfinished dream. Every siren. Every fucking siren! And New York City was *full* of sirens.

Tyrone Hunter lived each day in *terror* that maybe *this* day, whatever lay sleeping in him would *awaken*. David, on the other hand, had no sympathy for it.

"Know what your problem is?" David said as he and Ty sat in Ty's kitchen one evening. "I'm about to tell you. Your problem is, you spend w-a-a-a-a-ay too much *time* thinking about death. You spend your days and your nights wondering who's next, pondering and worrying about death and dying, and loss, and now . . . you're starting to become something lost and dying. Ty, this shit is *becoming* you! This, right here, this is what death is. It's the absence of *life*."

"If a *bullet* had killed them," Ty argued, "would you still fuck around and play with guns? Huh? Well, *sex* killed them! It's as true as the tag on their toes. Sex killed them, and I'm no longer a fan of the weapon that took all my friends!"

"Whoa! Get a grip, chip! You're starting to sound hysterical. Listen, you need to breathe some natural air . . . hell, it might just change your perspective. Open some damn windows! Better yet, let's just get outta here. C'mon, let's go out, baby boy," David insisted.

"What for, Duch? There's just death out there. Death in Levi's with a hard-on and a cock-ring, stalkin' our asses, literally."

"No. Death is in here. Life is out there! When hell freezes over, buy a fuckin' Dorothy Hamill wig, and slip on some damn ice skates! C'mon, Ty. Let's go dancin'. Don't you wanna dance anymore? Shit, I do! This whole thing is a conspiracy anyway . . . a conspiracy against us dancin' people. Just look around at who's getting it. Just us. You gonna tell me something that's been going on since time and creation suddenly kills us? But you know what? If I'm goin' down, shit, ya best believe, I'm goin' down dancin'. Just watch me, shakin my Black, faggot ass. 'cause that's how I fight. Ain't you the one who told me, 'never let the motherfuckers steal your joy'? Well, where that joy boy at? I liked him. Is he even in the building? Ty, I know you got dreams. You lettin' it steal all your fuckin' dreams, baby boy. Don't you want to be happy?"

Ty stared out his window at the twilight activity of the metro, and he didn't speak. He couldn't seem to find the words nor the strength to speak them. He did *that thing* he often did with his dreads, running his hands through them until they stood on end, like antennae, picking up the gist of his deepest thoughts. Finally, through slow and crazy tears, he managed to turn to his best friend in the whole world, and speak.

"I . . . I wanna be . . . something . . . some . . . thing . . . radical . . . something . . . fuckin' epic. I . . . wanna be . . . a happy . . . black . . . gay senior citizen."

CHAPTER SEVETEEN

Summer of the Great Fall

Sometimes the words we say, the words we choose to live by, can come back like these ironic little ghosts, to haunt us slow and painfully.

If I'm goin' down, shit! Then I'm going down dancin'. 'Cause that's the way I fight.

The dance is a fragile art. You leap and bound, spin and soar like a firebird, full of flames and light and music. But at any moment you can descend from flight and find yourself touching down *all kinds of wrong*. And all you know for sure is that the flame is still there, but the music in the limbs is gone.

JULY 4, 1989

It was the holiday, and David's leg had been bothering him again. It amazed him how getting older affected those parts of his body he'd placed the most faith in, especially when he was a tad younger and just a li'l more *spry*.

But dull ache or not, it wasn't about to keep the party-freak in David Richmond from running around town, looking to work up his freak's sweat. He called it dabbling. It was one of his favorite little euphemisms.

"Oh baby! I dabbled my ass off in the club last night. Oh, I see some new pants worth dabbling into."

Since he was a teen, David dabbled. Dabbling was his favorite pastime. In fact, David's dabbling was fast becoming his career.

On that July Fourth, as he checked his reflection in the mirror, dressed in his denim short-shorts and bright red tank, he said to himself, *You are still very much the hotness, David Donatello Richmond. So . . . let's let the dabbling again.*

Summer was the dabbling season. David's main dabbler-ee was a handsome young papi named Hector. He was tall, dark, hefty, and hot as a jalapeno.

They'd met in one of David fave spots, *Esuelita's* on West 39th and 8th Avenue. It was then, for David Richmond, a hot papi-shopper's paradise.

Hector could dance his thickly masculine ass off, and of course, so could David. The two of them scorched the floor that night—a hot night of hot music, hot striptease, and hotter lights. Somehow they fit, they clicked, they kicked it. Soon the little, lithe, dancing David was deep finessing a new move as he, and the heroically hung Hector were hotly, happily humping in Hempstead.

Hours passed, wine was imbibed, and so came that horny time for a bit more risqué sexual calisthenics.

He and Hector were engaged in a freaky fit of sexual inventiveness atop a spiral staircase. It was all so good, so hot, so right, so muy caliente, baby! But then, the friction became too intense, so intense, so powerful that David, the dancer, lost his prized sense of balance, and he took a nasty header downward. *AYYYYYYYEEEEEEEE!!!!!!!*

That fall, that treacherous fall . . . that loud, long, lingering fall, it broke David's left leg in three places. That loud, long, lingering pain-wrenching fucking fall would end David's soon-to-be fuckin' stellar dancing career!

He lapsed into a deep despair from which he would never, never completely recover.

The emergency room was bedlam, and David Richmond was its head banshee. He screamed, he cried, he bemoaned, and he bellowed at the tragedy of it all. David was a mad and muttering mess. He wanted sympathy. He wanted some understanding. He wanted his mama, but she was long gone.

He *needed* someone to understand. He needed his best friend, his confidant, his heart's other half.

"Where is *T-y-y-y-y-y-y-y-y-y-y-y-y?*" he cried.

But then, when the pain took a pause, when he was able to call Ty to tell him this terrible, heart-shattering news, David realized, he COULDN'T tell Tyrone Hunter THE TRUTH.

He thought Tyrone would only look at him, shake his head, and see David as some frivolously foolish fag foiled and fucked-up by his own fucking faggotry! David didn't think Ty would ever SAY it, but he'd think it the rest of his life. He'd wrinkle that fuckin' furrow of a brow and it would just *kill* David, and that look would slaughter him slowly with its silent judgment.

So, David wondered just how he could *work* this terrible thing. How, in this scary, crazy, stupid, mad, fuckin' unfair world could he tell Tyrone that his career was DEAD? As much as he hurt—and David hurt to his core—he somehow *knew* this death of his Art, this death of his heart and soul would only hurt Tyrone more.

And so David, being blessed with a wonderfully creative mind, wove a tedious tale of a "particularly treacherous step," a leap he was trying to perfect, that, in the end, went all kinds and dimensions of "*horribly wrong*." Yes, it was a dirty-nasty-filthy lie, but at least then he could hold his head up high, and earn some much-needed sympathy.

Sorry, Ty. I love you, baby boy. I do! But this one I'll take to the grave . . .

There, in that hospital, laid up in a cast from his swollen ankle up to his lovely, if promiscuous hip, David recited his revamped piece of fictional bullshit to Tyrone. The words were breaking *both* their hearts.

Ty gave great hugs. If David ever had any doubt that this man named Tyrone was his BESTEST friend, that day Ty stepped up and proved it. Love is a verb. This was something David always believed: *Love is a verb.*

Ty held him so tightly inside that hospital bed, it was like he tried to absorb David's pain, to take it all into his *own* body and somehow free David from it. Together they sniffed, they sobbed, and they cried such bitter tears to the death of David's long-standing dream. It was silently, quietly killing David—the hugs, the tears, THE LIE.

This was the only REAL LIE he would ever tell Tyrone Hunter—and he felt so fuckin' broken by it.

He'd thought he had found in Ty that one person he could tell *anything*, no matter how crazy or sick or unflattering, and he'd know it would be guarded from judgment. But David didn't trust Ty with this one ugly, promiscuous truth.

Maybe the line of trust had its own invisible limit—invisible until you'd *crossed* it.

But little did David know back then that Tyrone had his *own* dirt with which to contend, and he was keeping it very close to his dingy little vest. And a very unfashionable little vest it was, because, after all those years, he'd never told *David* about his lukewarm night with the deceptive Facey Depina.

And so, the tally in the naked honesty count was about even. Ty had lied by omission, and David, by creation.

But the fact remained, David's dance, his dream, his reason for being was done.

It was a lonely, low and abysmal period. David lost himself to a deep and devastating despair. Unlike Ty, David was not very good with depression. When David became dark, it happened so seldom that for him, things turned inward, and often violent.

He became susceptible to all sorts of psychosis and vile, shameless, un-Davy-like shit. Hard, rough and nameless fucks became his norm. David was very good and most adept at finding those self-haters. It was an innate skill for him. He would willfully locate a vato, a tough, a tatted-up gato, a macho cat, who liked to box, like Rico, and he'd let that battering bastard batter *him*. Pain let David know he was still alive. Sex gave him the drive to carry on.

This soon became a dark and spirit-draining odyssey, thick with the emotional beat-downs of beat angels, beat devils, and beat apartments with roaches and rats rounding corners like locomotives. David's train was lost. It roamed from station to station, john to filthy john, all the while trying to soothe an affliction that dare not say its name. Sometimes all he could do was look into his cracked, stained mirror and cry those why-did-I-ever-lay-down-with-this-musty-moody-macho-mad-motherfucker Blues.

He purposely avoided Ty. David reasoned that Tyrone Hunter had ways of saying shit without saying anything at all. There was this thing in Ty that David had discovered, a way Ty judged with words. David knew Ty's silences, and he was way too familiar with that brooding, disapproving, trick eyebrow of Ty's. So he figured Tyrone would just quietly moralize everything to death, just like David's father. This pissed David off the most, knowing his father, let alone Tyrone Hunter, was miles away from the concept of Perfection.

During David's extended affair with disappearance, oddly enough, within that absence, Tyrone went into a deeper writing mode. Sometimes in tragedy or in loneliness, one finds his art.

TYRONE'S JOURNAL READ:

When I witness someone's brilliance, I am instantly and most profoundly transformed. A part of me becomes a smaller thing, realizing I'm in the company of Greatness. It's like standing before some tall, lofty building and being diminished beneath its massive shadow. David's talent is a massive thing. Watching him dance is to watch a cosmos in motion. I know whatever talent I possess dims when he is in the room. His sun eclipses my moon. He is my friend, my Homeboy, my Hero, and unquestionably the finest artist I know. David is blessed with that magical something. It puts the balls in ballet, and the 'azz, in Jazz. It makes him taller, wider, and endlessly more sexy than the rest of us. When David dances, he becomes a different kind of beast. He is a glorious animal of movement from his arms and legs, to his neck, to his back, to every toe on his feet. Even in this city, this mecca of dancers, David's genius is unique. Seeing that animal go to work, it is a miraculous thing to behold. It has always made me so fucking proud of him, proud just to know him and to call him my friend.

I always introduce him to strangers by saying, "This is my friend, David. Duch, I call him . . . the Duchess of Incredible Dance."

It embarrassed him, I think. But I always meant it.

Now, this! This terrible thing has befallen him. I just don't know who he'll be now, or what will become of him without this joy in his soul that dances.

* * *

Tyrone's assessment of David came from a completely disassociative place. There was no ego involved. There was only LOVE.

Reading that passage aloud to himself made Tyrone cry. Cry hard!

Then, one day while nosing around for a peek of Ty's latest work, David happened upon that entry. He thought back to that painful day and wished he could erase Hector, risqué sex, and spiral staircases completely from his orbit.

He'd always known he was good. First, his mother praised him. She told him he was "blessed," and she made him believe it. Soon after, his dance teachers praised him, fellow students worshipped him, and his friends were all in awe of him. Yes, David knew Ty, a lover of art, had appreciated his gift. What made this so much worse, though, was that David never knew the degree, or just how *much* Ty *respected* his talent. He had not really known until he'd read those words.

And only he know his tragedy, the reason, the cause of it, was a lie, a convenient tale that he'd hatched for his own self-protection. Reading those words and knowing his . . . it re-broke David's heart.

How would Tyrone have felt, or reacted, had he known what really caused David's career's suicide? His sonnet would have been a tirade to his freakish friend David, the *so-called artist*, who risked a bright and promising career on a few mindless minutes of papi bliss.

No. Tyrone *chose to believe* the story his ears received. He believed in David's lie, and so, he deeply grieved for him. How terrible! How tragic! How gullible!

Ty did not place his trust in very many people. Those he did trust . . . he deemed them, Special. He had also mistakenly and even arrogantly believed he *knew* David. In some ways, he did. But how many of us ever truly *know* another person, inside and out? He knew David's heart. But Ty wasn't schooled in the tricks of David's mind, and he had no knowledge of that potential for deception. Tyrone took much stock in his own intelligence, his own intuition, his own perceptions. These, his tools as a writer, were supposed to be on the money, always fool-proof. And if not, what did that really *say* about *him*?

Tyrone Hunter was a naïve boy. When it turned out he didn't know, couldn't know people for the complex individuals they were, he took their foibles, their fuck-ups, their humanity as a personal affront. People he'd meticulously singled out, the ones he deemed to *trust* were not supposed to disappoint him. Hence, Tyrone Hunter, David's bestest friend was doomed to live in the company of disappointment.

CHAPTER EIGHTEEN

Facing History

1988-1992

Snorting, cavorting, and whoring around, painting the night-life red, tan, and brown in every city, town, hamlet, and island, Face Depina lived a fabulously sweet and spinnin' life. Suddenly, he was one of the *deified*. He fell in with a fast-track pack of spoiled, closeted playboys who languished in the joys and pains of the flesh, and they joined him in his hedonistic quest of snorting, consorting, trafficking, and laughing. They ate peaches on the beaches of Belize. In France, his famous mouth was known as La Bouche, and his busy penis, Le Baton Beige. While in Spain, he was El Toro Cremoso. Inside that new netherworld, Face became a divine being in a land whose beautiful denizens existed outside the lines of self-control and responsibility.

Beyond the Age of Excess trip, there were some particularly ugly incidents for which Face never fully took responsibility. But Face couldn't have any foul shit messing with all that fabulousness hurtling toward him. He knew he'd acquired a few ugly behaviors, but he had excuses: bad environment, bad breaks, bad influences.

If he fucked up badly, or hurt someone, he still never apologized unless it benefited him in some fashion. Later, Claudio schooled him on the ritual practice of sending flowers, but . . . "Why bother apologizin' for shit that happened in a moment? A moment is only here for so long. There . . . feel this one? Now it's gone."

And Depina's hectic schedule didn't allow for much self-illumination. One day he was posing in his drawers in Milan, and the next in a natty London Fog back dropped by Big Ben. Women and men were all over him, swarming like pigeons to a brand-new, wide-shouldered statue.

Women and men vied for his green-eyed attention as he donned matador pants and a cape to challenge a charging imaginary beast in Madrid. It seemed everyone loved him. He was showered with expensive gifts and treated to fits of ass-kissing extraordinaire, both figuratively and literally. And the sex, oh, the sexing was fierce, frivolous, free, freakish, and sometimes even felonious!

This was *The Good Life*. Away from the Nikons and Canons, the world was *his* to drink in, to fuck with, or to just plain fuck. But whenever he was alone, the sharpest part of his idling mind would rub roughly against the scabs of old wounds.

He was picking at the one he'd worn since birth, and it was beginning to bleed again. Under rainy London skies, he left his hotel room looking to escape the dead matches floating in that urinal of his hidden life. He was in a strange place and he wanted something *more* from the pace of that foreign night. He wanted to make the night freak inside its navy skin, shiver strangely from a little random excitement.

East-end-reed-thin boys of cockney fathers stabbed holes through their hurt in the doorways of Soho. It felt like the darkest part of home. That night Depina was spinning and full of the madman. He asked the right questions, copped the right bag, and joined the scag-fest.

Snorting horse was boss for a quick minute, though he'd sometimes get that abrupt urge to vomit soon after. But then came those insolent little tells: the vacancies of time and thought, that sudden clutch of despondency, those ill-timed nosebleeds.

And so, after yet another fabulous party, he decided to up the ante. There he lay, naked in another bedroom, next to yet another pale boy with another set of translucent eyes, who kissed slyly and was clever with his tongue. The boy rolled over and suggested in a woozy after-sex tone that they both ride a provocative little dragon called *China White*.

"I've been using since I was fourteen, mate. I'll fix ya, if you'd like, ya bloody bloke."

And the rest is addiction history.

Suddenly he'd found his new med, and it was a whole lot better than that Peruvian shit he'd *been* fucking with. It even had a *cool-jerky danger* to it.

Mainlining was the *real deal.* It was as if God Himself waltzed into his bloodstream and made everything tranquil and light, both radiant and radiating. For the first time, Depina could hear the music of himself, and he felt like he'd just grown *a soul.* Pain evened out, then vanished inside a floating mind made suddenly golden and wise, a mind wherein lay the answers to all questions, even those he'd never asked.

And then there were no questions, no answers, no worries. Only the exquisitely quiet hum of peace . . . . a peaceful existence.

It felt more than fantastic to lounge inside a crazy calm adrenaline of the new, to no longer sweat or stress the haze and horror of the old. *Ah! Smack!* He wanted to submerge his body, his whole mind, his reckless thrill-seeking soul in the cool crush tactility of it. It was such a radically different concept for the promiscuously nomadic, naughty by the nature of his gonads Depina to be thrilled, actually thrilled by a sense of calm.

By the time he boarded the plane in Heathrow en-route to Orly, he felt all *mooged* and synthesized, his mood marvellously modified. Everything in the life of his mind was now a fly glide of tranquil energies. He just wasn't the same Facey Depina anymore. Uncle Heroin was bouncing him on his thin and bony knee. Uncle? Hell! Mama and Poppa, too. It was his sister and his brother, his friend and lover, his teacher, preacher, and he didn't need anyone else, or any-motherfucking-thing else, except cash.

On the other side of the pond, shattered women and men he'd befriended, fucked, and fucked over awaited his long overdue return. Including Bliss Santana, who was by then in a bad way.

It was Tyrone who finally came to her rescue.

"Face, it's Tyrone. Bliss is in trouble. Have you seen her? Don't you care? She looks bad. Her fire's gone. She's losing weight. She showed up at my door this morning at 5:15, crying hysterically over your ass. It's got me worried . . . about her sanity."

"Well, who the hell asked you to worry? Mind your own damn business. Fuckin' drama queen! That's all you are. Better not be fillin' her head with no goddamn lies about me!"

"This conversation ain't about your fuckin' paranoia. Why don't you just once try being a fuckin' man? It don't pay top model dollars, but it's a noble gig. Tell Bliss it's over, and WHY it's over, man. Then maybe she can go on with her motherfuckin' life!"

"You sure it ain't her faggot-fuckin' life?"

Tyrone hung up. But he had become involved.

* * *

Bliss had come to Ty because she needed help. She was all hopped up on blow and delusions of grandeur, and she hooked him with her story.

She had recently tried to *work* her show's producer, schmooze and smile and do what smooth sexy women do to make *the suits* pay attention. She'd styled a plan for a new Black-Latina story line. But he flat out rejected it. So *the coquette* left the room and Bliss "Boom-Boom" Santana, the coke-charged seductress with a smart word and a "Lick my cat, you bastard!" for everyone, took over. She demanded a mad-outrageous salary. When the producer rebuked her, she went back to her Jersey roots and cursed him out, most thoroughly. Then, in a coup de grace, home-girl punctuated her tirade by hauling off and *spitting* dead in his face. As if that wasn't enough, she reached into her big, black, trick bag and whipped out a pair of cuffs. "I'll show you just who you're fucking with!"

TY'S HARLEM APARTMENT ROOF

Ty shifted in his chair. "And so, this fierce, fantastic jazz flower of a double-jointed woman *cuffed her own wrists* to a chair and had to be bodily escorted from the studio, crying and screaming like a formerly well-paid banshee. In one day, her part was recast and they cancelled her contract."

"As if she didn't know how cold showbiz could be," David said.

"She said she turned to her dwindling stash to recharge her broke-down bitch battery and to widen her scope. But besides her disappearing dope, the first person she tried to seek solace in was—"

"Please. Don't tell me. Let me guess: *Mi corazón*, Facey."

"You are correct, ma'am."

"But Facey was in Milan," David volunteered.

"Damn! You're vurry scurry. I know you've got it bad for The Man Who Would Be Fag, but hell, Duchess! You got some kind of trailing device stuffed in your Danskin, or what?"

"Don't be catty, gonad-breath! It's very unattractive on you. And, by the way, so is anything sleeveless. Pick up a barbell, damn it! Personally, I like to think of *my* Facey Face as The Once and Future Fag! All right, Pissy Poo?!"

"Well, I guess a girl's gotta dream, doesn't she?"

"You know, Facey's thinking about letting me do something different with his hair!" David angled his head and shook it in haughty *sniff-sniff* arrogance.

"Ummm . . . Bliss is the subject. Stick to the subject, please. And Ix-nay on Ace-fay, OK? I'm sick with it."

"You just *hate it* that Face and me are close, don't you? Because I won't let you say harsh shit about him without callin' you on it. That's how I do friendship. I'd do the same if *he* dogged you out!"

"You know what I *do* hate, David? How every conversation you have is about you and the *wonderfulness* of Face. It's like you *don't* see how he plays people until they *bore* him, then he just moves on to the next. I know you, David. You've always had *blinders* on when it comes to that cat. But you really *need* to see it. Because one day soon, he'll get bored and shoot some toxic shit at you, which will undoubtedly leave you quiverin' like Raid on a fuckin' roach. You'll be wondering, *What did I do? What the hell happened?* Well, what *is* gonna happen? Have ya even *thought* about that? I don't wanna see you in one of those three-cornered paper hats making a La-Z-Boy of your own excrement, mumbling, 'Facey . . . Facey . . .' Face it, he's a playa. I want better for you. Don't you think it's time *you* started wanting better?"

"See, Ty, that right there tells me you don't know jack-shit! Yes. He might be a little *complex*, but they don't come any *better* than Face!"

"*That's* your comeback? You makin' a joke, right?"

"No. I'm completely serious. Maybe you need to tell why you hate Facey so damn much."

"Ummm . . . why? You mean, besides the fact that he's always looked down on the rest of us?"

"Yes. Besides that . . . 'cause that's just your interpretation. Some people say the same shit about *you*."

"Oh. Really? Then those people obviously don't know me."

"Exactly! And that's just what I tell 'em . . . *all.* Ya'll don't know Ty. Trust me. That stick ain't *always* up his ass," David joked.

"Fuck you, witch! Fuck you, with the broomstick you flew in on!"

"But I'm serious," he insisted. "Something . . . something bad musta gone down between you two, because *you* don't hate without a damn good reason." David's eyes narrowed as he gazed at Tyrone in a way a surgeon might probe a gaping wound, pondering to see if he could close it, without leaving a scar.

"Let's see? Why would I possibly dislike Face Depina? You mean besides me trusting him enough to invite to my home, and then, him turning around and *stealing* from us? Or maybe you mean, besides the fact that his fuckin' thievery *destroyed* my family, and tore my parent's marriage apart?"

"Well, if that's true, that's very sad and très fucked-up. But he was a kid then. He's not anymore. And you really don't *know* him, or what he's been through, or the wonderful things he's done for me. He's introduced me to a whole new world. I think that threatens you. Does it? Well, cool it out. You're still my girl, friend. But you need to shut the fuck up on the subject of him playin' me. He only plays people he don't *respect*."

The cold bayonet of that word stabbed Tyrone slowly, and he wondered if the stun of it showed.

Why does he keep probing this shit? And why does he keep looking at me, like that? Does David know? Did Depina get high and babble his Depina-ized version of . . . Nah. I could see Depina doin' that shit to me, but not to Davy . . . unless . . . of course, he wanted to come between us.

"What exactly is going on in that dancing head of yours? What do you *think* you *know?*" Ty quizzed.

"I always pride myself on being a *good and graceful* queen. Not some cruel, bitchy, resentful shrew, like, well, some people. I don't speak nor spread rumors! I *give* good facts. You know that about me."

Oh shit! He knows. He definitely knows. Come on, girlfriend. Hit me with it! Let's just have our Geraldo *moment, take off our earrings, get to swingin' like two bitches, and be over it.*

"Tell me something, Ty. When did you get so concerned about Miss Bliss and her terminal New York times? Ya startin' ta sound like a princess all entranced by the Queen Mother! Please." He shooed away a bumblebee. "These things never work out. Let them handle their own risky business. She was just a phase, anyway." Traces of hope clung to David's every syllable.

"Well, for her sake, I hope he doesn't play her like that."

"Not thinkin' about switchin' teams, are you, queenie? I've *seen* that movie. You go through a drought, someone all soft and curvy shows you a li'l attention, and suddenly Ty, the sad young sodomite is magically cured by the Miracle of The Previously Unexplored Pussy? Somebody say, Amen!"

"Fuck you, up, down and sideways, David Richmond!" Ty spat.

"Well, at least you'd have better luck fuckin' *me*, than Ms. Bliss. Apparently you need a refresher lecture. Now, please, repeat after me: A woman, even a good, understanding, *sexy* woman is not, repeat *not* the boot camp for homo rehab. It's ridiculous for you or Facey or anybody who's runnin' scared and desperate to think so. It only hurts people. Just 'cause you can get it to stand up and cheer for the other side, please! A bored dog might lick a . . . *pussy* . . . cat. It don't make him any less a dog . . . . just a bored and curious dog."

"You forget that in the quest to be liked and accepted, desperate people do desperate shit. And when desperation rubs against desperation, it can make fire, or some other form of deeply sick pornography."

"That's probably true. But there's a limit to the things we can do with our dicks."

"But who sets those limits?"

"The owner. Fuck the rest."

"Yeah, David, but even *you're* insecure. We all are. And whatever the insecurity, sometimes you just want the world to see you as less of a freak. Face, he's obviously got some freak shit with him," Ty said. "And he doesn't want that fly shit to go away, so he's operating from a place of fear."

"I know about the fear. I'm tryin' to cure him and the *rest* of my friends of that."

"Please, David. Cure yourself! He ain't seekin' nobody's cure. He's too busy publicly dating beauties and doing his dirt on the secret tip. That's all he knows. And he's full of secret shit. Trust me. Queers either amuse or terrify him. So, he and his devils make a stab at being straight. Why? Because it's just so much more convenient, man!"

"Convenient? Fuck that! Who says anybody's life is supposed to be convenient? You are who you are, and you like what you like when you like it. That's the name of Facey's sex. He just needs to own that. There's a hell of a lot more *gray* than black and white out there. You're supposed to be this *insightful* writer, aren't you? Haven't you noticed that yet, *mijo?*" David asked. "See, I understand Face. I've been a student of his most of my *vida loca*. So all I'll say is, Face belongs to no one. No woman, no man, no one but The Universe . . ."

NATIONAL BLACK THEATRE, HARLEM

After her meltdown in the producer's office, Bliss Santana could no longer find work. She suspected she'd been blacklisted, which, she later found out was the truth. She tried to take her case to the press, but no one would touch her. No one, except Tyrone Hunter, and he had quickly grown to *like* her far more than he'd ever liked Face Depina.

One month after they'd met, there was a reading for Tyrone's play-in-progress, and Bliss Santana accompanied him. He'd asked her to read, and she did so most eloquently. Ty fell a little in love with the *fantasy* of her. But that fuzzy pink reverie went black, bronze, and green when Face Depina strode into the theatre. At that point, the winding road where Bliss and Face merged and intersected was filthy with skid marks.

Bliss was by now beyond furious with his chronically missing-in-action ass. Where was his support, his sympathy, his wide shoulder to cry on, his long cock to slide down and forget the darkest hour of her career catastrophe? After she'd helped launch *his* career, he *owed* her. Didn't he?

Now *he* stood in that theatre door, unexpected, unannounced, smiling, and causing little earthquakes just by hanging in the back, arms folded, looking like, well, Face.

Check 'em checkin' me. Shit, I could do anybody I wanted to up in this queer little group. Hell. See a few I already banged. Yeah. That's right. Depina's in duh motherfuckin' house. Look at poor Ty up there, still tryna be somebody. Look at his hair. What homey do, sit in the barber's chair and tell him, "Make me look like a goddamn fool"? Run a comb through that African mess, boy! Where's my woman? Oh. There she is. Gettin' kinda light in the ass, ain't you, baby? Bliss? Hey! Over here. OK, smile, Daddy's home. Come to Daddy. I said, come to Daddy! Bliss? Daddy's waiting. Bliss, come to Daddy, ya hard-headed played-out bitch!

After the reading, Bliss grabbed Ty's hand and they retired backstage.

Hey! What up with this shit? She tryin' to change him? So what now . . . she givin' that little fag a little head? Motherfuck! Is she hummin' him? Is she? Is he . . . ? Are they stank like that? Nah. What would she want with a fuckin' fag?

Face Depina checked his image in the darkened glass of the door. To his eye, he still looked fine. He turned around and saw their heads together, going over lines. He stared at them for a long time, and waited for that diabolical pussy-machine magnetism thang he slang to take effect. He'd expected kisses, maybe even an embrace from his quasi-homeboy. What he *got* was ignored. But Depina determined he'd make his presence felt, even if it stung someone.

"So. This here thing, this *play* needs a lotta work, huh, Ty?"

"Hello, Pascal. Actually, I think it's just about perfect," Bliss said.

Depina didn't like that defensive stance, or the way she and Ty *looked* together. The level of comfort they shared was all too evident.

"Tell me sum'n, how long you two been girlfriends? And what the hell you got to talk about, anyway?"

His questions died a silent death.

"Nice seeing you too, Face." Ty kissed Bliss's cheek, and whispered, "I'll call you." Then he walked away.

For a moment, Face Depina actually felt spurned. But in the larger picture, he was feeling too damn good to let small shit upset his axis.

"So, baby, let's grab somethin' to eat and party and fuck like it's 1999. C'mon. Grab your coat!"

"Can't. I got a doctor's appointment. Besides, you look . . . tired. Maybe you should get some rest. Bye."

"Yo, Bliss! Hold up! Wait a minute! So, you hummin' Ty, now? 'Cause you know he's a fag, right?"

"What I know is, he's my friend. Unique concept, isn't it, Pascal?"

"Friend, huh? Well, what your *girlfriend* say about me, huh? I *know* you talk about me!"

"Tyrone is far too busy and cool to spend his time *gossiping* about you. And what could he possibly tell me that I don't already know, huh? Bye-bye."

Face's question about whether Bliss and Ty were an item was not as far from the truth as one might have guessed.

Stimulated by Bliss's style, conversation, and mind, Ty couldn't help but imagine being with her. What would it be like? It was certainly doable, at least in his flinty imagination.

Every now and again, the thought stroked the dick of his mind, like once when she leaned in close, rubbed his thigh, looked into his eyes with those pale green lights, and said, "I'm starting to believe it's just not in a man to love completely. Even you think it's impossible for another man to love you totally and faithfully, right?" She cuddled close to him. "Maybe you're not so gay after all. Maybe you're just, terminally *tender* for men. Maybe you just romanticize the best in them. Did you ever think of *that*, my not-so-happy-and-gay friend?"

"Well, if I'm not gay, I've pulled off a damn good imitation of it. And believe me when I say there's *rarely* anything *tender* about it."

Yet, in those most vulnerable moments, in the thread-thin silence of thought, he'd revisited her words, and he'd wonder if she was right.

But he also knew it didn't matter because Face still rented space in her mind. A melancholy gaze would cloud her eyes. Then she'd breathe deep, and it would subside. But Ty knew. He'd seen that same struggling look in David's eyes. Both tried valiantly to overcome it, yet still suffered from that lingering sickness: the Acquired Depina Disease Syndrome.

David's case was just more overtly acute.

TY'S HARLEM APARTMENT BUILDING ROOF

"I know in my bones we're gonna happen. I even checked with Madam Zoreena, and ya *know* how accurate her predictions and stuff be. Well she lit a candle for me. Then she says she sees me 'walking hand-in-hand with a tall, impressive Latin man.' That's exactly what she said, Ty. Then, out the blue, I run into him, and he offers me a job that keeps me *very close* to his fine ass."

"Ah, Duch, no disrespect to the clairvoyant Zoreena and all, but what about Chaz?" Ty asked.

"Chaz? Please. Don't be ridic! I mean, I ain't mad at the brother, big and gruff as he be. But he's just too much *manimal* with a big ol' butt, big ol' body, and big ol' voice. He's always taking steps with them big ol' feet, and suckin' up *big* oxygen. Makes me nervous. Always brooding. Chaz ain't Facey's future. But recently . . . I've discovered something."

"Yes, Columbus . . ."

"Let's see . . . how do I put this *discreetly?*"

"Ya can't even *spell* 'discreetly,' so just spit it."

"Let's just say that when the native is restless, homey, and trust me on this, even the *horses* flee in fear. This brother's vine, it's . . . prehistoric! I almost expected to see *Tarzan* swingin' from it Just *ah-h-he-e-e-ah-h*, glidin' from one trunk thigh to the other!"

"Easy, baby. You're talking to a celibate queer, here."

"Please! Are ya chargin' for it, now? *Sell-a-bit?* Baby boy, ya can't even give it away!"

"So, what *else* is going on?" Ty asked.

David, however, was too busy *talking dick* to answer. "Listen to me! I'm talkin' 'bout record book bozack here! This was some *Ripley's Believe It or Not* type cock. Ridiculous dick! I seen it up close. I've scoped it, watched it do Slinky tricks. Every part of me winced! He couldn't be *doin'* Facey with it, could he?"

LOS ANGELES

Meanwhile, Face wanted to expand his budding thespian thing. So he flew to the West Coast with Claudio to see and be seen.

"Like it or not, Gloss Angeles is the spot pretty people pimp their potential," Face said.

The two rented a Mercedes and cruised Sunset. Conquering L.A. was always part of the Grand Depina Plan in his quest for total world domination. When flying on First Class Smack Airlines, there wasn't a part written Face didn't feel he could play. He'd accepted a couple of small roles as "male decoration" in some independent films, and it made him hunger for more. He was always chronically lousy at auditions. But one coveted role in a soon-to-be-major director's indie flick seemed picture-perfect for him. It wasn't the lead, but a potential breakout part in a drama.

He'd heard the talk about the pretty boy who hit the mother lode for being *only that*. Depina was determined. Almost as much as he wanted to fix, he wanted to show the world his chops. He read and reread with the kind of edginess needed for the part. Then, he actually did a pretty good screen test. Still, it was expected a Big Name Actor or hot newcomer would be the chosen player in the end. But the director had an aesthetic crush on him.

The rest is Lucky Pretty Boy history.

Face portrayed a conflicted young man, a hustler and a weasel who gyps a small-time hood, who in turn takes vengeance. In the end, Depina's character is responsible for his own mother's death.

It was a role he was born to play.

BROOKLYN, 1960

Two years after Mattie and Fonzy Depina jumped the broom, they discovered she had a rare blood disease, making pregnancy a dangerous affair. But Mattie loved Alphonze and desperately wanted to bear him a child. She was stubborn. She was willful and this was *her* sacrifice to make.

Mattie didn't tell her husband until the sixth month. Alphonze was furious and frightened. He pushed her against a wall, and suddenly she was bleeding. She panicked, thought she'd miscarried.

Like a madman on fire, Alphonze Depina rushed her to the ER. Things turned chaotic in the labor room. She was crying, breathing, crying, bleeding, crying, screaming, crying, and pushing to give the world a shiny new star.

It seemed as if giving birth was her one true mission, and a painful and unexpected mission it would become. Though, the baby was small, three months premature, the immediate concern shifted back to Mattie. There was so much blood; so many hands and bodies scrambling around her. In the end, not love nor doctor and nurses could save her.

Mattie would die in childbirth.

Alphonze Depina would be inconsolable. Though his son was strikingly beautiful, he wanted no part of "the little murderer."

Alphonze thought of smothering it, snuffing out its life as *it* had his beauteous Mattie's. *Flames.* Eventually he dropped *it* off at his sister's and disappeared into the sanctuary of alcohol, then, in time, hard-core smack. Alphonze never stopped loving Matilda or blaming the child he'd forever need to believe caused her death.

Flames. Bounced like an unwanted kickball from place to hard-luck place, Face never had a real foundation or any sense of permanence. *Flames.* Being exceedingly pretty drew others to him, but the child learned never to rely on anything, or *anyone*, or any feeling hanging around and existing for the long run. All friends, family, lovers—people in general—had expiration dates. *Flames.* Ironically, the intensity of his most memorable relationships lasted roughly *six months*. Such was the nature of things. *Flames.*

LOS ANGELES

Face had three scenes, one requiring emotional pyrotechnics.

Since his arrival in L.A. he'd been trying to wean himself away from heroin's seductive teat. But the pain coiled inside him, weakening his charm, making him nauseous and withdrawn. A day without smack was a day too long and distressing. What he needed was a little speed-ball, just to take off the edge . . . *Just one*, he thought, *and I can do this shit.*

When he strode back onto the set, his eyes were green windows, cracked by the telltale vandals of coke and smack. He stood with legs heavy as rocks, calling on strength, willing his brain into focus.

Sometimes all a man has left to *trust* are his bones. He trusts them to guide him, push him forth, and suddenly he's walking, talking, putting his own Personality Light Show until no one knows he's a crumbling fraud. Face did that shit to remarkable effect. Most *functioning* junkies do.

In that pivotal scene, the *lying* character he played had come home to find his mother, dead, murdered in her front yard.

It was a hard scene to depict. The script required a degree of depth, emotional surrender, and yes, real tears. And so, seeing this mother figure lying there, stilled by *his* lie, he began to cry. He stooped and roared. He slobbered in savage guttural grunts. He raged and wailed, he babbled in smears of snotty chatter. He cried, screeched, and he lamented the most brilliant tears a half-black, bisexual, closeted junkie had ever dared to cry, on screen.

But was it *acting* or was it something closer to a public breakdown?

Those sounds he made, those rants, howls, and caws of the heart, they were *outside of human*. He was more authentic than Brando, Pacino, Dean, or Denzel. Few men ever had the balls to reveal *that kind* of emotive intimacy.

He could only play that scene once. Luckily once was more than enough.

"Cut! Beautiful, Facey! Just beautiful. That's a print!"

But the wild tears didn't stop for Face. Every crippled feature in his aspect darkened, reddened, and wept. He crawled into a small fetal ball, and wept uncontrollably.

Witnessing this very real breakdown, and fearing for Face's sanity, a co-star ran over and tried to provide a comforting arm. But Face didn't want to be touched. How dare he or any of those others Hollywood motherfuckers touch him! He swung his arms wildly and he howled, "GET YOUR MOTHER-

FUCKIN' . . . . HANDS OFF ME! YOU AIN'T . . . YOU AIN'T . . . YOU AIN'T . . . MY DADDY!"

From deep within, he found the strength to rise from the floor and then he bounded away from the set.

In an attempt to lighten the atmosphere, the Assistant Director shouted to the crew:

"Those fuckin' New York actors!"

But this was not acting, New York or otherwise. This was Face Depina's blue moan, personified. This was the unleashing of a long-restrained primal cry.

Face Depina was, at his core, a user. In rare and coldly sober interludes, even *he* knew that. Only, this time, he'd used and abused his tender, unformed memory of the mother he'd never cried for. But this one particular act of using burned like a branding iron. How does a boy, or a man, any *real man* recover from that?

Yet for that fit of naked emotion, the film critics love him.

Six months later, Pascal "Face" Depina received an Independent Spirit Award Nomination for Best Supporting Actor.

CHAPTER NINETEEN

Bluesy Love Songs

JANUARY 1991

When Browny made parole, there were no loving arms left to greet him. Juanita wasn't outside waiting in the parking lot with a fresh pot of greens, ham hocks, and a ride back to a warm Dream Street apartment. If Browny were to record the soundtrack of his life, the title song would have been: "*Why My Arias Always Gotta Sound Like the Fuckin' Blues, Yo?*"

Making matters worse, the all-too-alluring call of *that rock* beckoned.

For the longest time, Depina was away, giving pretty face to crazy fly exotic places. Browny could never find him to hit him up for cash. He saw no choice but to sing in the subways for pocket change.

"Yo! Man. You got a voice. Why you down here, actin' like some Step-'n'-Fetchit fool?" a stranger barked.

Where the fuck is Face? I need to see that motherfucka! But it behooved Browny to sing because singing brought quick dollars and quick cash bought quick rocks. He had this hot new career going on with the rock. Even the other crackheads were beginning to call him "Rock Star."

Faison lost himself a little more each day. Was it one month or two before he was begging for loans, selling off his few belongings? Gone were his raggedy Mustang, his friends, his trustworthiness, a job, then another job, then another. None of it meant anything. Nothing mattered except that fucking *hunger.*

He often called Ty, using Trick's memory to secure cash. The cash was for the hunger, for the crack, and then the cash was for the help to quit the hunger for crack.

MESSAGE FROM TYRONE HUNTER LEFT ON FACE DEPINA'S ANSWERING MACHINE
APRIL 1991

"Listen, Pascal. I don't know the deal with you and Browny and I don't want to. But I finally got him to a clinic, and now he's AWOL. Damn fool seems to think that only you can help him. Everything's falling apart for him! He seems to think your life is intact. If ya got any decency left, and if you owe him like he claims, please don't turn your fuckin' back on him! 'Cuz I can't help him anymore. I'm out."

Face had assumed that whatever the lingering after-effects of prison, Browny could drink or smoke them away. But Browny was *not going away.* There was that phone call from Ty, and other things, too. Like Browny would suddenly *appear*—outside a corner store Face frequented or in the middle of Central Park during a fashion shot. Sometimes he was in a crowd, and sometimes he was all alone. Sometimes Face thought he'd only imagined Browny; that somehow the past or *his high* was fucking with him, playing with his mindset. But no. Browny *was there*, staring at him, smoking a borrowed cigarette, saying nothing.

So Face decided it was time to take him upstairs to his digs and buy his pathetic ass off, fucking once and for all! He wrote a check, a *nice* check.

But for Browny cash was not sufficient. "You tryna buy me? Nah. I ain't goin' out like that. A few bills, huh . . . for three years in hell? And it *was* hell, Pass-cow. I ain't the same big, tall, strappin' buck as you. Yo! Why was *you* shittin' bricks anyway? Huh? Was ya scared of the sound of them steel doors closin' you inside? Did ya figga you was too pretty for that shit?

"Scared ya wouldna survived, huh? Bet ya thought they'd like up, hold ya down, and take turns raping yo pretty ass . . . well, guess what? It don't matter if you pretty."

"Look, it's too bad you had to go through that. I never meant for—"

"SHUT THE FUCK UP, AND PAY ATTENTION! You ever hafta put on a fuckin' halter top? You ever have one real fight in your fuckin' life worth fightin' to the death for, huh? Well, between some con's poundin' fists red with your blood and them kicks to your insides something clicks, man. You realize, I'm gonna die like this. And for what? 'cause some motherfucker wants my ass? My short, thick, black piece of ass! What's a straight man's ass, anyway? His last piece of pride? Do it make him a punk if somebody take it? Why? Wasn't like somebody was battlin' for me or my ass to survive on the outside. So what I was fightin' tooth and nail for, when it was gonna get me took anyway, bloody or not?

"Men in prison, they ain't into that warm, fuzzy shit. Foreplay don't exist, except for *you* suckin' *his* dick." Browny paused long enough to wipe his mouth. "That first time hurt, man! And it never did *stop* hurtin'."

"You wanna know what kept me sane and alive? *You*, Pass-cow. You, and the future beyond that big, dark beast of a motherfucka drummin' down on me. I had me a future on the other side of that razor wire. That was all I needed to keep breathin'.

"I seen boys stop breathin', stop fightin' altogether. Getting' they jugular slashed or a rusty shank stuck in they scared shitless chest. I seen a young boy, even prettier than you, hangin' from his own sheet because he just couldn't take another beatin', another pair of women's panties, another man, another dick after diseased dick rammed up his cryin', helpless ass.

"Yo! Now you wanna offer me a check, and say we even? *I don't think so, Pass-cow!* You just don't' get it, do you? It ain't about the money, fuckin' asshole. I want a *life*. A *career*."

"I ain't God, Browny! I can't just snap my fuckin' fingers, and presto, you get a life!"

"I don't see why not. Yo! Ya played God before when ya guilted me into sayin' those four little please fuck *my* ass words: 'The stash is mine'!"

Depina almost wanted to laugh. Browny was the *ultimate* sucker. *Stupid, stupid motherfucker! Yeah*, you *copped* to it. *You got in the damn car, and shit happened. Didn't take much beggin', did it? Yeah, I said I'd hook you up. I was desperate, you crazy negro! All that time on the street, and you still don't know when you bein' played. Fuckin' hemorrhoid, that's all you are! Startin' to make me real uncomfortable. Need to have your naggin' milk-bump ass lanced. I know people, too. You don't wanna fuck with me, Browny!*

"Know what, Pass-cow? Once, when I was tryna build myself up into a big, strong *man* like you, I ordered the Charles Atlas kit from the back of a comic book."

"Yeah-yeah. What's your point?" Face asked, his buffed arms folded, his long legs spread wide in a defensive stance.

"Of course, Pass-cow. Yo! Wouldn't wanna waste yo time, you bein' one of them in-demand type motherfuckas. See, I got the kit, but it was just a lotta pictures of half-naked Atlas workin' out, and some instructions and shit. I felt ripped the fuck off! But they kept sendin' me more shit. Same shit. So I quit. Stopped payin' through the ass for some dumb-ass photos. Yo! Now, *you* pay attention. This is the good part: Mr. Charles Atlas, or somebody with his muscle camp, wrote me a letter 'bout debts. They was tryna shame me, sayin' how a *real man* pays his debts. Then they went all Oriental on my ass.

"They got this ancient Chinese sayin' that the worst thing any real man could do was to *lose his honor.* Without that, a man ain't nothing. They called it 'losing face'!"

"Yeah, so and . . ."

"Don't you get it, fool? You don't attend yo debts, boy. Ya ain't got no honor! You ain't no man! You, Pascal Punk-ass Depina, done LOST FACE, motherfucka!"

Depina eyeballed Browny, wishing he possessed the supernatural power to make him disappear, to make the world forget there ever *was* a Browny.

Little black singin' Sambo motherfucker! I could take his thick ass down, right here and now. Squash him like a fuckin' cockroach, 'cause that's all he is. I wish his little black ass fit in my microwave!

Still, that term *losing face* buzzed like an annoying black fly in Depina's aggravated ear—a fly he couldn't shoo away. As Depina phoned his agent to try to make *things* happen, Browny walked around the place, looking at all the new fancy shit that could've, should've, would've probably been his: the big screen TV, the top-of-the-line stereo system, the plush, Italian leather furniture, and that fly-ass view of Manhattan staring back in its steely majesty.

Depina hung up the phone, took a deep breath, wrung his long, elegant hands, and hit Browny with his latest plan.

"Listen, man, there's a role in this independent film I'm workin' on. It's got a nightclub scene that needs a singer. Now, hear me, Faison, *I can't say it's yours.* It's just my fourth film, and I ain't got that kind of power. But Benny, my agent, is gonna represent you this one time as a favor. He'll pull some strings, get you an audition, and the rest, pal, that's up to you."

Every feature in Browny's face lit up brighter than the Rockefeller Center Christmas tree.

"Yo! An open door . . . that's all I want."

As it turned out, Browny sang magnificently. But he wasn't *the right type.* The director hired him for his "incredibly melodious voice," only to use it as a dub for another, more photogenic performer, which turned out to be Face Depina.

Browny was livid. Homeboy was ready to go to the cops, the authorities, the press, to whoever might hear his story of how rising model-actor Face Depina was a dope addict and a punk ass half-a-fag, minus the balls to come forth and admit it. Depina realized his best defense was a good offense.

"Look! Don't be sweatin' me. I'm tryna make things happen, but it takes time, man. You say ya don't want charity. Bet, I can respect that. But stay here. Crush place, right? Plenty of room, lots of fringes. I'll make you my assistant. You can answer the phones, check my fan mail, whatever. I'll pay four bills a week, plus free rent and food. Hey, you can even take the money, pool it together, rent some studio time . . . Hell, you can record a CD, market it yourself. Sound like a plan?"

What it *sounded like* was Depina running scared. But hell! Browny had seen, slept, lived in, and been kicked out of far worse places. That fancy loft had *potential*, and so did Facey's plan.

"Bet. But only . . . for a few months . . . just until I got enough to do my thing. You know what, man? I might just have to change my opinion of you, Pass-cow."

"That's anotha thing . . . if you livin' in my crib, eatin' my eats, and receivin' a check with *my* name on top, you're gonna respect me! Try gettin' used to callin' me Face, aiight?"

Browny wasn't about to let this opportunity slip by, so he decided he could manage that. Actually, an entire family of misfits was harbored under Depina's roof. David, of course, spent a lot of time there, at least when Face was around.

One warm June morning, after a long night's freak, David reentered Depina's apartment to prepare for the Gay Pride Parade. In two hours, he created magic, transforming himself from a brown, downtown, club kid to a gold, copper, and gloriously platinum-wigged temptress.

Sometime during David's *tedious girl's work*, Depina returned and grabbed a quick shower. When he emerged, wet and naked to the waist, the ripe pacifiers on his chest resembling cinnamon Jujubes, the sight just about floored David.

In all his painted-up platinum regalia, Face, on first impression, thought that David was some freaky female intruder. But then David softly vamped.

"Oh my! Mr. Depina. Can't a girl have *any* privacy?" Then he changed voices. "Not bad, huh, Facey? I know. I see you're breathless."

"David? Da-a-amn! That's *you* under all that?"

"Yes, tís I, my love. I'm on my way to the parade. I really wish you would go . . ."

"Can't. Glitter ain't my scene," Depina quipped. Those ripe, brazen nipples entirely stole David's vision, not to mention his libido. "Besides, that damn queer-fest lasts all day and night. Ain't you got work to do?"

"Not to worry. I've picked three outfits for you." David laid out the selection of clothes he thought Face should wear that evening to a fashion awards show.

Still, Depina's nipples were whispering silent love notes.

"Know what would look really good on you, Facey?"

"What? The suede? The leather?"

"Me."

"A suede the color of your skin. I get it."

"No, I don't think you do. Remember when you hired me? You wanted a consultant, a stylist. But later, you wanted me to teach you a new word a day."

"Yeah. I remember. Yesterday's word was *insouciant.* It means cool, nonchalant, like me, right?"

"Very good. Well, today's word is *the word.* C'mon. Let's go to your bedroom and *spread it*, baby."

"David. I like havin' your little fly ass 'round here, 'cause you help me look fly, and I need to look fly, so I appreciate that shit. In fact, I'm kinda surprised how much I like your fly ass. In fact, I like most every queer bone in your little body, Davy. I just don't want *my bone* in it. Aiight?"

Color David Donatello Richmond devastated.

"You wounded me, Facey. You think I'm too delicate, to femme, don't you?"

Depina didn't want to say yes, so he kept quiet.

"Never judge *this book* by its smooth copper cover, Facey. Hey, I'm a dancer. You give me one chance between those sheets, and I will *turn you out* with my rhythm!

Depina took one hard look at him and broke into a booming round of laughter as he walked out of the room. Once the laughing ceased, Face peeked his head inside.

"Yo! Before you go, I need a touch-up, Davy, or whoever you are this week. You see these lines here under my eyes, they ain't pretty. People don't wanna see that."

"You mean *right now*? But I don't wanna be late!" Then, seeing the slightest upset claim Depina's mug, David quickly snapped, "OK, OK, I'll do it."

Touching Depina became the only fodder David needed to erect new exotic fantasies in his flaming mind.

It happens beneath a radiant sun, on a beach in Martinique, where Facey lies luxuriously along a mossy cliff. Ah! The ocean breeze rouses the peaks of his nipples. Like Facey, they burn so easily in the sun. He applies the elixir I created especially for him, smoothing it into his shoulders, his chest, and his belly where moisture collects like a pool of gold, and oh! I detect a stirring in his tight, black Speedo. He skims his hand along his striking pecan torso, massaging the slick fluid into one tightening areola. He slowly traces his hand down inside his suit. And I, shivering like a frond in a tropical storm, I watch him, as ever so slowly he glides his hand along his waistband. Then that suit descends down browning hips, thighs, knees, and he lets it fall to the green moss. Woo! I'm all *wet* by then. But suddenly his feet leave the moss, his thighs and chest become perpendicular. And Facey, being so tall, so lean, and long . . . I think he's going to . . . my, damn! He's going to suck his own . . . yes! A slow drop of liquid falls to those bee-stung lips. Just as he's prepared to receive his tip, the sun streams down in warm, honeyed light, and I, his watcher, make myself known. A sweat-bead forms at the lips of his excitement, and his sigh rises like a song on the breeze.

And Facey Depina sees me standing there. And gravity begs those long legs to the ground. And he smiles that sultry smirk. With no words between us, I walk to where beauty lies, and I fall, toppling to its chest, belly, and hard slippery prick. I'm warm and wet as his long greasy dick coasts between my thighs. We kiss slow and electric. We slide and moan as we hump pole to hard and glistening pole. Oh! My dancing legs spread in grand jetés. I look at him, and he knows my grotto is a warm, safe, and welcoming haven.

When his span journeys through me, it doesn't hurt at all. Once inside me, my hurting, his hurting, all the hurting, finally stops. A turbulent tide washes through my love-hungry soul, and I finally know the feel of him. Oh! Birds sing from wavering limbs of Banyan trees. All rivers flow into the boiling sea, and the sea foams like we do into the clamoring Atlantic. "Yes! Facey! Yes!" The feel of him embedded inside me is so fuckin' sweet and right and necessary that I bury my head inside his flawless pecan chest and silently weep.

Yes, fantasy can be an elixir for the lonely, unrequited lovers of the world.

But Face Depina had his own motto about sex with men: "The bigger the dick, the bigger the pussy."

Chaz, for instance. Though he might've been blessed with a *Superpenis Erectus*, he rarely used it to fuck. A contented submissive, he lived for the thrill of the whip, the agony of the victorious fist. He reserved his acres of ass and valleys of machismo for only the most robust of dominants. And Depina fit the bill.

Whenever Face breezed back into town, it became an event. That emptiness in the pit of Chaz's being would suddenly fill up. Depina's lean, shiny presence was his needle, and the junkie in Chaz would swoon as soon as Face entered *The War Room*.

Leathered-down, keyed-up, and flying in his skin, the High Hard One was still in good and sturdy working order. Face's chest would become a beating drum, his body, a seismic boom of driving bronze, his dick erect, thrusting through muscle, skin, and sweat. By then, The Williams Log was hard as iron, a mast wavering high from the fuck and the fuck's crescendo.

Flying and feeling strangely tactile, Face had a habit of touching himself, flicking his own nipples, grabbing his own ass while slipping into Chaz with forceful, jolting jabs. Submission was never better or wetter. But whatever the force of the fuck, it barely registered with Chaz.

"Punch it. Damn it. Hit me. Hard. Shit. Where's your force, you soft mothafucka? Hurt me!" he'd call out like a wildly different kind of creature, a creature addicted to its own slaughter.

One afternoon, when neither Face nor Chaz nor any other Depina hangers-on were around, David talked Faison into having his first facial.

"You *do* have a rich, dark, pretty complexion, black man. You just need a little exfoliation, that's all."

"Exfoliation? What the hell beatin' off got to do with my skin?"

"Honey? Were you always *so this?* I mean, so hopelessly, retardedly, grotesquely dense? Uncouth, yes. Ya never had any couth whatsoever. In school, all ya had was a mouth and those damn Farina braids that looked like they hadn't seen a comb or pomade since—"

"Bitch, I'll kick your—"

"Now, now . . . calm down, boyfriend! It *does* get better. I'll say this only one time, so you need to listen: Faison, you are so much more than a rock and a pipe. You bigger than that. God musta looked down and said, 'I'll kiss this one's throat so he'll sing like an angel.' Back in school, I had no doubt *you'd* be the one to shine. Well, stars shine, baby. Black holes don't. You a star, and you owe it to yourself to stop acting so defeated. If you ever leave that crack pipe alone, you'll be who you were *born* to be. You got some shine to you. Baby, your star quality just needs some work. Today, I'll start with your skin."

"You know what, David? You ain't half-bad for a little fruit. And I mean that shit."

CHAPTER TWENTY

A Season of Clarity and Blur

FEBRUARY 1990

Nelson Mandela was free after rotting twenty-seven years in prison. It was a time for jubilation.

On top of that, yet another singer had covered the song Ty wrote as a teen, and two other rap artists had recently sampled it, with platinum results. *Hunter luck* had struck again. Ty could not believe he was able to live quite comfortably off some freak beginner's luck. But those frequent royalties proved mighty sweet indeed.

Harlem was in the throes of gentrification, and the money enabled Ty to buy an apartment just off Striver's Row. Ty never acted like a black man with money, though. Ostentation was not his style. And so there were no jewels, no fly rides, no trophy sex, or high days and nights tripping on excess. He donated heavily to the GMHC, the United Negro College Fund, Meals-on-Wheels, the Red Cross, Hale House, and the Make-a-Wish-Foundation. Ty was nothing, if not charitable. And though neither David nor Browny were aware of it, Ty always put aside a little something for them, purchasing shares of blue-chip stocks in their names.

Was life fabu yet? From the outside, it seemed as if everything was mildy fabulous, but his interior felt deficient, his soul, empty.

A lifelong shutterbug, he took his camera to the streets on a mission to interview the city's downtrodden and disaffected. Victims of drug addiction, homelessness, and disease became the fruits of his new passion.

"What about *real* passion? You know, like a partner? Don't you want someone to share your life with?" David often hounded.

Davy wasn't wrong. At twenty-eight Tyrone was a man in sore need of getting laid.

"I seriously think you're undersexed, Ty. Lookin' like ya ain't had a decent blow job since Diana had a hit record!"

"Blow job? Not part of my new '90s vernacular. I'll settle for a mind job."

"Please. You'll nevuh meet a man with enough plumbing to reach *that* far, baby boy."

"A companion in the struggle would be hip. Well, besides your dizzy ass. I think a partner would be kinda doable. But that's a luxury, not a necessity, Duch."

Ty had taken some shots of Princess Diana when she visited Harlem's Hale House. She was holding a jittering little crack baby and everyone oohed and ahhed, *How brave!* A couple of those shots were published, and suddenly Tyrone became a *hot shit celebrity photographer* who was getting plum assignments to go out and schmooze with fifteen-minute cool ones in the hip-to-the-nanosecond downtown scene. It was either a part-time distraction or a slow death—he couldn't decide which, but he thought, *If it's got to be done, shouldn't someone do this shit cor-*

rectly? People have a need to know other people's business. There's a hunger for it.

Gossips were brazen bitches by definition, but Ty always tried to up that status.

He couldn't seem to *give away* a homeless photograph, or a story of an American Dream deferred. People didn't want to buy the *real* shit. People could see too much real, sordid, distressing shit in the city for free.

And so Tyrone Hunter became a kind of downtown dilettante, skulking around asking nonessential questions of nonessential people: Who's zooming who at 4:32 A.M. in the Cat Club's bathroom? Who was that blond on Grace Jones's arm, and *what duh hell* was she wearing? Who's disrespecting their twelve-step program, and what were they wearing for their public vomit? Who's stepping out on their old man with another man in a sedan? And just what were they *not* wearing? Who's hot, who's not, who's come out, who's back in the closet, who's strung out, doped out, played out, ovuh, and do we really care anymore what *they're* wearing?

It was another night of that stuff Ty termed "mindless megalomaniacal shit and tales from the metro maniacs." He slipped into his omnipresent leather coat, tossed his dreads into careless disarray, slid on the shades, and just as he headed out the door the phone rang. *Fuck it*, he thought. *The machine will pick up*.

"Hello. You've reached Ty Hunter. I'm most probably out doing good deeds and shit like that, so please leave your name and a coherent message, and I'll definitely holla back. Peace out."

On the other end, he heard no words, only breathing. Ty had no time for it. He was working on his mental mendacity-at-its-best mode. It was a special brand of fakeness he had to affect because, with all the turmoil around him, *Why should I really give a shit about your fuckin' stupid, wasted, shallow lives?*

He was *there* mentally, and had the night all scoped out . . . but then, that voice on the other side of the machine said its name sadly. Mr. Death was leaving another message.

That phone call was full of sordid, sad history.

Jimmy Lee "Razor" Morrisey had made more money than enemies, and more greens than Sylvia's famous Harlem eatery. When he walked his rooster's strut, you got the impression he'd seen one too many Eddie G. Robinson flicks. He was a broad caramel man, with a disturbingly large head. It was so large a dome word was Razor had to get his pimp hats custom-made. He never drove his Caddie, his New Yorker, or his new Mercedes S-Class. He was always chauffeured. Only two kinds of people existed in Razor's orbit: those who admired him, and those who were deathly afraid of him. He embodied power, juice, intimidation, and yes, much murderous intent. And he wore his prestige like a most fearsome sharkskin suit.

For Tyrone, a part of his naked heart would always belong to Trick. Trick's death never left him, nor had it settled itself into a dimmer, gentler memory in Tyrone's psyche. In the years since, it became more like a sensation of being robbed. There wasn't a day, night, or carefree moment when Trick Brown's demise did not wound him slowly. Once, Ty had a dazzlingly imperfect smile, where everything dark in his face would just blaze with brilliant happy light. That dazzle was gone, and that smile had long diminished. Razor had swiped it, just as he'd stolen the light from thousands of smiles before and since.

A large thing had been taken from him, and Tyrone never forgot or forgave its taker. Years went by, and still he paced inside a silent rage over Razor's lethal hand in Trick's death.

Yet, there was little he could do about it. Or was there?

Ty rarely left home without his camera. It was his third eye, his best eye. He photographed New York life in all its chiaroscuros of light and dark: A homeless man sleeping in front of the Met, a debutante ball on the West Side juxtaposed with an old woman in tattered clothes eating from a garbage can. Contrasts were the true stories of the city.

Harlem too, was a study in contrasts as the doers and workers kept rapid time beside the casualties of crack and heroin. Bodies were stockpiling, and Morrisey's rep as a major scourge around town was peaking.

Was it fate's accident that Ty saw him stepping out of a local numbers-friendly bar? Ty's loaded camera seemed to howl, *Shoot! Shoot him!* His hands literally shook as he brought that face into focus. He managed to snap a half-roll. Back home, as he developed the proofs, the face of that murderer came into view, and Tyrone's hatred only intensified. How smug and sure and Teflon-coated the garish gold rings on every finger, the fool's gold smile.

Just like the image of Razor's thuggish mug, within that instant, an idea came clearly into focus. It seemed predestined. Had Tyrone gone to school, earned his degree in journalism for this very moment of clear-eyed realization? *Damn it! Do the world a favor. Kill him with words and pictures.* Right then, Tyrone hatched a plan for an exposé on the dominant drug lords in the community.

The story received buzz after he sold his words and pictures to an underground rag. Ty then met with a producer, and soon the story appeared on *A Current Affair*, where Tyrone testified on what a few foul fat cats could do to ravage a community. His face was shadowed, but people paid attention.

Trick's ghost warned him: *Leave it alone, Ty. You the poetry man. Ain't no poetry in messin' with the Big Boys . . .*

But for once Tyrone ignored him.

Along the way, he discovered something even *he* had not bargained for.

Morrisey's family tree was more twisted and gnarled than an arthritic hand. Ty had suddenly, accidentally, stumbled over a root of this tree, and in doing so, he uncovered a few facts that could destroy Faison's chance at a happier existence.

Hard-headed bastard! Didn't I tell you to let it rest?

But the righteous, crusading reporter in his bones would not let it rest. Tyrone went straight to the source: Juanita Lewis.

"It's true, isn't it? Razor . . . he's your first cousin . . . and you never . . ."

"Yes. Yes, damn it! It's true. But please, please don't tell Browny," she begged—and Juanita was not a beggar by nature. "You don't get to choose who your family be. I'm ashamed. Been ashamed of him even before he started killin' his own people. I'm the one who started our neighborhood watch, remember? Believe me, Jimmy Lee ain't no friend or real family of mine. But if you told Faison, Tyrone, that would just kill him. It would kill us."

"But Razor killed Browny's only brother, Juanita! He killed Trick! And the slimy motherfucker just walked away from it. He's killing half of Harlem right now, and people walk by seeing and *not* seeing it! I swear, I'm not tryna hurt you. I like you. You're *good* for Browny. But maybe if the truth came out . . ."

"Destroy Jimmy Lee! Go on! I won't give a motherfuck! But, what about Browny? Ya just gonna end up destroying *us* in the process! Is *that* what you want, huh?" Then Juanita went in for the kill. "Don't you think *Trick* wanna see his brother settled down and happy . . . for once?"

It was a trying decision. Tyrone always felt just a little responsible for Browny. It wasn't so much a love relationship as it was an onus, a debt to Trick.

"OK, Juanita. It's not my secret to tell. But before he hears it in the streets somewhere, maybe he oughta hear it from you. He deserves *that* much."

Ty thought of all the consequences, then he boldly forged

ahead—without using real names. Still, it was evident that Razor was his main focal point.

Morrisey never bothered to read the news, let alone the city's underground papers. But the word did get back to him via one of his underlings.

"Tyrone Hunter? Somebody tell me, who the *fuck* is that motherfucka?"

"Ain't nobody really. Some faggot at a newspaper, that's all," a henchman offered.

"Well, he don't know me. But I'll tell you what, he's 'bout to . . ." Morrisey huffed, lighting the fat end of his Cuban.

Shortly thereafter, Ty was heading toward the subway when some thuggish cat approached him.

"Yo? You Tyrone Hunter, that writer?"

"Who wants to know?"

A black car with tinted windows quickly pulled onto the sidewalk. The back window rolled down and *that mug* he'd seen in his darkroom demanded, "Time we meet. Get in."

The thug forced Tyrone into the car and drove it away in a squeal of rubber.

"You got some beef with me, fool?" Razor's voice was as big as his head.

"Why would I?" Ty asked, shuddering in his skin.

"Now, see, *that's* what I wanna know. 'Cause word is, you's just a faggot. I got somethin' big and hard for yo ass. Ya might not like it, though," Razor joked, his deadly serious, seriously large head expanding. All the while he was stroking not his deadly cock, but the handle of a deadlier Glock. "What's yo beef? I don't know you, boy. Don't *wanna* know you, if you's tryna put me out of bidniz! Is it like dat, huh?"

Ty feared his odious ass. He feared for his own life. But the quiet wrath he'd maintained for years far outweighed his fear.

"I don't know what you talkin' 'bout, bruh. I'm just a man,

tryna do his job, that's all," he said, breathing in easy waves. Though he was beginning to sweat, he tried not to show any signs of stress.

"Well, the only *job* a faggot can do right is a *blow job*!" Morrisey rasped, as his boys laughed higher and giddier than most faggots ever dared to laugh. "See, that's the shit I don't understand. Why a weak-ass bitch like *you* wanna knock heads with somebody like me? Is you workin' for the *man?*"

"Nah. I'm working for myself. It's just a little part-time job, man. That's all. It don't pay much. I'm sorry if it upset you. I . . . I was just tryna to get ahead."

"I'm sure you get plenty *a head*. But why one black man tryna hold another black man down? See, I don't play that shit. You scared of me? You *should* be! Don't worry. I ain't gonna hurt ya, yet. I'm a bidniz man. Just wanted to see who you is, and let this little ride be yo warnin'. You keep writin' shit I don't like, and yo queer bitch-ass will be dealt with. Do we understand each other, punk-bitch? Huh?"

Tyrone Hunter shook his head. All the while, he was thinking of his next attack. With Razor's threat complete, the door opened, and Tyrone was pushed from the car as it neared the pier where working boys strolled and sedans slowed to barter before letting them inside.

"I just dropped the little bitch off in Fag's Paradise," Razor laughed as the car sped away.

Tyrone, though bruised and shaken, escaped with his life intact. But instead of mortal fear, he was overwhelmed by a kind of runner's high. Big and bad as Razor was, Ty could smell the fear one *meaningless faggot* had put inside the cocky air he breathed.

Nevertheless, that particular nightmarish ride had a sobering effect. In lieu of further stories, Ty wrote long words, took compelling pictures, and sent them to his congressman, both senators, and the district attorney.

In his own way, Tyrone became the catalyst in Razor's decline.

Within a few months, the tyrant had toppled. It was classic that he went down the way Capone had fallen. The IRS snagged his delinquent ass for failure to pay over eleven years of back taxes.

Razor strutted his bad-ass act a little too boldly on Rikers Island. An argument came too quickly and deadly when he was stuck with a shiv in his cell, and he bled out, and nobody cared.

That was the phone message from Mr. Death that stopped Ty in his doorway: Razor was dead. Maybe no one at Rikers Island cared, but Ty cared plenty. And when he finally did head out for the night, the air smelled a little fresher, the streets felt a little safer, and the ghosts in Tyrone's head haunted just a little less loudly.

DECEMBER 1990

Though his columns had grown in popularity, Ty felt underused. He decided to quit. But as he walked into his editor's office to shout the news, he ran into The One.

Blur.

Smart. Ambitious. Beautiful. Deceptive.

Blur Antonelli was a new jack law student, hired to cover the legal beat. When Ty saw him, he was thunderstruck. Not since the sad day he'd first laid eyes on Face Depina had he seen a more staggering arrangement of beige architecture.

Black and Italian features made Ty's eyes cling to Blur in awe of what lush beauty two races could accomplish together. His skin was not the preferred cup of rich hot chocolate, yet Tyrone was sinking inside its soft taupe shadings. His hair hung in loose dreads and fell like thick chestnut cocks to his unusually wide shoulders. His deep hazel eyes pierced Tyrone's discriminating core.

Suddenly, Ty's emotions were clumsy acrobats, tumbling, falling, fumbling, sliding around. He found himself wondering: *Are you here for me? Could you be the one? Shit! Baby, baby, please be the one!*

"Tyrone. I'd like you to meet Blur. Blur Antonelli," his editor said.

Well, hello! He's flawless. Not very tall, is he? Maybe Trick's height. Diz-zamn, you's a fine boy! God! Is there a mind behind all that fineness? If there is, I might just relax my rules about fallin' in dig with you smug-ass pretty boys. Please, please . . . do NOT open your mouth and squawk like a fool, 'cause I'm kinda feelin' you.

"Tyrone is one of our contributing editors," the bossman said.

"Well, hey, Tyrone!" Blur said, shaking Ty's hand rigorously. There was a trace of genuine excitement in his voice. "I read four papers every morning. But honestly, man, your column makes my day. Great stuff. It's perspicacious and consistently poignant. I digs, man. I digs."

Sometimes, the color in a person's voice turns on like a beautiful green light . . .

"Thanks, man. Good to meet you," Ty said, still holding Blur's strong hand. And all the while he wondered: *Who is this strangely beautiful cat, looking like this, talking like that, and rubbing my cranium with a mouthful of lovely?*

In a nanosecond's all-important *joint check*, Ty's eyes darted down—faded jeans worn at the crotch. He noted more than a suggestion of a piece. Blur Antonelli wore no draws, no boxers or briefs whatsoever.

You're a nasty boy, ain't you? Looking like somebody's casual dreadlocked sun god. And just how did you manage to use "perspicacious" and "poignant" in the same damn sentence, and somehow not make that shit sound even vaguely pretentious? Exotic name. Are you real, or something out of a dream . . . lugging ample penis, extensive syntax, AND you're a fan of my stuff? Oh, my goodness! Nuts up!

Ty was even more *intrigued* as he and Blur often found themselves meeting face to face, belly-to-belly as they quickly squeezed past each other in the narrow office hallways. With each encounter came a smile and a slightly naughty physical twinge. Each had already mentally undressed the other. Hell, Ty had already rubbered and fellated Blur between those mental sheets, and they'd yet to have a *real* conversation.

Then it came, that first minor heartbreak. Tall, rugged, and . . . *blond?* He'd dropped by to see Blur in the workplace. The two yapped it up, talking and laughing like intimate idiots. Ty immediately resented that handsome blonde's tall, stately, athletic ass.

But Ty was nothing if not *cool* in his carnal pursuits. He showed no sign of interest until he felt 99 percent sure that the attraction was mutual.

Come six o'clock, Ty collected his work, grabbed his coat, and headed for the elevator. Seeing Ty leaving, Blur quickly closed shop and made it to the elevator before the doors opened.

"Going my way?" he joked.

"I'm not sure yet, Blur. It *is Blur,* right?" Ty asked coolly.

"Yeah. Well, that's what everyone calls me. Actually, my name's Roger Antonelli Daniels. I'm a product of the whole Italian moms, black daddy, free-love hippie trip. Antonelli is my *mom's* maiden name," he explained. "Yeah, I know, I don't quite look either one. But I'm an Italianigga," he said as if he would never tire of defining himself.

Even though Tyrone hadn't asked his pedigree, it did save time.

"Right now, you're probably wondering about the *Daniels* part," Blur continued. "It's the name on my birth certificate, but I rarely use it."

Ding! The doors opened and the two stepped inside. Ty knew talking about one's *self* was most everyone's favorite subject.

"Does *Blur* have any significance?" Ty asked as he pushed the lobby button, wanting to keep their flow.

"I ran track in high school. Don't wanna brag, but I *still hold* the school record for the one-hundred-yard dash. Coach used to say, 'When you run, Antonelli, you're a freakin' blur zooming toward that finish line!' Soon 'Blur' became the nick, the name, the thing people seemed to know me by most."

"Interesting. So, uh, Blur . . . you're known for your speed, huh?" Ty asked with a touch of innuendo.

"Uh, yeah. But some things are better with modulation." He grinned, flashing the sexiest smile since, since, ever!

Good fuckin' answer, Mr. Blur Antonelli. Now, all ya gotta do is casually slide your hand along your crotch, and damn it, we can just let our soul song begin.

But Blur didn't grab the dick. Instead, he suggested they grab cappuccinos at the Black Sheep. The vibe between them was easy and comfortable. Blur was a brother with whom Ty could easily riff. He liked the warm glint in Blur's eyes, the rich sound of Blur's voice, which was a lightly sensitive baritone. Everything Blur said was like listening to brand new music, even when that music was blue.

"I've got the most dysfunctional family still raising hell on the planet, man," Blur confessed. "We started out in the 'burbs. Then the parents split. My mother's one cool chick. She was Madonna before Madonna was born. Maybe she was rebelling against Catholicism, or maybe she just had a thing for black men—married three of them. The last one was this bum with a perpetual hard-on. We were enemies from the start. I kept waiting for my *real father* to ride in on a big, black horse and rescue me. But he was a weak man."

Blur called his father, "a serial impregnator of the world's exotic women," explaining to Ty that he had a half-Swedish half-brother, whom he called "the Swigga." A half-Korean sister—"the Korigga"—and presently, the old man was down under, spawning a new tribe of "Austriggas."

"Seriously, I've got a mess of half-brothers and sisters. Two brothers I barely know are on lockdown, another's strung out on rock. I've got the cutest little sister you've ever seen. She's my heart. That's my *main* sib, Sabina, my bright tangerine girl." He smiled, though his eyes held a quiet sadness. "Besides myself, she's the only one who went to college. But . . . something really, really horrible happened to her. During her first semester." He swallowed hard and glanced into Tyrone's eyes, wondering if he could trust him. With one deep, soul-stirring look, he decided he could.

"See, she and some fast girl went to this club. Bina's not a party girl, and she didn't know what was out there. Well, she met some piece of shit, and he came on real strong. And her, being so new to dating, she didn't have the tools to reject him . . . and . . . and he raped her."

"Oh, my God, Blur! That *is* . . . horrible. Unfortunately, it's not so uncommon. But it's horrible," Ty said.

"You have to meet 'Bina. You can't really tell, but she's blind in one eye. It always made her sensitive and withdrawn. She's a real fragile girl, the last girl on earth who could handle something so fuckin' vicious! She hardly ever smiles anymore. After that, there was only one thing to for me to do: become a lawyer. A *prosecutor.* It's all I live for now, man. I just wanna bring some fucking justice back into this world."

Blur's story moved Tyrone.

There was something rare, shining, bordering on *heroic* about the dude. Unlike the others, so focused on the naked fact that Ty liked men, they'd forget to ask him about his own background. Blur wanted to know more.

"So, what's the deal with *you*, Tyrone? Somebody told me you were a kid actor. Then I heard songwriter. Someone else said poet, photographer, playwright? What the hell are you, really?"

"The *unknown* Gordon Parks, I guess," Ty offered. It sounded odd, even to him. Maybe that was how he came off, as either a Renaissance man or an unfocused kid who'd yet to grow the fuck up, and commit to a single career. "I wrote songs when I was younger," he admitted. "But that's when there was something to sing about."

"Yeah. Unless ya got a hip-hop flow and you can bitch to the beat, yo."

"Hey. Don't dis hip-hop! Sampling's been beddy-beddy good to me. 'Kay, the original plan: Have my first play produced on Broadway by twenty, my first novel published at twenty-one, my first Pulitzer by twenty-five, and then branch into scene writing. The short version: the reality of my life is I started out as a kid who acted. Never wanted to be. But I was cute then, and mama needed new shoes, and then a new living room set. But what I noticed from that, even at an early age is, there are some children who act, and then there are actors who happen to be children. I was always a very old child, but I never was an *actor*. So in a place full of umm . . . thespians, I rebelled by writing, reading, taking pictures. In some cases I've been pretty lucky. I love creating. So, I guess I'm an art mutt. There, I said it."

Blur's thought was: *You've done a lot of living between the sheets of books. But I bet you don't fuck much, do ya?* He suddenly realized he was *falling, not just in dig, but beginning to fall a little in love* with Ty. In love, when they hadn't even had sex. In love, when they hadn't shared the same dinner table, or car ride, or even the same bed.

He paid close attention to Ty's words, and the *Possibilities* in his carriage. The moments they shared, they felt so *romantic*.

"You know what? I'm that kind of man who puts it all on the table. No pussy-footing, just me, Blur Antonelli. So, you need to know this: from the moment we met, I mean, the instant I shook your hand, and gazed into your eyes, I was already falling for you, Tyrone Hunter."

"Whaaaaa? Whoa. Stop it! That's huge, and mad flattering, too. But *falling* for me? Falling for me . . . this cat you've only just met? C'mon now!"

"Who sets these time barriers you follow, Tyrone? It only takes a minute . . ."

"Well, that's kinda deep in a Tavares mid-1970s Disco kinda way, for real. I believe in attraction, at first sight. But love?"

Oh. So you think I'm playin' you, man?"

"I just met you, Blur. And no, I don't think you're a player, or a mack. Something, and I don't know what it is, but it makes me *trust* in you, in your sweetness . . . and your revealing heart. Maybe you're deeply in touch with that romantic who lives, to some degree, in all of us. So, thanks, Blur, for the beautiful sentiment . . ."

"I feel a big-ass but coming. . . ."

"But I'm not even sure if *real romance* between two men can exist in this city anyone. Hell! Did it ever really exist, without being laughed at, or crushed, or smothered or had deep gashes torn through the heart of it? Truthfully, I don't know if that's even in my future any more."

"Well Ty, I guess that depends on how *receptive you are* to another great love . . . *or the great love* . . . coming into your life. They may *already be* in your existence, just not revealed yet. God knows your heart, Tyrone . . . love is right there waiting for you . . . the timing just isn't up to us . . . this is where patience comes into play."

"Well, if I happen to find it, cool. It would be a wonderful *luxury*. But it's not a necessity; not for me. I'm a very self-contained and patient person. I've had to be. And, yes, God does indeed *know* my heart. You want to know the lonely part of that is?"

"What? Tell me."

"The lonely part is that sometimes, with the exception of David, I think God is the *only one* who knows my heart."

"Damn! I know the feeling, Tyrone. That's all I can say . . . I know the feeling well. Not too sure of what to say to you Ty . . . I mean, you've really *touched* me man . . . more than you probably realize. I wish falling in love wasn't so difficult for you, or as difficult as it has been for me, in the past. I wish it were easy to find that connection beyond the physical plane, and have it readily available and all the things that love is supposed to be, and all it's supposed to mean. I wish that the people, who touched us, more than we're even willing to *admit* to ourselves, were the ones we're supposed to be promised to *forever.*"

"Yes. That would be a beautiful gift," Ty sighed, as he thought about Trick.

"But, the world, and people in general, just doesn't work that way, man. So we're stuck in the trappings of romanticism and hoping that our lives will someday be that '*happily ever after*' we keep reading about."

"And of course, it doesn't happen. So, we find ourselves *longing* for it."

"Exactly."

"So you do understand. Wow. Aren't we both so brilliant, in our longing?" Ty laughed, although, it was a certain sadness he really was laughing at, or laughing through, and Blur detected it.

"Yes, I suppose we are. Sad, but true, isn't it?"

"True, but sad, it is."

Sometimes Blur thought talking to someone, like Tyrone,

someone of deep emotional intelligence was a GIFT . . . and a kind of life-lesson he was supposed to listen to and learn from and become stronger from having learned it.

"You're just too special, Ty."

"Yeah. I'm sure there's a li'l yellow bus for *special* people like me."

"I doubt that seriously . . . I think that bus belongs to the *rest* of the world."

He stared at Tyrone when he'd said those words. Tyrone stared back. He was so beautiful to the eye, so understanding and sensitive in nature. Blur Antonelli. He made a lovely picture, a romantic ideal. And though Tyrone had so longed for such a presence in his life, he wondered if it all were *too good* to be true.

"C'mon, bro. Let's break outta here!" Blur suggested.

Where would they go from there? The possibilities seemed endless. But Ty didn't think taking it to a physical place would be so wise, not then, not yet. Ty suggested a stroll through Tompkins Square Park, where maybe they sit for a while, maybe roll a tree, and vibe inside a night's cool breeze.

But as it turned out, Blur no longer smoked cheeb or drank, and he wasn't much of a nature boy, either. So, of all places for a first date, Blur took Tyrone to a live sex show. Ty didn't know whether to be insulted, or to take it as a form of public foreplay. He chose to think the latter.

The two walked into the small, red-lit room and took a seat. As Sade's "*War of the Heart*" played, a dark and rippling god sauntered onto the small platform. He was brawny, caramel-glazed supremacy from the tip of his shiny dome to his huge feet. A sensuous moneymaker, his G-string bulged thick with twenties. Every man sat erect, waiting to see what lurked beneath his leather jock. As he poured thick gold elixir along dark poking Jujube nipples, his eyes locked with Tyrone's. But Ty was not a cat in the habit of stuffing cash into baskets that cum. Cheap thrills and coppin' feels from paid sex machines didn't much interest him. Yet he still wondered, *Why is this man throwing his stuff at me? What's his story?* And when finally the leather jock descended: *Oh damn! That sure is a big ol'* . . .

Suddenly, a pouty blond joined the god onstage for a little interactive—though choking all the way—fellatio. For his second act, blondie was splayed across a wooden bench and deeply fucked to the entire Isaac Hayes *Shaft* soundtrack. Long after the blond came and the music ceased, Fuckenstein continued to *shaft* him to his own prodigious beat. Soon there was just him and the rhythm of the meat-beaters around him, pounding and jerking and staring—astonished. When at last the dark god shot, strange mouths gaped to catch his white-hot slosh. Even Ty wanted to whip *his* joint out before he exploded from writhing in his pants. But Blur just looked upon this fancy dancer with not a thrill nor *a boner* in sight. So Ty and his arousal both chilled.

"Did you like it? The show, I mean," Blur asked in the lounge outside the showroom.

"Far as *watching* goes, yeah, I sort of enjoyed it," Tyrone hedged. "But I noticed *you* didn't get into it much."

"I'm as kinky as the next bastard. But, my half-brother never did give me a hard-on. *Incest* just ain't my trip."

With those words, a *little sick feeling* crept into Ty's belly. *Half-brother? Why* had Blur taken him there? What kind of mad-ill shit was that? He was just about to ask that question when Blur explained.

"His name is Ray. Looks like my step-daddy, if you catch my drift. I've got no use for him, or his dong dancing. I'm all for an individual's right to dance the filthy-nasty if that's his trip. But truthfully I don't even think he's gay. Ray's just a cheap, cocky hustler with a big joint, and a habit. See, I've been monitoring this place. Look around, check the trade. It's just a front for a thriving underground drug business. When I make my fury in this world, places like this, and the motherfuckers behind them will cease to exist. And you can believe that shit." He said it coldly, but with such a sure and determined intonation, that it actually did make Tyrone *believe* him.

Ty found himself admiring the things Blur had yet to become. The prospect of all that power excited him, the same way the sight of a big, hard, Latin *pinga* excited the promiscuous pants off David.

Noticing Ty's physical excitement, Blur grinned. *So righteousness gets him hard!* He gave his joint a squeeze, and shot Tyrone a this-could-lead-to-some-serious-fuckin' look.

But it would be weeks before they'd finally *knock Timberlands.*

After work they'd hang out, and the conversation alone proved highly stimulating. They'd share kiwi and passion fruit, and listen like students to Billie's bluesiest blues. They attended off-Broadway plays, or they'd check the Yankees on the tube. Sometimes it *felt correct* for the two to just chill in silent meditation.

Was this Blur Antonelli, *The One?* Was he that exceptional being who could produce in Tyrone Hunter, a *Long Blue Moan?*

Sometimes your lips touch someone else's, and you *know* by the soft brush of certainty your heart's in trouble.

That magic night at Tyrone's, a month to the day since they'd first met, Ty was ready. Nothing if not prepared. He had everything: towels, oils, lube, candles, incense, condoms, and Najee's jazz. Tyrone was feeling, for the first time in a long time, fucky, lucky, and bursting with new semen. 'Twas the season to spew!

He and Blur kissed till their tongues hurt from the rattling, till their eager dicks cried tears and jostled painfully in an incessant grind. Blur's strange near-Egyptian beauty didn't cease at the neck. Fumbling, bumbling, Ty ripped open Blur's shirt to find his nipples hard, dark, and tight as stars. His chest, a heaving breastplate of golden skin, distinctly ripped. The slightest trace of pale-brown hair trailed his taut belly.

Ty licked his flesh, unzipped him, and oh! How immaculate this new penis seemed, so full of heat and veins, and skittering in his hand! Unleashed and erect, it swayed side to side. Its head wore a trace of chili-vinegar. Ty knew it could only get hotter, and it did. The minute Blur's long, naked *equus* meat touched his lips, its pulsing heat, its weight, its palpitation, the thrill of it throbbing in Tyrone's mouth instantly hardened him. He surged down. Even with a rubber, it felt hotter than cayenne pepper, sweeter than brown sugar melting down his wet trachea. Blur swerved those taut golden hips and lunged his nine-inch cure for loneliness deeper, deeper . . .

Blur—he came, he saw, he conquered.

Blur and Ty fucked for two hours and forty-nine minutes, and when Ty came up for air, it felt like *love*.

From the moment Ty hit Blur's groove, it was *certain*, a done deed, a fait accompli. Ah! In a sweet grunt of unity, Blur bristled and constricted around him.

"Go on. Give it to me."

And Tyrone pounded *love* into a man that night. And love's first thrust was sublime. Love was thick with power and drive, momentum and yes, that trickle of sweat. Love felt *present* inside that room, and it was full and rich with shudders and gasps. Love was there in the swoons and the pants, in the huffs and gusts of breaths. Love was there inside the eyes and the lungs and the heart, and in some deep guttural faraway place where Blur cried out, as he kissed his lover's face:

"Oh, T-y-y-y-y-y! Yes T-y-y-y-y-y-y! Oh shit, yes Ty-y-y-y-y-y-y-y-y-y-y-y-y-y!"

That fuck, their first fuck, felt more like design, like *making love*. It was excellent and uninhabited and new, and it was hot in all of its gooey-wet resplendence.

"Is this your baby?" Blur asked, huffing, puffing repeatedly. "Is this your baby?" It was Blur-speak for, *Are you close? Are you coming?*

"Yes. Yes," Ty chattered. "It's my baby!" And Love's first sublime hum came on like a quiet hysteria. And together they pitched and cried and sighed and shot, and they embraced so tightly for the longest time after.

And it was there, while cradled against Blur's racing chest, that Ty's mind sighed: *Be still my beating heart and cock. I'm laid up here with a man!*

Two months later, Ty was writing love songs again.

We're buying appliances, pooling finances / Even talkin' 'bout adoptin' a little knotty-head / The sex is electric, so stimulating / Each night I debrief him, and he purrs me to sleep / Now ain't we something', this world's never seen? / Ain't we somethin', my lover man and me?

When writing assignments took Tyrone away, Blur would feel his absence.

"Ty! You have no idea how much I've missed you, baby. Next time you go on a trip, you'll have to take *me* with you. These Tyrone-withdrawals are damn-near lethal for me!"

"Aww, stop the madness!"

"Seriously. I've *missed* you, man."

"You're just horny, Blur."

"Tyrone Hunter, what is your damage?"

"Huh? Excuse me?"

"I said I *missed* you. I *meant* it. When will you learn to just breathe and simply accept these things that come directly from my heart?"

Ty could only sigh to himself, and think: *Finally! I've found The One.*

But Blur's damn blond man kept reappearing. What were they to each other? Friends? Classmates? Buddies? Old lovers? Ty's curiosity was only compounded when Blur never thought to introduce them. What kind of game was he playing? Pride and the fear of appearing too possessive prevented Tyrone from asking that one nagging question, so it slowly ate at his jealous gut.

Still, Blur and Ty were volatile, passionate, and sometimes even apocalyptic when they rattled between the sheets.

When Blur's dwindling finances dictated, Ty suggested Blur move in with him. A hesitant Blur finally acquiesced. But when he made that move, he brought his tight ass, and a fat bag of manhood issues with him.

Unlike Ty, Blur wasn't *out*, and he'd no intentions of coming out. That simply wasn't how he rolled. He cared for Ty, but caring *too much* might spell trouble for his future plans. Leading a secret life made the one attempting to keep it a secret, corruptible. Thus, living with a man and establishing *a home* frightened Blur.

At times, Blur would get moody, never wanting to talk about his career disappointments, family entanglements, his issues with homosexuality. And the blond kept returning.

One day, fresh from a seminar, Ty came home to find them giggling like two secretive queens between the sheets of *his* bed. Tyrone was understandably enraged.

"What the fuck! Oh no. Not in my house! Get out! Get the hell out of my bed, out of my apartment, out of my fuckin' life!

And take blondie with you, you fuckin' asshole. I trusted you, you goddamn mothafuckin' lyin' ass bastard!"

"Calm down, Ty! Please. It's not even like that. This is my *brother*. My fuckin' *blood* brother!" Blur snapped. "I'm serious. This is my brother Lars."

"Fuck you very much, Blur! I'm far from stupid!"

But then the hulking blond pulled out his wallet and showed Tyrone his driver's license. Beneath his blond, blue-eyed mug it read true enough: Ingmar Lars *Daniels*.

"I told you my dads got around."

"One was a Swede," Lars added. "My momma, Greta."

So, color Tyrone corrected and dumbfounded by a *Swigga*.

When Sabina, Blur's "sweet chestnut sister," came to call, Ty was enchanted. He related to her soft eyes, her skittish movements, and he empathized with her fragility. She brought out a side of his savior complex.

"She's not *disturbed* in a pathological sense, just morbidly withdrawn, and afraid of people she doesn't know," he diagnosed. "Maybe it's just a case of social anxiety."

Ty bought a stack of self-help books, and genuinely tried to get through to her. But Blur would have none of it.

"What is this shit? She's not *yours* to fix! You got a hell of a nerve! *You*, of all people, playing the *shrink to my* sister! Well, Dr. Hunter, first, *cure thy-fuckin'-self*!" he blasted foully, hurling the books across the room, snatching his sister's hand and disappearing out the door.

Ty was both hurt and confused by that outburst. He'd meant no harm. He'd wanted to help. And just what was it about *him* that Blur thought needed to *curing?*

David told him, "Ty. Baby Boi, I thought you knew. You can't be getting up in *other* people's family. You just can't get too involved in that shit. It's too much history. There's way too much that you and nobody else will ever know, or much less figure out. So, your best bet is to just let it rest."

"Damn. I was only tryna help. I swear, I wasn't trying to *fix* her. But maybe you're right."

"Oh trust me. I'm right about this one, no doubt. And I gotta tell you, I don't *like* the way Blur exhaled on you, bruh. You didn't deserve that shit. Here he is, living in *your* apartment, eating *your* food, bringing *his* people there to *your* crib to chill. And then he's gonna wail on you like that? Oh, *hell* no! So, you want me to kick his ass for you? 'Cause ya *know*, I will."

"No, David." Ty chuckled. "Breathe, baby. Just chill! OK? I can handle this."

"Hey, all I'm sayin is, maybe he ain't *all* he represents himself to be. Maybe, he ain't *right* in the head . . . or the heart. And just maybe, you need to *ponder* that shit."

But what Ty didn't tell David was that Blur Antonelli would often explode. He'd vomit vile words and veiled accusations at Tyrone, and then leave, sometimes for days. During those occasions, Ty would be made to feel shattered, bewildered and lost. But Blur always returned humbled, with a bouquet of flowers, a contrite disposition, and offering some vague mea culpa.

A few months after the dust settled on the incident with Sabina, she was over again waiting for her brother Blur to take her bike riding. Tyrone was out persuing an art exibit downtown with David. Blur was showering and Sabina sat in Ty's living room, looking around at the things that had become familiar.

Then she glanced at the coffee table where a glossy men's magazine lay staring up at her. She began to stare back at it, and suddenly she became very, very agitated. Sabina was slowly losing control, and slipping into the darkest place she'd ever known. She began to moan and rock and cradle herself. All at once, she had to run, run or something horrible would happen to her again. She ran out the door, down five flights of stairs and into the street, crying and flailing uncontrollably. Blur, who'd heard the commotion, rushed in to find his sister had vanished. No one knew or could fathom why. Except Sabina, who had just looked into the eyes of her *rapist.*

The man on the cover of that glossy magazine was Face Depina.

CHAPTER TWENTY-ONE

Jacking Davina

Davy was decked out in full drag during the Halloween parade when he ran into an old friend from his days on the road. At six feet and three hundred pounds, Adeva was a fierce, flamboyantly maternal drag queen, strutting *toughly*.

Soon as Adeva saw him dressed as "Davina," she said, "Honey! Ya gorgeous! You simply *must* be in my show! It's an all drag revue. Maybe you've heard of it: *For Multi-colored Queens With Dreams Deferred When These Freakin' Platforms No Longer Fit*? I wouldn't call it a big boffo hit, but we do pack 'em into that little theatre on Sullivan."

And Davy, being such a natural ham-hock, he just *had* to say yes.

"Drag is only a costume for David," Adeva told a fellow performer. "He'll never be a fully let-out diva. He loves his manhood way too much. Quiet as it's kept, he can be very virile."

DECEMBER 31, 1990

The New Year's Eve show ran late, and Davina decided to leave the theatre in costume. That night he'd called Tyrone to ask if he wanted to hang out, but as usual his home-skillet refused. So there was Davina, all glammed up and no place to show. But when did that ever stop him?

As he tipped down the street, he thought to himself, *Miss Audrey Hepburn would be proud!* And it was true. Davina was rockin' this little black Givenchy knock-off *she'd designed*, and killer six-inch patent leather pumps. She went the whole nine. Had a pink chiffon scarf draped to dramatic effect along her *and* Adeva's Holly Golightly shades. A Virginia Slim blazed from her long, lacquered ciggie holder. She was cool like that, glam like that.

Yes, girls, Miss Audrey has arrived, and she is takin' no shorts!

Timbales played mad rhythms in Davina's chest when she spotted him by the bar drinking a Corona. Didn't he know Davina was a sucker for cool-pose *boricuas* with oh-so-smouldering eyes?

He was young, just out of his teens, with big, drooping Al Pacino eyes.

"*Hola*, *mami*. You lookin' *muy caliente!*" he purred.

Of course she was. But that was beside the point.

He sat next to her and began the novella of how he was dropkicked out of *la casa* for being a *maricón*. He'd just found his own place, and was determined to make it inside that Great Harassing City.

Davina felt for him. She sat listening and watching him watching *her*; knowing at least one of them was in the groggy stage of falling dick-first into some dizzy, crazy affinity. Did he have a sweet thing for *her?* He was certainly working that *cholo* charm, and Davina was snatching it up quicker than a two-for-one shoe sale at Screaming Mimi's.

He mentioned that he needed some "decoratin' tips for my new crib."

"Oh. So, you're inviting me home? How sweet. But I'm a lady, and I'm really not *that* easy, honey," Davina giggled, digging the kid's thick caterpillar brow, the mold of his hands and arms, and that way he had of stroking her warmly with those eyes.

"*Mira mami*, lookie here. My place is straight-up booty. Maybe you could give me ideas how to cook it. I mean, look at you. Yo! This place here is booty, but you dress it up, sittin' in here lookin' so fine and shit. Besides, baby, I never been with nobody like you. You like me too, don't you? C'mon, straight up, you know it. So, let's *do* this," he teased, shoving his shoulder playfully into Davina's.

There ought to be a law against butta boys whose eye-fuck is strong enough to make you say *Fuckit*. Davina found herself saying just that, thinking, *If this boy plays his pimp card right, he'll be purring like El Gato by night's end.*

Soon as they stepped outside, Davina began to hear new exciting sambas play in her lonely drag queen's heart.

"So, what's your name again, sweetheart?" she asked, wobbling behind.

"None of yo fuckin' business, faggot-ass bitch!"

The hairs under Audrey's elegant wig immediately stood at attention. Suddenly Davina felt That Shiver Thing: a cautionary reaction centered in her viscera. Why hadn't she felt it before? Was her barometer busted? She felt it now, though, in spades.

"What did you just say to me?" she asked, staring a hole through the back of his head.

"None of your fuckin' business, *faggot-ass bitch!*" he spun around and repeated.

"Look! Don't you be tryna ruin Davina's night, now! Ya hear? And don't take my evening attire to mean I'm some punk, aiight? 'Cause these heels *can* come off with a quickness, and I *will* kick your puny ass all over this uncaring street!" she proclaimed.

"Yeah, right. You know, you full-out faggots shouldn't be allowed out in public! What did you think, I'd let you suck my pipe?" The hood looked around. "I said, *you like suckin' pipe?*"

"Yes. I've been known to. But I like kickin' ig'nit ass even better!" Davina snapped, kicking off her heels.

Those meticulously painted nails came off in a flash, balled into two formidable fists, and Ms. Davina, aka David Donatello Richmond, sprang into ass-kicking action. Slow black and white visions of his earlier self pummeling some street kid in the ring danced through his skull.

"Knuckles up, guard your grill, you cowardly motherfucker!" David warned, taking a pugilist's stance.

Just then, another voice asked: "You like sucking pipe, huh, faggot?"

"Yeah. Look at this, bitch! You know it sucks pipe," still another voice chimed.

Hard boys streamed out of the alleyway across the street.

David turned. He was surrounded by six diabolical Brown and Black faces. A quick flood of panic rushed over him. But drag or no drag, he refused to go out like a sucker.

"Oh. So, you brought your boys, huh? Afraid you couldn't handle a soft, unsuspecting faggot by your lonesome? All right, Julio, Raul, whatever the fuck your names are . . . c'mon, bring it!"

What they brought was a tire iron.

"Ya like suckin' pipe, faggot? Well, suck on this!" With a blunt ram someone yanked the scarf at the back of David's neck and everything turned black. Strange how in that state of semi-consciousness, David's mind and body recorded every assault—the quick slam of a boot on his back, the taunts of "Take pipe, motherfuckin' ass-bandit," the stun of fist after fist, kick after kick hammering his flesh. They had no mercy for a dress-wearing, sashaying faggot on the prowl. They were crucifying him.

With malicious intent, they dragged him into the darkness of that sociopathic alley. With no one to see, they continued their battery.

They did it for fun, for shits and giggles. They did it because they knew they could. David was no longer fighting back. David *could no longer* fight back. It didn't matter to them. A swift and sudden kick to his mouth knocked out two teeth. But how *many* kicks would it take? How many times would that iron need to rise and plummet down, rise and plummet down, rise and plummet down before David could close his eyes and no longer *feel* anything? He wondered this, as he lay there, semiconscious. He lay there, waiting, just waiting for a neon sign from God.

Is God in this alley? his hurting skull questioned. *God? Do you see this?* The loneliness of his head wondered this, as the warm river of blood trickled, then gushed down, seeping through Audrey's little black dress.

The final humiliation came as the young thug from the bar ripped into *Ms. Davina's* purse, found a bright pink lipstick, and scribbled on David's bleeding forehead: FAG!

Then they ran away hyena-style, laughing, howling into the cruel Manhattan night.

ST. VINCENT'S HOSPITAL, JANUARY 1, 1991

It was some new cruel way to begin a New Year. A day later David lay there inside a hospital bed, in anguish, in shame, in a pain, so deep and thorough, it would not speak its rightful name.

His wired jaw prevented him from speaking at all. His only

communication was through pen and pad and those sad and questioning eyes.

"Know what hurts most?" he wrote. "Deception. Hurts more than a tire iron."

And deception had indeed hurt. What pained David worse was that people could be so hateful, so merciless, that some men would rather see him *dead* than to wear a dress. Who was he really hurting by wearing that dress?

What hurt David was that all his life, there were always people out to *get* him, simply because he *existed*. He wondered why those people had sought to *destroy* him, when he had never once actively *pursued them*, or made any sort of impure overtures, nor ever *courted* their ire.

Or had he?

"Is that all you can tell us? Average height. Brown skin. Caterpillar brow. Sad Pacino eyes. That your best description?" the patrolwoman asked, her Latina features contrasting against the pristine whiteness of the hospital room. She was a handsome woman, though her expression was one of vague, sympathetic boredom. "You've described half the population of Spanish Harlem."

The closest thing to a tear glistened, welling in David's left eye. But in steely queen's defiance, he refused to let it fall.

Maybe it's the price for being outrageous. Maybe it's just my lot to suffer the slings and arrows of outrageous fortune in this big, bad, hateful city. But like Ty says, I won't let those motherfuckers steal my joy.

David wrote back, "No Polaroid," and thought, *Am I supposed to say, "Uh, before you proceed to beat me down to a bloody pulp and break my face and my fuckin' stilettos, would you mind terribly striking a pose?"*

Something vital was missing from David Richmond . . .

something more crucial than his teeth. He could get new teeth. But what of the light, the sheer near-silver light that had always shone so bright in his aspect? His attackers had kicked that light clear out of David's eyes. Why hadn't the cops seen this, and collected the shattered pieces of it? Why hadn't the physicians noticed that vacancy, and just where was the cure for it?

For David, there was a bigger question than who his main attacker was: Where was his *support* system? And how the hell, with no insurance, could he afford his medical bills? He closed his weary, battered eyes and flipped through the Rolodex in his skull.

"If I told him once," Depina said to Ty, "I've told the little ill bitch a million times: 'It's risky enough being out there!' But he still takes that soft, saccharine-sweet faggot ass on the stroll like he's lookin for a beat-down! Fuckin' freak! Told him, 'Don't tempt strange men into shakin' yo tree without tellin' 'em bout that extra limb!' I don't feel sorry for his loose, stupid ass. I don't feel nothing. The phone rings at five thirty in the fuckin' mornin', and it's some drag queen callin' me: 'Face, honey, David's in trouble. He's hurt. They got him laid up here in the hospital, and . . . well, he sure could use a friend . . .' Well, I'm sick of his shit!"

"Excuse you?"

"Yo, Ty! Bitches get treated like bitches."

Ty searched Face's eyes for the foggy, tripped-out signs of a soul.

"Listen, I only came here because of David. He feels connected to the *real* Pascal. Remember him? David does. He's always been your champion defender. I'm asking you to do right by the brother."

"Yeah, that's funny. You, Dudley Do-Right asking *me* to *do right* by a brother. That's why we clash. You were always too righteous and bourgie for my tastes."

"Still trying to fade me, Depina? I'm not all hard and cold, but you sure as hell can't fade me."

"Everything you say *sounds white* to me. All you represent is a bourgie lie!" Face countered.

"Now look who's callin' the kettle indigo! I don't even know what you mean when you say that shit. Bourgie? Is it that I come from people who loved me, people who *tried* to keep it together? You resent that, don't you? I think maybe you hate seeing people happy. David was happy. Faison was *happier*, at least. I imagine Bliss was even happy once. Hell, I *know* my parents were before Hurricane Face blew in through our apartment window! Is that why you tried to sabotage them, is that why you stole the brooch? Yeah, I know all about it. Look me in the eye, damn it! I deserve to be looked in the fuckin' eye!"

Tyrone expected Depina to lie with a straight face. But for once he didn't bother.

"Oh, that. Don't worry, I'll write your mama a nice big check with interest," he said all nonchalantly.

Tyrone wanted to *hit* him. Hit him dead smack in his arrogant throat.

"You can't fix it now, Face. And you can't downplay the shit you do. Not with me. It won't work."

"But I can buy and sell your ass," Face bragged, though, by that time, it was a lie. The phone rang, and Face grinned as he walked backward to answer it.

"Talk sense to me," he said into the receiver as he waved to a little Korean man, who appeared to be unsure if he should enter that particular battlefield. He was carrying a basin full of suds, and was flustered about where to place it for Face's biweekly pedicure. "Yeah, I heard. Yeah. I got one of his *girls* here now, bitchin' about it." Tyrone heard, just as Face wanted him to hear.

"No. The other one. The one that thinks he's the shit. OK, Claude. I'll holla at you later. Cool. Sounds good. Hmm-m-m. Bet. Later, brother." Face hung up, then yelled at the little Korean man. "Damn it, put the tub down, ya little fool! Right there! Yes, in front of the sofa." He pointed. Then he turned to Ty. "Are we finished?" he asked.

"That was Claudio Conte? You call him *brother*? Interesting. Here you are, flaunting this light-skinned privileged life under the pose of *brotherhood*, and the *real* brothers you dismiss."

"I'll never call *you* my brother. You too fuckin' saintly for that gig! If I *did* have a brother, he'd be one hard and sexy bitch. At least Claudio *represents*."

"A bitch? I don't doubt it," Ty quipped.

"I used to laugh at you, Tyrone. Sometimes I still do. Now you want *everything* I got. My fame, my money, the women I already knocked out. Go on and take her, Ty. But I better warn you: Bliss uses her teeth."

With that, rage overtook Tyrone. It boiled up in his hand, and it made a fist, and it grew with heat and purpose, and it hauled off and swung. The punch landed square on Face's chin and bottom lip. This was no *bitch slap*. Placing his hand to the spot, Face sucked back a trickle of blood and laughed.

"Watch it, Ty! Fightin' over a woman? Ya bet not be lettin' her hum you! I'll fuck around and report your queer ass to the queer union, have 'em take away your purple carryin' card."

Ty was glad he hit him. He was also mad at himself for hitting him, but mostly *glad*.

"You're a pitiful excuse for a man, Face. The subject is David. David, damn it! Good, bad, black, or miserable, he's your friend. He's your fuckin' friend, and he needs you."

"You wanna talk about the little fag?" he asked, sitting on

his Italian-crafted sofa, removing his socks. He placed his precious feet inside the basin and his servant went to work. "All right. Let's talk. You say he's *my* friend? I don't know about all that *friend* bullshit. David's run outta time with me, and his shit is stale."

"Fuck you!" Ty yelled. "David is our history. Now he's down, and you're gonna walk away? Write him off? It's a pattern with you. You just *junk* people!"

"Damn right. I junk people who hit me up for money. I junk people who sashay into one of my shows lookin' like a black-ass Joan fuckin' Crawford on crack! David ain't Davy anymore. He's a fuckin' basket case, and I'm tired of him, his goofy dreams, and his stupid way of hittin' on me when he knows it ain't gonna happen. I'm sick and tired of his whole queer-ass *shtick*."

"What? Worried about the negative publicity? Relax. You could always put a spin on it, make it seem like you're one of the beautiful, sensitive, sympathetic motherfuckers that kiss known queens on the lips at all the right functions."

"Fuck you twice, mothafucka! I could always drop-kick your ass too, ya know."

"And I'd be a mess, wouldn't I?" Ty replied. "What would I *become* without *you?* Would I be a nasty drunk, strung out on rock, like Browny? Or maybe I'd be a tragic, muscle-bound marionette, like Chaz?"

"You steppin' out of bounds, now! Ya hear me, you Negro homoerectus with a confused dick! Ya leave it the fuck alone!" Face warned.

"Or maybe I'd just put on a dress and paint my face and step into that lonely trip of backrooms, suck-holes, and toilet fucks, thinking of *you* with every anonymous cock I suck, like . . . like . . . David!"

"That's it! Get the fuck out of here! Right now. I mean it. Out!" Face screamed, pointing to the door. He stepped out of his soapy basin and splashed his Korean pedicurist. His eyes were livid. Only when he was truly pissed did they have that strange green supernatural glow. *He* was now ready to hit *Tyrone*.

But Tyrone wasn't afraid of him, and no longer felt *punked* in his presence. There were things he'd wanted to say, hot words stewing and boiling.

"You know, Face, I can be a friend despite the way my friends might trip, fall down, and bust up the leg of that friendship. You think you're better than the rest of us? Truth is, you're not, and you never were. Browny's more talented, always was. I'm a lot more accomplished. And Davy's got more humanity in his tight hip-swinging ass than you can pull from your deepest opiate-addled imagination. But guess what? Fate smiled on *you*, even though you've never done a damn thing worthwhile in your fuckin' life. You're famous because of an accident of genetics! And this mad cool apartment and flier-than-fly lifestyle won't change the fact that you're empty and fucked up."

"I give less than a clipped fuckin' pinkie toenail what you think of me, Tyrone. And right now I'm wonderin' if I got any *real true blues* besides Claudio. Friends who understand me. You know, the kind that don't *want* nut'n from me."

"Yeah. Nothing but your *soul*! And just how do you *understand* somebody that's not even *real*, Face? You ain't real. I don't think you've ever been. Now *David* . . . he's real. Remember him? He's real and he's hurt real bad. You can either deal with that or *not* deal and just shoot up, and nod it all away. Do whatever the fuck you wanna do. Just don't dare talk to me about *Brothers* . . . cause on that and so many other subjects, you don't have a motherfuckin' clue. I'm out of here."

Face watched his road dawg head for the door. It felt like the end of *them*. But in reality, there was no *them*.

"Oh. One more thing, *brotha*," Tyrone added sarcastically. "We fucked once, and never again. Personally, I've never asked for a single thing from you, right? I'm not on a leash or a stipend. I don't bend to kiss your ass like your other sycophants. No, whatever I felt for you died a long time ago. Stupid-ass me. I keep forgetting to bury that stank fuckin' corpse!"

"Well, who the hell asked you to come here, faggot?" Depina's face reddened.

"You're right. I'm trespassing. This is *your* place. But I came here to remind you that somebody actually loves you. He loved you when you were nobody, when you didn't have a famous name, or this place, or anything. And now he's in pain. There's a lot of that out there. I figured maybe you could relate, just a little." Ty sniffed. "Pain. Hell, I smell it all up in this place. If you ever come down off that shit you're snortin, or shootin, you might smell it yourself, you stuck-up, counterfeit, mixed-up *superbitch*! Your life is a joke, Pascal. And *you* are the fuckin' laugh!"

Then he slammed the door behind him.

And I'm the laugh? Negro please! What a fuckin' queen! Always so goddamn dramatic! Well fuck his faggot ass and his faggot friend. I'm through with them.

Face turned and snapped at his pedicurist.

"Well? Whatcha waitin' for? My pinkie toe could use some buffin'!"

During the cab ride to the hospital, Ty recalled the first time he'd laid eyes on David: an openly queer teen, he wore a cape-like *shmatte* that was black with a lavender lining. His eyes were raccooned in mascara and he virtually glided down the hall. Ty reasoned that he *had to be* a dance major.

"Honey boy, relax those stiff shoulders and bre-e-athe. Walkin' 'round here like, like somebody's low-budget *Blacula*! Vampire vogue is very mid '70s. We'll work on you, though. Just relax, just bre-e-e-e-eathe, and be yourself, baby!"

These were Davy's first words to him. Now, in that cab, suddenly Tyrone felt haunted by the things he'd never said.

I never once told him how much I admire him . . . or how transparently beautiful he is.

Maybe he hadn't said it, but Tyrone always *felt* that when David finally grew into himself, he would be one of the most *lovely* and intriguing human beings anyone had ever seen. With "the Duchess," Ty saw no need to be plastic or malleable, or to live that schizophrenic existence he inevitably lived on the street. He wasn't required to speak several languages, use different gestures, vocabularies, demeanors, senses. His armor didn't have to be intact. The Core Tyrone, *the Ty no one else knew*, he presented to David.

David understood him, and Ty *got* David. Ty knew the whole gayer-than-thou thing was a costume David could change in and out of like a Broadway musical cast member. He knew David always feigned an absurd *machismo* around his father, and did so up until the day he'd died, because Daddy Richmond's acceptance loomed high in the sovereignty of David's heart. Though he'd never received it, David worked *hard* toward that goal of love and acceptance. Before he realized he could gather and create his own, the concept of family was very important to David Richmond. Thus, he would affect boxing, jock posturing, the "You should see the fox I'm datin', Pop" rap, and most any daring-do, short of marriage. Life around Poppa Richmond was a manly war, fought on a sunny beach of lies, but David thought he was winning.

His father *had* given him a spiritual base, from which David often toppled, yet it had always somehow sustained him. His father also saw to it that David learned to use his fists.

Knowing the Duchess could, if provoked, *swing* on an assailant and put a serious hurting on his ass made Ty feel easier. Only now it was one more reason to feel angry, confused, and guilty. Hadn't David *asked him* to hang out that New Year's

Eve? Hadn't Tyrone brushed him off again with an excuse that he'd finally shaken his writer's block?

Tyrone had been forewarned. The person in that bed would *not* resemble the David he knew. Still, he'd not been prepared for the shock of seeing that broken poodle of a boy, a tube extending through his nose, the heavy bandages, or the contusions littering that sweet face. He called upon the long dead comedian in him.

"Da-a-amn, baby! I know this place is a dump, but it looks like someone took one on you!" was his pathetic offer.

"Facey with you?" David scribbled anxiously.

"Uh, no, he's not," Ty hedged, a little poison arrow zoomed through his heart. "Maybe he'll bop through later. The Beautiful People keep different hours."

He saw the severity of the disappointment float across that battered aspect. Ty so wanted to say, *Why Depina, even now? Don't you get it, Davy? Depina doesn't give a shit about you!*

"So . . . how you feeling, Duchess? I mean, really?" Ty's voice was heavily laden by the weight of concern.

But there was now a thin shield, a membrane between them, and Tyrone felt it. It was like a fog had drifted into that room and filled the space between him and David. Though he'd tried valiantly to penetrate it, he could not—not fully. That wasn't David lying there now. It was a worn theatre marquee with a broken facade.

"Duch? I said how you feel?

"Like Garbo," David wrote, a limp wrist to his brow.

"Come on, Duchess. I've seen that movie. Garbo didn't really 'vant to be alone,' baby boy."

David wanted to say, *Thank God for you, Tyrone. If not Facey, then I'm so glad you're here. It's no fun playin' Camille all by my lonesome.*

"Davy, confession time. I had a plan. I was gonna come in here, whip out my dusty acting skills and *pretend*, just fake my scared ass off through this thing. But . . . I can't do it, baby boy. Look at you! You look horrrrrrah-ble!" Ty confessed, his tone colored by a mirthless chuckle.

David's head jerked in a familiar gesture that said, *Get over here and knock me a kiss.* Ty did. He placed the softest butterfly of kisses to his bruised left cheek. That's when he noticed it.

Oh! God! His teeth. His beautiful teeth! What kind of cretin would do this? I could kill those heartless motherfuckas! Kill 'em with my bare fuckin' hands!

Ty hoped the tooth horror wouldn't register on his face. But his voice was choppy with regret.

"What can I say, man? I should've been by your side last night. None of this shit would've happened if I'd been there with you. I'm sorry, man. So sorry . . ."

David scribbled, "Stop! Can't control me. Fuckin' cock-blocker!"

"But I never thought you'd wind up like this!"

Telegraphically, David said, *Save it. It's raw, ain't it? I know. Shit happens. Feces occurs. Not your fault. Whatever bleedin'-heart shit you're feelin', save it for that damn book you'll finish one damn day. Just don't clown me. Please don't stare at me like some soft, pathetic, eternal victim, 'cause when I'm healed, I'll have to kick your ass!*

There were a thousand things to say, and about a million apologies. But instinctively, Ty knew David didn't want them, nor was he in the mood to listen.

"I'll drop by later with some fashion mags and crossword puzzles. I could kick by your place and grab your most fetching robe so you won't be all assed-out in this joint, 'kay?"

Ty's words hovered on the silent, antiseptic air.

"Duch? Davy? What do you think? Would that be cool?"

"Thanks. Love you. Re-e-eal tired now. Sore," David scribbled, thinking, *Please just leave me the hell alone! I've had enough of this puttin' on a good face bullshit. Just go!*

"OK. I'll leave. But I'll be back. We . . . we all right, man?"

"Always," David scratched softly, turning painfully to bury his broke face inside his pillow.

As Tyrone left, David closed his eyes and *wondered why* Face hadn't come to visit. He thought about the phone call, and reasoned that Face was high at the time. He had to be strung-out, and not speaking with his right mind. How could he be? It was so cold and cruel. Everything he'd said left the saddest impression that Face didn't really give a fuck about him. *Why*?

Neither Face nor David shared the plug ugly truth with Ty, or the details of that desperate phone conversation. But Depina's final *fuck you* had deeply wounded David.

With Face Depina, you never knew which *face* you'd get. Would it be the Depina Brood or the Depina Grin? Would you be staring into the green pools of The Idol, The Moment Maker, The Boyishly Cool Heartbreaker, The Junkie, or The Jester? The one Face that David loved best was the dependable Face, the Face who remembered their history, who sometimes even said, *I think I love your fly little ass*, even if only with a wink of an eye.

But his *favorite* Face suddenly *turned all kinds of ugly* on David. That Face didn't wanna speak to *another freak in a fuckin' dress. Fuck Adeva*! No. He wanted to speak to the *original freak*.

"Whoever you are, fuckin' pervert, put David on the goddamn phone!" he demanded. "David. You there? What's the fuckin' profit in helpin' you? Huh? Ya ain't worth it. You done used that pitiful faggot routine one too many times. Now, if I paid your debts, would you wanna *work* it off? Ya know, I could turn you out, put ya on the street, and have you suck dick for profit. How's that, freak? What? Why you so quiet? Go 'head, tell me that shit *don't* appeal to you! Hello? David? You still there?"

After a long and painful pause, David handed the phone to his friend in drag.

"Whatever you said, you just broke his face. Are ya happy? Why you tryna hurt him? If this is about that stupid show, he apologized for that. He's sorry. But, he's, he's in trouble here. Please. At least come see him. You could talk, like you used to . . . Face? You know how he *feels* about you . . . David *loves* you!"

"Get a fuckin' life, faggot. And step the hell out of mine."

Click.

You stabbed me, Facey. I'm crouched down, doubled over in a wild pain. Don't you . . . see me? Don't you love me, even just a little bit? I'm bleeding, papi. Did you really mean it?

Had Depina meant to stab David with the thought-out precision of those words? If you asked Face, he'd say: "Yes. It was his moment, his time to bleed. Now get over it!"

Still, worst of all, *why*, after the last harrowing hours of disturbing clarity, had David become so *stupid?* Was he one of those *love me, please love me* people now? He'd always pitied those needy human beings, who, no matter what terrible thing was said or what vile thing was done to them, would still die *loving* their persecutors. David used to ask, "What up wid dat?" But, was *he* one of *those* tragically stupid people now?

Tyrone returned home, emotionally ass-kicked, and there, fresh from winning an important civil case, was Blur, stretched out on Ty's leather sofa. His locks were gone, replaced by a Caesar cut. But he was still hot in his staid wings tips, black socks, cock ring, and nothing else. He emitted his blatant *let's get fuckin' wild* gaze at Tyrone. And *getting fucking wild* was exactly what they were going to do.

Tyrone took one look at that nakedness and propelled himself at it. No talk. No hellos. No, *I missed your hot, yellow, ambitious ass, now knock me a kiss*. No. Ty threw himself at it with a bullet's speed. Soon, all he wore were his Nikes . . . and Blur's fat balls as a muzzle. Maybe the vein of that stiff shaft could stifle his tears. Ty was practically inhaling it. Blur reached down and smacked Ty's ass, his heart suddenly beating in raving rhythms that mirrored his frantic lover's. Tyrone's hands, mouth, and emotions were everywhere at once. The crush of prick, belly, and groin fur couldn't smother him. But he *wanted* to be smothered. Then Blur aimed two spit-wet fingers inside his lover's anus, jabbing them, and Ty gripped hold like an angry vise. And still he gulped and lacquered as if to drown in, be strangled or impaled by pure carnal abandon.

"Easy! Ease up, bab-e-ee! It ain't going anywhere!" Blur sighed, half-joking, yet close to erupting down that savagely sucking throat. "You're gonna make me shoot before we fuck!"

Ty pried away, stared into those cocky eyes of Blur's, and with his voice the closest it had ever come to sounding *menacing*, hissed, "Let's fuck."

He was stiff and dripping when Blur slid a rubber along his inflamed firearm. Tyrone was ready to launch it inside his lover with a speed and force uncommon to his sexual norm.

Pulling Blur's legs to the end of the sofa, he grunted and lunged hard and deep. Tyrone wasn't on a thrusting mission just to bust his nut. He could hear his own heart beating a thousand times a minute, and it scared him. Fucking might cure it. Fucking might just be the elixir. Fuck something! Fuck everything. Fuck hard, and come. Fuck and maybe the world would make some small kind of temporary sense again.

David was hurting and so was he, and so was Blur for being

there. Ty lunged with a swift velocity of pounding flesh, making the leather sofa beneath them screech from misery. Bucking and sweating, his wounded eyes filled with a wildness Blur Antonelli had never seen.

"Fuck! Fuckin' wild, Tyrone! Easy, man! That shit hurts!"

But it didn't ease the ire or calm the ineffectual fire in Tyrone's loins, heart, head, cock, and balls. With every hard and punishing lunge, he saw David's battered face with its missing teeth, multiple bruises, and heartbroken eyes. He remembered the embarrassed way those beautiful honey eyes could barely look at him.

Tyrone's now vengeful dick stabbed at the image of Face Depina for the heartless way he'd dismissed David. He slammed those faceless thugs, those motherfucking gay-bashing bullies who'd taken something unspoiled and precious and *felt* from little David.

Blur roared the *roar* of a near-raped lion. The noise brought Tyrone back to the time, place, and *reality* of this weapon he punched headlong through his lover's anus. A lover howling in anguish, shaking and shooting, trembling, ejaculating from the pain of a man inflamed.

Shooting sparks rained in a gush to Tyrone's pounding chest. He dismounted Blur and heaved, and the anger shot clean out of him in violent white tears. And it seemed he couldn't stop shooting, hurling his hurting seed past Blur's dizzy head. It leapt from the cliffs of his pain to the floor like wet, white suicides.

CHAPTER TWENTY-TWO

Vampires, In Leather and Fur

JANUARY 1991

Chaz Williams walked in on Face in the War Room performing a crude act on a young, blond prince. Howling mad, Chaz proceeded to go off, and he tore up the place. The nude-boy offender, turned petrified, ran screaming nakedly from the loft.

The incident was later squashed . . . and that night, the sex between Face and Chaz was hotter, wetter, better than it had ever been. Things were back to being kinky-as-usual, until about two weeks later when the same lusty blond prince in question approached Face Depina at a film opening and boldly kissed him hard on the mouth.

Face was quickly taken aback. He was, in fact, a bit mortified. Face Depina had *rules*, and chief among them was: he just didn't do *public* displays of affection with other *men*! Recognize!

He thought he'd played it off before the swells, and felt he could say it was a très European thing to do. But Chaz saw it, and Chaz was not amused. And Chaz reacted in a decidedly and most *uncool* fashion.

"Motherfucka! Don't you ever put your nasty, dick-sucking lips on him! Mangy son of a skinny bitch!" he blared.

Then Chaz hurled off and hit him—hard. Just once, but one punch from Chaz Williams was more than enough. Blond boy landed soundly on the red carpet, completely unconscious.

"My bodyguard. He's *mad* protective of his . . . umm . . . client. Just got a little carried away, that's all. It's cool, it's cool," a quick on his feet Depina told the curious watchers as the paparazzi flashed and clicked away. It seemed an *almost* reasonable, *nearly* plausible excuse.

"Fuck you! Bodyguard, my thick, black ass! You think anybody believes that shit anymore?" Chaz bellowed.

"Shut up, Chaz. Shut the fuck up, man!" Face warned through clenched teeth, his cool-face evaporating, his skin manifesting a visible sweat. Face Depina never sweat in public—not unless he was paid to, and it would appear *sexy* on a magazine cover or a billboard.

He felt very *raw* in that instant. He felt—naked—and *not* in a sexy Face Depina way. He felt practically outed on that New York street!

What does a model do when caught inside in a publicly embarrassing moment? If you're Pascal "Face" Depina, you skip the damn movie, quickly push your "bodyguard" back into your shiny limo, and you speed away into the curious Manhattan night.

JANUARY 1, 1991

Bliss Santana waited in a rented Jaguar in the West Village. It was that misty twilit hour custom-tucked for sleepwalkers, tardy vampires, and men who believed tricks were for kids.

The Jaguar was parked in a prime spot, just outside Face Depina's loft.

When he finally bopped home from a long day's journey through another abusive night, she saw him and shouted.

"Pascal! Pascal! It's me. Get in. We need to talk."

Oh no! Not this clingy bitch! Not today! Not now!

"Hey Bliss. What's goin' on?" he said in the chronically bored voice he usually reserved for those tedious people with vaginas.

"Pascal? Pascal! It's me. Get in. We need to talk." She opened her leather trench to reveal the soft, light-caramel planes of her nakedness.

Face Depina thought to himself. *Aw shit! This crazy, desperate freak! I can't do any more sick chicks!*

"I'll get in, but just a minute 'cause I'm feelin' sick and I'm real tired, Bliss."

The two took off onto the Westside Highway for a harrowing ride Face Depina would never forget. With eyes blurred with tears, Bliss took a deep breath and she said it.

"Here's the story: I'm pregnant. It's yours. Do we abort or what?"

"Awww, Bliss. C'mon. Don't be yankin' me tonight. You, *pregnant*, for real?"

"For real," she said, taking his shaky hand and placing it on her belly. "Wanna feel?"

But all he could feel was ill.

"Seriously? You're pregnant, and it's *mine*? Not Claudio's or Julio's or maybe *Ty-rone's*?" He said the last name with a particular emphasis.

"No. Sorry, Pascal. But I'm not half the whore you take me for."

He held his head in his hands, rubbing his eyes, trying to make it all go away.

"Bliss, you *know* how I feel about kids. I don't want none.

Never did, and you knew that. Trust me—I know—nothin' worse in this fuckin' world than some unwanted kid! Are you stupid? Did ya think you'd keep me this way? No. No babies. Not now, not ever! Damn you! You shoulda been more careful."

He looked wired and nervous. He was starting to tic inside his skin. By then that creepingly familiar gnaw settled in his belly. He knew what it was.

"Pull over! I'm sick. Pull the fuck over!" His voice was shrill as a police siren.

It wasn't an easy trick, pulling over on the Westside Highway, but Bliss found the skinniest of shoulders.

Face got out, turned around, and vomited up all that was left inside him. *She's pregnant? A baby? And it's mine? Fuck, fuck, fuck, FUCK!*

He opened the door and got back inside.

"Get rid of it," he said simply, with green eyes weighed down by a sickly seriousness.

"So, we abort," she said coldly, staring at the white lines of the highway exploding beneath the wheels of the now speeding Jag. She applied more pressure to the gas pedal.

"And you need to slow the fuck down! Your ass is *too* damn emotional for me."

"My ass is fine. The sky," she said, "look at all those colors. You know, the sky hasn't cried in such a long time. But I think the clouds have been meaning to," she said.

"What the *hell* you talkin' 'bout? Just take me home!" Face clutched his belly and leaned against the passenger window.

"I'm talking about crying. Don't you want to cry with me, Pascal?"

"Fuck no, I don't wanna cry!"

"Then would you like to *die* with me?"

"Don't fuck with my head. I'm sick, damn it!"

"Yes. I know you're sick. And except for that *one* time,

three-and-a-half months ago, I've long stopped fucking with you and your sickness!"

She looked at him and wondered in that moment if his beautiful pitifulness had succeeded in driving her crazy . . . and if she was crazy, could she stop *being* crazy if she just simply said, or screamed, "NO"?

"Pascal, you said to get rid of it. So I'm about to, right here and now."

It was that first yellow shout of dawn. The highway hadn't yet been overtaken by rush-hour traffic. The road was dotted by delivery trucks and eighteen-wheelers, lots of them, zooming, zooming, zzzz zzzzooming by. The speedometer glided from seventy to seventy-five, pushed up on eighty.

"See, now I know you're crazy. You better stop fuckin' around, Bliss! Slow down!"

Eighty became eighty-five, then ninety.

"Slow down, Bliss! Baby, slow the hell down! See? See that, you just missed that last exit. What you doin'? Take your foot off the gas, you fuckin' crazy, pregnant, stupid bitch!"

Nothing he said registered. Even if it had, *she* was feeling sick now. Sick of his voice. Sick of his promiscuity, his moods, his friends, his jiggling Lolitas, his excuses . . . the whores, the boys in leather, the groupies. She was sick of how he and the rest of it made her *feel*. Most of all, she was sick of loving him. But she couldn't stop even though she wanted to. She wished there wasn't a baby in her womb. And she wished it wasn't his. She wished it was Tyrone's. Maybe then it would be kinder, gentler, more loving, and *healthy*.

"Oh God, I'm so sorry, baby," Face cried out just then, out of fear. "I'm sorry. Sorry for everything. Everything, you hear me?"

He'd said *everything* as if he *knew* he had *it* and had given it to her and their *baby*.

"I never meant to hurt you, Bliss. I don't know why I do shit sometimes. I'm sorry. I mean it. Now, please slow the *fuck* down!"

"People used to say we looked good together, Pascal, and you ate it up. We were elegance walking hand-in-hand with a fuckin' freaky little lie. They even wrote about us in *Vogue*, remember? I doubt they'll recognize us as that same beautiful, brown, green-eyed couple after our violent abortion. Do you think? No, of course you don't. You never do."

"Slow. The fuckin'. Car down, Bliss. Please! Slow down before you kill innocent people!"

"Nobody's innocent anymore," she said.

"Yo! Bliss! Look out for that truck! Get away from the fuckin' truck, Bliss! Please, slow down!"

"You, ummm . . . afraid of trucks, Pascal? See? There's still *so much* I don't know about you. But I know you used me! I was a perfect beard for you, wasn't I?"

This mad-crazy bitch is doin' one hundred miles per hour on the fuckin' Westside Highway!

"That's why I'm naked under this coat. Your public will think we were two insatiable lovers who couldn't keep our hot hands off each other, and that we were fuckin' our brains out when we reached our wailing, bloody-red climax. See, even after everything, all the madness and shit you've put me though, I'm still trying to protect my man! Now ain't that love?"

She swerved around one eighteen-wheeler into the lane of another. Horns blew.

God, not like this! Not with this crazy bitch! Do something to stop this shit right now. Say something!

"Bliss, this is stupid! Look. Let's don't be stupid, let's be crazy. Let's do completely nuts. Let's get married. I'll . . . I'll marry your ass if you want! You hear? We can do this. Bliss, we could raise the kid together. Bliss, slow down! Bliss, baby, you hear? You my boo. Bliss, there's a kid in this shit. Slow the fuck down, baby. Slow the fuck down, baby . . ." he finished in a whisper.

And the baby in that whisper reached her. She eased off the gas, and she did slow the fuck down. A baby was worth more than this. A baby, even sick, was worth more than him or her or them together.

A baby. My baby! This is my baby!

Suddenly sanity reentered the blood-red room of her vanity, the part she only let herself see came back into focus. She wasn't poor or defenseless or a babe in the jungle. She could make it alone. Fuck that tortured pretty-boy junkie crying and begging beside her! This was still *her* baby

DECEPTIONS AND REFLECTIONS

LATE FEBRUARY 1991

A still secretly pregnant Bliss Santana was just two-weeks out of rehab. Her senses were clearer, and her most rebellious attitude had remained: FUCK PASCAL FACE DEPINA!

The only person she wanted to see now was Tyrone. The entire time she'd been detoxing, *his* was the only face she could imagine beyond the pain, beyond fog, beyond the fear, beyond the What If.

Bliss Santana set out to make a most delicate, deliberate and *devious* series of moves on Tyrone Hunter. She was in part trying to convince herself that she was slowly but surely falling in love with him. But Bliss had other motives as well. If she could convince Tyrone that her baby was *his*, then life would be far more normal and perhaps for the first time ever, *tranquil and serene*.

Although it was freezing outside, Bliss wanted some cold, fresh air. She'd shown up at Tyrone's apartment begging him to take her for a walk. It had recently snowed and the streets weren't yet plowed. Ty, ever the comforter, grabbed some blankets and they went up to his rooftop.

"What's going on in your head, you dizzy broad?"

There was a marathon of crazy/sane thoughts running in the lonely silence of her mind.

"Once again, the men in my life leave me in pain and blankets. Why? Damn it. Why, Ty?"

"Because, that's what we do. We're all variations of bastards, you know."

"Bastards I could do. I've done plenty. But where have all the *good* bastards gone?"

"Bliss, baby, that's . . . that's an oxymoron."

"If you're all bastards, are there any left who aren't underage, unemployed, or *uninterested* in a good woman? Or hell, even a bitchy Jersey broad like me? We're not so bad, you know?"

"Nah. You're *so* bad, I know," Ty concurred, as he watched a wild gust of wind blow havoc through her black hair. She looked so beautiful, and yet so troubled. He put his arm around her.

"We're born givers, you know? We give life, and breath, food, comfort, and sex, even head when we don't want to, and why? Because . . . *that's* what we *do* for our lovers. But men, they never give back. Men are takers of a woman's best stuff."

"Hey, I was just kidding when I said we're all bastards. Don't believe that. We're not *all* thieves and takers and emotional pimps and shit. Once we get past the fear and learn to *trust*, some of us can be some rather sensitive mofos."

"Sensitive?" She chuckled sadly. "Please. Would that word describe any part of Pascal 'Face' Depina?"

"*Sensitive?* Face? Let's not get *crazy!* Besides, I thought you said you were *over* him."

"I say a lot of things. The heart lies like a son-of-a-deluded-bitch, even to its owner sometimes. Don't hold it against me."

"So . . . it's still all about *him*, huh?"

"God, I wish it wasn't!" She sighed, staring blankly at the skyline. Below, the frozen residents of Harlem drifted about the streets like elegant vagabonds.

"People come to this big, bad, impossible city with heads full of dreams, and this place butchers them. Me, I managed to conquer it in my own little way."

"Of course you did."

"But don't you see? The urban fairytale ain't enough if I've become a princess and failed at being a woman!"

"Full of metaphors today, aren't we? It's too cold for them. What is it you think you've failed at, Bliss?" Ty asked, growing impatient.

"The things I wanted most are so common that they would be a joke to most people."

"I promise I won't laugh."

"First, answer this question for me. What is love, Ty?"

"Aw, Bliss, c'mon! It's way too cold out here for this!" Ty shivered.

"No, I want an answer. What is love?"

"Well," Ty sighed and exhaled a smoke ring. "*Heinlein* said: 'Love is that condition in which the happiness of another is essential to your own.' I kinda believe in that. It convinces me, that I truly love David. And wonder where he is, and how he is . . . and . . . I hope he's safe . . . and happy."

There was a tear forming in Tyrone's eye. Bliss didn't notice it. Bliss could not have cared less. She wanted, *needed* answers to her *own* predicament.

"Don't give me some egghead philosopher bullshit, you over-educated son-of-a-bitch! What is love to *you*?"

Tyrone wiped the tear from his eye. He gazed at the gray Harlem sky and sighed. "I don't know. I guess, love is being naked, raw, honest, your fullest, most real self, flaws and all with another person. It's having it all, even the ugly shit, returned to you in a way that's real and enduring. That's the nutshell version, I guess."

"That's not very romantic. I want more. I want someone's eyes to warm and sparkle like the Twin Towers all lit up when they see me. I want him to smile when he says my name, and even when he thinks of me. I want to be all his eyes see. I want to be *wanted*.

"Sounds like you're asking to be . . . *adored*."

"Maybe. And what's wrong with that? I'd be willing to return it in full. Yes, I'm passionate . . . and overwhelming sometimes. It's who I am. Bliss Santana, dammit! But I'm just a woman who needs the comfort of a man. And the tragic thing is, I'm starting to believe no man will ever love me—not completely. And I *know* I'm worthy of love."

"Of course you are. More than most, Bliss. Hell, I love you," Tyrone said, looking deeply into her eyes.

But as soon as he said it, he sensed time stood frozen on that rooftop. He felt as if the concrete beneath them were opening up, and he was falling through it with her. Wherever it would land, however they descended, it would be some deep and inescapable place.

"I thank God for you, honey boy. I really do. You're the only one on this whole fucking ice-cold planet who loves me for me."

He kissed her then, out of friendship, sympathy, curiosity, a million different things, and that kiss was comforting.

For Tyrone, comfort or some fitting imitation of it was needed. With Blur among the chronically ambitious and thus, always missing, along with the strange and heartbreaking disappearance of David, comfort was such a rare commodity.

Sometimes, we will do whatever and *whomever we can*, just to remember that sensation of comfort, just to know its warm visitation again.

TWENTY-THREE

The Past is a Hard Song to Dance To, Yo,

MARCH 1991

The Duchess was still nowhere to be found. Always one to dance away from the constrictions of his situations, with the assist of a most resourceful drag queen, David had skipped out of his hospital room. But then, he perfected his queerest act of all. David had vacated his West Village pad and left no forwarding address.

Ty had been frantic. He'd placed call after desperate call to mutual friends, and turned up nothing.

"Why do people leave like that? It's like he just fuckin' died on me! Where is he, Blur?" a hopeless Tyrone asked what had become a suitcase of rhetorical questions. "Is David out there? Is he somewhere walking alone in this narrow-minded place, with all its narrow-minded hates and fists? I don't know where he could be, or if he's even in the city. Do you think he's still in town?"

"I don't know, Tyrone. But I've never been his keeper," Blur Antonelli said over the phone. Blur was in DC, making politically advantageous moves, and had little sympathy for David and dancers and disappearing acts.

"You know, since being on the streets, volunteering at the soup kitchen, and just paying attention, I've stopped wondering why so many of us are stone drunk, or sucking pipe, or sticking a needle in a good vein at three A.M. I've stopped wondering why so many people are escaping and just saying 'Fuck it all!' I understand."

"Well, I don't, and never will. I don't understand why there's even such a thing as crack, or horse, or even drag queens," Blur stated bluntly.

"That's because you never once tried to understand David, or any of my friends. A thousand people in this city will say fuck it today. Someone is saying it right now. They're saying 'fuck it' to life, or they're *fucking life* and its jagged little fucking days to shit. Or they're smoking, dropping, snorting, shooting something, anything, as long as it makes the mean and vicious shit go away. I really do understand the urge to say fuck it."

"Maybe it's just a 'fuck it' generation," Blur added.

"No. You're a lawyer and you don't even see. These are lost and shaky times, Blur. It's so much easier to say fuck it when you're lost."

Was David *lost*? It's easy to get lost in New York City. Tyrone imagined ghastly scenarios: David alone, in pain, and babbling in the Bowery. David carted off to Bellevue by the men in white. David bombed out of his mind on Thorazine, moving from place to place like an aimless ghost. David addled by amnesia, sleeping a sleep swept clean of dreams.

Ty read in the *Village Voice* about the brutal murder and burning of a drag queen, and wondered if somewhere out there David hadn't suffered the same kind of appalling slaughter. *No, I would know. Trick taught me to know. David's alive.*

Carrying David's picture, Ty walked the streets, cased all the haunts Davy once frequented—Area, Danceteria, Limelight, America. Where the fuck was he?

"Have you seen this cat? He's five foot six, 130 pounds, delicately muscular. His name is David."

Think like Davy. Where *was* that Wednesday Night Hot Body Contest? More than once, Ty stood in the middle of Washington Square Park and shouted from the top of his scared and frustrated lungs, "David Donatello Richmond, where the fuck are you?"

If anyone knew, they weren't telling.

Ty saw Davy's disappearance as a personal rejection, though he was stymied for a reason. He blamed everyone for the vanishing. Face, for obvious reasons. And Adeva, with that silly tribe of drag queens. He blamed David's own foolish quest for love and attention. But most of all, *he blamed himself.*

Then David was gone so long, Ty grew pissed at him. *If I do ever see him again, I will kick his little troubled ass, and then I'll kiss him.*

David couldn't explain it at the time. He didn't want to explain, because *telling* it was far too painful. But after that beating, a vital light had gone out in his head, and he realized it was up to him to fix his faulty wiring. It was the season for self-examination.

Do you really love yourself? Are you addicted to sex, or are you just a contact junkie? Will you ever find Face waiting for you on a Martinique beach, in a backroom's darkness handing love's cock to you like a gift? How far does love go? Where is all this lo-o-ove getting you? What is it giving you, David, but a chronically broken heart, broken ribs, broken teeth, and broken feelings?

* * *

A Pale Blue Room.

Dr. Ted Horowitz was a balding man in his mid-fifties. He wore wire-framed John Lennon specs housing pale blue eyes that were keen observers. He had a tendency to scratch his wrist at signs and subtle gists of deception. Initially, with David, there was excessive wrist-scratching until they managed to scratch beyond the surface of the truth.

"There's a very telling saying in my profession," Dr. Horowitz told David. "If it's hysterical, it's *historical.* In other words, whatever triggers a destructive behavior usually has its roots in childhood."

"My father was *all* I had. Without him, I would've had nothing to rebel against. I'm the man he made me, and he never learned to love the queer in me," David confessed. "I'm here to get well. And I'm not gonna if I don't tell the truth. See, Doc, my mother raised me on MGM musicals. Sometimes she'd wake me up at 2 A.M. so we could watch Fred and Ginger, Fred and Cyd, Fred and Rita, or Fred alone just tappin' up a storm. See, she *understood* the dancer in me. When I was accepted to The Dance Theater of Harlem's children's program, no one was happier than my mother. She came to see my final recital—alone. My father couldn't be bothered. But she, oh, she was very proud. On the way back home she was telling me *just how proud* I'd made her feel, and then she was . . . tryna . . . say something else . . ."

David began to cry. "My mother was a very *graceful* woman. But all that grace, it suddenly left her. Then . . . she sort of *slumped* forward. A massive stroke. She was gone. I was *hysterical.* My father, he was something else. He never forgave me. I mean never! It was *all* my fault. Me and my faggot dancing! I really do believe he *wanted* Rico to beat that little faggot dancer out of me. He never understood that if Rico coulda, I woulda let him. Now I'm a broken boxer, a broken dancer, a broken little faggot, and I still like dick—even when the world wants me to believe this ain't the Decade of the Dick. Well, screw my father and *fuck* the world! I'm not gonna stop being gay, even if I do stop having sex with men."

"David, are you OK?"

"No! Why the fuck do you think I'm here?" He laughed, as he often did to cut through the pain.

"Well, if you feel you're ready, I'd like to hear about Face Depina."

"Oh! God! You don't ask for much, do you?" David sniffled, drying his eyes. "High school was sweatin' season for curious fags. I saw a *vision*, and I *had* to know, 'Who are you? What are you? What are you into? How big is it? How dark is it? Can you make it do tricks?'"

"Seriously, David, this man's affected you in ways only you, your heart, and your mind can reveal. I think it's crucial that we talk about it."

"Ah, Facey," he began, his eyes clouding over. "He doesn't want me. I know that now. He wants a man he can spit on and still respect, like Chaz. They spit on each other, you know? Some people say hello. Those two hock on each other's faces and it becomes something almost *sacred*. I can't compete with that."

"David, you're talking around the subject," Horowitz reminded.

"A long time ago, I taught him how to *dance*, and we shared our own private tango. We were people of the night, ya know. I remember the stars and streetlights cutting through the darkness that sharp, cold, winter night, and how we laughed. We were all coming back from the recording studio after we'd cut our first song. We were high on the idea that we were about to be somebody.

"Tyrone's folks were gone, so we partied at his place, getting drunk on Hennessy and high on Facey's spacey weed. We laughed like we were all such good friends, like the way I wanted it to be. But we never all got along at the same time, except when we were singing. Well, Ty and Browny passed out, and Facey and I sat up talking. There was a moment when I felt so *safe* that I broke down and told him my childhood horror story. He felt sad for me. And in return, he told me *his* horror story. He'd never told another soul those things. It all came spilling from his mouth. I knew he wasn't acting. NO, Facey was *being real* with me. Suddenly, I felt closer to him. He'd never let anyone get that close, and once I got there, I thought I'd never lose it. It was in his eyes. We'd shared *this thing*, this *hurting thing* that most people would never even know about either of us, let alone understand.

"We were having the quietest conversation with our eyes. Then he went into Ty's bathroom, and after a while, I followed him. It seemed like he was *waiting* for me, just waiting for me to come inside and go down on his sadness. For a minute, I think I actually sucked that sadness away.

"When it was over, that big, pretty, sad boy kissed my forehead and whispered, 'Thank you, Davy.' I never heard him sound more tender or fuckin' sweeter.

"But then, he acted like he was *too drunk* to remember any of it. We were *one* person that night, Doc. And he pretended like it *never happened*. Why? Did reaching that honest place with me make him feel too naked? Well, my attitude's always been, 'let's just be naked with each other, baby.' Naked can be beautiful and revolutionary, too.

"For days his scent was everywhere, everyplace he was. He can pretend until we're dust that he was stupid-drunk. We were *both* drunk, Doc, and *truth* was our elixir.

"The other day, I saw this man. And I use the term as limply as an über-queen's wrist. He was berating his lover out in the street, just talkin' all kinds of cruel shit. 'Look! I don't want yo ass! I don't like bein' 'round no *faggots!* Brothers want somebody to come strong and hard like Black men should!' he yelled. It was my father and Rico and Facey all over again. I can't tell you how that affected me, Doc. Once, you said 'the goal was self-acceptance.' Well, I *do* accept me. I ain't ashamed of who or what I am. I happen to like men. I happen to be a superb fellatrix. I embrace that part of myself. It's my nature. People who think I'm *vulgar* can kiss this faggot's natural black vulgar ass!" David declared.

What Dr. Horowitz realized was that what David feared more than anything was the thought that he'd someday be alone.

"The lips, the throat, and yes, the anus, they're such selfish masters. They want what they want, and they usually get it," David announced. "Today's my birthday, Doc. I didn't get what I wanted. But that's OK. I'm here, I'm queer, and damn it, by now you must be used to it!"

"What was it that you wanted, David?"

"Why, a gold-plated Eveready battery-operated foot-long dildo, of course!" He giggled. "No, seriously, I wanted me some new love. Hell, it ain't even gotta be new. Like Luther sang: *Any Love.*"

For the most part, the boxer kept his guard up around Horowitz. The doctor was fairly sure that David's lisping, mincing queerer-than-thou spiel was a ruse. It seemed to color his speech when he was being comical or defiant. But his voice turned to a smoke and gravel baritone those times he allowed his truth, his *core truth* into the room.

"I used to want so many things, simple things, really. You think I'm *fine* now? You shoulda saw me at fifteen. I was ma-a-ad-crazy-sexy-cute. I had wild limbs, and a *desire to live, dance, love, and do everything twice. I had energy, and this do it fluid juice* runnin' through my veins. I was comin' into myself, and comin' all the time *with* myself. Sheeee-e-it! I was a raw piece of hot fruit, just dyin' to be plucked from the vine. Remember being fifteen, Doc? Fifteen, when everything was new and in working order? All you're lookin' for is the opportunity to *work it.*

"I used to see straight people in love, walkin' hand-in-hand, kissin'. It seemed like the whole fucking hetero world was kissin' to remind me just how *wrong* my nature was. But what kind of freakishness lives inside me that makes me so fuckin' unworthy of love, huh? Hell. Every song on the radio was a love song. Didn't it ever occur to those songwriters, many of them queer, I'm sure, that queer fifteen-year-old copper boys needed love too?

"So I learned to *front* for love, for respect. I learned to hold the dick, scratch the pubic scratch, walk the cool, hip, simian bop, throw a rap. Hell, I did whatever was required of me to snatch a little piece of love from the jaws of suffering. I used my charm, my muscles, my fists, and finally, my tongue. I wrapped my lips around Rico and something in that pulse *felt* like love. Well, I know now that ain't love, and that's OK. Right now I'll settle for the respect to walk down any street and not be called a *faggot*, not be reduced or dishonored, disrespected, discarded, or *dissed* in any way. Even if I'm flamed-out to my boa-flourishin' extreme, I want people to look in my eyes, and see me, Davy, because what the fuck does the rest of it really mean anyway? See, David! He's a helluva cat, and a kitten too, sometimes.

"I'm pretty sure I've had more sex than most of your patients. Trust me on that. Yet, I still remember the few sweet times somebody made *love* to my ass. No pun intended. But what I keep missin' is that one in a million motherfucker who loves me for me. Not because I'm a fly dancer, or because I'm available. I want a man who sees all the good shit inside me. Then we could fuck till they hear our hot howlin' asses in Hoboken.

"Taking inventory, today I glanced in the mirror, naked, and

I didn't blanch once. Well, maybe Black folks don't blanch. But I thought, 'G'on girl! You ain't so vile.' Got this nice, smooth, copper Venus skin. My friend Ty once described my eyes as 'luminous orbs of amber fire,' and I *like* that. Still got a dancer's body, and I got it the hard way. Plus, I got an ass like a Chevy pickup. So what if I tend to laugh a little too loud, or swish just a little too much. I don't live for the comfort or approval of uptight assholes. I'm a good person. I've been around, Doc. I see how people are. I realize I don't *have* to be a good person to achieve great sparkling things, or to have great things thrust at me. But I am. I've got a good heart, too.

"I have a life. But it's not the life I want. I have friends. Some are gone, and some don't want the same things I want. When I'm feeling alone and unappreciated, I go to the theaters. There's too *much* loneliness out there, Doc. Sometimes you have to swallow it before it swallows *you*, whole. But in those hot places I go, loneliness sits erect inside a stranger's fist, and it says, '*Hello. Look at me! I'm just like you!*'

"You find a strange kind of popularity in those places, Doc. And everyone's cute in the dark. So I go down slowly on loneliness. I make it sigh and melt away on my tongue. Because, believe me, this is one Sissy-of-Color who truly *knows* the flavor."

The doctor looked on, surprised at last by the raw honesty of David's words.

"Now, some judgmental people might think that's pathetic or sluttish, or dangerous these days. And maybe they're right. But those nameless motherfuckers, shining and erect in that theater, they're *all* my lovers. Doesn't matter if they're Black or Brown, White, Red or Yellow. When loneliness comes down and it hurts too much to talk about, they need to sink inside something moist, deep, and boundless as their own freakish longing. Maybe I *am* just a whore—a little man who dances and dresses in drag sometimes. But I'm an *artist*, damn it! I create pleasure. If you could ask any of those men spinnin' under my tongue, they'd swear I was some rejected angel come to light on them. And when they unload, I spit it out so quietly they can't even hear their loneliness hitting the cum-stained floor, Baby Doc!"

Davy wiped his willful mouth, refusing to be ashamed. The room grew quiet with the silent rhythm of things felt, but left unsaid. David had taken to smoking. His hands fluttered about, tapping, reaching into his chest pocket, needing, itching to light a cigarette. But he knew it was prohibited in the doc's office.

"Well, Doc, looks like you've got your work cut out for you."

"Next week, David, I'd like to delve more into the issue of your private life."

"Day-yum, Doc. Do it *get* any more private? I'm runnin' out of material!"

That night David drifted into the Adonis Theater. A man bathed in flickering silver light sat next to him. His breathing, his lust came in a scent that rose slowly between them. He gazed at David. David ignored him. Then this man exposed his erect and bronzed beauty. David quivered. With no words, only hot eyes and that disembodied sigh lust sometimes makes, David went down on him.

The man tasted restless as the night—long, hot, and lonely.

When the magic was over, David expected nothing. It came as a happy shock when this burly brown shadow kissed him and said, "Oohhhh! I want more of you. Let me take you home and make love all night with the lights on."

It was an invitation David seldom received, and it sounded like Latin jazz, like salsa and the harp strings of an erotic heaven all at once.

His name was Carlos. David liked the way he rolled the *r.* Together, they stood, letting their cocks lead them up the aisle and out into the warm, enigmatic night.

A different David walked into his next session proclaiming, "I'm in love, ya'll! Sweet, sweet, thick and juicy, gooey-rich *love*, Baby-Doc! His name is *Car-r-r-los*. He's a big ol' luscious russet daddy who doesn't fuck. But, *ay caramba*, he makes slow, levitating *love!* And *love*, my sissies, is The Best Dick of All! I tell you, this is *big love! Mira! Mi hombre es gusto! Mi corazón es muy GRANDE!*"

"Random encounters ask nothing more of us than gonadal interest," Dr. Horowitz offered. "True love rarely happens in an instant, in the course of a night, or a few weeks. What is it that you love? Is it the physical, or is it something spiritual you feel you've found in this Carlos?"

"It's both, Doc. He calls me 'Puppito.' Just the sound of it gives me a big ol' warm-fuzzy. He looks at me with shiny eyes like I'm somebody precious. And the sex. Oh! God! Have you *evuh* had a man spend an entire hour on your nipples? Just your nipples? Pulling, licking, slowly suckin', I mean to the point of being worshipful. Tellin' you how special they are, how special *you* are. And when you come, damn it, you want to cry from the pure and joyful nut of your *soul*! That's *bliss*. And that's what Carlos gives me nightly."

The doctor crossed his legs to hide his own erection.

Yet, for all of David's happiness, there was a stopwatch affixed to his dance with the concept of bliss. The night they'd met, after David had gone down on him, after walking up the darkened aisle together, and after arriving at Carlos apartment, David saw the bottles, the meds with the elongated names;

names he had slowly become accustomed to . . . he saw them, and his heart crashed to the floor, because, he suddenly he *knew*. Carlos was sick.

David's saddened eyes questioned him.

"Yes. They're mine," Carlos finally admitted. "And I would've told you before . . . but, I saw you, and you saw me, and somethin like, like *lightning* crashed in that theatre. I know we both heard it. And the thunder was so loud; it was all either one of us could hear. So I don't think you woulda heard me say: 'No. No! Don't do that! Don't go there, papi! Let me put a rubber on, first!' No. Don't think you woulda really heard me, David . . . because there was too much thunder going on between us."

David wanted to cry. He'd always coveted a man with an inherent sweetness, who'd spoke in poems; who made even the awful things, the most *terrible of shit*, sound romantic, and less jarring to his soul.

Carlos was sick, and he *should've told* David before anything transpired between them.

But he didn't. And for his part, David didn't ask. And David didn't provide a rubber. And now that he knew, David didn't even feel betrayed.

He just felt incredibly sad.

A part of David, that part which was never once tested, *knew* somewhere in his marrow that he couldn't and wouldn't be *so damn lucky*. He'd never asked if someone was sick, and he would become mildly offended if someone asked him, if he were sick. His attitude had become one of a poetic providence: *Hey, I don't know you . . . and you don't know me. But we've both been around the block, haven't we? You've probably got it. Don't you? I've probably got it, too. So maybe we can pretend until we forget that IT even exists. And maybe we can cheat the gods, and find some temporary shelter, some short-lived pleasure in our sick and blessed ignorance.*

It was crazy, and it was fatalistic. And it was the price David was willing to pay for the promise of something that felt, even just a little, like *love*.

WEEKS LATER

"The other day I was walking home from the clinic with Carlos. He has his good days, and his bad. This one wasn't such a bad day until some *punk* yelled as he passed us, 'Fuckin' faggots! Hope you all fuckin' die from that shit!'

"I ain't nobody's punk. It made me so mad, I *know* I coulda kicked his ass! But there's Carlos, dying a little more, and my fuckin' back's against the wall and I can't kick *everybody's* ass. And the world's tellin' me to *be a man*, and all the time it keeps kickin' me in the fuckin' balls!

"Doc, if you listen very closely, you can hear the sound of balls breakin' all up and through this room, and this city. Sometimes I just wanna cry for days. We've all been beaten down, broken down, black-balled, gay-bashed! We've been told we're too this and not enough of that! Can't be trusted. Despised worldwide. Diseases takin' us out like fuckin' assassins! Multi-colored motherfuckers workin' 24-7 tryna break your spirit! It's hard, damn it. It's hard!"

The room was full of emotion. David's eyes watered. His face was breaking in two. Dr. Horowitz thought maybe, just perhaps, they'd reached a breakthrough.

"Well," he said, "*you* more than most understand the crush of that kind of isolation, pain, and humiliation. So you might very well want to hit something, strike out, break or take something because you feel some part of your being has been broken and taken from you. It seems to me that experiencing some of mankind's ugliness would give you better insight. If fighting against the power outside you isn't working, maybe you need to fight *for* the power within. Trust whatever you believe in—God, divine justice, karma, or whatever to take care of the confusion, the ignorance, and all the rest of those mean and hateful things out there."

David embraced "Baby-doc" for the first time before leaving.

It had begun to storm. Rain and wind whipped his skin like shards of broken glass. David headed home to Carlos. They kissed for thirty minutes, then *did it* doggie style on the kitchen table. Between thrusts, Carlos sighed, emitting the poems of Federico García Lorca to David's taut, cocoa bung hole.

When it was over, Carlos noticed tears in David's eyes.

"Puppito, what's wrong?"

"Nothing. I'm just happy to be out of the rain."

TWENTY-FOUR

The Play Is the Thing

OCTOBER 1991

It was a Sunday afternoon, when, out of the clear indigo-blue, Tyrone's phone rang. Because he was on his computer and didn't want to lose his flow, he let the machine answer.

"Imagine, if you still can, you're sittin' in the dark," the voice on the answering machine cooed. "A large, dark man stands behind you. You turn, and all you see is *crotch*. Lots and lots of crotch. I mean it's all up in *your face*. And unless he's packin' a plantain wrapped inside a double pair of tube socks, he's well, *huge!* And the music and the drums, and your pulse are all thumpin': 'Gotta get you some. Go'n get you some!' Are you with me?"

Ty dashed to the phone asking, "*Whoisthis*?" though, through weary, rainy eyes he already knew.

"It's your queerest half, baby boy. I'm ba-a-ack. Have you been a good boy? Of course you have. Wanna hear somethin' unbelievable? So have I, and we both know that's so much *harder* for me."

"Duchess! You fuckin' heartless, negligent, absentee bitch! Where the hell have you been? *How* you been? You know I've got gray hairs worrying about your callous, uncaring ass! Would serve you right if I stopped caring and junked your ass altogether."

"Please. You couldn't if you tried. Tonight, we'll get very drunk, and we'll talk and laugh and cry and maybe I'll try to explain it all . . ."

"I've met this wonderful man. His name is Carlos. I've never been happier. You'd like him. He's a poet of the heart." Then David's face hardened. "But my poet's leavin' me, Ty, in a very un-poetic way. We're running out of reason and rhyme. And the saddest part is, I think I know now what it is to be *truly* devastated."

"Do you need anything? Does he? Tell me what I can do," Ty said.

"Yeah. I need you to tell me something good and wonderful and true about yourself, 'cause I've missed that."

"Well, let's see . . . I missed you, man, and missing my peeps, it's made me very introspective. I'm writing again, from the soul. Things are happening." Ty launched into a tale about irony—about how youthful disappointment can lead to adult fulfillment. "Remember me telling you about this white cat who tried to kick a young, ambitious brother's creativity to the curb?"

"Oh, yeah . . ."

Neither man acknowledged remembering the other, though Feld recalled the tall, brown boy in green corduroys with something to say, but who lacked the experience or mastery to say it. And Tyrone most definitely recalled a terse, slick taker of dreams.

Tyrone had to remind himself that he wasn't a glutton for punishment, since this time he'd been recommended to Feld by the editor of a lifestyle magazine.

Feld now presided over his own agency, and sitting across from him at a large oak desk, Ty noticed he'd acquired this *Omar Sharif* thing. Those clinging, dark Pepsi-Cola eyes. That old-world mustache, cut thin, but not so thin as to be *merry*. The thick bank of mixed gray waves that had begun to recede a bit. At forty-four, he was a striking man—suave, polished, urbane. A seasoned intellect emanated from his cosmopolitan demeanor, tailored Italian suit, and perfect manicure. He smelled divine—subtly French, and expensive. Ty would invent all kinds of stories about a man such as this. *But why would I bother? It's not like I'm attracted to him . . .*

"This has promise," Feld said, tracing the pages with a sensuously thick index finger. "There's potential here. But this is all very . . ."

Uh-oh. OK, you elitist fuck, you better come correct with me or I'm out!

"Your characters talk a lot," Feld said, followed by, "Take a deep breath. That's not necessarily a bad thing. I feel this could be reshaped somehow. Mamet's big now. Lots of realism and gritty language. What do *you* think?"

What Ty thought was, *Bet! Then let's do this!* He'd never set the world on fire with his first *enfant terrible* diatribe. But with this, a play about the cool skin of strangers, the cruel heartbreaks, fast flirts, the false starts and flutters of love, and the pain of being Black and gay in the diseased and fear-ridden '80s. Yes. This, he thought, might be his own small masterpiece.

The work was rewritten, but not without many arguments,

creative differences—maddening battles, tantrums, and tempestuous shit. Ty wrote and Feld critiqued. One artistic clash of wills resulted in a blowout:

"Don't you dare question the legitimacy of these feelings! These are *my* feelings, damn it! Every black and blue one of them! Either you want it real, or you want it fake. And if you want some comfortably fake shit, you best find yourself a beige synthetic writer. This is what it is, and if you can't relate, fuck you, this play, and the rest of this fake, half-baked shit!"

Neither gave in, and Tyrone walked away from the project, unwilling to surrender completely to another man's wishes, to give up *his* good fight. He would rather have written for free and never let another soul read his words. After a week of silence, Feld called him. The two talked and squawked like two opposing intellectual bitches. Then Ty thought of Trick, Jerome, Jazz, and all the rest. And he agreed to forge ahead.

There were more demands, more changes, and more disagreements. But then a rather miraculous thing occurred. The play, in previews, received *extremely* favorable notices. One early review read: "Electric! Angry and hopeful. *Bestest Friends* is a play of biting characters and razor-sharp words that cut through the pathology of our times. This story attaches itself to the thinking gay brain like a tumor."

Ty was quite happy with the reviews, though he took particular exception to the *thinking* GAY *brain* reference.

"See? Why do they have to constantly *do* that, Conny? This isn't a play just about, or just for gay people, or black people, or gay black boy people. It's about the *humanity* in *all* people. Didn't they *get* that? I mean what the fuck? Leave it to the media to try and limit a brotha by giving my work a backhanded compliment."

But by the time the show reached off Broadway, there was a buzz, and the word-of-mouth was: *Baby, pay attention!*

Tyrone was pleased that most everyone he knew came to see

the opening of his long-nourished creation. David, and a nearly sober Browny, the guys from the paper, folks from the magazine, people from his writing class, student friends, his college drama professor. Even Face showed up, with Chaz—of all people—in tow. Everyone was surprised to see Face blow through, Tyrone, especially. Blur, with whom Ty was "on again," was off once more, working his wares in DC, so he sent flowers.

It was a fantastic opening, followed by a fabulous party, but before it was over, Tyrone left. He went back to his apartment to be alone with his thoughts, and to quietly commune with Trick's ghost.

You should be here, man. You should be here, laughing, dancing, and drinking. You should be here makin' love with me until we're both fuckin' raw! All I got is a fucking ghost whispering the way in my ear!

But you ain't never needed me to do this, Tyronni. You the Poetry Man. You make things all right. Did little white Dorothy need that Great and Powerful Oz cat? Shit, no! Neither do you. All you needed was a peep inside your private heart. Now, how about a life? Don't ya want one of them? You cheat me and everyone who ever believed in your ass if you don't live your motherfuckin' life, Poetry Man. This here is your time. What you need to do is get your ass back to that party and dance like we'd both be dancin'. Live a life, Ty!

"A life? A life, Trick? Haven't you been watching? That was one of those tricky Trick dances I never did get quite right."

It's all in the steps, homey. The first one is a left, then a right, and before you know it, you out the door, Trick advised before his voice, and perpetually crooked-smiling image, disappeared.

When Ty opened the door to head back to the party, there stood Feld. Ty was surprised, but happily so.

Tyrone had noticed that while the play was in previews, Feld had stopped wearing a wedding ring.

"I came by because you left the party before I could tell you I'm proud of you, Ty," Feld said. "I've watched you work, struggle, question, and explore. And you've developed into a very good writer. More importantly, you're an extraordinary young man. And I like you a great deal. But being around you, lately, has been fucking with my perspective. I just can't do it anymore."

"What are you saying? That . . ."

In one leaping action, Feld grabbed him by the collar, silencing his words with the sure and blunt punch of his hardened flesh.

"I don't know about you, Ty, but I think we're good together," he said, eyes fixed, lips dangerously close.

Tyrone experienced an uncertain flush of weirdness. What was Feld going to say? What words of wisdom, warning, or woe was this agent whom he now considered a friend going to say?

"Your play is about truth, isn't it? When you break it down, there is just the truth, right? Tell the truth! Just say it!"

But before Ty could say anything, Feld grabbed him by the swing-low. Feld's lips moved in close, then suddenly were on top of Ty's, smashing hard, strong, and savage, saying everything he'd wanted to say, everything he'd felt and tried to hide. In one burning flash, Ty's blazer was ripped away.

"I've wanted *this* since the day I met your cocky green corduroyed ass," Feld said, his large hands tugging at Ty's sweat-soaked shirt.

"Ummm . . . Conny . . . are we about to do something . . . dangerous?" Ty asked.

"Yes. Very dangerous. But it's been a long while since I last did dangerous."

Shirts flew away.

As Feld boldly locked the door, Ty found himself strangely at odds with *a whole other aesthetic*: A thick and shaggy pelt so dense the man's nipples were barely visible. Everything about Feld was shaggy and heaving, and the pipe down his leg was threatening to burst through the seams of his tuxedo pants. Feld ran his lips along Tyrone's torso, feasting on the lean brown slopes of his shoulders and his chest. He gripped the firm dark nipples, suctioning each keen tit. With hands tracing, racing over each other's flesh, they fell to the sofa, gripping, groping at zippers.

Yes! What a beautiful dick you've got, Tyrone, Feld thought, staring at Ty's ringed phallus. Dipping down, he coated Tyrone in slow and sensuous sucks and tried to swallow the spike to its root. Ty studied the pulsation darting between Feld's bushy legs. It was more than an ample *schmeckel.* It was hard, sturdy, and attached to a man Ty could respect. Just in that moment as Ty was trying to decide whether to descend, or not to descend, the buzzer buzzed—and it buzzed loudly.

It was David, with a bottle of Dom and a big Hawaiian gift of a celebratory shlift.

"Sweetheart? Open up! I know you're in there! Don't start playin' the *star* with me, ya literary bitch! I still got a key, you know?" he said in a singsong reminder. "Don't make me use it!"

"Ignore him!" Feld insisted, sucking, gasping, running hands along humping curves of cheeks. His slurping nearly drowned out the noise of the rain, buzzers, and indecision. His tongue lashed feverishly at Tyrone's crevice, lapping, teasing its dark bud out of hiding. Ty stroked a trailing web down to what lay plush pink and rigidly poking from Feld's fist.

"Yeah, let's see if we fit," Feld hissed.

Ty gazed at those thirsty brown eyes and that raw-red erection.

"Dammit, Ty! I'm growin' old and *haggard* in this fuckin' hallway! All right?" Davy huffed. "You bet not have nobody in there . . ."

"This . . . this can't happen," Ty said suddenly. "We can't let it. This wasn't meant to be, Conny. We both *know* that." Ty pushed away, tucked himself away and buzzed up David.

"So . . . it's the *race* thing, isn't it? Isn't it?" Feld insisted. "Admit it! You're afraid I wouldn't be the right *arm piece*, huh? Not the *acceptable* scenery for your pro-black stance?"

"Man, please. You should know me better than that! It ain't political—just too damn personal. And this place we were about to go, it's not a *professional* place, Conny. I'd like to keep you and your presence in my life, but only as a friend and a *professional* colleague!"

It seemed a most *ridic* statement, considering he was still *wet* with his colleague's spit, and that irony was not lost on either of them.

"Besides," he added, "in my experience, friends last longer when they're not fuckin' each other."

Feld eyed him with vague disgust as he quickly dressed. He felt *used.* Maybe it *was* political. Maybe all Ty ever wanted was to be a success, at any cost.

David entered, flying through the door, bottle in one hand, playbill in the other.

"Oh my! What have we here? Hello," he said dubiously to Feld. "Leaving so soon? Why Tyrone, you little coquette!" he teased, rolling his eyes.

"Shut up, David! It's not like that."

"No. Not when *I have a key*, I guess it isn't. Well, Mr. Feld, you're welcome to share in some bubbly with us . . ."

"Thanks. But, no thanks. Three's a mismatched crowd." He exited, leaving the door open in his wake.

"Well, I just *hate* to be the saboteur!" David yelled. Cocking his head around the corner and watching Feld walk down the hall, then, noting the open door, he said, "*Symbolic*, don'cha think?" As David removed his coat, he sniffed the air. "Mmm. I just love the way that man smells. So worldly, so damn sophisticated. It's all Paris, and Greece, and (*sniff*) moist *dick!* And . . . (sniff) sweaty azzzzzzzzzzzz? *Ooooooooob*! What duh fuck? I'ma tell somebody! Where's Ms. Liz Smith at . . . or that thick one from *Sista 2 Sista*? Hell, I needs to tell *somebody* about this!"

Ty grimaced. "Oh . . . shut the hell up, *Swish* Cheese!" David smirked devilishly.

"Well, mon petite *Tyronique*, looks like timing *is* everything. You know my antenna was up all evening long. You! Escaping in the dark of night from your own damn party? Strange that. Then, I come here, and find you, all caught-up in mid-swerve with the dashing Mr. *Almost* Sharif? Stranger still. Now, I know (*sniff*) from the *whiff* of things, that situation was pregnant with all kinds and varieties of *raunchy* possibilities . . . and ya *know* you wanna tell me, so let's get our party started, shall we?"

The champagne opened with a *pop*, and flowing white foam exploded into the air. Ty sipped, but remained quiet, reflective, and a bit freaked about the night's most recent event. David wanted dish. Ty wanted contemplation. But David *wanted dish*, damn it!

"So," Davy asked, bringing the suds to his lips, "my youngish, but rapidly aging black man, you sure there's nuttin' you wanna *tell* me about you and the oh-so-dashing Mr. Almost Sharif?"

There *was* something to tell him, something Ty couldn't quite believe himself. There was no denying a part of Ty might've enjoyed a little interracial bozack to *shmeckel* mambo with Feld. But that vital Africanus Ambitious Rex who dwelled within would've forever questioned what part *emotions and dick* played in his success.

In the midst of champagne and chitchat, the phone rang and a half-drunken Ty allowed his machine to take the call. Suddenly, Bliss Santana's voice filled the room:

"Hey, honey boy, it's me. I am so sorry I couldn't be there

for your big night. If you're celebrating, then good for you! But listen, we have to talk. Hon, it's about Tyra. Oh, I can't do this on the phone. I'm in Atlanta, but I'll be in New York next week, OK? We're talk then. I love you, honey boy. Bye. And Ty—Congratulations!"

Now there was yet another question to alight the night, and it was left to David to ask it.

"Who the hell is Tyra?"

TYRONE WOULD SUDDENLY RECALL THE WINTER OF DAVID'S ABSENCE

One seasonably chilly day in Chelsea, Ty and Bliss were walking together when Ty happened to catch their reflection in the glass of a passing car. *Hmm*, he thought. *Interesting couple*. For a split second, he'd forgotten who they were. He thought he looked sexy with her on his arm.

"Bliss Santana, stunning Blacktress, do you realize, this is the first time I've seen you *clean*, in the bright sunlight? "You look *new and exquisite*," he said, and he meant it. "Ah, Bliss. Daddy's proud, baby-girl."

"Well, it's about time, don't you think? A month in rehab can make you sit inside your own stillness, and realize all the shit in your life. Ty, my whole fuckin' life was about big hair, big jewels, big drugs, and big men. Well, I'm downsizing now.

"Coolness. It's a very '90s thing to do."

"Sometimes a girl needs a new face and friendlier eyes to show it to," she said. "I'm starting from scratch. No crutches, no pretty-faced assholes, and no more fucking anesthetizing," she proclaimed in that seductive scruff of a voice. Tyrone actually believed her.

"You know, sometimes the best way to *get out of yourself* is to get involved in something larger," Ty told her as he lead her *not* to a glitzy premier or a groovy downtown über-club, but to a bare-knuckles soup kitchen in the heart of Chelsea. There they helped serve and feed 150 strangers. A frequent volunteer to that and other shelters, Ty had gotten to know many of the people there.

"That's Sonny over in the corner, in the frayed hat and raincoat. He lost his whole family in a fire and gave up on life. The lady in the black scarf, she lost her job and after two months was evicted. Had to leave her kids with a sister until she could get it together. Then the sister up and moved. Took the kids, and never told her where. No job, no house, no kids, no hope."

And so the stories went.

Bliss noticed that Sonny's attire seemed vaguely familiar.

"Tyrone? *Please* tell me that man's *not* wearing the 450-dollar raincoat I bought you two Christmases ago!"

"Oops, sorry! But it never *was* my style. Besides it was a very *dry* season."

If Bliss was pissed she didn't reveal it. Instead, she shook her head, exasperated, yet exhilarated.

"This is some fuckin' date, you stupid-ass bastard! But you know what, it's just what my spoiled and pampered ass needed. You think it would be all right if I came again, and maybe brought some clothes and things I don't need anymore?"

Ty looked at her and smiled, glad that his prized instincts were on the money.

What a rare and beautiful man you are, she said in her mind. *A person like you should have a powerful force of love in his life.*

But at that moment, he didn't. He and the ballistically ambitious Blur were once again on the outs.

Back at Bliss's apartment, as Ty was saying goodbye, the look on her face became strangely devious and tangibly sexy. Something had grown between them. Bliss Santana *had* play, and the play was the thing. She gently touched his hand, and she kissed each finger softly, and then she placed his entire hand upon her left breast.

Bliss! Stop! This ain't gonna work, baby girl!

She placed his hand lower and then lower, and lower, still. He was amazed at how easily she'd made tears in his hand, and how she turned misunderstanding into flashes of lightning.

"Come to Mami," she purred.

And she fashioned a place for him to fall, a net of moist wet skin to catch his sad and endless longing.

No rubber was involved.

OCTOBER 1991

"So. Guess I have to give it *one* mo try. Who the hell is Tyra?" David asked.

"Tyra? I . . . I think she might be my . . . daughter."

A champagne-swilling David stood up quickly, very quickly, and then he promptly *fainted.*

"Well, mine or Face Depina's," Ty said.

But David was out cold and did not, *could not* hear that little addition.

TWENTY-FIVE
This is Not My Beautiful Decade

THE '90S

It was the dawn of Generation X. No more slick, glossy extravagance. Everything was downsized. Even the Gulf War proved a streamlined affair. It was time to keep it real. Real as gangsta rap, real as a Rodney King beat-down. Real as the L.A. riots. Real as the unrest in Crown Heights, Brooklyn. Real as a gay sailor slaughtered in a public men's room.

Rapists, racists, race and race violence, sex, the sexy, and sexual abuse, proud gays, club kids, and homo-haters were screaming obscenities on talk TV. Oprah Winfrey, Sally Jesse, Phil, Geraldo, Jerry, and Ricki—everyone came to shake and speak freely from the lips of their asses, and get their fifteen minute groove on. As TV screens grew bigger, phones became smaller, and cellies were glued to most every ear. Personal computers gave way to the Internet.

The city elected its first African-American mayor. Tyrone was a major campaign fundraiser.

A sprawling disease clenched its indiscriminate fist and took on new prisoners.

In late '91, Magic Johnson got *it.* Upon receiving this sobering news, Tyrone placed a call to his number one homey to ask the question most everyone asked that November night.

"David? Did you hear? Did you hear about Magic?"

"Yes, I heard. And apparently that Johnson *ain't* so magic."

"Not funny, David! This shit should be a freaking *clarion* call to everyone. Even *you*!"

"Me? Well, I did spend *some time* in L.A. But I swear, we never once knocked Nikes! Or in his case, clacked Converses," he deadpanned.

"David, I'm serious. Please! I want you to finally get *tested*."

The silence on the other end was deafening. David didn't like Ty's tone or this invasion into his sexual business. Most of all, David didn't want to face the reality on the other side of that test.

"Maybe . . . maybe I don't wanna know. You ever think of that? Maybe I wanna live my life without fear. Maybe I'll die not knowing."

"Oh yeah? Well maybe you're just a pointless, unapologetic asshole on a *suicide* mission. Maybe you're *not* as decent and right-handed as I *thought* you were, down deep. Maybe you're just some fuckin' casual serial killer on the lam. Ever *maybe* think about that?"

David abruptly hung up on him. The two would not speak again for a long time.

Tyrone had just about had it with David and his chronic fits of irresponsibility. Ty had also had it with Blur, who was so busy fighting, scratching, and clawing his way to a higher position in city government that Ty had become a non-entity in the meteoric scheme of things.

With friends and part-time lovers such as these, Ty was glad there were other things, other places and other people worth his time. His flight was booked, his plans were made.

The following day Tyrone left the U.S.A., and the Third World awaited him.

NOVEMBER 1991

Ty grew a soul in Africa. More precisely, he realized the existence of his soul in Botswana amongst the Bushmen moving across the Kalahari Desert. They were a yellowish-brown people, short in stature, yet so tall in spirit. They worked cattle posts and farms, spoke in hypnotic clicks, and each year, after the first rains of November, they moved en masse twenty to thirty miles from their villages. And Ty photographed them throughout this heartening sojourn. Their survival depended upon killing prey with poison darts and digging up roots of plants for food. Still, they trekked through the desert toward a new home.

It was a humbling experience, and it succeeded in teaching Tyrone just how little was needed to replenish one's life, to start anew.

SPRING 1992

Ty was back in the states working as a photojournalist for *Current* magazine when he got a call to fly out to the West Coast. His editor wanted him in L.A. to cover the Rodney King verdict.

Tyrone, like most of the country, had been watching and waiting for America to show her true colors. Ty would be there for the aftermath.

From the back of a rented van, he managed to freeze-frame the flames of unrest. It was not glossy, not glamorous, but an up-close and deadly personal view, in black, brown, and bloody. While the electronic media videotaped the stunning ravages of a Madness Incarnate, Ty's stills illustrated a profane savagery waged by the Frankensteins that injustice created. He saw men, women, kids, whole families enraged. He captured people running in tantrums, looting in droves, frantically pulling drivers from their vehicles, bashing heads, beating them down and screaming "Fuck the police!"

For three days a city burned. For two of them, Ty didn't sleep. There was no time to sleep.

His photographs had cold-cocked the public with the brutal truth. This violence as a spectator's sport granted Ty yet another of his bouts with miniscule celebrity. But he did not *want* celebrity, especially at any cost.

"In this country, you kill someone by inflaming words, by fists of automatic weapon, and suddenly, inexplicably, you become The Shit. Kids are killing kids in schools. They wanted to be visible, to be discussed on the news, to have their name on the country's collective tongue, even just for a moment. What does that say about us? There is something inherently wrong with this concept because there's no honor in it. Sadly, we live in a country that erects its killers and does not honor its honorable, its poets of the heart, its angels of the spirit," Ty wrote in an opinion piece.

He wanted *better* from life, but the riots and current events put a tragically sad face on his childlike view of the future.

Sometimes Ty thought he was born to feel things deeply, too deeply sometimes—and that the pain in him might be generic—not wrapped up in God, or lost lovers, or ego, or mother, or father, or race, or sexuality, or even disease.

And with all the wars and worries, riots and ruination swirling around him, there was still that little war of the heart surrounding Bliss Santana. After their last encounter, Ty was bewildered. In those most bewildering times, he turned to the friend others couldn't see. Ty began talking out loud to a ghost again. "I'm perplexed, man. I mean, I like Bliss. I do. I find her fascinating and sexy, and most times she's pretty cool. But to tell the truth, this shit scares me. Maybe it's vanity, but kinda reminds me of myself. She's always wanting what she can't seem to have . . . and yet it never stops her from wanting it. Face, the Face Depina she wants or imagines she wants, he's as dead as you are. And she can't see that."

CHAPTER TWENTY-SIX

Goodbye, Hello Again

LATE SUMMER 1992

While getting his blackjack fix on in Atlantic City, Ty's father collapsed and suffered a fatal heat attack.

Ty and Blur were on the outs again, and Tyrone didn't even try to find him. He had no lover to calmly stroke his dreads, to soothe or spoon him to sleep, and he thought maybe he didn't *deserve* one. Most of all, he *missed* David. He'd placed call after desperate call to David's crib. But David never returned them. Tyrone had killed the friendship.

"Duch, please answer. How many times can I say I'm sorry? I opened my mouth and I hurt you. David? I'm jack back from another funeral. Got another one on Wednesday. Seems I've painted myself into this role where everyone blows their noses on my sleeve.

"I met a man whose job was collecting nipple rings, cock

rings, wedding rings from the bodies of elegantly deadly boys. He said the worst place he ever found someone dead was just outside a tearoom—corpse's pants around his ankles, a night's worth of stranger's DNA all over him. I don't ever wanna see you elegantly dead on the other side of a glory hole, David. I'm selfish like that. When I love someone, I'm way too candid, and sometimes even cruel. So shoot me. There's a Timex in my head, and it's ticking off time. Where are you? I always thought we'd endure this shit together. David, how's it's gonna turn out for us, bruh? Straight up. What's gonna become of us?

"Sorry for this message. I guess I've outgrown or outraged the friend I haven't outgrown. But you're my friend, aren't ya, Duch? So how many apologies do I have to leave before you step out of your chilly dance of intolerance? Look, I opened my mouth and I hurt you . . . out of love. I'm sorry for lovin' you that much. Goodbye."

David was home, and he'd heard this pitiful version of Tyrone courting his sympathy. But just like all the other messages, he chose to ignore it.

Ty could have simply said, "David, my father died today. Come quickly. I need you, Duch." If Ty had only said those words, then whether David was still upset or not, he would have surely come running. But Tyrone didn't say it. He didn't want David's sympathy. He wanted the *love* back.

Say what you will of Faison Brown (and people said or were apt to say all kinds and varieties of shitty madness), he understood *the importance of support*. Browny managed to contact David.

"Yo, David. You got yourself a friend in Tyrone. Ya ain't gon find no better. Shit! Let's face it, ya don't deserve none. Ain't sayin he perfect, yo. But he *good* people. You know his father died, right? Well, he did, and the funeral's Wednesday. So, yo . . . is you gon be a *bitch*, or is you gon be his *boy*? Huh?"

TY'S EULOGY FOR HIS FATHER

"Funny thing about secrets: Sometimes they can sit still and untouched, like so many figurines gathering dust on an old shelf. Secrets, they were our family possessions. They did not leave the house, and we did not share them—not even with ourselves. There wasn't anything so sinister going on inside our tiny box in the sky. No. We simply went about robbing ourselves of feeling and living our quietly tragic lives. Because of this, for as long as I can remember, I've walked around with something *gigantic* and unshared in me.

"I've no skin-memory of the texture of my father's arms wrapped around me. This isn't a daddy dearest eulogy. You see, there were two kinds of men in my family: the *bums*, and the workers. My father was a *worker*. He'd come home each day in that bent, broken-down waltz of overworked bones, and I'd think, *Oh it's just Pops, home from another day of just-a-slavin' for The Man.* He'd pitch some tired utterance at me, and then he'd be gone again.

"But there were always decent clothes on my back, food on the table, and my mother was a ghetto widow crying herself to sleep each night. Though I've no doubt anger was a very real part of my father's composition, we were never victims to anger blind rages, never bombarded by its words or fists. In his way of thinking, he was a 'man' because he provided. If we didn't ever get to toss a ball, or have a conversation for more than three minutes, it's because he was always too busy, or too tired, or too afraid. And the little monster he spawned now stands before you with a sharper mind, newer clothes, a better education—and I flaunted those things in his face. Shame on me! Shame on us!

"I'm older now. I understand the complexity of men who spend so much time locked inside their skulls that they never get to *live* what's in their hearts. For my father, respect was never a given. It didn't come on the job, on the corner, or on the shelves of any liquor store. And respect didn't come calling with a malnourished wallet. For my father, respect showed his best face during a night of poker, or a game of twenty-one in Atlantic City, and later Vegas.

"'You never did understand the things I do for me,' he once told my mother as he headed out the door and into another superstitious night. Well maybe we never did. But we each could've tried just a little harder. My father leaves behind a shamed and broken son. He leaves to grieve him, my mother—who has been a proven phoenix, and who will no doubt rise again. He leaves behind a new blond companion, and a host of muttered voices that now sound, just a little, like *love*."

When Ty's eulogy was done, he looked out inside the crowd, and standing in the door in his own sedate suit was David. Later they embraced very tightly. In that moment, all was forgiven.

"I can't even remember. Am I the good twin or the evil one? And which of us is supposed to say 'I'm sorry' first?" David asked.

And then, together as if they were still members of the long ago Da Elixir, simultaneously, harmoniously, they spoke.

"I'm sorry, baby boy." They hugged again and broke apart.

"Ty, I know this is a sad day . . . a tragic day and a very heavy time for you. Why don't you come with me tonight? Screw the always absent Blur! You know he's The Anti-Nelly anyway. We'll just get you some new bone. Bet we could rustle ya up some BBBs."

"Excuse me?"

"Duh! Some big black bone, or some big brown bone. Hell, might get fancy and find you some big ol' imported bone. But please trust and believe me, bonage is *needed* here!"

"Imported? *Whaaaaa*? You mean, like some big ole Brazen Beluga Bone? Is there some of that in town this week? No thanks, Davy . . . but I've got a BBB of my own, thank you."

"Yes . . . but you ain't *that* young, or that hung, and you never were *that flexible*. Listen, Ty, there's one surefire way to shake off the remnants of a sad memory day. You can come out with us, and just be wild and young and gay again. Besides, there's a high that comes from shovin' your hand down a new pair of pants, man—and you missin' way too much of that good shit!" And Ty sighed.

"Welcome back, David Richmond. You are still such a 'mo. But I love that 'mo in you. Thanks for coming, Duchie."

They embraced again. Ty kissed his cheek and winked at him. Then he went off to play his version of Superman to and for the grieving others.

WEEKS LATER, TY WAS TALKING TO A GHOST AGAIN:

"Today I saw a young black man playing with his son in the park, and it beautiful how natural they were togther. And overwhelming sadness came over me. Today, I realized how much I *miss* my father. He wasn't always strong or smart, and he wasn't always my hero, but damn it, he was my dad! I wish he was someone I could've taken my stuff to . . . I wish we could've been friends, and . . ."

"Ty? Tyrone? Who you talkin' to? Please tell me you were just on the phone and NOT buggin' the fuck out!" David, key in hand, had stopped by to drop off a shirt he had designed.

"No, David. I wasn't on the phone. And I'm far from *buggin* out, as you call it. I was just talking to Trick."

"Trick? TRICK? You mean . . . dead Trick. Been dead for mad years, Trick?"

Ty immediately regretted his confession.

"Hold up, wait a minute! You been smoking on some bad weed, baby boy? I know they got some ganja out there that will totally fuck with your senses. Tell me you smoked an ounce of that shit. Tell me you're all blitz-blasted or blunted on reality. Tell me *something* before I have to call Bellevue on your ass!"

"I haven't been smoking anything. Trick is real, and I'm still regular," Ty said calmly.

"Hold on. I'm gonna have to sit down for this one."

"I never told you how tight we were."

"So tell it."

And so, Ty recited the story of his shortened relationship with Trick, and then of his long, ongoing relationship with Trick's ghost. Through it all, he kept looking around as if waiting for word from Trick, or permission from the cosmos to speak.

"We shared an energy. We still do. A spiritual connect that makes me think we probably walked this earth together before. I knew him, before I knew him, and when I met him, it was like *home*. I know it sounds crazy, and if it is, I've been crazy for years. But Trick is here. See, we were on this road together and it was a short-lived, but very cool, Electric Avenue, OK? And now I know he's left this physical plane . . . but a part of him remains here, for me. I can feel it."

"Trick's here. Oh yeah," David mocked. "There he is with a diamond in the back, sunroof top, digging the scene with a gangsta's lean, mmm-hmmm-m-m."

"Fuck you! He's here. If you don't see him, or feel him, then you're not supposed to." It all sounded perfectly sound to Tyrone.

"Ty, I love you. Even if you crazy as a shithouse rat, I'll still love yo crazy rabid ass. But this is scarier than Madam Zoreena's parlor that Halloween night the woman made fire in her hand. Is he here, right now?" David asked incredulously.

"I feel him over there by the chair. I feel the vibrations of him laughin'. He knows you don't believe me."

"That wicker chair by the window?"

"Yes."

"Well, what does he look like? Is he still black as coal? No disrespect. Or is he white, and all see-through?"

"He's not like Casper, ya wiseass. He's not some murky ectoplasm movie ghost. He's like a shadow or *flicker of light*. His voice is in my head like I'm wearing headphones, or like I'm imagining it in my thoughts. But it's his voice. *His* voice! Sometimes, not so much anymore, his face will flicker inside a shadow. He's different from how he is in my dreams. In my dreams, he's whole, real flesh, and fully tricked out. Here, he's just pieces of light and wisdom, comfort and counsel and sometimes, just company."

"Hey, as long as he's not some vengeful *haint* wreckin' up shit, then we cool. My southern grandma, she used to talk about these *haints* comin back mad that they'd been done wrong, so their earthly shit ain't finished. They come back raging, makin' life hell. But let's don't dwell. In fact, let's not talk about this shit anymore, 'kay?"

And so, they never did.

APRIL 1993

In the Clinton Age of "don't ask, don't tell," a curious David was asking.

"Hey Tubby . . . ummm . . . I mean Ty . . . so just how much you *weigh* these days?"

David might've asked, but Ty wasn't telling.

Always the queer iconoclast, Ty didn't seem to mind aging. He'd fallen out of his gym routine shortly after snagging the fair and coveted Blur Antonelli. Then Blur never bothered to clarify himself within their blurry relationship. Then Blur had his own place, his own haunts, his own friends, and his own lofty agendas. Then Blur, for the most part, was gone and there weren't any new prospects.

Ty was now in his early thirties and beginning to look *every single day* of it. He'd gained twenty-five pounds sitting on his ass ambitiously trying to be brilliant. Then David started calling him "Richard Poundtree" and "Salami Davis, Jr." and that shit began to hit the fan of Tyrone's ego.

So Ty joined another gum, and he began to witness a strange new phenomenon: beefy brothers, V-shaped bodies, men with deep tans and terribly terrific teeth. These men were not just hunks, but astonishing *hulks* with shaved scrotums, shaved crotches, and waxed legs and asses.

These beings swarmed and coalesced throughout the city. It was something to see. Queer young men were no longer walking around looking sick. Suddenly the bars, the baths, the streets of Chelsea, the boys of Riverside the east and west side, the bangees of Harlem and Brooklyn and Queens were vogueing their stuff in better machines. The beach boys deep in the Pines and in the Hamptons were transforming into the buffed, the clipped, and the grotesquely sublime. This tribe of strutting stripped down stallions was becoming a new, hyper-masculine trend.

One warm day, while he and David were sunning in Washington Square park, watching one fantastic ballooning creature after the next file by, Ty complained.

"Look at this shit. I don't get it!"

"But of course you don't 'get it!' Celibates rarely do. I think that's the whole concept, Blackie Gleason."

"You know what? You spit one mo fat joke, and I'm all over yo gag fag azz! Aiight? Besides, who says I'm celibate? You don't know everything. Maybe I'm doing a whole new genre of strange," Ty hinted.

"Well, whatevuh endeavuh's clevuh, Trevor. Please. If you're doing *anything*, besides pining for *Blur*, the Anti-Nelly, it would be a mad piece of *strange* indeed," David snapped.

Another magnificent hulk passed them, and David gave him the kissy face.

"I swear this is like the Invasion of the Titty Men. NYC is beginning to look like a Wonder-bra ad. And it's just *not* hot," Ty said.

"Oh yes, it is hot! Seeing so much of this naked bodacious beef, it gives me hope for the future."

"How so?"

David grew reflective. "Well, Carlos, for one thing. If the sick ones are getting well, it could mean something promising for him, and for so many others."

"Yeah. That is a hopeful thought, Duch."

Then, David's mood and his face brightened again. "Besides, it's the season of beef, and I was always rather . . . ummm . . . carnivorous."

"Truer words never spoken."

"Hey, gay boys are *supposed* to be beautiful. Didn't you ever get that manual?"

"Nah. I never subscribed." Ty said.

"Well, sure beats the hell outta flannel shirts, faded Levi's, and that oh-so-tired mandatory lip-hair."

"If you say so."

"And I do. So face it, baby. The Clone is dead. Long live the New Clone!" David trumpeted. "If an *aging* brother wants to compete with common *bar bait*, he needs *body*—cut, ripped, shredded body, I tell you! But . . . *you* wouldn't know anything about that, would you, *Thick* Wilson?"

Tyrone punched him in his bulging biceps, *hoard*.

Lately, David had been doing more than simply eyeing bodies.

MAY 1993

As with the majority of David's stories, it all started out innocently.

Enrolled in his final year at F.I.T, The Fashion Institute of Technology, he'd become the popular old sage. In one class there was a kid, a cute copper boy who'd been kicked out of his home. David would often encourage him. Then, one day, the boy showed up in class, battered and badly bruised.

David took the painful sight of him very personally.

"I've been through it all, baby. Violence is an American birthright. This suffering you're going through, it ain't new, papi. I've felt it, and sometimes even now, I still feel, too. It hurts like hell. But it's necessary, 'cause it's gonna make you stronger. That's what the Universe is telling you right now: 'Be strong, Gabrielle! Be brave, be the best damn human being your spirit will allow!'

"Here we sit, suffering in this skin, and yet we're creating these little masterpieces every day. Don't you see the connection? You nevuh create better, more beautiful, or more vital than when you genuinely know the taste of suffering.

"Now, enough with the queen mother hen act. Have you reported this ghastly shit? No? Well, I happen to *know* a few people. First, let's take your picture. That'll be our evidence."

David and his new friend hit the precinct to report the latest in a disturbing series of attacks against gay men. It nearly amused David that the decade had spawned a name, a phrase for this special indignity. They filed a "hate crime" complaint, and David, even more than Gabrielle, was determined to see justice done.

Instead, they were promptly disrespected, mistreated, patronized, and dismissed—in that order.

Embarrassed Gabrielle, seeing the uselessness of it, wanted to just let it go. But *not* David. He felt if he were famous, the incident would've received more attention, more hype, more press, more headlines. And suddenly it occurred to him that he wasn't and never would be that world-famous dancer of destiny. He'd never get his chance to win a Tony, jet propel to the Wintergarden's stage, kiss some grand dame on both cheeks, gush, scream, and profusely thank his lover by his masculine, not doubt Latin name.

Now it seemed both he and Gabrielle were companions in their suffering.

"Let's get you home and cleaned up," David suggested.

David called Tyrone, hoping to get some press in his downtown rag. But Ty had gone to Atlanta hot on a story, and unbeknownst to David, Ty and Blur had just recently reunited, for the umpteenth time.

Now, Blur "the bore" the "Anti-nelly" was staying at Ty's crib, yet again. Blur and David were never good friends, though both had managed to *fake it* for Tyrone's sake. But Ty wasn't there, and Blur saw no need for the tedious pretense or façade.

Hearing Blur's voice, David politely asked for a legal referral.

"Why? What is this about, David? It's always something with you, isn't it?" he snipped. "What is this latest drama?"

Though his attitude stunk on ice, David simply sighed, and instead of reading him the riot act, he recited the story of Gabrielle.

"Oh, so some kid in the family queens it up in public, no doubt under *your* influence, and he gets beat down. Why am I not surprised, David? You want some advice? Gratis? OK, here's a piece for free: tell the kid to walk like a fucking man in the street. Being gay doesn't mean he has to be some fey and frilly little *bitch* on prowl. You tell him *that*, and just maybe he'll make it in the world."

Click.

"Oh. No. He. Didn't!"

So much for *knowing* people.

As David applied iodine to Gabrielle's battered face, he saw traces of himself in that tender skin, the not-quite-brown-eyes, and the firmness of those limbs—at eighteen. Gabrielle was a slight kid, which made his beating all the more senseless. For a moment, David wondered if his friend could see their physical and spiritual resemblance. He wondered if he'd noticed their mutual interests, their similar circumstance, and if he did, was that why *his* jeans *quaked*?

"See, it's real hard becoming somebody large. I know people who've tried all their lives to be larger than they really are, or were ever meant to be, you know? But the hardest part of being large is keeping the size of your soul intact through that whole metamorphosis . . . because that's the true shit. That's the gold and the goal. You wanna be able to look in the mirror and know that you and your God are cool with the human staring back. That person in the mirror is the only role you're responsible for in this little B-movie we call life, baby boy."

David's new friend smiled sadly, and then he slowly rose his head and gently kissed the wisdom that had formed on the surface of David's lips.

THE NEXT MORNING

"I slipped. Damn it, I slip sometimes. That's why I feel like so much wrong, rank, rancid, stank shit. No, don't look at me—I'm positively vile. I slipped, damn it! I should be allowed one or four fuck-ups in the duration of this relationship, shouldn't I? Men are such bullshit beings. Myself duly included. I like to pop the yang, and shake my thang, and see if it still works. I think that makes me human and gay, with an anxious dick. I'll love you forever, Carlos. I do and I promise, I will! But sometimes, I just get so scared, because, for once in my life, I didn't want to slip and fall into some scandalous unforgivable shit. Not now. And don't talk to me about no rubbers or coughs, sores or tests . . . I slipped. Damn it! Let's get over that shit first!"

Those were the words David said to himself inside the morning's mournful mirror.

Carlos lay dying in a hospital, and David was already cheating on his corpse. He felt awful. He felt sub-human.

DR. HOROWITZ'S OFFICE

"When I went to see him that last time, I was prepared to talk to him, to *tell* him what had happened . . . only, he couldn't hear me. There were all these crazy rhythms in that room. They clicked and churned and hissed and beeped, and even I couldn't dance to any of those rhythms. But those rhythms, they broke the silence. They filled in the gaps, the blanks, the words that fought to escape my throat.

"I wanted to say, 'Hey, papi. Those sores seem less purple. Your KS scars, I think they're going away. You seem much stronger today . . . and maybe this new drug they're giving you just might . . .'

"But I couldn't say those things. I knew they were all lies, and besides he couldn't hear them. So, I wanted him to take my *silence* as LOVE. I was silent because words will never make any more sense to me. Words like 'the plague,' words like 'faggot,' like 'junkie,' like 'gay.' Words like 'thrush' like 'SIDA,' like 'AIDS.' I'm sick of them! They've stopped making sense. So silence was better. I wanted him to take my silence as *love*. I realized the simplest moments, like the wink of his eye had become, now and forever . . . my *keepsakes*."

"I understand, David."

"Do you? Oh, Baby Doc, it's so hard for us to forget pain when it's loud and coming from deranged places. It's hard to forgive punks who have screamed on us in the street, or the people who we thought would always *love* us . . . until they *know*, until they belch that masculine smoke of intolerance in our faces.

"And Carlos knew his share of it. Suddenly all that time spent being estranged, it seems a sin to me. He'd send his family birthday and Christmas cards, and each of those cards, those sentiments from his heart, they always came back, 'return to sender,' left unopened, unfelt. Where was the *love*? Carlos was bubbling over with it. And shame on all those judgmental bastards! They missed it. They missed s-o-o-o-o-o much. Well, I was blessed enough to get it. And I was glad.

"Then, near the end, a *forgiving* few wanted to filter into his room, to whisper these lost words of love. Love, when he couldn't even talk to them now. It was senseless and tragic. It was a *waste* of love.

"On his last night, because he so adored the poetry of Lorca, I wanted to say strange poetry of love so close in his ear, to whisper them in scat silences over the misunderstood jazz of his and my own life. But he couldn't hear me, the nurse said. So, I hoped he took my silence as love. The unconditional kind he always sought, and rarely received." David sighed.

"It was a very transcending moment for us. Then, we were interrupted by the Mask People. Everyone wore a mask there. What were *they* all hiding from?

"I dried my eyes. Wouldn't dare give them the *pleasure* of seeing me cry. That's when I noticed, in all those blipping, churning, hissing, clinical fucking surroundings, someone had brought my Carlos flowers. They sat far away from him, by the window. I noticed some petals had fallen, and the rest were wilting. How *ironic* was that, Doc? His flowers were dying, like him. Like us.

"You know, sometimes, I think. And sometimes I think, I think too much. But I think this world is a Stupid Test of Love, and most of us are failing, miserably."

David, in a moment of utter weakness had cheated on Carlos. Carlos died soon after, as if he *knew*.

His passing had a profound effect on the terrain of David Richmond's soul. Though it was not wholly unexpected, there was just no preparing him for the reality, or the emptiness.

He sat on the floor, debasing himself, cursing himself, cradling himself. He could not eat. He could not sleep. All he could think to do was wail—wail inconsolably, and for days. He called out to Carlos. He hoped for a ghost, a visitation like the one Ty claimed he shared with Trick. But for David there was nothing but that stun of stillness.

"All I truly had was The Universe, and Carlos's last request: Live your days and nights with fire. And once I'd left the floor, once I dried my eyes, once I could begin to *feel my own life* again, the firebird in me made a list.

"Dear Universe. This is what I'm asking to come inside my life. Please don't send in the clowns. No heads, either. No knuckle, crack, or chicken-heads need apply, 'kay? He's got to have some looks, style, personality, ambition. Some spirituality wouldn't hurt either. Let him be real. And please let him know how to dance—at least hustle, and I'll take care of the rest. This is your boy, David, signing off."

OCTOBER 1993

"Ty, my dear, The Universe *listens*. Things are pickin' up in the booty department. I done found me a new man! You know me. I always do. Distinguished. Latino. A real gentleman, and he's older, by about fifteen years. Been married, divorced, got the T-shirts and two teenaged sons as consolation prizes. And now he's got me. Face it, didn't we all know I was just a lost boy searchin' for his daddy? Well, Victor's a Papi. And he only spanks me when I want him to. He wants a partner, not a wife. But what he really wants is to open a club, a downtown lounge. Says that's the next wave. I can relate to an ambitious hombre who ain't desperately seeking the long-time wedlock headlock, cock-lock jammy. He just wants a commitment."

"Hey, if you're happy, then I'm ecstatic," Ty said. "So you're committed to being Victor's partner? Commitment is like a seesaw with two sturdy asses on board. You do know what happens when someone gets *off*, right?"

"Oh, Ty, sweetheart, you're such a boringly biological boy. I've known *that* since I was twelve!"

"You know, it just occurred to me, jokes aside, you've never been on a seesaw. They frighten you, don't they?"

"Yes. Seesaws, circus clowns, people with no fashion sense, rainy days and Monday's always get me down. Plus, some other stuff I don't wanna talk about."

Not long after, the men in David's mercurial life were finally introduced.

"Ty, meet my architect, my new papi, and the builder of that erection in my heart . . . mi hombre de la corazón, Victor."

"Hola. Very glad to meet you, Victor," Ty said as he grasped Victor's large, strong hand. "Now . . . run, papa! Run as hard and fast as you possibly can!" Ty warned.

David's face fell.

"But why?" Victor asked, confused by Ty's knowledge of David's scattered history, along with Tyrone's warped sense of humor.

"Well, finally, FINALLY David's found himself a good man, a true and decent man," Ty said. "And he *will* corrupt you. This, I promise," Ty added with a wink.

"Joo *know* I'm a *good* man? How?"

Ty grinned with happiness, and he said, "I just know."

Though silently, Ty thought: *This must be a good sign. I don't have that overwhelming urge to dash home and take three hot showers after shaking this man's hand. Good work, Duch!*

TWENTY-SEVEN

We Should Get Together More Often

NOVEMBER 1993

There is more life in the city on Saturday nights. More death, too. More beer sold to more agitated drunks, more bridge and tunnel traffic, more friction, more threats, more punks, more tits and dicks to be idolized. There is more potential for smoke and fire. There are more chances to meet, connect, to dream and to find some meaning. In short, in a Crazed and Carnal City, such as New York, whatever one's choice of merchandise, Saturday nights presented more.

The clock of Ty's wall read 10:15. For him, it was a time to kick back and just breathe. But some restless brothers were far too erect to sit in front of their VCRs slapping their lovelies in violent masturbation techniques. And one such brother, troubled by the trials of being Browny, wanted to escape the madness and just get his Saturday night's freak on. He decided to ring Tyrone. The crazy thought was: Maybe they should take their diversely different dicks out on the town and try getting them wet together.

Tyrone felt the invitation had *other* sleazy fingerprints all over it.

"Yo, Ty! Check it: Meet me outside the Zebra so we can both get our jungle illness on. Don't give me no shit either. Step outta that damn cave, ya fuckin' hermit! Just be there at 11:30, and cleaner than the Board of Health! Ya heard?"

"No can do, Browny. Got a deadline and I'm runnin'—" *Click.*

"Damn bastard, with a chronically criminal record!"

Ty gazed out of his window. The night was full of speed, full of life, full of neon-lit activity. The night was so young it was almost illicit. He decided just maybe he'd acquiesce. Blur was always busy, or out of town, and lately Ty wasn't feeling very bound to that tediously tenuous relationship.

And so, weighing his options, he showered quickly, dressed, and stepped into the metro.

When he hopped off the subway and bounded up the steps onto 14th Street, a thin rain misted the cool city air. The quick and maddening energy of natives moving, going, and doing played against sounds of salsa and the slow swis-s-ssh of traffic. *Yes, it's good to be out among the living*, he thought as a large throng of night-people muscled toward the club on East 11th Street.

"Yo, baby, yo! I told you I'm 'posed to be up in here, yo!" he heard as he approached the Zebra Den. The sound of that 'yo', it was unmistakable. Ty looked, and there stood an overly-emoting Browny, talking loudly, drawing a crowd, hands flying in a fit that way his well-loved brother's once did. He was rocking a vintage George Raft gangsta-style, navy pin-striped zoot, complete with matching *spats*. He looked like a cross between a ridiculously cool jester and Cab Callo*wayward*. He was arguing vociferously with the doorman, desperately trying to cop a freebie, a slide-by, a get-in-where-he'd-fit-in.

As dark, moody, and difficult as Browny could be, he was

still *Mr. Five Boroughs*. Wherever he went in the city, people *knew* him.

"Browny! You lookin' *stoopid*, man!"

"Yo! Browny! You got that *five* you owe me?"

"Hey, Browny. Still listenin' out for you on the radio, dawg. Where you at?"

"Yo! Check Browny out! Rockin' that dope-ass suit! G'on Browny!" They'd laugh or pat his back. It was almost as if he was running for mayor, except most of the folks who knew him, well, they didn't vote.

Now he was all argumentative, animated and actively pissed at some overly stressed doorman.

"Yo, man! You no habla English? Mira! Moola! Dinero! Faison's got plenty bank!"

If he had any Presidents in his dubiously baggy pockets, they rarely saw the light of Harlem or the village.

"Yo!" he yelled. "Yo, Ty! Over here, yo!"

After so many years out of school, and still most every sentence out of Browny's mouth began or ended with a big, loud, "*Yo!*"

"Yo, Ty! 'Sup. They actin' like they don't *know* me up this hovel! But it's cool, I ain't stressin' the small stuff."

Ty simply addressed the doorman. "He's with me. If that's a problem please tell *Coco* his friend *Ty Hunter, the nightlife writer* is outside waiting. And he's gettin' increasingly more pissed."

Any *friend* of Coco's was, well. . . . The two were granted entry.

"*Love* the suit," Ty said wryly.

"Yeah, I know. It's fly as hell, yo. But Fuck all that! Look at *you*, lookin' like you look. You dressed like *that* in high school, yo. When you go'n get you some *glamour*, bwoi?"

"I'll get the glamour when you get the class. I think *both* of our orders are on layaway. And by the way, *why* am I here?"

Browny's reddened eyes answered for him. Three months out of his latest rehab adventure, and apparently he still *wasn't* clean.

"The theme tonight is 'for old times sake,'" he said cryptically. It sounded like the shit liquor made men say.

Oh Browny . . . Browny . . . Browny? What's it gonna take, man? How many times after all these years, have I wished you clean, sober, and singing your foolish ass off? But you don't hear me, though. Ty wondered.

If he had his way, Ty wanted *better* for all of his old friends and associates. He wanted David to slow down the partying, to find his artistic legs, and to dance again. He wanted Face Depina to connect with the soul of his inner *Pascal.* And he wanted Browny, clean. And if *happy* wasn't his fate, then at the very least, *contented* in his skin.

Inside, the first floor was a darkened cavern alive with a driving mix of muscle boys, gogo girls, bangee boys, and party girls in varying degrees of undress. Andy Warhol was dead, and as David had recently proclaimed, "So ends the wild downtown party as we real fly boys knew it." Now it was sprinklings of club kids hyped on crystal meth, second-tier fashion models, R&B semi-artists, and local celebs, perennial posers, and gangs of young, weaved-out chicks. It wasn't a specifically gay or babe-a-licious crowd, and those present were either twinks or homos-disguised-as-street-thugs or demi-fabulous people who hadn't come to stay.

Needless to say, Tyrone hated it.

Browny ordered his vodka straight-up and perused the hard-core party freaks. But something in his temperament signaled there wasn't much freak left in his party game.

Truth was, Faison didn't want to get drunk that night. He wanted to achieve a blessed state of wonderful numbness, an everything-go'n-be-all-rightness. Ty stood next to him, expecting him to *say something*, let him know what was up. But

Faison only bobbed his baby-dreadlocked head and modeled his zoot like a lyrical gangsta.

"C'mon, let's walk, yo," he said.

On the second floor a more tranquilized crowd settled down to watch the live show.

"Mad lovelies up in here tonight."

"Where? Where they at?" Ty deadpanned.

A balding, tuxedoed bloke tickled the ivories and he crooned almost woozily:

"*All the lost young sodomites,*
Slowly disappear into the night,
Where men will come
To dim the lights
My ears detect
A humming song, tonight . . ."

The inherent sadness of the song affected Ty's mood. He thought of the few lovers he'd known, the ones who got away and those taken by the times, and melancholy overtook him. But when he looked at Browny, he thought it strange to see him on the verge of crying.

"Yo. Step into the john with me," Browny ordered.

"What for? Ya know you ain't nuttin' off me."

Browny grabbed Ty's arm and forged a way to the men's room. Glancing at that strangely Trick-like expression, Tyrone suddenly knew something *was* wrong; desperately wrong.

"It's Jonathan. Jonathan's sick. Very . . . very sick, man . . ."

"*Jonathan?*" Ty asked. "Jonathan," he repeated to himself. "You mean . . ." Suddenly the name, the face, the association all melded into one realization. Oh! *That* Jonathan?

"Yeah. Final stages, yo. And it's just a fuckin' waste, man. Such a fuckin' shame."

A shame? It was *more* than that for those who knew him. In

a town of tedious tack-heads and raggedy mustangs, Jonathan was a true Cadillac of men. He had a big, pure, altruistic heart and had taken in many strays over the years. Browny was, in fact, one of them, but Browny was *not* gay by nature. Gay for *pay?* Queer for a beer? "Faggot for a habit," he once called it. Perhaps. Gay out of *gratitude?* Probably not. But Browny's disdain for "*sissies*" had lessened over the years, and if he had to count his true blues, at least two gay men would complete that puny total. Jonathan was his best friend, and gay, and he'd probably saved Browny's ass from spiraling into the deepest depths of alcohol, crack, and emotional hustling.

But then, Jonathan was everyone's friend, protector, coach, father figure, confessor, and all around decent cat. Ty had once written a feature on him, but he didn't know the full extent of Jon and Browny's history, or the complexity of their trip. He figured that Jon, who was nobody's fool, saw Browny's potential to be something better, to exist beyond the broken toilets of life.

Jonathan Rodgers had saved Browny, gotten him clean, and bailed him out of scrapes countless times. And now, in return, Browny couldn't save him.

"Ty . . . not many people know this shit . . . but I tried to kill myself, once. Just once, yo." Browny confessed. "I was young and little and black as tar. I was tryin' real hard to be somebody, yo . . . and nobody gave me a fuckin' chance. Man. It's a rough motherfuck to be young, Black, and hurtin'. I mean hurtin' real bad. But, yo! Big Jon, with his big-ass Buddha wisdom, made me see only one of them conditions was permanent." He chuckled. "So you know what he did? He threw away my fuckin' pipe and flushed all my best shit, yo. Then the big, bloated bastard locked the fuckin' door so I couldn't get out. What that motherfucka do *that* for? All I wanted was to get the hell outta there and finish myself off.

"Man, I cried, screamed, begged, bitched, and tore his

fuckin' livin' room apart. I woulda beaten him to death, too, if I coulda. Yo, I had to fuckin' hurt him somehow, so I went crazy, hauled off and threw his Mr. Leather Cleveland trophy out of his tenth floor window."

"Browny, nah!"

"Yup. My angry ass just watched that fucker smash into a thousand gold pieces, yo. And ya *know* that damn trophy was his pride and joy! But get this shit, Ty: instead of kickin' my crazy vandalizin' ass all over the South Bronx, Jon *held* me. That's all. Held me so fuckin' tight, he put new bruises all over me. And through all that hurt and pain, all that wild shit I was feelin . . . for the first time in my fuckin' life, I felt loved, yo. That man showed me much love." Browny examined his stricken reflection in the mirror.

"Yo, you know Jon was a real big motherfuckin' bear of a man."

"Yup. I remember, *Big Jon*. He *earned* that name, too."

"Well, you wouldn't wanna see him now. Breaks my balls man. Just breaks my fuckin' heart. Last week, he got on Harley, rode that loud fucker into the crazy night, and crashe it into a pillar under the Brooklyn Bridge. Yo. I guess wanted to go out *his* way. He didn't get his wish, though. N he's all kinds of busted up, and he's so sick and I . . . I . . ."

Tyrone watched that inarticulate language of pain across Browny's face. He saw how his fingers were entwine if clutched in a useless prayer. Browny's lost eyes searche ceiling for something to cling to, and Ty embraced hi seemed such a wasted gesture. But there they stood, two lives, two more casualties in a world of mean and diseas tle things.

Had he called just to cry with Tyrone? Strangely, ne them was crying.

Then, suddenly, a shrill voice entered the cage of skull, asking that question he himself was afraid to cause he feared the answer. The words boiled on his lips like troublesome cold sores. *Were you and Jonathan ever . . . together? Have you been tested?*

Tyrone didn't *want* to know. It was all becoming just too sad—Alexis, Marlon, Ari, Fat Don, Kwali, Jerome, Leon, Essex, Jazz. Ty had kissed the dead lips of too many young, beautiful men—Black brothers, White and Brown brothers, gay and straight. The phone would ring and it would be *Death* placing
nother collect call. Someone was dying. Someone just discov-
ed they had it. Someone died, their funeral was last Thursday,
d *why* hadn't Ty been there?

ften he'd thank God that in his anal retentive rubberized
ney through road posts, yield signs, and blinking yellow
the awareness was such that promiscuity was not an op-
till, there was always fear. Rubbers did rip. Men did lie.
takes one. One night. One man. One lie. One fuck to
period at the end of a sentence he hadn't yet finished
ow Browny? Tyrone was not ready to stare down at
orpse and mourn his small, unfinished life.

nted to tell you to make sure you heard it from me
spered.

y said. "I know. So, you wanna book from this
What?"

n't nothin' more to say about it. I just wanna
. He ain't' got no insurance, and . . . I was
." Browny was about to hit Tyrone with his
grouping for a benefit in Jonathan's honor.
oup, a group of rowdy club-kids entered
wny all chicken-shit.

, toast Jonathan, and party like it's all we
vin' like two soft bitches, yo."

r, Ty ordered a club soda, and Browny,
d in a corner, they nodded their heads,
their eyes wore the glaze of two se-

cretly shell-shocked victims. They shared the saddest of toasts to Jonathan.

Time passed. Ty was thinking and living inside his head again. When he casually glanced at Browny, he noticed a marked change. All at once, Browny's face was different. His eyes were brightening like mood rings as he stared ahead, smiling like some brand new idiot. Ty peered in the same direction. He now saw what had magically brought on that big, goofy-ass, gap-toothed grin. Through the thriving dance of humanity, a tall silhouette swaggered. It seemed for a minute that all attention shifted. Heads turned, eyes widened to embrace this strobe-lit phantom. Shadows lifted slowly, and the realization hit—it was Face!

Face is here? Damn. I don't see or hear from him in months. Then I step out with Browny's ass, and . . . coincidence? Or is Faison stalking him?

Face, meanwhile, was at a zenith of his Afro-Portuguese physical appeal. Café au lait sin personified. He was indeed, the fucky ideal, and he looked *exceptionally fine* that night.

Now that Face was in the Zebra Den, lookin' weirdly mahhhhvelous, would he bother to acknowledge Ty or Browny? Would he clutch the jewels and grace them with a few moments of his effervescent presence?

Club voices rose in the air: "You know who that is?" "Damn! He fine!" "I don't do men, but he's so fuckin' pretty I'd do him!"

Face loved it! He gave them a view of that famously fine profile, to the left, to the right, and the few queens in attendance screamed: "You betta *work* it, baby!"

The man was pushing up on thirty-three, a substance abuser, and still so drop-dead stupid-fine that it was incomprehensible—especially to Ty, who wondered: *Has he had work done?* Everyone could see the brother was still butta—the six-foot-five, two-hundred-and-ten-pound definition of the word.

"Madison Avenue created this *monster.* But what the hell *we* 'posed to do with it?" a voice asked, followed by a big, dark claw gripping Ty's shoulder.

Ty turned and there was Chaz. Chaz, with that tough, long-suffering mug tinged with the sadness of a restless yet silent narration. Amazingly, he was *still* braving it with Face. Watching them over the years was like viewing a long, very tedious, very brutal S/M flick. Only no one watching that kinky little flick of theirs was beating-off to the sight of it. Least of all, Ty. Still, Tyrone and Chaz were esoterically intimate, and often flirting in spite of themselves.

"What up, Bub?" Ty shouted, smiling as he and Chaz embraced full and hard. Holding and beholding Chaz again, Ty couldn't help mentally telling his dick: *Hey you down there, you better be still now!*

"Damn, Bub, when you start keepin vampire hours?" Chaz joked in his ear.

"Bub, please! Ain't ya heard? I'm one of those vintage vamps, from way back!"

Chaz chuckled. "Oh is that right, Bub? Sho coulda fooled me."

"Bub" was short for *Bubba,* someone either of them could be.

As other hangers-on of the Depina entourage sifted through, Face rested his beauteous backside at a table in the shadows, his star quality darkening like a lunar eclipse. Was he *live,* Memorex, a flicker of virtual reality? Ty realized it *had* to be real, because Chaz was *still* in his arms. Chaz, the devoted and ever true, was always there, bringing up the rear, so to speak.

"Yo Chaz-Bear." Browny tapped Chaz's gruesomely wide back. "What it look like? Think I can holler at Mr. Facey-Face a few?"

Chaz shrugged. "I ain't his manager, man. Suit yourself.

And just what up with *that suit*, anyway? Come on, Ty, uh *Bub*, let's me and you dance."

The club music boomed Soul II Soul's "Keep On Movin'." Chaz, who looked, oh-so-*Gigantor* in his white T-shirt, made his move. He grabbed Ty's wrist, and they proceeded to the floor. It was wild, and Ty felt like a true native again, dancing among the mad mad-sexy people. One song flowed into the next, and Tyrone was too busy getting his necessary groove on to notice Face had given Browny the usual brush-off. In mid active groove, he saw Browny walking away and assumed he was heading for the rest room.

"Easy, Ty, *I's* an old-aged vampire," Chaz shouted, sweating like somebody's field slave. "And *you-know-who's* staring holes through us."

"Really? And I should care?" Ty said, working his shoulders in a who-gives-a-fuck-move.

"Well, we have our rule. And one of them is I shouldn't' be dancin' with no *mens* in public. He's probably all pissed now. I'm getting a soda. You want anything?"

Ty shook his head no, and thought: *Please. Grow some balls, Chaz!*

Ty and Chaz had almost *happened* once.

TWO YEARS EARLIER AT FACE'S LOFT:

"Face? Please. He's in Milan, or Japan, or one of them "an" sounding places. Probably sucking on some strange Italian dick, or licking some exotic Japanese clit. Do you really think he gives a shit about what *we* do?" Chaz had asked.

And warm blood began to flow and flood all through a brother as Ty suddenly recalled David's mortal fear of what Chaz *allegedly* had. His shifting eyes fell below, and, *Oh, my goodness! David ain't lied! Bruh, look at what you've got!*

What Chaz had "on *swole*" was a mad anaconda, crawling along his thigh and over it, stretching, reaching across that reckless space between them. Hard as it was, and it was *hoard*, Ty left before he would have an even *harder* time saying *no* to Chaz's offer of a momentary *man-to-behemoth* mambo.

And now, as club music rumbled, Face made a cool, ambling journey, coming to an impressive standstill beside Tyrone. He grinned as if a mere grin could erase all time, distance, and acrimony.

"So, Ty, what's *your* bag, huh?" he asked, softly slurring his words in that refined purr from his last commercial.

"My bag? Gucci," Ty replied, and Depina's' face stretched into a portrait of thirty-two dazzling capped and captivating pearlies. They clutched hands and bumped shoulders like old partners who'd once popped collars. It felt odd for both, but lukewarm and familiar too.

"Been meaning to call ya, 'cause it's been a while. And just so you know, I phoned in a few favors, and those punks that *jacked* David, well they won't' be jackin' nobody else no time soon, *trust* me," he said.

"What? Say again. You did what, man?" Ty cupped his ear and yelled over the blasting music.

But then Face thought better of playing the hero. Why cater to Ty? Where was the profit in it?

Ever since Da Elixir's beginnings, Tyrone had unwittingly reigned among them as "The Patriarch." It was he, Ty, who had written the hit song. He was he, Ty, who'd made very good money from it. It was he, Ty, who'd doled out stipends, in increments, making the rest of them, in a sense, his trust-fund babies. Though Tyrone's original intent was righteous, in doing so, he'd been thrust into the role of more than just the group's leader. He'd become their *father figure*.

Face Depina had no love for father figures and for whatever else Tyrone Hunter represented. Suddenly, *telling Ty* of his good deed reeked of some desperate kid seeking his *Daddy's approval.*

Fuck you! I don't need your damn respect, he thought. And so Face dropped the subject.

"I'm pretty much livin' out of hotels in Europe and L.A. these days. It's *hoard*-rough being me, man," he joked. "Tell you what. Tennis, next Saturday at Crunch, bet? Look, I gotta book. Promised Calvin I'd step into his new boutique, and ya don't wanna piss off Calvin. That bitch holds a mean grudge. Must be all that *Bronx* in him. Anyhow, it's all the way on the Upper East Side. So, Boss. Tennis? Call me. I mean it."

"Yeah, yeah, whatever," Ty said to the air, knowing he'd see Face again in six months to a year—if then.

"Ewww! Ty-ro-o-one! Honey, you are lookin' *too* tired tonight," a coming from behind him said. Ty turned, to see David, dressed in tight, black drag-queen gear, tittering in a mock girlish laughter. "Cucumbers might help, honey! They are *more* than a cheap sexual device, yanno. Trust me, a couple over those eyes will work wonders, darling." *Mwah, mwah.* He kissed both of Ty's cheeks.

"Tired? Me? Witch, please!" Ty replied.

"Tyrone, I *know* you don't think ya cute in that 1985 leather! Times and fashion change! When will you? Or *have* you? Please. I'll just have to stop hangin' with you entirely, if ya continue to roll so . . . so archaic!" David teased, plucking at Ty's jacket. "Look, I keep tellin' you to stop by my salon for a complete fashion makeover. You *can* afford it, yanno!"

"Yes, I guess can afford it. Though I hear your prices are to the north of outrageous."

"Honey please. Beauty costs. Leave the ugly and tediously unfashionable for the poor."

"Hmm . . . you've become such a snobby li'l bitch in your old . . . ummm *queendom*."

"Watch your mouth, honey!" David snapped.

You know, it was one of my *better* investments, kickin in with you on the salon. But I did as a silent partner. Don't wanna cramp your . . . umm . . . style."

"Cramp *my* style? Please. As if *you*, or anyone else could," David said in an almost rude tone.

"I'll have to drop by more often. I will. I promise."

"Coolness."

But tell me something, is it me, or does tonight suddenly feel frighteningly like a *reunion?*"

"A reunion?"

"Yeah. Da Elixir. We're all here in the same place, in all our wasted, faded glory," he said, eyeing his best friend's costume up and down.

"Faded what? You'll have to excuse me. I'm flyin' on *X Airlines* tonight. But yes, Facey is looking a bit *faded* these days. We all knew he'd hit that wall sometime," David joked, again kissing both of Ty's cheeks.

"So . . . I'm guessin' that tonight you're Ann-Margaret in her *Kitten-with-a-whip* stage?" Ty speculated. "But why didn't you go with the white boots shaking a mad fringed tail feather a go-go Ann? By the way, how did your meeting with the people at Ailey go? Will you be designing next season's costumes or what?"

"First of all, please, check yourself," *she* admonished, spinning around. "I'm Emma Peel, damn it! Get yo leather bitches correct. Secondly, I did the Ailey thing. Met with the peeps. Complete yawn. A mess*! Dame* Judith, uh, Ms. Jamison, if you're nasty, was straight trippin'!"

Ty didn't know what that meant. David had always *loved* him some Judith Jamison. She, was his goddess-ideal of dance. He wasn't making any sense that night. Maybe it was the X. Even though he wasn't getting any younger, he was always experimenting with the trippy-hippie shit. Ty wanted to scold him, but he let it go. Besides, hadn't David *stopped* dressing in drag?

"I'm just back from a wake, hon," David volunteered.

"Oh? So what did you wear?"

"Why *this*, of course," he said, spinning around. "It was *a formal* affair."

"Anyone I know?"

"Rue DeDay. Didn't you hear?""

"Stop it! Really? Oh, God no! I didn't even know he was sick!"

"He wasn't. Good queen. Horrible ba-a-ad judge of traffic. Glitter all over the place!"

"Oh. Sad. But isn't it queer?" Ty mused. "I'd almost forgotten there were *other* ways for us to die. So where's Victor tonight?"

"Didn't wanna come. I'm flyin' solo," David answered in a clipped, that's-the-end-of-that-subject tone. "And how are you and Mr. *Blur* this week? I gather you don't see each other much. So, at this point, is it strictly dickly?"

"Nah, Wholly ass-holian," Ty admitted. "I still love fuckin' him. Sometimes I think if I hit it right, I might just fuck him out of blindness and he'll *come* into seeing."

"Well, ain't it hopeful to fuck so?" David snipped. "And just what's the bloody deal with Facey? You know, usually when I'm on X, I wanna just run up and kiss err-body, but he gets *no* kisses from me. Did you see the way he dissed little Faisoni? I mean, damn. I know it's *his* world and he's like *the bomb* and all, but Faisoni didn't deserve that shit. Sometimes I wonder about Face, staging his little star tantrums. He's so hopelessly déclassé!"

"Duch? Tell me you're not throwing *shade* on the shady low-low. Has the decades-long crush finally been stomped?"

"Well, I've just opened my eyes to a *few* things. Therapy can do that. I'm tryna love from a distance. It's healthier. I forgave all the ugliness. Forgivin' is what I do. But even my artistry can't make him crazy-pretty anymore. He dropped by the Salon as if nothing bad had ever happened between us, asking me to *style* him for some event. He put his arm around my shoulder, and foolish me, I agreed. But over at his place, he gets one of those notorious nose bleeds of his, flips out, *ejects* me, and fires Browny!"

"I didn't know that, Duch. You never told me."

"No biggie. Business thrives. I always land on my stilettos. It's Browny I'm worried about. With him and Face, there's nothin' but drama. I smell it swirling around like skunkweed around them. I used to think Faisoni was just a natural born hater, and would always be. But no, mon cher. This definitely goes deeper."

"Well, there was way too much *ego* for that one loft to handle. Face it. Depina's always had big probs with ego management. Even *you* must've noticed that little flaw in his otherwise *sterling* character." Ty joked sarcastically. "And Browny *never* liked him, so that whole living arrangement thing was a queer piece of strange and unusual."

"Indeed it was. God, I need to kiss somebody, now!" David said, scanning the room for new kiss victims.

"Ummm . . . David? Maybe you can set off your little kiss-fest later? I understand Browny's going through some stuff."

"Yes. We *all* are. Must be that going-through-stuff season again, you think? Facey can be a fuckin' unappreciative pig to the people who love him. But he's *not* alone."

The silence between them, even in that room of roaring sound was deafening.

"You know something? You can take some mixed-Negroes out of the South Bronx, but ya can't make 'em wipe they asses!"

Ty wondered what the *hell* David was going on about. He

detected a new attitude in David and it went beyond the drag. Was David upset or *mad* at him? What had he done or not done to offend his little friend now? Ty couldn't imagine what it was, but instinct told that yes, there was definitely a certain stink to his and David's relationship of late, and it had risen between them in recent months. Ty wanted to ask him about it, and he'd planned to—only, this wasn't the *place* for that delicate discussion. And then, Tyrone remembered he hadn't seen Browny in the last fifteen minutes. Had he left? Was he OK?

Meanwhile, outside the Zebra Den, in the deepest blue tinge of nocturne, wandering artists, suffering faces, trendy kids, heroin boys, working girls, leather men, and subterraneous hip-hoppers merged on a night full of stars and unforeseen calamities.

The Depina entourage prepared to enter its stretch limousine, and Face turned to flash that Depina grin and wave the customary blasé wave one last time.

Five shots rang out.

Hot metal flew, direct and keening with purpose. Hot metal flew, found its target and quickly exploded through human flesh.

The street hushed. Two men fell to the pavement. One of them was former model-of-the-moment Claudio Conte. The other was Face Depina.

CHAPTER TWENTY-EIGHT

The Death of Hip

THE NEXT DAY

Browny was running on a full tank of scared shitless. Suddenly, he was being treated like a prime suspect, so he blustered, bitched, and re-bitched to the cops who'd bogarted Juanita's place.

"Yeah, I ain't surprised somebody busted a cap in his ass, the conceited, lyin', son of a mixed bitch! I ain't gonna lie, yo . . . I ain't never liked him. No big thing. I don't like the way people treat me at the bank. Yo, I don't like how them Korean grocers don't wanna touch my hand when they give me my change. But I ain't shot none of 'em."

Shit-talkin' aside, Browny had no alibi. He did, however, have a long history of cop-hatin'. The feeling was entirely mutual.

The pundits were calling it "The Male Model Melee."

In the crowded hospital waiting room, David was hysterical.

"First Martin Luther King, then John Lennon, now *Facey*? This is madness! What the hell is this beastly world comin' to? *Who* would do this? Why you think those bastards in white won't even let us see him? You think he all right? You think he still look like himself?

"I think you should listen to yourself. He's alive. All right? Celebrate that shit!"

"Do you think he was shot in the face? Why won't somebody tell us what's gon on? Why ain't they telling' us anything?" David begged for an answer.

"They probably know who did it, I guess, and an arrest is imminent. Or else they don't know jack. Now please try to calm down," Ty said strongly, then, looking at the sobbing wreckage of his best friend, he asked, "You need a good, strong, bitch smack, Duch? 'Cause I got a coupla those left in me."

"No. But a good, strong bitch's hug would help."

Tyrone swooped him up in his arms.

"Who would want to kill him?" a scared David whispered.

Get a fuckin' grip! Who the fuck wouldn't? The list of New York names alone was staggering! And Depina's enemies were global in scope. To know Face was to hate the shit he did on the regular without apology. But why was everything so hush-hush?

It was common knowledge that Claudio Conte had received a flesh wound to the shoulder. Once released, he was busted for possession of an unlicensed weapon. Surprisingly, it was his first offense.

"Look," Ty said. "I've said more than once, 'I'll kill him!' And for as long as it took to say it, I meant it," Ty whispered inside their embrace.

"I know," David said softly. Then, after a pause, "I know *everything*."

"Everything? Like what, Duchess?" Ty asked, stepping back.

"All about you and Face, and the DJ booth. And I know why you never told me. And I've hated you for it. But I'm tryna get over it. Best friends are supposed to tell each other shit. You're not a very good best friend. You're still, my friend, but . . ."

"David," Tyrone sighed, exhausted by the one secret he'd kept between them. "Please. Don't even finish that sentence. You *know?* You know nothing but *his* version. And you didn't come to me. Why? What does that say?"

"It says: It must be true. Besides, why would he lie? You're not exactly the supermodel catch of the day. So, it must be true. You and Facey, you broke my fucking heart."

"I didn't come to you because I love you harder than my own fuckin' kin. And I never wanted to hurt you. I knew it would hurt you. And it was meaningless. But I knew you wouldn't see it that way. So why bring meaningless shit into the picture?

"You know that picture of us," Ty continued, "where we've got our heads together with the same goofy expression? I look at that picture and I smile. Love's all inside that picture. I look at it, and I see two twins. And over the years we've argued over who's the good twin, and who's the evil twin, and it's always been a joke. Please don't see me as evil now. There was never a lie, any meaningful lie between us. Only an omission. There's a big difference, baby boy."

"Yeah, whatever. You and your *words*," David said, dismissing him. "Whatever you say is gold. You see a photo of friendship? If you remember, *you* set the whole damn thing up, how to pose and how to look to get the right effect. There's a *metaphor* for your ass. In the movie of your life, you *direct* your friendships. The rest of us, we're only actors. Well you're not fuckin' Cecil B. DeMille. And you're not Spike Lee prettying up the ghetto scenes of my life!"

"What you talkin' about? I don't do that . . . I . . ."

"Some people don't understand this thing I call friendship, Ty. They don't know how to live *in* it, or to stay in it. All they know is how to stand like a little crippled god over the scenes, tryna control it. And they decide, 'This is what I'll do, and this is how I'll act, and this is how I'll handle things.'"

"Calm down! I don't know what you're talkin' about . . ."

"All these years, I thought you were the *good* twin, and I was the *evil* one. But the truth is, you're *not* so righteous, my friend. In fact, you're kind of a slutty little closet *whore!* And you're not a very good queen, either. You could use a few lessons in Telling Sexual Secrets 101. So I thought maybe I'd just keep a few secrets of my own. Well, here's one for you: I've *hated* your self-righteous ass for three years and counting."

"This, this is crazy. Seek more *help*, David. Not only is it crazy, it's so fuckin' *hypocritical* coming from *you*. So, you've NEVER neglected to tell me the TRUTH about something, Duch? Never?"

David quickly, a little too quickly, answered.

"No! Never."

"Oh? So, I guess I should keep *pretending* I still believe that bullshit you fed ME about how you broke your fucking leg, right?"

David looked wholly stupid for a moment. *So Ty knew? The one lie he'd ever told Ty, and Ty knew it?* Strangely, that fact only made David angrier.

"You told me some bullshit, and I *cried* with you. You looked me straight in my eyes and you *lied* to me, and I *still held* you. I *know* what happened. I don't know *why* you couldn't just trust me with the truth, but I'm sure you had your reasons. Did I *hate* you for it? No. And I never would. I just felt quietly sorry for you, David."

"OK, so now you know. Yes. I broke my leg fuckin' around

with some meaningless trick. There, I can say it. So I guess you thought you had some *power* over me, holding that secret?"

"Who *are* you, Duch? Why would I *ever* do that to you? You know I would never *do* that, don't you? Some things are just too damn *painful* for us to talk about, and so, we don't. That's how I treated your truth. But you thought I'd use that tragic fall to have some *power* over you? What the fuck? You're painting some picture of a cat I don't even know, and calling it *me.* I love you. I always will. But, fine, you just keep *hating* me, David. But hate me because I *betrayed* you. Hate me because I *stole* something from you. But don't come in my face, talking about hating me over some bullshit! Wake the fuck up from that fantasy, David! The *fact* is you never *owned* Face Depina. No one ever did. And I'm still your friend, that one friend who never once—"

"Disrespected me?" David snapped.

"So, you don't want to listen to my side? OK. Then, we're not having this conversation."

"There you go, playing the fucking director! Cut! You think you got the *power* to say we're not having this conversation? Well, fuck you!"

"I'm not playing anything. I'm just being *Ty*, remember him? Maybe you don't remember Ty because you tell him lies, and then decide to *believe* in the people with a long history of lies and deceit. No, you don't even remember me or *who I am*, because Face and your wild-ass brain have devised a whole other truth."

"Fine. Go ahead. Try explaining yourself. The *short* version, please." David sat and held his head.

"It's simple." Ty sighed, took a deep breath, and began. "That night was the quickest mistake I ever regretted. But I didn't do it to you, or against you, or in spite of you. In fact, *you* weren't even in the room. I thought I was doing it for myself, my baser self. My dick worked fine that night. He's already *Depina-ized* his version, I'm quite sure. Suffice is to say, it was a long, hot, sweaty lie. He sucked me, I fucked him. He then launched into a performance art piece called: 'I'm *not really* a homosexual. But I might get to play one on TV!'"

"What? Come on, Ty!" David scoffed.

"That's what the boy *told* me. I couldn't make that shit up. It's vintage Face. Think about it."

David did, and, for a second, he let himself chuckle at the thought of Ty thinking he'd rocked Face's world, and then, Ty's sweaty, horse-face falling to the floor when Face Depina announced it was all *an act*. That was such rich shit, classic shit, *laughable* shit!

David figured he'd probably forgive Ty's deceptive ass one day. But *not* that day. His *first* concern was Face.

The cop's immediate focus remained on Browny. Ty hired him a lawyer, who got Browny out of custody. But he wasn't cleared of anything. Several people had witnessed his animated exchange with Face at the Zebra Den. Browny trried to explain it.

"Yo! I asked him if he wanted to put *the group* back together for a benefit. And he laughed in my fuckin' face. Then I asked for a loan, man. He owed me, yo! And I only did it for Jonathan. I swear, it was for Jon's bills. And he dissed me in front of his fancy friends. And they was all laughin' at me and my *suit!* Yo! And I got pissed, and I booked . . . I've been madder than that at his ass and ain't tried to kill him, yo."

Meanwhile, in the venerable chambers of a well-known city judge, a promising, politically ambitious young lawyer met quietly with the esteemed and politically well-connected adjudicator. The young lawyer told the judge the story of a fragile girl and the *terrible thing* a certain man had done to her. But there was no evidence of the deed. At best, it was a case of "he said, she said." The young lawyer proposed that if said alleged man, who'd recently been shot by said fragile girl, would not press charges, the young woman would never speak publicly of her motive, and would furthermore agree to seek psychiatric care in a facility of the good judge's choosing.

It was a solution that, the judge agreed, seemed best for all parties involved.

DECEMBER 1, 1993

FOR BLUR ANTONELLI, IT WAS A TIME FOR ENDINGS . . .

"Tyrone, please! No painted black thumbnails tonight!"

"It's a show of mourning. You know that. I do it so I'll always remember . . ."

"Tyrone, you're not wearing that to this dinner. You know people will ask why."

"I have no problem telling people why," Tyrone said, adjusting his tie in the bathroom mirror.

"Well, it's queer, and its eccentric, and I'd prefer you didn't wear it," Blur said bluntly.

Ty had already agreed to fashion his braided mane into a sedate ponytail, and now the man was bitching about his fingernails? Instead of jumping in his face, as he'd taken to doing of late, for once, Ty remained silent. He removed the polish and quietly accompanied Blur to the firm's reception honoring a senior partner's anniversary.

Ty remained in the background as he'd been instructed. Blur danced with the lovelies. Tyrone watched. Blur adjourned to smoke cigars with the big boys in the parlor. Ty sat at the bar. Blur made an obvious pass at the coat-check girl. Ty was not amused. For one rebellious moment he thought of stopping the swing band, seizing the mike, and announcing that he and Blur would soon celebrate their own anniversary as long-time apocalyptic lovers, and were thinking about adopting a Korean kid.

But, he chilled.

When they returned home, it was on.

"You know, I've had just about enough of your straight man act. It's way too fucking fake for comfort. You stand there, in your little suit, spouting your little ideas on justice, crime, punishment, and manhood, and you don't have a clue. Ever think maybe you're just a little man in a little suit?"

"Oh, good. The mature and oh-so-*enlightened* Tyrone Hunter spews another height joke. What was it you once said about name-calling? Wasn't it supposed to be an act of *the guilty and insecure?* Everything you do just makes you another desperate *fag*, another slave to some man's validation of you. Well, that's your trip, not mine!"

"What the hell are you talking about?"

"You! And your *needs*! I'm sick of them! Ever think I might want a *discreet* partner who acts like *a man* in public? And how many times have I told you, don't grab my fuckin' hand in the fuckin' street!"

"Actually, I'm trippin on desperate fag needing *validation* theory. If you think that, I mean *really think* that, then you never knew *me* at all. How many times have I gotten along without *you* by my side, in my bed, or in the same damn city? Please. If I ever needed someone so desperately, it certainly wasn't *you.* So don't even try to paint me as some clinging bitch, because that little black dress won't fit my ass."

"So, *you've* taken to wearing dresses, too? I knew it was just a matter of time."

"If you wanna insult me, please, get some new material, Blur. Your words were never strong enough to do the trick. But your *actions*, *they* insult me. I watched you tonight, and one epiphany finally came to light: I used to *admire* all the things you wanted to become, and now all you've become is this *thing*."

"I know how to play the game. Apparently, you don't have a clue about how they do things in the straight world. Maybe you should take some lessons."

"Who the hell am I living with these days? Lessons? I don't need lessons in being a liar. I like the *real* me just fine, most days. But at the risk of sounding like a sixth grader with a crush: Do you *like me?* Sign your real name in my slang book, and let me know."

"Don't be ridiculous!"

"No, I'm very serious. You need tell me how you feel. Just tell me, and I can take it. I challenge you to say the words, Blur! If you don't wanna be *who* you are with me, then maybe you need to be someone else, *someplace* else. I'd rather do alone than do time with your insecurities."

"I'm only showing you a few things you need to correct."

"Correct them for whom? Myself? Or for *you?* If you're so uncomfortable with *who* I am, then we have a serious problem here, bruh!"

Tyrone remembered their sex life in the last few weeks. How, when the two grew hot and sweaty as Coke bottles at a Fourth of July jamboree, he'd lie inside that confusing afterglow and think, *Damn! You never stop blowin' me or my mind. You're fuckin' heroic between these sheets. Too bad you're a fuckin' fraud in life!* Now all those thoughts he had given no tongue to, he could say them aloud and not give a shit about the repercussions.

"You're strictly homosexual, Blur. You like to kiss men, lick men, and get fucked by men. Preferably in the dark. All that makes you is a homosexual. Take it from me, you're a fantastic homosexual. But I don't think you've ever been gay, and I don't think you want to be."

"That's not the case."

"No, I think it is. Every one of your friends I've ever met is deeply homophobic. They make *fag jokes* around you, and you *laugh*, harder than all the rest. Do you hate yourself *that* much? What do they really *know* about you, or me, or us for that matter?"

"That's none of their business!"

"What the hell are you so ashamed of?"

"What the hell are you so fucking proud of? You, and your damn parades, and your crazy faggot friends. This whole damn crusade, it makes me sick!"

"Damn it, finally some truth breezes into the room. You don't want a relationship with me or my friends or the rest of the world. You just want to fuck and suck in the dark, and walk tall and straight in the sun." Tyrone laughed. "Fuckin' David was right. Again."

The name alone says it all, Ty . . . Anti-Nelly.

"Please don't bring *him or her or it* into this fuckin' conversation!" Blur fumed.

"Watch it, now! You disrespected me because that's just what *I've let you* do. But no more! And don't you ever *dare* disrespect David! Trust me. You don't want that fight."

"Why? What is he to you? Your *bitch?* Your lover on the side? I thought you liked men!"

"What the hell would you know about *manhood?*"

"I know this much: I know when to say fuck you! And fuck queer David! And fuck whatever queer agenda you're on! Fuck moving to Westchester and setting up house with me, too. In fact, fuck *us!* Fuckin' forget about us altogether!"

"Are you sure?" Ty asked. "Are you really fuckin' sure? Because, trust me on this, I can get straight-up *amnesiac* on your ass!"

Blur left with two suitcases, a suit bag, a shaving kit, and not another mumbling word.

The Face Case was magically hushed. The official word:

"The act of a probable stalker." Browny was seared, but not badly burned.

Blur campaigned mightily for the esteemed adjudicator in the next election, and in return was appointed to a politically advantageous position in the district attorney's office.

Depina's wounds were not catastrophic: two bullets to the posterior region, a little gunpowder on his ego. In a star exit, under the sneaky shroud of night, he left the hospital. But while there, secrets were revealed and unlocked—the kind of secrets one only discovers after a complete physical examination, including the necessary blood work.

It was all in the doctor's face. He delivered the sentence plainly.

The cinema in Face Depina's mind played a reel of events, mistakes, faces and places he wanted to snatch back from the deepest depths of forever.

He became drawn, and withdrawn. He was decidedly low-key. He stopped seeing Chaz altogether. There would be no more carnal battles in The War Room. He broke it off coldly, never gave a reason why.

There were lots of messages on his various machines. He listened to the distressed, "Facey, are you OKs" from the usual jaded set. There were hounding messages from the press, annoying ones from Browny, and some deeply unsettling ones from Chaz.

It was too much to deal with *straight*. He needed something to take the edge off. Who was he gonna call? For legal reasons, he had to distance himself from Claudio, at least temporarily. *Maybe Browny?* he thought. But those damn dealers Browny knew stepped on, cut, and manipulated the purity of the shit. Who had the *good shit?* And where could he fix? And just how *quick* could he fix?

He thought of a cat who hung out in Tompkins Square Park. When the cat saw Face's desperate condition, he decided he'd have a little strung-out junkie fun.

"You want it, big man? Huh? You want the good shit? Well, suck me off!"

Sometimes, when a man knows he's drowning, he goes down peacefully, with no fight left in his limbs, no last minute protest of desperation, and no desire to rise again.

Chaz Williams, fresh from the gym and convinced the breakup was just a whim, another mood swing, decided to pay a visit.

Face, in his haste to fix, had left the door unlocked. Chaz walked in on him and his dealer thug. Seeing those two together, an apoplectic Chaz abruptly stormed out.

Back at his apartment, he drank and drank very heavily. Chaz straight was a gentle giant, but Chaz polluted was Mr. Hyde, squared. Few knew what lay on that terrifying side of his eerie silence. Those who did shivered in its wake. Realizing he possessed an inner psychotic, Chaz rarely revived him via the bottle. But he did that evening. Things began to eat away at his gut. Then, in the middle of the night, he returned to Depina's loft, carrying something extra dangerous in his pants.

Face lay sleeping, naked and alone. Chaz stood over him, loving yet hating how peaceful he looked in his *fixed* and satisfied post-coital slumber. It would've been so incredibly easy to just shoot him in his naked balls. Maybe Chaz would junk the place, make it look like some crazy trick had gone berserk. He thought of the public ridicule on top of the recent shooting, and imagined the headlines:

"Face Shot in Pinga! Details at eleven."

How sweet and fitting that would be.

Chaz had quit his job, and he'd forsaken friends. Even his

prowling lifestyle had ended that torrid night in Spike's Den. And for what? Some vacant-eyed, pretty-boy junkie? The sight of him burned hot coals in Chaz's eyes. He slowly stroked the metal of his .45 as if it was the last true lover he'd ever have.

Face often slept with his mouth open. Chaz very quietly brought the barrel to Face's lips, slid it softly along the bottom one.

He wanted Face to wake up and beg. As he inched the barrel deeper, his lover stirred a little. Chaz pushed in deeper still. Face began to roll his tongue along it, sucking it as his hand played between his thighs. Chaz could see him growing aroused.

After a few perverse moments, Face's eyes shot wide open. He stared directly at Chaz, seemingly unafraid. His stone fearlessness took away Chaz's base homicidal instinct, and Chaz removed the gun.

"Go ahead. Do it. Do it, man. Do it, and do us all a favor. Come on. I'm right here waitin' baby. *Come on!*" he yelled. "Look at you! All that dick and no fuckin' balls! Pathetic. If you had real balls, you'd just do it!" Face said, staring Chaz straight in the eyes.

Instead of pulling the trigger, Chaz Williams felt a tear pull down his cheek.

"You do *love* me, don't you?" he asked pitifully.

Back in Harlem, Browny's woman had once again drop-kicked *his* junkie ass. It was Juanita's last-ditch tough-love effort to get her man clean. She wanted him off crack, off booze, off self-pity, and off that perpetual merry-go-round and sometime savior, Face Depina.

Finally, Browny broke down and told Juanita his whole ugly, confused, stupid, nonsensical Face story.

Shocked, speechless, and appalled, she still put him out.

But knowing now the despicably sleazy tactics of Face Depina and the way he'd played *her man*, well, Juanita Lewis just wasn't having it.

A wrathful Juanita was a thing no man wanted to endure, because that wrath was just too fantastic! She'd gained a lot of weight in the '80s. Truth be told, she was a sister with an acute ham hock dependency. But by then she'd grown in spirit, and in love too. All that ire coming from a woman of her size and threat, loud and ghetto-proud with her shit, a woman with a fluency of the "motherfuck" language cussing and punking you, hand on her hip, fingers in your face—it was too much. Standing away from it, you could see in her wrath the wild, freestyle, Thelonius Monk art of it. But up close it was like fire, and that day Face Depina was her gasoline.

"Mr. Depina, Face, whatever yo motherfuckin' name is, I know everything," she said, folding her arms, getting her posture in gear for that erratic figure-eight-head-and-neck-swerve-thing she did.

Oh, nah. Here it comes at me. This mad-ass black Buick's about to stomp on the gas. And I'm high and sore, and I'm sick, and she don't care! I need to get high and look at that Buick. Ain't no stoppin' it.

"You been jerkin' my man around all this time, ya punk bitch! Do you know the cops was all over his ass when you got shot? Did you know that they came in *my* motherfuckin' place, *broke* through my door, and tore up stuff in *my motherfuckin'* house? And Faison, he ain't been nothing but loyal to you, motherfucka. Oh! So now you's about to do right by him. I don't think you got enough to pay him what you owe him. But, Mr. Face Depina, you *will* make it right!"

This shit was the last shit Depina needed. He *needed* to cop, to fix, and quick, and he told her.

"Look, I'm takin' care of things with Faison. Hell, I'm always cleanin' up after his ass. But that's between me and him.

It's none of your damn business! Now go away. Please." He said this arrogantly, using his lowering eyes as brooms to brush her off entirely.

Only Juanita was not a piece of lint on the shoulder of his new Versace.

"Who the fuck you think you're talkin to? Huh, motherfucka? You need to know, you don't mean *shit* to me! You think you *know* people? Well, hell, I'm Juanita Ruby-Mae Lewis, from Harlem, USA, baby, and I know people, too. People who would just as soon as *cut* ya than look in them fake-ass motherfuckin' *white-boy* eyes of yours! No. You don't wanna fuck with me, little mixed boy! Hell, I'll kick yo motherfuckin' ass myself, 'cause you ain't all that!"

"Please. Just . . . just go *home*, woman."

"Listen up, you fuckin' junkie! Yeah, I *said* it! I know *all* about you. And what I don't know, I can figga. So you gonna *listen* to what I got to say. My baby needs help, and you gon get him in Daytop Village! I understand you still got *some* power, so there won't be no long waitin' list to get him in. Y'all *need* to go in on the buddy plan! But your habit is your damn business. Now, once my man is clean, and I'm *sure* he's clean, me and him is gettin' married. And you, you payin for the wedding! Oh yes, I don't stutter. *You payin'* for it. You buyin' *everything* from the flowers to the motherfuckin' silk socks on his feet! We'll be honeymooning in Jamaica. And thank you for that, too. And when we get back, there will be a check in our mailbox with *my man's* name on it. A check for fifty thousand dollars. And by the way, *orchids* is my favorite flower."

"Oh. I get it now. Now I *see* why you and Browny hooked up. Y'all *special motherfuckas.* Straight-off-that-li'l-yellow-bus *special.* Glad ya found each other, though, 'cause you're both a coupla seriously delirious bitches. Now leave! Book, bitch!" he sneered.

"Bitch?! Oh? So, I'ma bitch? And *delirious*, too? Really? Well, this delirious bitch is about to get fuckin' psychotic!"

"Too late, trust me. That Buick done left the lot, baby," Depina cracked in his private desperation.

But he was not the *Aramis* Man in those old commercials. He wasn't, as the catch phrase said, "*Ready For Anything*." And he certainly wasn't ready for Juanita Lewis's trump card.

"Did I say psychotic? Maybe I meant, what's that word? Oh yeah, *pyromaniacal*!"

Face's mouth dropped open and all the air rushed out. He had to sit, and sit quickly. He sat, and he winced. His ass still *hurt*. Bullets tended to do that. He wondered what she knew, how she knew, and what she planned to *do* with what she knew.

"I know somebody who *knows* somebody who got all kinds of stories about some boy who burned a whole lotta property up in the South Bronx. And this wasn't *no little* kid who didn't *know* shit. No, this kid was old enough to *know* better. Caused *a whole lotta* property damage, too. Now, I might be all *delirious* and shit, but I figure, destroyin' a whole lotta property, causin' all that damage must be some kinda *criminal* act. Ya think? Seems to me, if they *caught* the motherfucka, he'd be lookin at a whole *lotta* cell time. Well, he would, when they finally bring his motherfuckin'-fire-startin punk ass to justice. Ya think? But ya know, them cops *still* ain't never solved that motherfuckin' case. Maybe . . . just maybe all they really need is some bitch, some formerly *delirious bitch* to provide 'em with a good, solid lead. Ummmm . . . Motherfucka? You don't *look* so good? You all right? *Delirious* bitch to homeboy . . . please, come in . . . Homeboy? Are you *with* me?"

It was a *lovely* motherfuckin' wedding.

CHAPTER TWENTY-NINE

Peace-out, Baby Bwoi

MARCH 1994

Floss Angeles seemed a perfect fit for a cool, hip, ambitious, smack-addicted, terminally ethnic New York actor.

He rented a little place on Sunset. The thought was, after that *one* memorable role, in an indy flick, his once critically acclaimed ass would be the new Flavor-of-the-Month, and he'd be offered all types of phat cash and challenging roles.

Unfortunately, Face's agent was unwilling to risk his reputation on an idling addict, and so he rarely submitted Face for parts.

In short, life in L.A. was not Facey's blue, kidney-shaped pool! He wasn't "funning the sunshine, playing just to play," or becoming that crazy-paid denizen in his actory-foolish dream. He was just another hopeful in a city full of hopefuls, stranded amid the palm trees, sun-drenched plazas, highways, freeways, and lavish ways of L.A. It was a Whole New World out there, only this one didn't say, "*Hello, Facey! You fine motherfuck! Welcome to L.A. Mr. Swifty Lazar's reserved a table at*

Chasen's. Mr. Geffen would like to see you. And please don't forget to return Steven's calls."

"Yo, Claude, it's me, man. Times here are hoard as fuck. You go to Hollyrock, and the real estate's prettier, things seem friendlier, the people, the clothes, and the cars are finer. And everything's marvelous. But this town will drain the heart and talent right out of a motherfucka! Everything ain't fake, just a helluva lotta pretend. But I'm hangin' in, baby. You know how I do. Hey, Claude . . . every now and then, check in on Chaz for me. I cut him loose but . . . What you mean, he don't like you? You got a dick and a whip, don't ya?"

In addition, modeling had turned a cold, padded shoulder on Face. Black men who *looked* like *black men* ruled the catwalk now. The Era of The Light-Skinned Pretty Ones was ovuh. That phenomenon, coupled with Depina's chronic instability, his absences, and the jittery phantoms of his increasingly visible addiction, made him dispensable.

Junkies tend not to acknowledge a changing of the guard, of clothes, or of a decade. Face was primarily an '80s-thinker. And that thinker was looking craggier, less the hunk du jour, and more like yesterday's graying statue. He resembled a puny scarecrow, stripped of its vital stuffing. You knew him from that omnipresent Kangol, but what was he trying to hide? That perhaps Face Depina was no longer the shit? You could see the once-famous bones of his face, every one of them, exposed, gaping, and even the eyes were a sickly green color that his skin was beginning to match.

MAY 1994

No new monies were flowing in, and a cash-strapped Face was busy shooting up the dough he had. He'd scan the trades, go on open calls, put on a T-shirt, his leather, or his best suit to meet and greet and read for The Suits. He'd haul out the dusty charm, but something about him was just a little askew, the eyes weren't the same luminous green. The skin and smile were less vibrant. In certain slants under the cruel L.A. sun, one could see that he was balding!

"Yo? What's supposed to happen to folks too cool for New York and too cold for L.A. anyway?" he asked of Conte, who was still busy funning in New Joke City.

"I know how it is, Facey. That's why I left the biz. You're hot, you're cold, you're cute, you're over. It's enough to make a nice Italian boy go crazy. Hey! San Francisco is a good place to go crazy."

"Nah. I miss my friends, man. Hell, I even miss you, and my little fag David too."

"Then come home, man. We can be on Fire Island by the weekend. Nuts up!"

"I can't."

"Why not? Just come home!"

"I can't, Claude. I. . . . I don't look like me anymore," Face confessed. "And I'm broke as shit."

But not everything looked as bad as Face.

"Say," Claudio said, "when was the last time you talked to our accountant?"

Face had totally forgotten about those boring-ass money talks Conte forced upon him. But those talks had been lucrative.

"You know what?" Claude said. "You can thank me later. Just come home, pretty boy. Come the fuck home and help me count some of this brand new moola!"

JUNE 1994

Maybe it was *better* in New York. People wore more clothes, they coolly covered up, and everything wasn't so wide-fuckin'-open. The hardest thing to do is to *try* to act normal, *be normal* when normal is a drive-in movie and you're watching it far away from inside a hazy window. Normal was a two-dimensional flick, and he wasn't the star. Hell, he wasn't even *in* that prosaic little pic. All Face could do was feel his habit, and try to conceal his habit, and all the while he was yielding to nothing else in the fucking world but the motherfucking habit.

Back home he could always get a runner to deliver heroin to his crib, hang out there, shoot up there, OD there. This was, after all, New York, and there were worse places to wake up dead.

There was a growing group of mean street boys who'd drop by just to watch him, fascinated by that addict's palsy claiming his face, and the slow ballet against gravity as he'd nod his pitiful nod. And they would goof on him mercilessly. The once famous Face Depina was losing weight, losing hair, and losing time.

"Yo! This motherfucker here, he used to *be* somebody!" They'd laugh.

"Angel? Angel, is that you laughin at me', ya punk?" Face asked in his elongated way, through a haze of faceless Puerto Rican boys who once, not so long ago, were just *dying to* meet him.

AUGUST 6, 1994

Even if his success was only a fit of serendipity, Face Depina thought, *Maybe, I'm entitled to a little bit of better.*

But then suddenly *better* had turned its sunny face. That dizzy spiral of days where everyone wanted Face—"Get me Face"—had spun off the calendar. All at once that cool leather coat of fame had played out of style. But he thought he could stitch a new one, because his needle and his fixings were in a metal box beneath his bathtub.

Sometimes the elixir betrays you. But even then, there can

be a blessed state of placidity. Even then, in that final jerk of quietude, perhaps for him, there was a *long, blue moan* in the end.

The plaintive howls of his dog Sasha caused a disturbance in the building. Someone called the cops. There was nothing they could do. When EMS came to pick up the body, no one recognized him.

So gaunt, so wasted and blue, it took a mortician's artistry to make Face Depina resemble the man he used to be.

The few who saw him in those final months had guessed his story would end badly. Knowing him, in that limited way some people allow you to know them, it would be easy to say he never wanted anyone to see him looking *like that*.

AUGUST 7, 1994

"He kept talking about being sick and tired. Life was becoming this crazy movie beauty contest, and he was chicken shit about his looks changing. He was talking about ending the flick before his audience got bored. He was shooting up all the time, behind closed doors, all alone. But it wasn't just about *anesthetizing* the pain anymore. Face was shooting for death's door—I know that. The biggest thrill wasn't the high. The biggest thrill was in not knowing, not *caring* if he nodded off and never woke up again. That's what it comes down to when you're sick and tired all the time. So many nights I'd find him strung-out, on that edge. I had to smack him around, throw him in a cold shower, walk him across the room like a cripple. He'd curse me: 'Motherfuck you, Claudio! You fuckin' fake-ass Guido bastard! Get the fuck outta my goddamn life! You ain't NO fuckin' God! This is between me and the Real Guy!'

"Guess I finally realized what he meant. Facey wanted to wake up *dead*. We had a way of sending each other these messages. He was my friend. You don't want to see your friend looking so pitiful. So I said, 'Facey, you know what? I love you, man. You say the word and it'll be done. I'll do it myself . . . 'cause I love you that much,'" Conte claimed in a late night phone conversation with Bliss.

"And I would've done it too. Sure, I'd miss him; miss him like Hell. But I was *already* missing him, Bliss. See? Facey, the Facey *I knew* and loved, he was already dead and gone months before the coroners came to pick up the body."

AUGUST 10, 1994, FACE DEPINA'S FUNERAL

"Pascal. What can I say about Pascal? He was Adonis and Venus too," her eulogy began. "I looked at him and my molecules hummed. After you met him, they never quite stopped humming, did they? The first time I saw him, he was standing on the set, illuminated from behind by a spot. I noticed how tall he was. Men like my father, men with Latino blood, they seem taller than the rest, because that's how a man stands when he's out to prove something. Pascal moved in a slow sway toward me. The light left his wide shoulder, and another settled on his face. My God! A cool Savannah breeze swirled over my arms and every part of me was Goosebump City. Ice-green eyes cut over the room and landed like warm emerald and bronze butterflies all over me.

"'You're, uh, Bliss, right?' he said. 'Hey, Bliss. I'm Face. So, you ready to do this thing?'"

"Who was he, anyway? Was Pascal a scared little boy or a cocky son of the streets? Was he a sly fox or a sad and shelterless puppy? Whoever he was, strange, isn't it, how the things we find ourselves attracted to . . . sometimes wind up making us cry?"

Bliss, at that point, was crying.

"Say what you want about him, but Pascal 'Face' Depina was so *notorious* in his sway."

No one quite knew what the hell she meant, but it fit somehow.

Atop the closed coffin sat a photograph of a younger Pascal Depina, the statuesque idol. He was indeed something to look upon, with that dreamy mix of features which were part Newman, part Belafonte, part something only a marriage between African/Creole/German and Portuguese angels could summon. It was a stark and a violent contrast to what he would later become.

Tyrone:

"I doubt if he ever read the book, but Face reminded me of a quote from *The Picture of Dorian Gray*: 'It's better to look good than to be good.' Maybe a part of him wore the skin of a secretly scarred kid. But he learned to overcome it, cosmetically, at least. I remember he had this move in high school. He gave people the peace sign. He'd put his two fingers very close to his face, so if you didn't respond, the sign became a scratch of the nose, a rub under the eye. If you didn't acknowledge him, screw you! You'd never *punk* him. It was a very cool move. Face was the Duke of Cool Moves. The freaky, sexy ones usually are.

"It would be a lie to say we were friends. I tried, but he always made it hard. Most times I thought of him as a pretty fool . . . pretty lucky, pretty damn cruel, and pretty unappreciative of his *gift*. His duality confounded me. I believe passion and coldness coexist inside us all, but Face's stuff stretched the limits of human contradiction. He wanted to be noticed, and once he was, he grew to hate it. He wanted to be loved, yet held disdain for those who tried like hell to love him. He wanted to know pleasure, yet he seemed to almost enjoy inflicting pain.

"Was he in some kind of private pain? If so, it never really showed or photographed. His outside distracted us. Maybe beautiful things make us selfish. Even as we age we don't want to see beauty grow old. So maybe, just for us, he decided he wouldn't. When he did, he didn't let us see it. Guess the Duke of Cool Moves struck one last time.

"I'll miss him . . . the way Batman might miss The Riddler if The Riddler ever took his bag of tricks and left Gotham City for good. Peace, Face."

Browny to Juanita:

"Listen to Ty talkin' about him like he was some-damn-body. The Riddler! Sheeit! Yo! I'm keepin it real. Real is my spiel, yo! Do you think I came here 'cause he was my *friend*, *my partner*, *my boy*? Oh, hell no! I needed to see if the motherfucka was *really* dead. Yo! Wouldn't put it past his slick, devious ass to cook up some scheme, some bullshit. I thought the mofo was slicker this year, though. But I guess the motherfucka really is tag-on-the-big-cold-yellow-toe-dead."

"Shhhhh!" Juanita hushed. "Not in God's house, baby."

"Once there was this gorgeous, *gorgeous* time when we were all living our dreams," David began. "I know some of y'all expect me to get up here, scale that gender fence, and act a fool, but today the fool has left the asylum. I see no need for folly anymore. Facey's gone. And I *loved* that boy. Some of you know that. And the cherry on the cake of my outrage is that the world gets so judgmental of behavior . . . when it's only human. The way we are, and how we got there, it's called the survival of human beings, baby. I could tell you a few stories about it. But this is for Pascal Ornate 'Face' Depina, devout hell-raiser of our emotions. How many of you know there was a kind of *sadness* to him? Not many, I bet. It was probably his biggest secret. He kept that beautifully cool unflappable *other* Face in check, so the rest of the world would miss that sad thing in him. I saw it once or twice, and it broke my heart. He ached like the rest of us human beings, squared, and he'd take that ache out on us or whoever was there. No matter what kind of love or friendship or solace we offered, he'd take it like a hungry, desperate thief. And maybe he silently resented us for being such chumps. Whatever we gave him, it wasn't enough. See, I know, he was stamped as *damaged* goods from the moment he first breathed air. That was his heritage, and no amount of idolatry could ever fix that. He didn't *trust love*. When a child is never given the keys *to* love, the possibility of being able to *accept* love dies a little more every day. So maybe we should take comfort in what he was able to give."

Sitting there, Ty's mind drifted back to one shining night in October 1991 . . .

"Hey, look at us being civil. Having cocktails and sharing war stories. We've never been quite *this* civilized. This shit feels so . . . *Old Acquaintance*."

"Whatever, man," a confused Face said, never a fan of old Bette Davis movies. Face was in a strange mood, looking everywhere, everyplace but in Tyrone's eyes. Then he just decided to ask Ty the question that had plagued him slowly.

"So, after all these years, and all that harsh shit, I guess you don't hate me anymore. Huh?"

"Man, please. I never hated *Pascal*. *He* was *aiight*. Well, most times, anyway. I just never liked '*Face*' very much."

"Damn! Are ya drunk tonight, Ty? Or am I just *too high* to hit you? You said that shit straight out. Always been you . . . straight-out with it."

"Only way I know how to be. What's that the kids say these days? Just keepin' it r-e-e-e-eal."

"Yeah, *whatevuh*. But sometimes a man can be *too* honest, and too real."

"Since that's never been how *you* roll, I'm guessing you must have *heard* that somewhere," Ty jabbed.

"Ow! See? That, right there . . . *that's* why we clash. People expect *me* to be a prick, a bastard, a son-of-a-cold-hearted-bitch. But not *you!* You try to go out of your way not to be . . . to most people. I know your trip better than you do, baby. You like to go around livin' your life like you never want anybody to ever say anything *bad* about you."

"Well," Ty began. But when he contemplated the truth of that statement, he thought, *Damn! What the fuck? Did Face Depina, of all people, just unriddle me?* "Well, I'm a gay, Black man who's fairly successful—no target there, huh? But what if I didn't want foul shit said about me? What's so wrong with that?"

"It's useless. If mugfuckers can't find somethin' negative to say about your ass, you think that'll stop them? Nah. They'll just make shit up. You think you gonna go to heaven 'cause of that do-good shit? What if there's no heaven, Ty? What then? All you did was waste so much fuckin' time *and fun* tryna be better than the rest of us. Ya think I'm a heartless bastard? Hey, maybe I am. I admit it. But every now and then, *Ty*, you'll say shit, or do shit, or just *think* shit, so HOARD, you out-bastard the worst fuckin' bastard in me. I'm not blamin' ya for it. I understand it. Maybe it's just the way we survive."

It was the opening night of his play and he'd never expected Face to show. But there he was, *notorious in his sway*, saying halfway nice things, semi-provocative things, instead of bent and ugly things. If Ty looked beneath that cool, unflustered display he might've realized Face was going through something. Face, in his own way, was assessing his plight.

"Tonight was cool. You did decent work, man. I kinda thought I might've seen *myself* up on that stage. But it's like I didn't even exist. I saw Davy all over the place, a little bit of Browny, too. Still holdin' on to them damn grudges, huh? I didn't think you'd resent me forever, man," Depina said.

"Awww . . . Come on, man. Don't make me have to say something *nice* to your ass. Oh, what the hell. Here it is: I never hated you. I don't even resent you, anymore. You just . . . *disappoint* me sometimes . . . too many times. But that's *my expectation* trip, not yours."

"So you was trippin'? All these years, you were just trippin? Is that why *I'm* not in the play?"

"You? Who ever once *got you*, Face? I know David *thought* he did . . . but not really. And who could write you on paper, man? You're a straight-up enigma. And by the way, that means . . ."

"I'm not stupid, Tyrone. I *know* what that means."

"For me, a character isn't real unless he unravels who he is, and lets me *see* him."

"Oh, I remember once I unraveled and you *seen plenty*," Face quipped.

"I wasn't talking about your dick, man. I'm not talking about all the shit you've pulled. I'm talking about *why*. But you'd never give that up, would you? Sure, I could've put some vain-ass pretty boy on the page, but he would've come off as pretty, and empty. I don't think you're *that* pretty or that empty, man. I just never knew who the fuck you really were . . . or what filled you up."

"Don't get this twisted, man, but you and Davy, you share everything like chicks with your fuckin' periods. I never wanted people seeing me bleed. Just ain't my trip."

Wow! That half-drunken tidbit speaks volumes for the man under Depina's skin, Tyrone thought.

"But I sat in the audience," Face continued, "and watched those people sayin' things out loud. And I gotta tell you, I was almost jealous of your flow. I even remember some of the lines and shit—like that thing about respect. What was it? 'Snatch Joy! Snatch respect'?"

"Snatch JOY! Snatch respect! Just snatch it any way you can. With your fist, with your lips, with your heart, with your example," Ty recited, slightly amazed that Face had paid attention.

"Yeah, that's it. You did all right for yourself, by yourself. This fuckin' thing looks like it's gonna be a hit. What's that they say? *Boffo*, baby."

He said it as if he knew it—and as if in some secret part of himself, he might even be *proud* of Tyrone. It was a Good Moment. The two of them, they'd never had many of those.

"Hey, that's a thick watch you've got on," Ty commented, gazing at the chunky, gold-plated Rolex gleaming on Face's arm.

"Ah! You like that, huh? It is pretty fly, ain't it?" Face smiled to himself. "You want it?"

"Yeah, right. Sure," Ty joked.

But Face began to remove it because he was serious.

"Nah, Face. I've never been into flashy stuff. And I'm not ready to sell my soul to Beelzebub. But thanks anyway." A kind of quiet distress settled on Depina's countenance.

"Ty? You ever think we're losing ourselves, our *spiritual* selves, and just becoming these people who have a lotta shit?" Those haunting eyes for the first time searched Ty's for confirmation.

Ty looked at him with a real sense of awe. And he hadn't done that in years. Well, not since he'd laid eyes on the Depina penis. *Spiritual selves*?

"Losing our spiritual selves? Yeah. All the time," he slowly answered. "In fact . . ."

Then someone, perhaps Mr. Destiny, tapped Ty's shoulder, and Broadway's newest playwright had to leave what promised to be an interesting, possibly even *mind-bending* conversation.

* * *

Tyrone wondered now if things would've been different if he and Face could've learned how to *talk* to each other. It seemed the only good thing in being enemies was that at least they knew where they stood.

Who was Face, really? Ty had tried to solve the riddle. On occasion, he'd asked Face about his mother, and Face had invented stories of loveliness, bravery, and of sacrifice. But were the tabloids right? Was his father a chattering derelict? When Ty asked about his heritage, most specifically Alphonze Depina, Face shot him the look of a thousand deaths. Some things were better left unsaid.

David stood, finishing his eulogy.

"The saddest thing of all is because he looked like a fantasy, everyone expected him to *be* one. I wish I could've told him the secret. I know it now. The trick is this: just let people see the *real you*. Let them love, hate all the things that you are. Those who still love you, they're the ones who came to stay."

Later, stylish men in black and matching sunglasses removed the coffin, and the people who knew bits of Face and pieces of Pascal gathered outside in the street. Ty had never seen the Duch look more lost. Ty grabbed his arm.

"Tonight, if you want," he whispered, "we can just get pissy drunk. Talk all night, or not talk at all. Whatever you feel would be the proper requiem for your Facey, I'm down to do it with you. I just don't want you going into some dark place all alone."

"I'm fine, Ty. Death, sex, and funeral dirges, you know how they affect my libido. Tonight's a night for dancing. Maybe, if I throw myself *hoard* enough into the music, I might just dance myself to death. Then I won't see my Facey in every tall, fine man's physique. I'm dancin' tonight, baby. You can come with me if you want, but ya damn sure can't stop me!"

Bliss Santana joined them on the street. Throughout the

years, she and David had never been in such close proximity. Now there they were.

"Well, hello, Miss Bliss. At last we meet."

"So, *you're* David," she said, managing the slowest of smiles.

"Yes. I *be he*. And I need to tell you something," David began.

All at once, both Ty and Bliss held their breath.

"Once I had this crush. God! So many of my stories start out that way! He was a very long, lean and lovely Puerto Rican boy from Newark. But this fool, this loco could *not salsa* to save his pointy-toe-shoe-wearin' life. So, cute as he was, I had to drop-dip him. But as a goof, we once tipped into this dance school. You remember working at Arthur Murray's, teaching those Latin steps to them old rhythm-free people?"

"Another lifetime ago," Bliss responded.

"Well, you were *something* to see in that lifetime. You, in that tight, yellow dress with the feathers on the side. I thought, oh my God! Ay caramba, mami! Wow! Look at her! Just look at *her go*! You were too pretty for that place. It was a waste of time. But every now and then, one of those rhythm-free men got a step right, and something in your face brightened and you let loose. Suddenly, you were Rita Moreno in *West Side Story*—hair flying, dress gliding, so free and sexy. You were a spirit. We should all be so free and sexy," he finished sadly.

"Free? Isn't it sexy to think so," Bliss said.

"I'm going to hug you now, Bliss," David announced. "Now don't get skurred. It'll be very short and sweet, but sincere. Are you ready?"

"Yes, I think I am." She planted her feet firmly.

David's hug was very much like him: short and sweet and sincere.

"God bless, Bliss. Goodbye, Ty. We'll talk." He kissed his best friend's cheek, then David slowly walked away.

Later in the day, Browny appeared at the grave site to share one last sip with the dead.

He thought about that day, so many years ago, when it seemed as if their lives would be golden. It was hours before their first live show. Ty, David, Face, and Browny were teens, sitting peacefully on the train, envisioning a future so bright they'd all have to resort to sporting Wayfarers.

Browny imagined his own exotic Paradise.

"When my career jumps off, I'ma be like, fuck y'all! For real, yo. Fuck you bastards! I'ma build me a mansion on a beach in Bali, and just cool the fuck out, eatin' peaches with some bikini-clad honeys!"

"Hell, you losers can eat the dust from my crush, fat-ass, fully tricked-out, mint-green Mercedes. Yeah, I'll probably go to Hollyrock, make a few pics, and marry a couple starlets. Then, I'll just get fat and bald and talk about what hot gold shit I *used* to be," Facey Depina predicted, high on weed, Hennessy, and dreams.

"Hmmm. 'Marry a couple starlets,' Facey? Somehow, I just don't see that in the cards for you," David teased. Face gave David a smirk and shot him his middle finger.

"Now, as for me, well, I see myself giving a Royal Command Performance," David predicted. "And after my pas de deux with hopefully some Nubian Nureyev, everyone will be agog. But I'll still be a rebel dancer, so I'll rock a bloody, bawdy, blooming jock to tea," David joked in veddy proper English.

Then Ty chimed in, as only Tyrone Hunter would.

"Well, later for the Brits, boss rides and Bali. If any of you future egomaniacs even think about trippin' around me, I'll write a nasty tell-all about your rich, sad, pathetic asses," he promised.

* * *

Strange he would remember that day, and the teenaged Pascal "Face" Depina. Odd, how he'd suddenly remember the dreams of the others. If only Browny were Fate's Author, he'd want to rewrite an entirely different future than the one he and the rest would come to know. Considering everything he'd been through, and everything he'd known, he still felt cheated, gypped in the card game of life. And there sat Face Depina at that table, always dealing from the *bottom* of the deck. Now that dealer was in his grave.

"Peace out, ya miserable bastard," was all Browny could think to say.

Everyone wondered what happened to Chaz. Was he too distraught to deal with the death of his most tempestuous lover? Some would say yes. Five hours after hearing the inevitable news, Chaz Williams suffered a seizure. It was later diagnosed as a brain aneurysm.

Later still, yet another figure appeared. Angel, Face's teenage friend-turn-betrayer, came to say his own farewell. A thin bruise of a man, he had no words. He simply poured a shot of bourbon over the grave.

LABOR DAY, 1994

In a deeply reflective mood, Ty sat at his writing desk, talking to the spirit of Trick.

"Obviously, I've got nothing going on, or I wouldn't be stuck here talking to your ghostly ass. It's Labor Day. Jerry still ain't found a damn cure for those kids. Muscular dystrophy has gotta be one behemoth-sized bitch! Over thirty years of telethons and still no cure. So what are our chances for a panacea?

"Nothing and no one is so young or pretty anymore. Face is dead, the rest of our goatees are graying. This disease is a teen.

For my last birthday, Davy bought me a speed-bag. When I punch it, it becomes anyone or *anything* I want it to be. Can you guess what I want it to be?

"Well, Browny's finally landed a singing gig. He shifted his repertoire from pop to jazz and blues. He knows a little something about the latter. Just loves to flex those falsetto flourishes. The kid's not half bad, though. But didn't we all know that? You know Browny. He's got so much energy and all this crazy potential. And if he could just conquer those damn demons once and for all, maybe things'll turn out alright for him. I hope so.

"And the Duch is now officially a High Priestess of Fashion. Maybe that's what he was meant to be second. He tested positive, you know. He wanted to get drunk one night, so we did, and he told me. We cried for days. Sometimes I still do.

"But David is a *firebird*, for real. Today at Wigstock he decided it was time Davina retired. It was her last public appearance. Nothing quite as sad as an old queen. Well, maybe there are a few sadder things. It was a damn good performance, though. Every year someone steals the show and manages to outdo the most outrageous. This year, in my unbiased opinion, that thief was David. In that three-foot-high Afro wig and six-inch spiked heels, the dancer was stepping lively."

CHAPTER THIRTY

And Then There Were Two

LATE AUTUMN 1994, NEW YORK CITY

"The last time I saw him, he was outside The Blue Note in a heavy rain. He stood in the middle of this mean, metal and steel-shouldered city with no fuckin' umbrella. He had on his good overcoat. His 'jazz coat,' he called it. It was black wool, long and flowing, and it hung along his wet shoulders in a way that made him almost *elegant*. When he saw me, he smiled a little. But his eyes, they seemed so weary and bankrupt of any real joy. Maybe it was his time. It seemed like life had finally just wore him the fuck out."

In another time and place, David wondered why there was no music written especially for the dejected, lugubrious dancer. Where were the Blue Boy Waltzes, and those Bruised Bangee Boy Ballets? He would've, and most certainly could've danced the rhythmic bluesy shit out of them. He was in constant search of the right music, and the right singer or dancer who understood and who had an answer for his Blues Condition.

And then, suddenly, Victor arrived, and all music was beautiful, lovely, vital, alive! *Look at him . . . my man. My dark, dominant, delish, thick-donged daddy!*

To the strains of a sultry samba, Victor asked David to dance. David grabbed his hand and comically took to the floor, walking the Enchanted Walk—he called it—his head haughty, his limbs mimicking a stiff Bea Arthur meets Bela's Count Dracula glide.

They were alone at last inside the moody dive they co-owned called Cool Relax.

The old cat with the crying guitar, Browny and the singers backing him, all the players and martini slingers had gone on to tear down and kick around what was left of the evening. Outside on a small moonlit street, seedy elegance walked side by side with the hip sneers of leather boys. Ferocious pairings and terminal wet dreamers converged with the liars and cheaters and the fictions of an empire. But inside, the cavernous room was brought alive by the soft Latin jazz of Ray Barretto, a favorite of Victor's.

Something in Victor's fragrance had always intoxicated David. Even after a night of entertaining, he smelled as if he'd just stepped out from a dip in the warm Caribbean Sea. He smelled and tasted like a new piece of humankind. Now, David's eyes were glued to that protrusion in his pants. Victor's gaze asked, *Are you ready to be seduced, puppy?*

Though, at forty-nine, he was composed of more bulk than muscle, Victor seemed to bulge muscle all over whenever the two of them slow danced.

"Music OK, puppy?"

"On nights like this one, right here, right now, no other music exists."

"So . . . Joo in a good mood?"

"The best," David replied, beginning to spritz down his lover's thigh. He wanted to rip those trousers off Senor Love Daddy, expose that proud papa's pinga to the atmosphere.

"Good. I have something to say to joo, and it's harder than I thought."

"Oh, yes. It *certainly is*, Papi!" David chuckled slyly.

Victor sighed in a warm, erotic trail down David's neck. Anticipation raced through David.

"What is it?" he asked. Then, not being used to things going so right for him and unfamiliar with things *staying* right, David suddenly panicked and immediately thought the worst.

"What? Please. Please, tell me you're not sick."

"No. I'm fine. Pressure's down." Victor smiled as David silently breathed a sigh of relief. "Wait here. Papi's gonna show joo a night joo'll never forget!"

He vanished, and David lay inside some speechless dream, mad with love, happy in his skin. *Whee-e-e!*

Suddenly the jukebox ignited—"*In Your Eyes*"—and the blue lights dimmed into the softest of indigo. David heard breathing, jagged breathing, and soon realized those breaths came from the amplified speakers surrounding the room. Ooh! Victor was the Real Deal Master of slow seduction.

"I'm coming . . . closer. Can joo feel me? No. Don't joo turn around! Eyes closed! Breathe . . . Breathe with me . . ."

David obeyed. He inhaled and then exhaled slowly, feeling Victor's naked presence behind him.

Buttons flew.

Music played.

Pants cascaded to the floor in a heap.

Bodies were bathed in electric blue. And their breaths were not breaths, but small puffs of wind, the kind that make a candle flicker and a flame grow tall. A large, brown, benevolent husk was rubbered.

Atop the bar, David's legs became like straws, thrown over Victor's beefy shoulders. With a smile of seasoned recklessness, Victor aimed through that beckoning brown starfish.

"Aw-w-w!" David groaned, washed in those wet Latin eyes,

his limbs vining, entwining his lover. Victor pulsed within him, methodical and slow, and David fastened on as that nimble hollowed place in him conformed with a "Whoa!" to love's profuse width.

"Aw! Aw-w-w! Yes! Do me! Bust that piñata, Papi!"

He gripped the bar's rails—wincing, smiling, meeting, kneading Victor's thrusts.

Victor grunted, catching David's frantic limb and whipping it, inciting sensuous riots in him.

"Joo feel me, puppy? Shit, jess, joo do!" His gruff beard raked David's neck and he planted his kiss there. David trembled, dripping, wet with sweat.

"Yes! Don't stop!" he roared, as Victor bore down. "Tu mesientes, puppy. A la chingada—claro que si!" David danced beneath him, a quaking, shaking body of joy incarnate!

"Oh, yes, I'm . . . I'm gonna come for you, Papi. Only you, Papi!" he cried as he erupted.

Victor too vibrated at his deepest depths. And the gush was so strong, both lost gravity and fell to the floor. They laughed hysterically. Victor cradled Davy in a coat of fur, heartbeats, and laughter, their bodies full of jazz and sweat, their chests filled with rapid thunder.

David sighed a short breathless song, and, for once, it didn't sound anything like the blues.

"Joo all right, puppy?"

"I'm all out of words for 'all right,'" he panted.

"Joo happy?" Victor asked.

"More. More than happy. I could lie here ass-naked with you all night. Hey! Let's do it and not give a damn when the cleaning men come tomorrow. I'll just wave a foot over your back. 'Good morning!'"

Victor laughed. David often made him chuckle. Then he suddenly rose and walked across the floor.

Oh, Papi! Look at him, damn it! I gots me a man.

Victor returned, grinning, holding something behind his back.

"What you got there, Papi?"

"Jess a little something for joo, of course."

"But you don't have to, baby. You've given me . . . Look, be careful! You don't want a spoiled little maricon on your hands," David giggled.

"Well, this should spoil us both," Victor said, whipping out a small black velvet box.

How do you tell someone what you've only begun to realize yourself? How do you translate that with him, you are the most complete man, person, human you will ever be? Your journey has left you bruised, battered, and bewildered. But not bitter, because you've learned and you've survived. And now, in that most excellent hour of your journey, you're ready—ready to release the long, blue moan.

"Oh my goodness, Papi! It's a ring! You're giving me a ring? What does this mean?"

"Everything," Victor said. "*Everything*."

The two made love again before falling naked, engaged, and fast asleep on top of the bar.

Dave had a dream.

It started out magnificently in that special violent arena where machismo clashes and sensitivity bleeds crippled red rivers. They called it "The Sweet Sport," and the Champ and the Contender were going at it, dancing, shuffling, mixing it up. Jab for jab, the sting and stun of fists flew and tagged and cut and jabbed, and soon the river began to flow. With a flurry of uppercuts and a frenzied exchange of blows, each fighter scored points with the judges. But that vile virulent virus of a Champ remained unaffected. Still, even money was on David Donatello Richmond.

Initially, both boxers gave as good and hard as they got, and the hyped crowd settled in for a masterful night of pugilism. But by round four, the Contender's arms grew heavy, his dancing legs weary. He looked a little wobbly, a bit dazed. He was fading, his will oozing away like the blood trickling down his forehead. Worst of all, he was dropping his fists, not guarding his grill. The crowd began to boo him, hiss him, thinking he would throw in the towel.

Wearily, he gazed back to his corner. No support there. He lumbered forth, resting his head in the hills of his opponent's chest. A few harmless body blows to the opponent's impenetrable torso, the Contender backed away and saw the Champ grinning behind his mouthpiece. Then it happened: the coup de grace, the death blow. It came in a hellish right cross to the nose. It hammered out a spectacular sanguine mist, which drifted slowly across the canvas like a fizz of shattered rubies.

The Contender fell hard.

The hushed crowd watched, shocked, silent.

The referee shouted the count: "One, two, three, four, five, six, seven, eight, nine ten! He's out!"

In the corner of the defeated Contender, Daddy Richmond and Rico Rivera chastised mercilessly: "You let your fuckin' hands down. Why? You forget everything I taught you, damn it!" And, "You useless boy. Always was! Thought I could make a man out of you. But you ain't no man. You ain't nothin! Wipe that blood from yourself and put on a fuckin' sundress, bitch!"

Why wouldn't they disappear, just leave him alone?

"I ain't gotta listen to you bastards anymore," David shouted. "Hell! Be gone! Vanish!"

And so they did.

And in their place, there stood Tyrone. It was a *young* Tyrone, smiling and holding something gold in his hand.

* * *

"Oh! My God! I had that dream again, Papi."

"Relax, puppy. It's just a dream. It doesn't mean anything."

"No, I think it does. Madam Zoreena's foreseen hurtful things. I was afraid she was talking about you, Papi. Your heart. Your blood pressure. But now I'm not so sure."

"Joo dream different, puppy?" Victor asked.

"Well, it starts out like before, where I'm pummeled to a bloody pulp. My father and Rico are tellin' me how *worthless* I am. But finally I'm strong enough to make them go away. Then *Ty* appears. But it's Ty from high school, with that long, skinny, horse face and the Sal Mineo hair.

"And he's holding this big-ass trophy, smiling his biggest, most goofy grin, and he's telling me, 'Screw the judges, Duchess! Screw the oppressors. Screw 'em all! You're the bravest champion of all the queens and all the queen's men!' I'm *so happy* to see him there. And when he says it, I believe him. I think, yes, damn it, I am a champion! But just as I'm about to hug him and bleed all over my goofy, horse-faced bastard, he disappears. I mean, he was there, and then, he was gone. The shock of it, it made me wake up. And now, I'm scared. I feel *scared*. What does it mean?"

A kiss exchanged energies. Between David and Victor Medina there was only silence.

Face Depina was dead.

Bliss was living with HIV in Philadelphia with Face's daughter.

Faison Brown, who was quickly becoming a draw at Cool Relax and other cabarets in the city, had just purchased Juanita a full length, big-ass mink coat.

And Ty . . .

After two successful plays and a marginally well-received novel, a sense of fulfillment had eluded Tyrone, and that lustrous light at the end of a long tunnel seemed at best anticlimactic.

"It's funny, David," he'd said not so very long ago. "I worked so hard because I thought the end result would be some money shot into happiness and self-contentment. But you know what? It never happens that way. The money shot is a pitiful little dribble, and the moan of contentment is so low . . . you can barely hear the shit. I've wasted so much time waiting for that *money shot*. Maybe there's more to contentment than a long, blue moan."

"Speak for yourself, baby. I'm perfectly happy just to moan with Victor. Well, happy is a concept. But I am content."

"Are you really, Duchess?"

"Yes, I am. And yes, I *mean* it. Even at this advanced age, even living with a muscular virus—with the right partner, contentment is a doable dance."

"Well, I'm so glad for you," Ty confessed, his eyes blurring with tears. "I'm glad because you *deserve* it."

"And you? You still dancin' around 'happy' instead of grabbing it by the dick?"

"I'm not grabbing much of anything. Maybe happy is something *outside* of me, outside of this world I've inhabited. But *I know* there's some meaning out there somewhere. And I'm going to find it."

"Ty . . . my sad, but lovable horse-faced friend, must I remind you, yet again? Tell it to the The Universe."

"Ah, yes, you and The Universe. You know David, maybe the The Universe doesn't always turn out the way we plan. Maybe *we* turn out the way The Universe plans."

In the midst of losing friends in life, losing lovers, losing his bearings, Ty had become haunted by his inability to find a lasting *spiritual* center. It had worn him down. He'd spent his life attempting to create *better in his self*, in others, and to write or sing, to photograph, or carve something beautiful out of the pain of existence. But he grew tired of trying to show the world his scars, and its scars. It was time to concentrate on the business of healing them.

It had been building . . . forming, erecting and becoming taller in his mind, this Higher Calling, this second level to being a human being.

The metamorphosis began in November of '91, with his first trip to Africa.

Something in Africa, in that time he'd spent wiping the sweltering foreheads of dying children, had resonated in him.

And how he wished Bliss hadn't lied about Tyra being his child. Though he'd forgiven her, and it left a raised scar on the complexion of his future. He thought maybe, if he ever found someone *real*, he could adopt a child to love. Maybe he could impregnate a willing lesbian friend. Maybe he could father a child of his own. Maybe, *maybe*, life is full of fucking maybes.

But children were alone and dying on a dying continent. Disease and famine were ravaging both coasts and rocking the interior.

Imani's letters from Liberia were troubling.

Dear Ty,

I write you tonight with a heavy heart. Inside the capital of Monrovia this conflict has already claimed over one hundred fifty thousand lives. I believe there are even more. Today a baby was born in my hands. Tonight a child died in my arms. So many others are losing their way. Mothers, fathers lie dying beside their children. But Ty, though people are barely holdin' on, some are holding to survival, even in the hot and dry faces of death. I see them, and I am humbled. Even through famine and disease and the guns of rebel factions, these people, my people of the sun are striving to survive!

It was a dawning of an epiphany. In the final analysis, even staring into the eyes of death, the best of us strive for some kind of existence with dignity.

There had to be *something* Ty could do.

He decided to once again trek to Africa, this time to escape the lies and liars and riots and fires of his life. He approached several editors about embarking on a photojournalistic project on Africa's children. He was promptly rejected. Ty didn't care. Fuck them! He was strong-willed and independent. He went on his own.

Tyrone left for the Motherland with the intent to do better by the world. En route, he wanted to see Paris, just once.

The night turned suddenly golden in the City of Lights. He could appreciate Notre Dame de Champs, The Arc de Triomphe, and still dream of that New York moan of jazz and speeding yellow taxis that ignored black men. He could still dream of lovers, homeboys, church ladies, and bars and nights when an audience rose and screamed, "Author! Author!"

He was walking down the Champs Elysees, snapping photos, when he thought he saw a face—a vaguely familiar, if slightly older face. Nah. It couldn't be him, he told himself.

It was Paris on the cheap, complete with the seventy-dollar-a-night dive on a winding Parisian street. Inside the lobby, he saw that face again, and that face recognized him.

"Ty?" a voice asked.

It was a mug Ty hadn't looked into for nearly twenty years.

"Omar? Omar Peterson? What the hell are *you* doing here?" an astonished Ty asked.

"Starving," he said. "I've been living here for two years. I'm an artist now."

"Really? An artist? Who knew?"

"I did. Sometimes I feel like I'm the only one who knows.

So you're a writer now, huh? I read the reviews of one of your plays. Shit, Omar, keep it real. I went to see it, Ty."

"Oh. So *you* were the one."

"So, Ty's in Paris," Omar said in disbelief. "Damn. Is life strange or what? So, how long are you here for?"

"Until tomorrow."

"Oh," Omar said disappointedly. "Well, then you have to come with me. I wanna show you something."

What Omar showed him was *his* Paris. The one sprinkled with jazz clubs, out-of-print bookstores, and porn shops. Then he insisted they venture into a little art market where several of his paintings were for sale. One of them was titled "Sad-face Lust." It was an oil of a young, naked, black man, alone on a bed, a single tear drifting down his cheek. That young, long-faced man bore a remarkable likeness to a young, long-faced Tyrone.

"I must've done about a hundred sketches of you, man."

Ty stared at the portrait for a long time, silently.

"Why?" he asked.

"I was a little obsessed, I guess. I knew I'd hurt you. See, there's this *look* you used to get when you were hurt and tried like hell not to show it. But I could see it. It was all in those damn *Ty eyes*—so intelligent and sad. Sometimes I close my eyes and I still *see that look*. It wrecks me, because I knew I'd put it there. I'm sorry, Ty. I'm so damn sorry I ever did that to you," he said. And the colors in his voice wore all the hues of sincerity.

The two left the market as it began to pour. Instead of taking the Metro, they ran through the raindrops, laughing like fools. By the time they'd reached the hotel lobby, they were both drenched.

"I've got a bottle of wine in my room. It was a gift. A Chateau something and it's like over a hundred years old. You wanna . . ."

Tyrone's first instinct was to say no. *Hell, no!* He was on his way to do noble work, and he hadn't come to Paris for some bang-bang, peace-out thang.

"Well, just walk me to my room so I can get out of these wet clothes," Omar suggested. Tyrone accompanied him.

"You look good," Omar said as they stood outside the door. He soothed away a bead of rain from Ty's ear.

Then Ty saw inside of Omar's eyes a hunger as deep and wide as Somalia. And as Omar went in, there were traces of Kenya within his kiss. After all those years, the taste of betrayal was in no way evident. That one longing, lunging kiss said a million wasted things, spoke a thousand formerly hard homeboy utterances.

Omar opened the door and nudged Ty inside. Right away, as if it was something he needed to do, he ripped Ty's leather from his wide shoulders.

"So . . . ummm . . . where's the wine?" Ty asked.

"Fuck the wine! For the longest time I've waited to make things right with you, to do *better* by you than I did all those years ago. Before, I was just this scared and confused punk-ass. I was a kid. Well, I'm a man now . . . a proud, *gay* man." His hands pulled and tugged at Ty's rain-soaked shirt.

Africa waited. Yet Africa was in Omar's face when he turned to plant another kiss on Tyrone's lips.

Omar moved along Ty's neck, licking downward, suckling earth-brown tits with a hunger that seemed almost brand-new. He ran his lips against the slopes of Ty's chest and his shoulders. Ty could not resist. With hands tracing, racing the contours of each other's flesh, they fell to the bed—gripping, groping, their zippers unzipping.

Yes! Omar thought.

Ty's engorged member was looped in a leather-braided ring (a gift from his first *real* lover, Trick Brown). Omar took him in hand, and he slowly, assuredly swallowed him.

And the noise of his slurping drowned out the sound of the rain. And his tongue warmed and colored Ty like a beautiful sepia dream. Omar rose.

"Let's do this, Tyrone. I can take it like a man . . . wherever it leads."

Ty eased Omar's legs apart and he slowly entered him. Omar watched. His eyes were taking photographs of Ty's near-handsome face. He would remember that devilish grimace each time Tyrone lit into him. And together they moved with the flow of water in a buoyant, warm, and fluid rhythm.

There was only the sound of the rain, the clapping of their flesh, the noise of a gasping rubber . . . and their heated breath.

It seemed to last forever, until finally a feeling of consummation welled and grew so intense that Ty had to retreat.

"Oh! Yes, yes, shit! Omar-r-r! It's my baby!" he cried, ripping off the rubber within an inch of its life.

Tyrone arrived in a white torrent on Omar's furry chest.

It was then that Omar pitched and whirled inside that bed in Paris. His charge leapt high to the fuzzy rocks of his belly as Tyrone's essence slowly rolled down his torso.

Yet, even in that eerie afterglow, Ty wondered what had really changed. Even if he cared for the man lying in his arms, thoughts of caring *too much* distressed him a little. Where would all that caring lead?

Sensing Ty's uneasiness, Omar cradled him tightly. He ran a hand through those tousled copper dreads.

"I'm home," he whispered. "I'm here, Ty. This time, I swear man, I ain't going anywhere."

"Well, I *am*. Remember? Tomorrow, I leave for *Africa*."

Omar lifted his head and he kissed Tyrone, and it was returned, slowly. And slowly their tongues spun toward the open dark continent of each other's mouths.

It was an exchange of spit, a duel of lust, of ache, and of need. And it tasted like, *goodbye.*

Sometimes we find ourselves staring into the wilderness of another spirit's eyes, and all that is left between us is a sigh, or a moan. But it's OK. A moan is also a survivor's sound.

Strange, the things The Universe hands us . . .

Tyrone Hunter made his way to Africa, and he was killed in a plane crash heading home.

With Imani by his side, his body was flown back to New York.

Part of Manhattan, of Harlem and the Village had trouble processing the shock of it.

"Damn, 'Rone? Yo! Always thought out of all of us, *you* was the lucky motherfucka," Browny eulogized in his own special way.

David could not talk. All words, all sentiments fell through the trap door of his broken heart.

The services brought out a who's who, and a who's *that*(?) from Ty's years of do-gooding. There sat a speechless David with Victor, Faison with Juanita, sharing a pew with a most inconsolable Bliss and her daughter, Tyra.

The sight of Blur Antonelli pushing through made David want to rise up out of his silence. He wanted to kick the bastard dead in the throat, and wail all over his politically ambitious ass. But in a last show of good Christian etiquette, David somehow chilled. He was surprised by the presence of Omar, and stunned by the gathering of family and homeless friends who attended Tyrone's homecoming.

As far as memorials went, this one was almost funeral-perfect.

Loyal to the end, Ty willed his savings, a part of his royalties, even his ghostly apartment to David.

And so it became *his* chore to go through Tyrone's things. And in that painful undertaking, he discovered some of Tyrone's most recent journals.

What were you so damn busy trying to tell the world, ya dead half-beautiful bastard? Why couldn't you be a little like me? Why couldn't you ever, just once, grab life by its big nappy balls and milk the motherfucker dry?

There were so many questions and no one, much less Ty, could begin to answer them now.

And then he came across the last passage Ty had written about him, and it read:

Today I am no longer David's mother. I've officially given up the gig. Besides, he never put in an application for another mom anyways. I'm sorry I've wasted so many fucking years misusing The Truth of our friendship. The Truth is this: He might've stopped boxing long ago, but David remains my champion. I think I realized that again today. Today, I saw him at Wigstock, rocking the crowd in his big hyper-blond atomic Afro wig. He was dancing and shaking his little wild ass to "I Will Survive."

It was like he didn't have one sad bone in his entire body.

Later, as I watched him, falling safe and contented inside Victor's arms, I wondered: Why am I worrying? David's fine. All HIV-positive queens should be so fine. He's got friends, and a good man who's big in the pants, and he's even got this thriving fashion career. And every now and then when his eyes get weird and teary, I'll ask him if he's all right . . .

"Duch? Are you OK?"

But he tells me those tears are because he's "HAPPY! Happy, damn it!"

And you know what? I have to believe he is . . . because he looks so much like that queer copper kid I used to know at fifteen. That one I knew and loved, when all the world's stages were just ahead of him.

So I'm not gonna worry about David, or his mercurial ass any-more. The Duchess is happy . . .HAPPY, damn it!

And to that I say: Bravo! You go, baby boy!

Snatch Joy! Snatch respect!

And David, who had been raving about the utter unfairness, David, who'd cried the wild muted tears of a grief-stricken fool for three weeks straight, slowly closed his eyes. He mused about that kid, that long, horse-faced *almost handsome* boy called Tyrone.

My God! What a friend! What a spirit!

When he opened his eyes, he thought he saw something for just an instant. He thought he'd perceived a flash, a quick piece of Light zipping past the corner of his eyes. And for some queer reason, the *idea* of that *Light*, it made him smile.

THE END

About the Author

LM Ross is a New York poet, novelist, and columnist. But his true heart is that of a poet, and most everything he composes contains a certain jazz-tinged rhythm. He was first published nationally while in high school, and in the succeeding years his work has appeared in well over 200 magazines, journals, and anthologies including: *African American Review*, *Black Writer*, *Catalyst*, *Class*, *Essence*, *Free Lunch*, *Gypsy*, *Haight Ashbury Literary Journal*, and numerous others. He was featured prominently in the landmark "In The Tradition, An Anthology of Young Black Writers" and recently an excerpt from his latest novel was published in "Freedom In This Village."

LM also records his life experiences, poetry, rants and reviews in an online blog called One Moanman In Time. You can peep him out at http://bluemoaner.journalspace.com/

LOOK FOR MORE HOT TITLES FROM

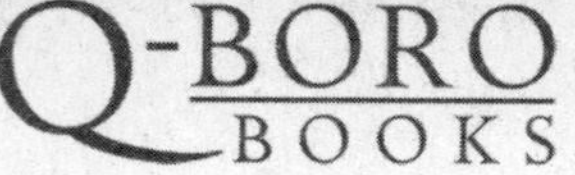

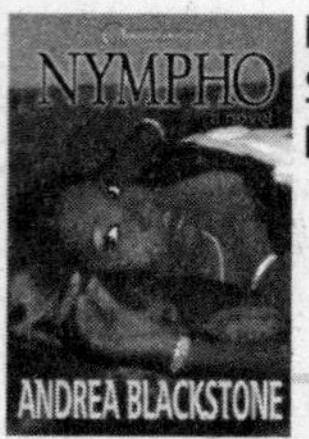

NYMPHO - MAY 2007
$14.95
ISBN 1933967102

How will signing up to live a promiscuous double-life destroy everything that's at stake in the lives of two close couples? Take a journey into Leslie's secret world and prepare for a twisted, erotic experience.

FREAK IN THE SHEETS - SEPTEMBER 2007
$14.95
ISBN 1933967196

Librarian Raquelle decides to put her knowledge of sexuality to use and open up a "freak" school, teaching men and women how to please their lovers beyond belief while enjoying themselves in the process. But trouble brews when a surprise pupil shows up and everything Raquelle has worked for comes under fire.

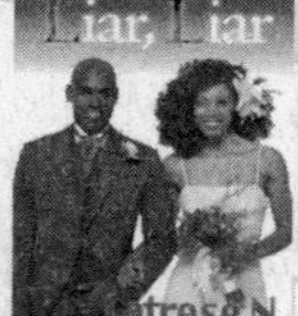

LIAR, LIAR - JUNE 2007
$14.95
ISBN 1933967110

Stormy calls off her wedding to Camden when she learns he's cheating with a male church member. However, after being convinced that Camden has been delivered from his demons, she proceeds with the wedding.

Will Stormy and Camden survive scandal, lies and deceit?

HEAVEN SENT - AUGUST 2007
$14.95
ISBN 1933967188

Eve is a recovering drug addict who has no intentions of staying clean until she meets Reverend Washington, a newly widowed man with three children. Secrets are uncovered that threaten Eve's new life with her new family and has everyone asking if Eve was *Heaven Sent*.

LOOK FOR MORE HOT TITLES FROM

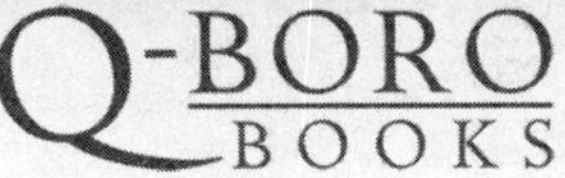

DARK KARMA - JUNE 2007
$14.95
ISBN 1-933967-12-9

What if the criminal was forced to live the horror that they caused? The drug dealer finds himself in the body of the drug addict and he suffers through the withdrawals, living on the street, the beatings, the rapes and the hunger. The thief steals the rent money and becomes the victim that finds herself living on the street and running for her life and the murderer becomes the victim's father and he deals with the death of a son and a grieving mother.

GET MONEY CHICKS - SEPTEMBER 2007
$14.95
ISBN 1-933967-17-X

For Mina, Shanna, and Karen, using what they had to get what they wanted was always an option. Best friends since day one, they always had a thing for the hottest gear, luxurious lifestyles, and the ballers who made it all possible. All of this changes for Mina when a tragedy makes her open her eyes to the way she's living. Peer pressure and loyalty to her girls collide with her own morality, sending Mina into a no-win situation.

AFTER-HOURS GIRLS - AUGUST 2007
$14.95
ISBN 1-933967-16-1

Take part in this tale of two best friends, Lisa and Tosha, as they stalk the nightclubs and after-hours joints of Detroit searching for excitement, money, and temporary companionship. These two divas stand tall until the unforgivable Motown streets catch up to them. One must fall. You, the reader, decide which.

THE LAST CHANCE - OCTOBER 2007
$14.95
ISBN 1-933967-22-6

Running their L.A. casino has been rewarding for Luke Chance and his three brothers. But recently it seems like everyone is trying to get a piece of the pie. Word of an impending hostile takeover of their casino, which could leave them penniless and possibly dead. That is until their sister Keilah Chance comes home for a short visit. Keilah is not only beautiful, but she also can be ruthless. Will the Chance family be able to protect their family dynasty?

LOOK FOR MORE HOT TITLES FROM

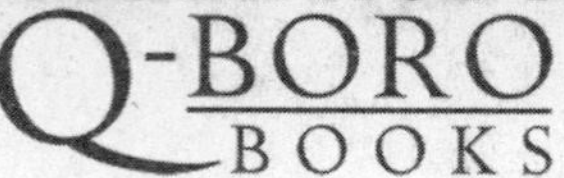

DOGISM
$6.99
ISBN 0977733505

Lance Thomas is a sexy, young black male who has it all; a high paying blue collar career, a home in Queens, New York, two cars, a son, and a beautiful wife. However, after getting married at a very young age he realizes that he is afflicted with DOGISM, a distorted sexuality that causes men to stray and be unfaithful in their relationships with women.

POISON IVY - NOVEMBER 2006
$14.95
ISBN 0977733521

Ivy Davidson's life has been filled with sorrow. Her father was brutally murdered and she was forced to watch, she faced years of abuse at the hands of those she trusted, and was forced to live apart from the only source of love that she has ever known. Now Ivy stands alone at the crossroads of life staring into the eyes of the man that holds her final choice of life or death in his hands.

HOLY HUSTLER - FEBRUARY 2007
$14.95
ISBN 0977733556

Reverend Ethan Ezekiel Goodlove the Third and his three sons are known for spreading more than just the gospel. The sanctified drama of the Goodloves promises to make us all scream "Hallelujah!"

HAPPILY NEVER AFTER - JANUARY 2007
$14.95
ISBN 1933967005

To Family and friends, Dorothy and David Leonard's marriage appears to be one made in heaven. While David is one of Houston's most prominent physicians, Dorothy is a loving and carefree housewife. It seems as if life couldn't be more fabulous for this couple who appear to have it all: wealth, social status, and a loving union. However, looks can be deceiving. What really happens behind closed doors and when the flawless veneer begins to crack?

LOOK FOR MORE HOT TITLES FROM

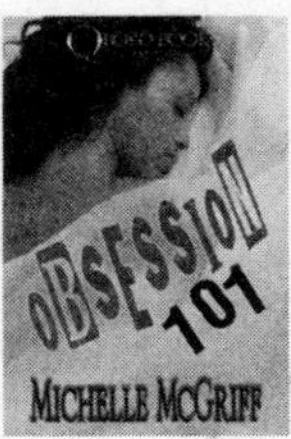

OBSESSION 101
$6.99
ISBN 0977733548

After a horrendous trauma. Rashawn Ams is left pregnant and flees town to give birth to her son and repair her life after confiding in her psychiatrist. After her return to her life, her town, and her classroom, she finds herself the target of an intrusive secret admirer who has plans for her.

SHAMELESS- OCTOBER 2006
$6.99
ISBN 0977733513

Kyle is sexy, single, and smart; Jasmyn is a hot and sassy drama queen. These two complete opposites find love - or something real close to it - while away at college. Jasmyn is busy wreaking havoc on every man she meets. Kyle, on the other hand, is trying to walk the line between his faith and all the guilty pleasures being thrown his way. When the partying college days end and Jasmyn tests HIV positive, reality sets in.

MISSED OPPORTUNITIES - MARCH 2007
$14.95
ISBN 1933967013

Missed Opportunities illustrates how true-to-life characters must face the consequences of their poor choices. Was each decision worth the opportune cost? LaTonya Y. Williams delivers yet another account of love, lies, and deceit all wrapped up into one powerful novel.

ONE DEAD PREACHER - MARCH 2007
$14.95
ISBN 1933967021

Smooth operator and security CEO David Price sets out to protect the sexy, smart, and saucy Sugar Owens from her husband, who happens to be a powerful religious leader. Sugar isn't as sweet as she appears, however, and in a twisted turn of events, the preacher man turns up dead and Price becomes the prime suspect.

Attention Writers:

Writers looking to get their books published can view our submission guidelines by visiting our website at: *www.QBOROBOOKS.com*

What we're looking for: Contemporary fiction in the tradition of Darrien Lee, Carl Weber, Anna J., Zane, Mary B. Morrison, Noire, Lolita Files, etc; groundbreaking mainstream contemporary fiction.

We prefer email submissions to: candace@qborobooks.com in MS Word, PDF, or rtf format only. However, if you wish to send the submission via snail mail, you can send it to:

Q-BORO BOOKS Acquisitions Department
165-41A Baisley Blvd., Suite 4. Mall #1
Jamaica, New York 11434

***** By submitting your work to Q-Boro Books, you agree to hold Q-Boro books harmless and not liable for publishing similar works as yours that we may already be considering or may consider in the future. *****

1. Submissions will not be returned.
2. **Do not contact us for status updates.** If we are interested in receiving your full manuscript, we will contact you via email or telephone.
3. Do not submit if the entire manuscript is not complete.

Due to the heavy volume of submissions, if these requirements are not followed, we will not be able to process your submission.